NO L OF
SEAT RY

COLUMBIA BRANCH
RECEIVED
MAR 05 2016

SLOW BOAT TO CHINA
AND OTHER STORIES

MODERN CHINESE LITERATURE FROM TAIWAN

MODERN CHINESE LITERATURE FROM TAIWAN

EDITORIAL BOARD

Pang-yuan Chi
Göran Malmqvist
David Der-wei Wang, *Coordinator*

Wang Chen-ho, *Rose, Rose, I Love You*

Cheng Ch'ing-wen, *Three-Legged Horse*

Chu T'ien-wen, *Notes of a Desolate Man*

Hsiao Li-hung, *A Thousand Moons on a Thousand Rivers*

Chang Ta-chun, *Wild Kids: Two Novels About Growing Up*

Michelle Yeh and N. G. D. Malmqvist, editors,
Frontier Taiwan: An Anthology of Modern Chinese Poetry

Li Qiao, *Wintry Night*

Huang Chun-ming, *The Taste of Apples*

Chang Hsi-kuo, *The City Trilogy: Five Jade Disks,*
Defenders of the Dragon City, Tale of a Feather

Li Yung-p'ing, *Retribution: The Jiling Chronicles*

Shih Shu-ching, *City of the Queen: A Novel of Colonial Hong Kong*

Wu Zhuoliu, *Orphan of Asia*

Ping Lu, *Love and Revolution: A Novel About Song Qingling and Sun Yat-sen*

Zhang Guixing, *My South Seas Sleeping Beauty: A Tale of Memory and Longing*

Chu T'ien-hsin, *The Old Capital: A Novel of Taipei*

Guo Songfen, *Running Mother and Other Stories*

Huang Fan, *Zero and Other Fictions*

Zhong Lihe, *From the Old Country: Stories and Sketches from Taiwan*

Yang Mu, *Memories of Mount Qilai: The Education of a Young Poet*

Li Ang, *The Lost Garden: A Novel*

TRANSLATED AND EDITED BY
CARLOS ROJAS

NG KIM CHEW

SLOW BOAT TO CHINA

AND OTHER STORIES

COLUMBIA UNIVERSITY PRESS
NEW YORK

COLUMBIA UNIVERSITY PRESS
Publishers Since 1893
New York Chichester, West Sussex

cup.columbia.edu
Copyright © 2016 Columbia University Press
All rights reserved

Columbia University Press wishes to express its appreciation for assistance given by the Chiang Ching-kuo Foundation for International Scholarly Exchange and Council for Cultural Affairs in the preparation of the translation and in the publication of this series.

Library of Congress Cataloging-in-Publication Data

Huang, Jinshu, 1967–
[Short stories. English]
Slow boat to China and other stories / Ng Kim Chew ; translated and edited by Carlos Rojas.
pages cm. — (Modern Chinese literature from Taiwan)
ISBN 978-0-231-16812-0 (cloth : alk. paper) — ISBN 978-0-231-54099-5 (ebook)
I. Rojas, Carlos, 1970– translator, editor. II. Title.

PL2865.C426A2 2016
895.13'52—DC23

2015027378

Columbia University Press books are printed on permanent and durable acid-free paper.
This book is printed on paper with recycled content.
Printed in the United States of America

c 10 9 8 7 6 5 4 3 2 1

COVER DESIGN: KEITH HAYES
BOOK DESIGN & TYPESETTING: VIN DANG

References to websites (URLs) were accurate at the time of writing.
Neither the author nor Columbia University Press is responsible for URLs
that may have expired or changed since the manuscript was prepared.

contents

introduction

NG KIM CHEW AND THE WRITING OF DIASPORA

NG KIM CHEW'S 1990 SHORT STORY "The Disappearance of M" revolves around the recent publication of a (fictional) novel, *Kristmas*, that is described as a virtuosic tour-de-force and receives rave reviews around the world. The novel is compared to *Ulysses*, and there is even discussion of nominating the author for the Nobel Prize. Critics in the United States applaud *Kristmas* for being "the first work to cross Malaysian literature's ethnic boundaries," while writers in Malaysia are energized by the international attention the work has received. The novel is published anonymously under the initial "M," however, and no one has any real idea who could have written it. There are, however, some tantalizing clues, such as the fact that the manuscript was sent from a P.O. box in West Malaysia and the postage was paid from a Chinese bank account—suggesting that the author may have been from Malaysia, and may also have been ethnically Chinese. As a result, discussions in Malaysia of the novel's literary merits overlap with debates over its national, ethnic, and even linguistic characteristics, as the work's global appeal helps catalyze a reconsideration of the significance and limits of regional literary identities.

Composed near the beginning of Ng Kim Chew's literary career, "The Disappearance of M" anticipates some of the characteristics of the literary oeuvre for which Ng himself would subsequently become known. Born in 1967 in the Malaysian state of Johor, Ng grew up in a poor village in a rubber forest. In 1986 he went to Taiwan for college, where he received his B.A. and Ph.D. in Chinese literature. He is currently a professor of Chinese literature at Taiwan's National Chi Nan University, and is also a prize-winning creative author in his own right, having published six volumes of fiction over the past two decades. Focusing on the interethnic and multicultural environment of Malaysia and Southeast Asia, Ng's fiction probes the distinctive peculiarities of the Southeast Asian region he calls home, while helping interrogate some of the basic conceptual paradigms through which literary production itself is understood.[1]

ON TAXONOMY

Near the beginning of "The Disappearance of M," there is a description of two literature conferences that have been convened in Malaysia to discuss the publication of *Kristmas* and its potential implications. The first is convened by the Malaysian Writers Association and is attended by hundreds of Malay authors, while the second is convened by the Malaysian Chinese Writers Association and is attended by most of the significant authors of Chinese descent residing in Malaysia. Both of these groups want to claim the novel as their own, so as to help raise their international profile—despite the fact that they know virtually nothing about the work's authorship or origins. If fact, there is even debate over the language in which the novel is written. The work is primarily in English, but includes passages in a variety of other languages ranging from Japanese to Javanese, and even oracle bone script. There is speculation that the text at hand may not in fact be the original version of the novel, as participants at the first conference insist that "Malaysian literature must necessarily be written in Malay" while those at the second conference resolve to try to "locate this M and, if possible, find the original 'Chinese edition' of his novel . . . if, that is, you believe he must have written it in Chinese."

This question of how to classify *Kristmas* speaks to a broader set of questions of literary taxonomy. In the modern period it has become conventional to categorize literary works based on their language of composition or nation of origin. For instance, French literature is typically understood to be literature from France written in French, just as Japanese literature is literature from Japan written in Japanese. This sort of classification is useful to the extent that it helps to validate coherent literary traditions and communities, though many literary texts and phenomena do not map neatly onto the contingent configurations of the nation-state.

In recognition of the inherent limits of categorizing literature in primarily national terms, therefore, it has become popular to use language as a basis for classifying bodies of literature that fall outside of existing national boundaries—particularly as a result of processes of colonialism and migration. For instance, Anglophone literature is English-language literature originating from outside of Britain, and Francophone literature is French-language literature originating from outside France. Conversely, there has also been a move to recognize *subnational* categories, which is to say bodies of work positioned outside of what is conventionally viewed as the dominant national tradition. For example, in their analysis of Franz Kafka's works, Gilles Deleuze and Fèlix Guattari developed the concept of what they called minor literature, referring to a body of literary production nominally written in the language of a dominant national literature but which nevertheless challenges many of the assumptions and values of that same tradition. Similarly, there has also been growing interest in literature written in languages other than non-dominant languages, including works by ethnic minorities, immigrants, and aboriginal populations.

In the case of modern Malaysian literature, meanwhile, the nation-state in question is an artifact of British colonialism. The modern state of Malaysia is a multilingual and multiethnic entity that was derived from a group of British colonies known as British Malaya. When these colonial territories were formally unified into the Malayan Union in 1946, ethnic Malays accounted for just under half of the population while ethnic Chinese accounted for nearly 40 percent. The British initially kept these Chinese communities separate from the local Malays, and following the establishment of an independent Malaysia in 1963, the new government developed a set of policies that were ostensibly designed to encourage cultural diversity but which in practice prioritized Malay culture. As a result, the nation's Chinese minority has been encouraged to retain a distinct identity, resulting in the production of a body of literary production by Malaysian Chinese authors, including works not only in Chinese but also in Malay and even English.

This latter body of literature is frequently referred to as *Mahua*—using an abbreviation consisting of two characters, each of which has several different shades of meaning. On one hand, the *Ma* in Mahua is short for either the modern nation of Malaysia or for the former confederation of British Malaya, which historically included not only the region that is now Malaysia but also Singapore, the Philippines, Brunei, East Timor, and parts of Indonesia—suggesting that *Mahua* marks either national or a more general regional affiliation. On the other hand, *hua* is short for either *Huawen* or *Huayu*, meaning the Chinese language (in its written and spoken forms, respectively), or for *Huaren*, meaning people of Chinese descent—suggesting that *Mahua* literature is determined either by its language of composition or by the ethnicity and origins of its author. Unlike literary categories such as Francophone or Anglophone literature, which merely use language in place of the nation as their defining criterion, accordingly, the portmanteau word *Mahua* may refer to a nation, a region, a language, an ethnicity, a culture, or to any combination thereof. The result is a taxonomical category structured by a logic of what Ludwig Wittgenstein calls family resemblances, wherein natural categories are defined not by any single necessary and sufficient condition but rather by a more fluid set of overlapping conditions that are in dynamic interaction with one another. Mahua literature, accordingly, occupies a marginal status with respect to both Malaysia as well as China, regarded as a subtradition within Malaysia and largely ignored in Mainland China, even as it simultaneously dramatizes some of the conceptual indeterminacies that characterize national literatures themselves.

It is precisely these sorts of conceptual ambiguities that are foregrounded in the debate, in "The Disappearance of M," over whether the novel *Kristmas* can be held up as an exemplar of Malaysian or Mahua literature. The "M" under which the novel is published, accordingly, could potentially stand for either *Malaysian*, *Malay*, or *Mahua*, and part of the work's appeal lies precisely in the degree to which its identity is a function of an indeterminate variable.

ON AUTHORSHIP

"The Disappearance of M" follows a local reporter, Huang, who has been assigned to investigate the authorship and origins of *Kristmas*.[2] To this end, Huang travels to Taiwan, where he meets with several Mahua authors based there, including Zhang Guixing and Li Yongping. He ultimately concludes, however, that that none of them could possibly be

"M," given that their Sinophone, Anglophone, or (Taiwan) nativist tendencies appear to be too strong to have permitted them to produce a boundary-crossing work like *Kristmas*. Huang then returns to Malaysia and proceeds to a village deep in a rubber forest to investigate a news report of a mysterious visitor from Singapore he suspects might be the author he is looking for. By the time Huang arrives in the village the visitor has already left, but after speaking to a local family Huang develops a hunch that the visitor may actually have been the famous Chinese author Yu Dafu, who is generally believed to have died approximately half a century earlier.

Born in China in 1896, the historical Yu Dafu went to Japan in 1914 for high school and college. In 1921, while still in Japan, he helped establish a literary organization known as the Creation Society and also composed one of his most influential stories, "Sinking" (Chenlun), about a Chinese student in Japan whose feelings of national self-loathing are intricately intertwined with intense erotic yearnings. Yu returned to China in 1922 and became one of the leading figures in China's May Fourth Movement, which promoted a new politically progressive literature written in the modern vernacular rather than in classical Chinese. Ng Kim Chew, however, is more interested in a series of developments from near the end of Yu's career. In 1938, Yu Dafu fled China during the War of Japanese Resistance and relocated to Singapore, where he became actively involved in the local literary and cultural scene. In particular, he sought to promote Chinese-language literature, arguing that Southeast Asia needed to produce a "great author" writing in Chinese in order to secure the region's position on the global stage. Four years later, Yu left Singapore on the eve of the Japanese invasion, ultimately ending up in the Western Sumatran village of Payakumbuh, where he assumed the identity of a Chinese businessman named Zhao Lian while also secretly working as an interpreter for the Japanese military police. One evening in 1945, a visitor came to Yu's home and asked him to step outside, and he was never seen again.

Although it has generally been assumed that Yu Dafu was executed by the Japanese military police, several of Ng's stories explore the possibility that Yu might have somehow survived his abduction and secretly lived on for decades. For instance, Ng's stories "Death in the South" and "Supplement" revolve around the discovery of evidence that Yu may have survived his apparent execution, and describe a quest for the legendary author and the texts he may have left behind. In both cases, Yu Dafu's apparent postmortem existence is used to offer a commentary on the ability of texts to travel through space and time, creating an intricate web of identity that both reaffirms and profoundly challenges recognized national literary traditions. In "The Disappearance of M," meanwhile, Huang remembers that Yu Dafu had been fluent in a number of different languages, and speculates that if he did in fact survive his presumptive death he might have gone on to pick up several more, thereby making him an ideal candidate to have written *Kristmas*. If so, the global attention that the novel received would have helped realize Yu's earlier dream that Southeast Asia might produce a literary masterpiece that would help drive a reconfiguration of existing configurations of world literature—though the fact that Yu himself did not relocate to Southeast Asia until late in life would have added an additional complication to the essentialist assumptions implicit in some of the discussions of Malaysian or Mahua literature.

ON TRANSLATION

In "The Disappearance of M," the novel *Kristmas* is described as having "mixed up a number of the world's languages, thereby creating a unique new written language." Even as some characters in Ng's story speculate that the published version of the novel may actually be a translation of an earlier version composed in either Malay or Chinese, others note that given the interplay between different languages in the "English" version of the novel, "the novel is literally untranslatable." Jacques Derrida, in his discussion of Paul Celan, makes a similar point when he observes that "everything seems, in principle, *de jure*, translatable, except of the mark of the difference among the languages within the same poetic event."[3]

One of the distinguishing characteristics of Ng's own fiction, meanwhile, is precisely his attention to this "mark of the difference" between the various languages that appear in his stories, including different dialects of Chinese as well as Malay, Japanese, English, and other languages. Although most of these linguistic elements in these stories can be translated effectively into English, it is significantly more challenging to preserve, in translation, the heteroglossic character of the original text. That is to say, even if every element in the original text were to be translated faithfully into English, what would inevitably be lost in translation would be the *differences* between the various languages contained within the stories themselves.

This issue is compounded by the fact that the precise relationship between the different languages in Ng's stories is not inherent in the original works themselves, but rather is contingent on the linguistic background of his readers. As a Malaysian Chinese author who usually writes about Southeast Asia but who publishes most of his works in Taiwan, however, Ng writes for a variety of audiences, each of whom will approach his works with varying degrees of familiarity with the specific dialectal and foreign terms that he uses. Many Anglophone readers, meanwhile, may be unfamiliar with the Chinese dialectal and foreign-language elements in the stories, and in this volume I have tried to strike a balance between fidelity and intelligibility—striving to preserve the heteroglossic feel of the original while making some discrete adjustments to maintain the intelligibility of the English translation. In some cases, such as the terms *Tuan* ("the gentleman") and *tolong* ("assistance"), Ng himself includes a parenthetical explanation of the foreign-language terms, which I translate as well. In other cases, I either add a short explanation to a foreign word or else leave it to the reader to deduce the meaning from the context. For instance, I note that a *kám-á-tiàm* is a convenience store and that an attap hut refers to a palm hut, while leaving it to the reader to figure out that a batik shirt is a kind of traditional garment and that a *cempedak* is a kind of tropical fruit.

ON TRANSLITERATION

In the description, in "The Disappearance of M," of the meeting of the Malaysian Writers Association, the names of the participants are identified either by abbreviations (e.g., "Author A," using the roman letter "A"), Chinese phonetic equivalents (e.g., "Mohammad" is rendered as 莫哈末, which would be pronounced "Mohamo" in Mandarin), or by alphabetic romanizations (e.g., "Anwak Ridhwan," which is printed in caps in the text and with no corresponding Chinese version of the name). A similar pattern of transliteration can be found throughout Ng's oeuvre, as he frequently uses either Chinese characters or roman letters to provide phonetic renderings of words and phrases from other languages. In translating Ng's stories into English, I have similarly used transliterations for elements in the text that resist translation, including proper names, specialized terminology, and onomatopoeic words. I use *pinyin* as a default romanization system, though I have used alternative spellings when they are provided within the text itself, and for proper names that already have an accepted spelling (including for Ng Kim Chew's own name, which would be pronounced *huang jinshu* in Mandarin, although the author prefers to use a romanization of his name based on the Hokkien pronunciation).

One of the central characters in the final story, "Inscribed Backs," is identified as Mr. Yu and is introduced as a "coolie expert" who has spent decades researching the transnational trade in Chinese laborers, or coolies. The story's narrator learns Mr. Yu has been secretly investigating the origins of some mysterious tattoos that he once glimpsed on the back of a coolie. Years later, after having already retired, Mr. Yu invites the narrator to join him on a research expedition to look into the tattoos, but is struck by a car before they are able to come up with any useful leads. He ends up in the hospital in a coma, while the narrator shuttles back and forth between his hospital room and the home of an elderly Chinese woman who—in collaboration with her lover, an Englishman identified in the text as Mr. Faulkner—had owned and run a Singapore brothel. Over many leisurely afternoon teas, the elderly woman tells the narrator a story that contains clues as to the origins of the tattoos, in the course of which she refers in passing to *a different* Mr. Yu, whom she describes as a "world-famous author."

Although the surnames of these two men have an identical pronunciation in Mandarin (*yù*), they are actually written with different characters. The surname of the first Mr. Yu is rendered with a relatively obscure character, 鬻, which means "to sell," while the surname of the second is written with the character 郁, which means "fragrance" and is also the surname of the historical Yu Dafu. To avoid confusion, I have transliterated the surname of the first figure as *Yur*—using an alternate romanization system that indicates the tone using variations in spelling of, rather than with diacritic marks[4]—in order to differentiate it from the precisely homophonous surname of the second figure. While "The Disappearance of M" revolves around a mysterious text and a quest for its author, who may or may not be Yu Dafu, in "Inscribed Backs" a similar quest for the authorship of another mysterious text ends up hinging on an interpretive gap that opens up between Mr. Yu[r] and his homophonic namesake, who may or may not be Yu Dafu. The silent "*r*" that I use to visually mark the graphic difference between these two homophonous characters symbolizes the story's own fascination with a diasporic process of textual dissemination.

ON APORIAS

"The Disappearance of M" concludes with a section in which the journalist finds a newspaper containing an article titled "The Disappearance of M," which mirrors not only the essay he himself is writing but also the text of Ng's story itself. The article describes a conference convened to discuss *Kristmas*, and includes transcriptions of remarks made by a number of the authors in attendance. As he does throughout the story, Ng uses the names of actual authors, including Chen Zhicheng, Fu Chengde, and Zhang Dachun, and as a result the passage revolves around a mirrored interplay not only between the embedded text and the story itself but also between the contents of the story and the literary field within which it would come to be positioned.

It is implied, in other words, that the content of the newspaper article found by the story's protagonist mirrors that of the essay that the protagonist is himself in the course of writing, which in turn presumably mirrors the contents of Ng's story itself. The result, as the embedded article notes, is "an absurd situation [in which] a group of Taiwan authors in the work were critiquing fictional characters who shared their name in a work by the same title, even as the fictional characters themselves were simultaneously critiquing a work by the same title." It is fitting, therefore, that Ng's story concludes with a reference to Zhang Dachun, a contemporary Taiwan author who is known for his playful intermixing of fiction and reality. In particular, Zhang's novel *The Great Liar* (*Da Shuohuangjia*)—which was published in 1989, a year before Ng wrote "The Disappearance of M," and is explicitly alluded to within Ng's story itself—is an ambitiously metatextual exercise in which Zhang would read the morning paper every day and then incorporate fictionalized elements of these news stories into the next installment of his serialized novel, which he would then publish in the paper that same evening. Accordingly, the observation attributed to the story's fictional Zhang Dachun—"Don't you know, reality itself is actually so fictional"—neatly encapsulates a key premise of Ng's general oeuvre.

Although "The Disappearance of M" contains what are perhaps Ng's most explicit reflections on the interweaving of fiction and reality, many of his other works also allude in suggestive ways to historical and contemporary events. For instance, his 2001 story "Monkey Butts, Fire, and Dangerous Things" positions the first-person narrator as caught in a power struggle by proxy between two mysterious figures—a character identified merely as "Elder" and another character who is described as being his "most powerful rival." The story offers considerable evidence that this Elder is actually a fictionalized version of Lee Kuan Yew, the first prime minister of Singapore and the cofounder of the People's Action Party, which dominated Singapore's politics for the three decades that Lee was in power. The Elder's antagonist in the story, meanwhile, is a caricature of Lee Kuan Yew's main rival, Lim Chin Siong, who originally partnered with Lee in founding the People's Action Party but later broke with him to establish his own political party. The two politicians traded barbs in their respective autobiographies, both of which are alluded to in Ng's story. In addition to these two figures, Ng's narrative also makes passing allusions to Lee's successor Goh Chok Tong (referred to as "that premier . . . to whom I handed over my seat") and to former president of Taiwan Lee Teng-hui (described as "that long-chinned Japanese who recently stepped down in Taiwan"). Moreover, not only is "Monkey Butts" structured as a semitransparent *roman à clef*, the story itself revolves around a similar interweaving of reality and fiction, as the fictionalized Lim Chin Siong character is found to have fallen into a sort of delirium, in which every night he dramatically recites speeches and other oratories he finds in the old newspapers that have been provided to him, and views himself the political leader of an (imaginary) "People's Republic of the South Seas."

In "The Disappearance of M," meanwhile, one of the peculiarities of the final newspaper essay—a portion of which is reprinted within Ng's own story—is that it has been heavily redacted, ostensibly by the authors who are quoted within the piece itself, and as a result the text explicitly draws attention to its own limits. We find different versions of this sort of linguistic aporia throughout Ng's oeuvre. For instance, his stories frequently contain empty squares and ellipses marking points where text has been deliberately left out, and they also often feature parenthetical interpolations in which a meta-narratorial voice corrects or expands upon something the narrator has just said. At a couple of points in "The Disappearance of M," the narrative slips from a third-person narration into a first-person voice, whereupon a meta-narratorial steps in parenthetically and corrects himself, noting, "uh, it's not me." Similarly, "Deep in the Rubber Forest" contains a couple of handwritten passages (in Chinese) inserted into the printed text, while the story reflects on how something intrinsic to a handwritten manuscript is always lost when the text is printed.

Ng's stories also incorporate a number of nonsemantic graphical elements that underscore the inherent limits of the text's intelligibility. In "The Disappearance of M," for instance, the protagonist discovers a document with a mathematical formula: $M = M_1 + M_2 + M_3 \ldots + M_n$. Different, and seemingly more nonsensical, versions of this formula are cited later in the story, including $M_1 + M_2 + M_3 \ldots Mn,n_{\in}N_0$ and MN,K < NLOO. In "Monkey Butts, Fire, and Dangerous Things," meanwhile, the narrator discovers a document titled "Secret Files from Malaya's Communist Period," listing a number of former communist activists. The list, however, becomes increasingly incoherent, and by the end it consists entirely of meaningless graphic elements such as *c/o* and # & * ♀. The most extreme example of this practice can be found in two stories from Ng's 2001 collection, *From Island to Island.* One text, "Supplication," consists of a single paragraph of meaningless symbols, while another, "Untouchable," consists of six pages of completely black paper. Both texts function as purely perlocutionary utterances, in that they do not attempt to transmit meaning directly but rather, through their very existence, they effectively interrogate the limits of language as a communicative practice.

A thematic correlate of this fascination with linguistic aporias can be found in a scatological motif that runs through many of Ng's stories. "Death in the South" and "Fish Bones" both conclude with allusions to human excrement, while "Monkey Butts, Fire, and Dangerous Things" and "Supplement" contain discussions of anal sex and rectal cavity searches. This scatological obsession is most obvious, however, in

"Dream and Swine and Aurora," which features an extended discussion of the stench of pig shit. The protagonist is a pig farmer, which carries complicated connotations in a country where the majority of the population is Muslim and views pork as taboo while a large ethnic Chinese minority regards pork as a defining part of their cuisine. The smell of pork shit, accordingly, may be viewed as a symbol of this kernel of cultural difference—this limit point of cultural translatability. At a textual level, this overdetermined significance of pigs in the story can be observed in the author's somewhat mysterious decision to render one of the story's final references to pigs as a handwritten—rather than a printed—character, thereby lending it a sort of mysterious totemic quality.

ON DIASPORA

A character in "The Disappearance of M" notes at one point that not only does *Kristmas* include a variety of different modern and ancient languages, "there are even some portions written in oracle bone script!" Oracle bones were divination texts used during the late Shang and early Zhou dynasties from around the second millennium B.C.E. For much of recorded history, the very existence of these inscriptions had been entirely forgotten until they were serendipitously rediscovered at the end of the nineteenth century. It was quickly recognized that these inscriptions constituted a version of the Chinese language that antedated all other known versions and consequently provided compelling evidence of the language's underlying transhistorical continuity, though some of these characters differ so much from other extant versions of Chinese that they remain undeciphered to this day. The result is a body of writing that represents not only the remarkable stability and persistence of the Chinese language but also the possible loss of meaning with which language is perpetually confronted.

In many of Ng's stories, oracle bone inscriptions signify not only the historical continuity of the Chinese language but also its inherent discontinuities and potential ruptures. In particular, Ng uses this ancient script, together with its contemporary reinventions, to underscore the extraordinary plasticity of the Chinese language as it circulates around the globe. In "Inscribed Backs," for instance, there is a description of a figure who resolves to create a literary masterpiece—what he calls a modern-day *Dream of the Red Chamber*—by inscribing a vast text onto the shells of ten thousand tortoises. The Englishman known as Mr. Faulkner, meanwhile, takes inspiration from this project and attempts something similar—but rather than inscribing characters onto tortoise shells he instead tattoos them onto the backs of actual men. Given that he barely knows Chinese in the first place, however, the resulting text is virtually unintelligible—a precise mirror image of the similarly unintelligible oracle bone script that inspired it.

In "Fish Bones," meanwhile, the protagonist re-creates ancient oracle bone divination practices by scorching turtle shells until they crack, and then inscribing the shells with text written in oracle bone script. In this case, the protagonist is haunted by the disappearance, decades earlier, of his elder brother, who was seized on account of his affiliation with communist resistance groups. For the protagonist, the antiquity of the oracle bone inscriptions comes to function as a metonym for his melancholic attachment to his assassinated elder brother, as well his more complicated relationship to the underground communist movement that was indirectly responsible for his brother's death. During the Japanese invasion, a militant arm of the Malayan Communist Party had led the resistance, giving ethnic Chinese a particularly prominent role in challenging Japanese aggression. After the war, the British encouraged the communists to turn in their arms and disband, and while many did, some instead went underground and recoalesced into a group dedicated to carrying out a guerilla war against the British. This insurrection, technically known as the Malayan Emergency, lasted from 1946 until 1960. The insurrection was declared suppressed in 1960, but even after the establishment of independent Malaya in 1963 the Malayan Communist Party remained a destabilizing force. The result was that even as the communists played a critical role in helping to secure Malaysia's independence, they subsequently came to be viewed as a fundamental challenge to the Malaysian political authority. In "Fish Bones," meanwhile, the elder brother's communist sympathies lead not only to his death but also produce a traumatic rift within his family, while at the same time providing a ground upon which the younger brother eventually comes to understand and reassess his own identity.

The Malayan Communist Party also plays a critical role in "Monkey Butts, Fire, and Dangerous Things" and "Allah's Will," both of which feature a protagonist who has been exiled to a remote island as a result of earlier communist sympathies. While in one case the protagonist is deprived of virtually all human contact, in the other he is being stripped of virtually everything that had previously shaped his identity, including his family, friends, his language, and even his name. In particular, the protagonist of "Allah's Will" is forced to take a vow never to speak, read, write, or even think in Chinese for the rest of his life. He agrees, and keeps his vow for more than three decades, but eventually becomes worried about slipping into oblivion after he dies and, taking inspiration from early Chinese writing such as oracle bone script, decides to create a cryptographic version of his Chinese name, which he hopes may serve as his epitaph. The irony, however, is that he writes this epitaph in an invented script only he can read, meaning that after he dies the epitaph's communicative function will necessarily be negated—unless, of course, someone translates the epitaph into a language that others might understand.

In fact, the story "Allah's Will" may be seen as doing precisely that—translating and explaining the meaning of the epitaph for the benefit of the story's readers. As a result, the corresponding text (which is not reproduced within the story itself) is presented as being both cryptically opaque and also fundamentally transparent, and its significance lies partly in the way in which its conditions of intelligibility oscillate depending on its presumptive audience/readership.

I, meanwhile, translate that story and others into English. Beginning with "The Disappearance of M" and concluding with "Inscribed Backs," this volume includes translations of twelve short stories composed between 1990 and 2001, each of which was included in one of Ng Kim Chew's first three collections of fiction: *Dream and Swine and Aurora* (1994), *Dark Night* (1997), and *From Island to Island: Inscribed Backs* (2001).[5]

NOTES

1. For useful discussions of Ng Kim Chew's work in English, see Jing Tsu, *Sound and Script in Chinese Diaspora* (Cambridge: Harvard University Press, 2010); Allison Groppe, *Sinophone Malaysia Literature: Not Made in China* (Amherst, NY: Cambria, 2013); and Andrea Bachner, *Beyond Sinology: Chinese Writing and the Scripts of Culture* (New York: Columbia University Press, 2014).

2. The reporter's surname, Huang 黃, which is mentioned in the story only in passing, is written with the same character as Ng Kim Chew's own surname (though Ng uses a different romanization).
3. Jacques Derrida, *Sovereignties in Question: The Poetics of Paul Celan* (New York: Fordham University Press, 2005), 29.
4. A version of this practice is most familiar in the doubled "a" in Shaanxi province, conventionally used to distinguish it from the nearly homophonous Shanxi province immediately to its east.
5. The stories appear here in the order of their initial publication. More recently, Ng has published several more collections of fiction, including *Earth and Fire: The Land of the Malay People* (2005), *Memoir of the People's Republic of the South Seas* (2013), and *Fish* (2015).

CHINESE TITLES AND ORIGINAL PUBLICATION DATES

Collected in *Dream and Swine and Aurora* (夢與豬與黎明) (Taipei: Jiuge, 1994)
"The Disappearance of M" (M 的失蹤) (1990)
"Dream and Swine and Aurora" (夢與豬與黎明) (1991)
"Death in the South" (死在南方) (1992)

Collected in *Dark Night* (烏暗暝) (Taipei: Jiuge, 1997)
"Deep in the Rubber Forest" (膠林深處) (1994)
"Fish Bones" (魚骸) (1995)

Collected in *From Island to Island* (由島至島) (Taipei: Rye Field, 2001)
"Allah's Will" (阿拉的旨意) (1996)
"Monkey Butts, Fire, and Dangerous Things" (猴屁股、火與危險的事物) (2001)
"Supplication" (訴求) (2001)
"Untouchable" (不可觸的) (2001)
"Slow Boat to China" (開往中國的慢船) (2001)
"Supplement" (補遺) (2001)
"Inscribed Backs" (刻背) (2001)

SLOW BOAT TO CHINA

AND OTHER STORIES

the disappearance of m

THE BAMBOO BRIDGE consisting of a string of V-shaped joints opened up like the skeleton of a prehistoric dinosaur. The bamboo was as thick as a man's arm, with each of the "vertebra" in the middle being as thick as a man's leg, and were connected together while facing inward. The V-shaped bamboo joints were stabilized by parallel bamboo poles, which were bound together with thick ropes. At one end of the bridge there were a couple of towering rubber trees and at the other end there was a waterside pavilion.

A man was standing next to the two trees. He reached out and stroked the thick ropes, feeling how strong they were, then carefully observed the scene in front of him while idly waving away mosquitoes with a tattered newspaper. Beads of perspiration covered the entire exposed surface of his body, and his shirt was completely soaked with sweat. He panted as he carried a large bag, then took out a couple of newspapers, placed them over the leaves on the ground, and sat down. He opened another newspaper to a section titled "South Malaysia News Edition," whereupon his eyes came to rest on a text box next to an advertisement for imported condoms in the bottom left-hand corner of the page. The box contained an announcement titled "Young Singapore Man Mysteriously Disappears, Whereabouts Unknown," and the accompanying text read:

(*Reported on the 19th of XX*)

An unidentified young man arrived recently at a location about three *li* from the city center. He built a stilt house, where he lived for more than three months. According to two nearby rubber plantation workers, the young man disappeared two weeks ago. While the police investiga-

> tion concluded that he had left on his own accord, some people suspected he was actually an opium addict, though it appeared they had no proof. In his room, locals discovered several manuscripts, so perhaps he was an author. . . .

When the man saw this announcement he had just returned from Lion City (Singapore), where he had been visiting Fang Xiu. He had obtained numerous documents, but failed to come up with any useful leads. This announcement, however, struck him like a thunderclap, and he felt as though his entire body was strumming with inspiration, as his exhaustion from the preceding several months immediately melted away. He quickly categorized the materials he had collected and stuffed them into a three-foot-long cabinet. After riding a bus for more than an hour, he had to walk along a narrow mountain path. Asking for directions along the way, he eventually made his way here.

"This bridge . . ."

The bridge made a deep impression on him, since he had never seen anything like it . . . half-suspended over the river like something out of a dream. After he left the city, the sound of traffic and crowds faded away, and all that remained was the sound of birds and monkeys jumping from tree to tree. He watched intently as though on a field trip, then held the railings and stepped onto the bridge.

He stumbled forward, staring intently at his feet. All he could see were the weeds peeking up out of the water. Between the weeds, there was only clear water so deep you couldn't even see the bottom, in which there were fish swimming around and dragonflies laying eggs. The weeds pushed him forward toward his destination. After a long time, the scenery began to change, and he glimpsed the reflection of an attap palm hut. He leapt onto the floor, causing it to sway back and forth, then wiped away his sweat and glanced back at the path he had just traversed—and felt even more strongly that, apart from its brown color, it looked just like the skeleton of a prehistoric dinosaur.

Even though he was well aware that the hut was empty, he nevertheless hurried forward to knock on the door. The door was unlatched, and when he knocked it swung open on its own accord. The evening light made the inside of the room appear quite dark. He dimly saw that on the floor there was a box of matches and an oil lamp, and he removed the lamp's cover and lit it. He put down his suitcase and took off his shoes, socks, and coat. He quickly lit an incense stick, at which point the cloud of mosquitoes surrounding him began to disperse. He opened two windows, then rolled up a newspaper and used it to brush away all the cobwebs in the room. Only after sweeping the floor did he finally begin to feel at ease. The ground was covered with books, some of which were still open. He examined their covers, and discovered with surprise that they included works like Li Yongping's *Jiling Chronicles* and *A Lazi Woman*, Zhang Guixing's *The Sons and Daughters of Keshan*, Pan Yutong's *The Stars Last Night*, Lévi-Strauss's *The Savage Mind*, and so forth. In addition, there were also a handful of novels in English, Japanese, and Malay (including the unofficial history, *Sejarah Melayu*). Piled up with some toilet paper in a corner of the room was Fang Beifang's *Tree with Deep Roots*, Fang Xiu's *A Draft of a New Malaysian Chinese Literary History*, Ma Lun's *Group Portrait of Singaporean and Malaysian Chinese Authors*, together with a tattered copy of the *Daodejing*. There was a side table on which, in addition to some ink, pens, and a typewriter, there were also several dust-covered pages of a journal, which were weighted down by a piece of wood. On the first page was written in uneven script:

You still don't deign to notice
Every petal of depression that I have shed.

Astonished, he examined these pages one after another, and found that some of the other pages had some odd mathematical symbols, such as $M = M_1 + M_2 + M_3 \ldots + M_n$, as well as strange numbers such as 22/505, NEW, 23 22+1, and so forth. He took out a pen and wrote everything down. The last page was a sales receipt, at the top of which was written (with supplementary annotations in parentheses): "May 25th, 1 packet of tea (Chinese virgin tea), 1 box of mosquito incense (Goldfish brand), five bars of soap (Lux), talcum powder (Pureen), toothpaste (Heiren), half a *jin* of sausage, ten eggs, five kilos of rice, one bottle of oil, one packet of salt, clothes detergent (Fast White), shampoo (Follow Me), face cream, and kerosene."

In a crack in the floorboards, he found a Malaysian Chinese Bank withdrawal receipt to the amount of M$500, together with a deposit receipt for a postage parcel. The house had only a single room, in the corner of which there was a simple set of cooking utensils.

He washed a pot, ladled out some water to rinse some rice, then used one of the remaining dry matches to light a fire. There were two sausages left, and one egg. . . . Through the window he saw a bamboo fence extending toward a grove of trees growing in water, and guessed that that was where the bathroom was. It was set up so that after relieving yourself you could ladle up some water to rinse yourself. He felt as though he had rediscovered a "stilt house."

After nightfall, he cleaned up and prepared to conclude the investigation he had been pursuing for several months. Early the next morning he would conduct some final interviews, and if there were still no conclusive results he would have no choice but to concede defeat. He could vaguely make out a dim light in the dark forest, and speculated that this was probably coming from the house belonging to the people who filed the report. What would they do if they saw that a lamp had been relit here? Everything appeared to have been secretly planned. At the crossroads he had relied on his intuition to select this road, and in this way had found this place that perfectly matched the description he had read in the newspaper announcement. He opened his sweat-stained notebook, then closed his eyes and pondered.

It had all begun with a single interview.

On July 8th, a "National Literature Discussion Panel" was urgently convened on the second floor of the Hilton Kuala Lumpur Hotel, with more than three hundred participants—all of whom were Malay authors—in attendance. The lighting was bright yet soft, while also sentimental and poetic. Everyone present, though, was very solemn. Author A spoke first, in his capacity as the moderator, and his report dealt with something everyone present had already heard about through the grapevine: that there was a respected colleague who, writing under the pseudonym M, had published a novel in English (titled *Kristmas*) that had attracted the attention of numerous critics in the United States, to the point that even the *New York Times* had taken notice. In addition to giving the novel their highest praise, some university professors wanted to nominate it for the Nobel Prize. The *New York Times* therefore assigned someone to investigate the author's real identity, but they ultimately found that "no one knows anything about this person." It turned out, however, that the manuscript had been sent from some location in West Malaysia, and the postage had been charged to a Chinese deposit company, and from this information they obtained their first clue: that M was probably Malaysian.

The *Times* reporter immediately called up the Malaysian Writers Association and the Chinese Malaysian Writers Association, telling them that some people in the U.S. wanted to know who this M was, and adding that the *Times* would be particularly interested in obtaining documentation concerning the specifics of his biography or other works he has published. With this, the two writers associations received a piece of good news that the literary world had been waiting for ever since the founding of the nation: a "great author" had finally arrived.

Then, the moderator of the panel—whose name was Mohammad—reduced the matter to two key questions:

(1) Who is this author, and what is his or her ethnicity?
(2) Can a work published in English count as "national literature"?

On every attendee's table there was a book that was as thick as a brick. On the front cover there was an image of a bronze *kris* sword, while on the back cover there was a blood-red dragon.

Initially, everyone assumed that the author was sitting amongst them, and therefore they all turned around and looked at one another—focusing their attention on those attendees (such as Anwar Ridhwan) who had achieved notoriety for their fiction, and particularly those who had received international literary awards. . . . The poets, meanwhile, were rather nonplussed by the fact they were not considered to be realistic "possibilities," and therefore hoped someone would come forward to resolve this situation as quickly as possible (thereby putting an end to the speculation that the author might be ethnically Chinese). At the same time, these same poets also hoped that M might *not* be among those in attendance, so that everyone would thereby remain functionally "equal." The entire auditorium grew silent for a moment, as everyone permitted themselves to exchange a knowing and embarrassed smile but at the same time couldn't help but sigh in relief. Then, someone raised the possibility that "perhaps the author was in fact Chinese?"

The subsequent discussion was even more one-sided, with virtually everyone taking the position that, from the perspective of national culture, Malaysian literature should definitely be written in Malay. In other words, even if someone managed to win favor in international literary circles with an "English edition" of a novel, it could not be considered a work of national literature—because Malaysian literature must necessarily be written in Malay.

"This is a fundamental principle!" K proclaimed loudly. He was also a novelist.

Osman Awang saw that things were not going well, and therefore interrupted his announcement and shifted to questions such as, "How might one promote the status of Malay literature in international literary circles?" Speaking as a journalist, he made a variety of random gestures, with spittle flying everywhere. He then noticed a reporter from *Nanyang Business Daily*, who had been furiously scribbling in his notebook with his head bowed, waving him and the other journalists away. At the door, the reporter hailed a taxi and immediately proceeded to the Selangor Chinese Assembly Hall.

The old and elegant Chinese Assembly Hall was brightly illuminated, and inside it was already full of people. In the entrance there was a red carpet with the words, in white, "The Malaysian Chinese Writers Association and the Malaysian Chinese Literature Conference." The reporter shouldered his way to the front and posed for a group photo with Yuan Shancao, Yu Chuan, Hong Quan, Fang Xiu, Fang Beifang, and others. After a quick glance around, he saw that most of the important authors had already arrived, including Wu An from East Malaysia.

Wearing thick black-rimmed glasses, Wen Renping was speaking. He asked plaintively,

"Why didn't we know that we had such a colleague?"

Apart from Wen Renping, who was wearing a batik shirt, Wen Rui'an, who was wearing a Western suit, and Fu Chengde, who was wearing a traditional long gown, all the other attendees were wearing ordinary shirts and pants. Wen Rui'an was solemnly speaking with an author of detective novels, and based on the documents he had acquired (including the news from the tabloids), he concluded that M was probably someone in attendance at the conference—though it was also possible that he wasn't.

"Based on the text," Wen Renping retrieved a copy of *Kristmas* from his briefcase, "we can speculate as to the author's biographical background . . . which we may narrow down to one of three possibilities." He then proceeded to analyze each of these in turn: "The first possibility is that the author is the son of a poor family who never received any formal education, in which case he would be a complete autodidact who had been writing continuously for many years. The authors who fit this description include Ding Yun and Yu Chuan." Upon hearing this, Ding and Yu were extremely moved, and their eyes misted over. "However, based on what Ding and Yu have published up to this point, there is no indication they are remotely capable of writing anything of this caliber." Upon hearing this, Ding and Yu immediately blushed bright red. "The second possibility is that the author is a graduate of Nanyang University who is currently in his forties or fifties, and who had leftist tendencies in his youth. He would have written in many different literary styles, and representatives of this group would include Fang Beifang and Meng Sha." Fang's and Meng's faces immediately lit up with delight. "However, these sorts of authors place too much emphasis on realism, and as a result their works feature too much reportage and not enough art." The sound of teeth grinding could be heard coming from the crowd. "The third possibility is that the author could be someone who studied in Taiwan, where he would have absorbed the results of Taiwan's development of vernacular Chinese fiction and have been nourished by European and American literature. It is even more likely that he would have studied in a department of foreign languages. Authors belonging to this third category include Li Yongping, Zhang Guixing, myself, Pan Yutong, Shang Wanyun, and so forth." At this point Wen Renping discretely left the microphone and returned to his seat, his face scarlet. Wen Rui'an replaced him at the microphone and happily announced,

"As for myself, my English is not very good, so don't even think it! Pan Yutong, however, would definitely be a possibility."

"It's not me!" A tall man stood up and interrupted him, then sat back down again.

"I'm sorry, Mr. Pan. In saying that it could potentially be you, I didn't mean to suggest that it necessarily *was* you." Wen turned again to the audience. "However, I'm afraid that Pan's works are too incompatible, and in this respect Ms. Shang's limitations are even more evident. The others whose English is good and who have achieved success in their writing include Zhang Guixing and Li Yongping. I already contacted both of them, but they are so deeply committed to writing in Chinese that they wouldn't even dream of writing in English. Mr. Li is even more insistent on making sure that his works not be published in foreign language editions, and I hear that he now plans to write in a variant of ancient Chinese seal script, using a combination of pictorial and homonymic elements. . . ." He heard even more tooth-grinding from the audience. "As for myself," he lowered his voice. "This," he lowered his voice even more, though he didn't stop talking. "*Yi yi . . . ya ya . . .* ," his voice gradually became completely muffled.

The person who grabbed the microphone was Meng Sha, from the realist school. He declared that regardless of how good the work might be, it still couldn't be considered "Malaysian Chinese literature," for the simple reason that it was not written in Chinese. "I leafed through it, and found that it contains not only English but also Malay—including both modern Malay and a lot of classical Malay—as well as Javanese, Arabic, Bali, German, French. . . . There are even some portions written in oracle bone script! Can you imagine?!"

Tan Swie Hian, who at the time was a leader of the modernist camp, came over, attracted by the commotion, and proceeded to grab the microphone from Meng Sha. Holding a sheet of paper, he began to read,

"Based on the judgment of American critics, this was the first work to cross Malaysian literature's ethnic boundaries. It has mixed up a number of the world's languages, thereby creating a unique new written language. Because it is so multifaceted, the novel is literally untranslatable. In fact, strictly speaking it is not even written in English to begin with. In terms of its genre, it resembles a 'Malaysian calendar,' and is as extraordinary as *Ulysses*. At the same time, it has also absorbed the strengths of several different cultural traditions . . . including the Indian, Chinese, and Greek traditions . . . and has integrated them into a coherent whole." When Chen finished reading, he melted back into the crowd.

The modernists and the realists immediately found themselves at loggerheads, to the point that they virtually overturned the entirety of Fang Xiu's New Malaysian Chinese literary history. In the end, Fang Xiu, in his capacity as a "historian," finally cried out,

"Please quiet down. . . . Everyone, please quiet down. . . . What is the use of making such a ruckus? The key thing now is to locate this M and, if possible, find the original 'Chinese edition' of his novel . . . if, that is, you believe he must have written it in Chinese." With this, he called an end to another tedious Malaysian literary history debate.

The notebook lying open in front of the lamplight had been composed in a serial manner, one page after another like a novel. He closed the notebook, rubbed his sore eyes and then, using his arms as a pillow, lay down on the floor. By this point it had already been several months since those two literary conferences and the media was gradually beginning to calm down again. It was only with considerable difficulty that he had managed to secure his editor's permission to take a three-month vacation to try to track down information regarding M's whereabouts. He had contacted, interviewed, and met with virtually every living Malaysian Chinese author he could find. He withdrew several years' of savings from his bank account, and in October he accompanied a cohort of elderly women on an "Overseas Chinese Returning to the Homeland" expedition to Taiwan, where he met with Li Yongping at Yangming Mountain, after which he proceeded to Yilan, where he met Zhang Guixing. Li and Zhang both received him warmly. Li took him for a stroll around a cemetery near Yangming Mountain, inviting him to savor some of the freshest air in Taiwan. He was quite surprised by Li's height and appearance, and if he were to have run into Li in the street he might well have assumed that Li was a pig butcher or a fish monger, and would never have expected that such an ugly fellow would be an author. Mr. Li said that he had already heard, whereupon I (uh, it's not me) . . . *he* told Li frankly that, as far as literary ability is concerned, there were at most only a handful of Malaysian Chinese authors who were even capable of writing a work like *Kristmas*. Apart from English, their knowledge of Malay and foreign languages (including ancient languages such as Latin and Sanskrit) would have had to be quite good, not to mention the fact that two pages of the novel were written in ancient Chinese oracle bone script! Li smiled warmly, then said,

"Don't waste your time on wild goose chases. Maybe the novel was written by some Chinese writer living abroad who wanted to pull an elaborate stunt. This sort of thing is of absolutely no consequence."

Li Yongping's meaning was very clear—he preferred to write his own works in a kind of "untranslatable Chinese," and didn't deign to try to ingratiate himself with those immature American critics and that peculiar institution of the Nobel Prize. Under the shadow of Li Yongping's arrogant dismissal, he arrived in rainy and humid Yilan, where the humidity made him feel as though his entire body were covered with the sort of moss found in northern Taiwan.

Zhang Guixing was wearing thick glasses, and was very quiet. He was neither tall nor thin, and had a dark complexion with traces of the East Malaysian countryside. Together, they strolled along the edge of a field, each holding an umbrella. Like Li Yongping, Zhang was grinning, though for very different reasons. He said quietly,

"What does it matter who it is? Is it worth it for you to go to so much effort trying to figure it out?"

He bowed his head and considered for a while, then finally said slowly,

"I'm not sure why either. . . . I just know that this is very important to me. Perhaps you didn't know, but even though I'm a journalist, I'm also very interested in creative writing. I've even secretly composed several stories and poems. . . . I don't know, I just feel that if I'm going to maintain my resolve to continue writing, or to affirm the future of Chinese-language literature in Malaysia, then I must get to the bottom of this."

He wrote up his conversation with Li and Zhang and sent it to the *Nanyang Business Daily* for publication. In the remaining few days, he visited several iconic sites in Taiwan, including Taipei's Longshan Temple, the Zuoying Confucius Temple, the campus of Taiwan University, the Chiang Kai-shek Memorial Hall. . . . He meditated for a while in a few old Tainan temples, then had an epiphany. Of course, he had also suspected some Taiwan author might be playing an elaborate prank on everyone, but based on these particular Taiwan authors' nativist, Americanized, or Sinified tendencies, he eventually decided that it was simply not conceivable that they could have written the novel in question.

Before leaving Taiwan, he also paid a visit to Chen Pengxiang in Taipei. Upon hearing Chen's amused laugh, however, he knew it was time for him to return home.

With the air full of mosquito repellent, he crossed the border between reality and fantasy, feeling as though he were floating in midair and peering down at all of the places he had visited, including North Malaysia, South Malaysia, East Malaysia, and even Singapore. He began to feel as though he were lying on a boat, which was floating gently in the water. Moonlight was streaming in through the window and over his body. The boat rowed past the plains, and was floating into the middle of the water. The moon continued to follow him. He suddenly got up, and realized he had already reached the shore . . . a sandy beach covered in a thick layer of spongy leaves. He stepped onto it barefoot, and could feel the moisture and softness of the leaves. There was a dark forest full of tall trees, and as he walked he looked around, and suddenly noticed that the leaves were covered with jellyfish-like objects. He leaned over to pick one up and open it, and noticed that it resembled a human face. . . . He put it on his own face, then leaned over the water to look, and another figure appeared to emerge out of the water. He looked carefully . . . it was Shang Wanyun. He was astonished and tried again . . . now it was Zhen Gong. He tried again . . . and again . . . Finally, a young man with short hair and thick eyebrows appeared to emerge out of the water. It was himself! He awoke with a start, and noticed that the soles of his feet were wet, and that outside everything was enveloped in fog. Inside, it seemed as though even the lamp was covered in dew. Seeing the light of the lamp in the fog, he felt a surge of warmth.

He abruptly stood up, as though he had suddenly remembered something, and began looking around the room. Apart from the Group Portrait of Singaporean and Malaysian Chinese Authors, there was also a pile of other photographs, including individual portraits of every significant Singapore and Malaysian author. He gazed at that photo portrait of the unusually talented but prematurely deceased Chinese author Tie Ge, who had come south from China but was then killed in a massacre during the Japanese invasion, and he sighed deeply. He found a youthful picture of Wen Rui'an, remembering the potential implicit in his essay "Dragon Crying for a Thousand Miles," whereupon he was silent for a long time. He lay there, his thoughts adrift and his body feeling as though it were floating again. Who *is* this M, he asked himself as he gazed out into the darkness. He had considered every author included in standard literary histories, and it seemed as though virtually none of them was a plausible candidate, while those who were in fact potential candidates had already explicitly denied having had any involvement with the novel. Could it be that M wasn't ethnically Chinese after all? Could he be Malay? Indian? A face appeared in the darkness, going from indistinct to clarity, from black and white to color. . . . It was a man, it was Yu Dafu.

He walked over to an attap hut where, in the wall-less tea house, a live Yu Dafu was drinking with some companions. He went up to them and asked Yu Dafu,

"Didn't I hear you had been killed by the Japanese?"

Yu glanced at him disdainfully, then replied,

"Who said I died? Who saw my corpse? Couldn't I have gone into hiding? Haven't you ever read a knight-errant *wuxia* novel?" This body that apparently belonged to Yu Dafu had gained a lot of weight, and his belly was now so big that he couldn't even see his own feet. From the reporter's research, he knew that Yu Dafu had already known many foreign languages, including German, Japanese, English, Malay, and Dutch. . . . And perhaps over the years he had also managed to learn Javanese, Arabic, and Sanskrit. . . . The more he thought about it, the more likely it seemed. He took the copy of *Kristmas* out of his satchel and handed it to Yu, who signed it and handed it back to him, then immediately burst into laughter. . . .

"If this were a *wuxia* novel . . ." he reflected. At this point the sound of splashing water could be heard coming from somewhere nearby, as though an enormous fish was doing some sort of calisthenics.

In the swinging of the bamboo, he woke up and heard the sound of frogs croaking.

"Hey," a child pushed the door open and stuck his head in, "Who are you, and why have you come here?"

He reluctantly stood up, but a quick glance revealed that at the end of the bridge there was a young girl wearing braids and a green dress. As the bridge rocked back and forth, her dress waved in the wind. He was instantly transfixed, and when he opened his mouth to speak, no words came out.

"Hey, what are you staring at? You still haven't answered me! That's my elder sister you're ogling at. How could you be such a pig?"

The girl looked at him for a moment, then slowly walked away. He called out to her, as though he wanted to say something, but his hand paused in midair. The boy was about six or seven years old, and examined the room for a while. He rubbed the sleep from his eyes and stretched. The child asked again, "Who are you?" He replied listlessly,

"I'm a reporter."

"What does a reporter do?"

"He writes for newspapers."

The child told him that it had already been half a month since they last saw a light there, but the previous night the light suddenly appeared again. His father thought that "that crazed mandrill had returned." Because it was already dark, no one was allowed to approach, since they were afraid that there was a cocaine-snorting hooligan there. Knowing that the child was about to say more, he quickly prepared his pen and paper.

"That fellow, the really thin one—Mama calls him *bamboo pole*, my sister calls him *cockroach*, and my father calls him *four-eyed monkey* or *mandrill*. He likes to play with me, and I learned all of my Chinese from simply hanging out with him. My father says that he is a crazed mandrill and doesn't allow him to get too close to us, concerned that he might take an interest in my sister. He taught me to play the flute (but who would I play for?), and I would take him to go catch fighting fish and hunt jaguars. He seemed as though he had never played anything before, but appeared to like it. Sometimes while watching the fighting fish in the jar, he looks like this (the boy extended his neck and stuck out his chin, his eyes bulging like a fish's). When he gave me the fighting fish, I never imagined that that meant he was about to leave. We don't have any neighbors here, and there is rarely anyone for me to play with."

The boy rambled on and on, and then suddenly asked,

"Are you hungry?"

He nodded. The boy took out a bundle (wrapped tightly in a newspaper) and opened it. It was a baked sweet potato, and emitted a fragrant aroma. He offered his thanks.

"I thought that when he returned he would bring some back . . . like he used to."

He carefully observed the child standing in front of him, and from the boy's incessant chatter he detected a hint of loneliness. He asked the boy his name.

"They call me Bird's Egg," the boy replied cheerfully.

"Do you know that uncle's name?"

"I'm not sure—I simply called him *Uncle*. I didn't need a name for him. Maybe my sister knows. She also knew him well."

Encouraged by this information, he resolved to interview the entire family.

"He was always writing something. Sometimes he seemed to be very unhappy, and would rip up everything he wrote. Sometimes he was quite content, and would shout with delight as he jumped into the water, declaring that he was a fish. One night I caught some lightning bugs to give him, to make a blue lamp that flew around the room, and we jumped and shouted together. Later, he told me he had finished a long poem, then took out some money and invited me to have some chocolate. You know, I didn't have any other friends, and sometimes he would sit there like a bump on a log reading his books until my parents called me, whereupon he would grab a candle and walk me home."

Once the boy started talking, it seemed he couldn't stop. He recounted every incident he could remember, including how this Uncle would send notes to the boy's sister, and so forth.

After they finished their sweet potatoes, he took out a miniature tape recorder and a notebook, then proceeded over to the family's house. The boy skipped along in front of him, and after they had walked about a hundred feet they heard dogs barking furiously. The dogs ran up to them, baring their gleaming white teeth, but the boy scolded them until they finally retreated. They walked through row after row of rubber trees, until they finally arrived in front of a stilt hut. A middle-aged woman welcomed him with a smile. He introduced himself, explaining that he was a reporter and that upon reading the news he had come to interview them, and the woman responded loudly,

"It's no use reporting this to the police. They once sent over some officers, but they left after looking around for just a few minutes. They had no desire to go inside. I hear that the newspaper wrote up something or other, but the resulting article was smaller than a piece of tofu. . . . By the way, how may I address you?"

"My surname is Huang," he said. "You can call me 'little Huang.'"

A young woman brought him a hot cup of coffee, but then insisted on going back into the house, never looking him in the eye.

The middle-aged woman sniffed and sighed, her wrinkles revealing a kind radiance.

"We only have this one daughter. Children from the countryside nowadays are all like this—they don't have any manners at all. . . .

"At first no one knew who he was, but suddenly he took out a leather briefcase and directed a group of people to build a house. They worked very quickly, beginning at dawn and finishing the same day before the sun had set behind the mountains. We had never seen anyone build a house over water, so we asked him about it, and he explained that he liked water. At the time, my husband remarked that he was somewhat crazed.

"He is very refined, and as thin as a chopstick. Initially we assumed he was a cocaine addict, but later we discovered that he was actually quite cultured and animated. Every time he saw me, he could politely call me, *Ah Fan, Ah Fan.* He was definitely an educated man, and extremely erudite. What we couldn't understand, though, was why he had ended up coming here. Maybe Ah Qing knows. If you wait for a moment, you can ask her yourself.

"You couldn't really tell his age. He could have been in his thirties, but could also have been in his forties. In any case, he was probably under fifty. . . . On the other hand, perhaps he was in his fifties after all. . . . At any rate, it was clear that he hadn't aged as quickly as those of us accustomed to doing hard labor. I once asked him where he was from, but he just smiled and said that he came from somewhere far away. . . . You could tell that he often relied on harvesting rubber to make a living, and would chain smoke one cigarette after another. Perhaps he was simply trying to keep the mosquitoes away. At the same time, he seemed to be pondering something. He wasn't afraid to touch caterpillars, and sometimes truly resembled an idiot. . . . The first time I saw him emerge out of the rubber forest, I was truly astonished. From a distance I couldn't tell who he was, and therefore assumed he was up to no good. You know that when we rubber-harvesting women see a stranger, we always pay close attention. During that period there were a lot of bad people. . . . Once, he was wearing his usual striped shirt, black pants, and was leaning against a rubber tree staring blankly at something—which turned out to be a tiger-headed wasp nest. . . . I noticed that the closer I came to him, the more scared I became, and I carefully examined whether or not he had any strange tendencies. . . . At that time there were many crazed men who would remove their pants to flash women. . . . But he remained completely still, as though he were a mannequin."

She kept passing him crackers and other things. He could vaguely hear the young woman in the house talking to Bird's Egg. It seemed as though they were discussing something. . . ."

"Who told you to be so talkative?"

". . ."

Then, he heard someone sweeping the floor. It was an indistinct and random sound.

"He was often like that. Sometimes he would squat on the fallen leaves, then would cock his head as though he were listening to something, appearing very intent. Eventually, I mustered the courage to ask him what he was listening to, and he pointed to the tree, cocked his head even more, and told me to listen carefully. I paused and looked and saw that it was a rubber tree seedpod that had split open, and sap was going *drip, drip, drip, drip* all over the branch and onto the ground. His finger was moving in time to the sound. I was rather startled, fearing that it was true that he was somewhat crazed . . ." The woman paused, and added,

"Then, there was the time I saw him squatting in the counter staring at something next to a pillar, examining the eddies of sand. It turns out that out he was catching ants to feed to the aardvarks. This must have been something Xiaowei taught him. At any rate, he was a very peculiar fellow. . . ."

The tape recorder clicked to a stop, and he quickly flipped the tape over. The woman grew quiet.

"One day before he disappeared, there was a heavy rainstorm while we were harvesting rubber. My daughter and I rushed to finish, and he also came out to help us. Smiling as he got soaked, he said, 'Quick, quick!' [she imitated his voice]. He said that the rubber sap was so white and fragrant that he really wanted to drink it, not to mention a lot of other things. Then he said that it was too bad that he wasn't as quick as I was . . . That night, my husband took a flashlight to go pick some durians, and suddenly saw a man standing on a mound of earth, which startled him so badly he almost collapsed. It turned out that this was *him*. He had a cigarette in his mouth, and was gazing up at the moon. He seemed to be mumbling something, or perhaps he was singing 'The Sun is Rising.' . . ."

At this point the woman began to look rather worried. She paused for a moment, before continuing in a somber voice,

"I could tell, from the expression with which he always looked at Ah Qing, that he was interested in her. But he was too old, and we had no idea what kind of work he did. Moreover, Ah Qing was simply too young . . ."

The humidity level gradually dropped, and once the fog receded the sun reclaimed its rightful position over the earth. He thanked the woman, then reflected for a while under a jackfruit tree by the door. He had a strong feeling that he had come to the right place, and perhaps . . . He recorded in his notebook a summary of what the woman had said. Perhaps the answer could be found somewhere between the lines? Did that hypothesized Chinese edition really exist? And why did M (if that is indeed who he was) have to leave? Where did he go? Was he even still alive? . . . He was assaulted by a string of questions. He smelled the aroma of ripe jackfruit, like in March when bees start visiting flowers, and as he was pondering these questions he sensed that someone was behind him. He abruptly turned around, and saw that it was that girl in the green dress. She waved to him, indicating that he should follow him, and he sprang to his feet.

"I've been waiting for you for several days already." The girl was quite clever, and her brows were marked by the grace and melancholia associated with Song lyric poetry. They stared at each other for several seconds. He estimated that she couldn't be older than eighteen or nineteen, yet he felt he was not her match.

In the winter, there was the sound of rubber tree seedpods splitting and dry branches cracking. The girl then said,

"According to local custom, I have to tell you a story:

"He was an odd fellow. He wore round May Fourth–style glasses, his hair was cut so short that he could be mistaken for a student, and he was as thin as a cockroach. But he looked at people with a piercing gaze . . . and was rather grim. My parents never let me approach him, but the only reason they offered was simply that they had a bad feeling about him. He was a rather fickle fellow. I rarely went to help my mother, except for on school holidays. I know that he often used his interactions with my brother to secretly observe me. I've seen that sort of look too many times—I could easily recognize that kind of lust, which was like dryness seeking moisture. That particular day—the day he was helping my mother harvest the rubber—he secretly passed me a note:

You still don't deign to notice
Every petal of depression that I have shed.

"He lent me many books to read, always asking my brother—that meddlesome Bird's Egg—to bring them over to me. Most of the books were literary works, including poems, essays, and novels, and many were by Taiwan authors. Sometimes he would insert a note into one of them, imagining he was in love. When I encountered this sort of situation, I would ask Bird's Egg to immediately return the note to him, and to tell him not to send me any more books. . . . Upon receiving the note I sent back to him he would immediately panic, and therefore I would then simply ask him to come over and apologize. . . . This forest is very large, and sometimes I would catch him hiding in the shrubbery trying to spy on me, since he always forgot that his glasses reflected light. I, however, was too lazy to do anything about this. . . . My mother has always suspected that his disappearance somehow involved me, but who knows? I was merely a passive figure in all of this. . . ."

The girl spoke in a soft and deliberate manner, as though placing great emphasis on punctuation marks. She led him over to a well, and they sat down on the wooden edge.

"If I may, what is your name?" he asked.

"Are names important?" she asked with a smile. "At any rate, I never knew his name either. . . . I once heard him explain that he was constantly changing the pennames under which he wrote his manuscripts, and was always claiming other writers' manuscript fees. . . . I heard that at one point or other he has 'poached' the name of every Mahua author alive." She handed him a bundle she was carrying in her breast. "These are some documents I saved after he disappeared."

He accepted the documents while describing M's disappearance . . . and his own quest. Based on his analysis, he concluded that M must be somewhere on the mainland, maybe hiding out in some remote town so as to avoid the media. . . . Perhaps he was teaching in a rural elementary school somewhere, and publishing something every now and then. But a long search had so far proved fruitless.

By chance, he discovered a newspaper article . . . which described a man's mysterious disappearance. . . . The girl listened quietly, occasionally cracking a mysterious smile. He read through the documents one after another, until he reached one that said:

Even a heart that has long been cold still has some impulse. I can't change my old habits. I never expected that even here I would encounter such a pure young girl, like a moonlit flower. But I'm too old. Forget it, forget it. I don't want to harm anyone or anything. I fear attachment, and particularly beautiful women.

Based on this fragment, we can probably conclude that the author was in fact Yu Dafu, since Yu always got worked up after seeing pretty girls, and furthermore the document cited a famous passage composed by Yu himself. It perhaps also makes sense to link Yu Dafu and M, given that Yu himself once wrote that, "If only there could appear a great author, it would change the fate of Mahua literature." Unfortunately, Yu Dafu disappeared in 1945. The reporter recalled his dream from the previous night. Another fragment read,

White cloak, you are impossible to forget
Let the third month recede into the past. Let it.
Flower blossoms fly in the breeze. White cloak,
may you appear in my long works
to be eternally serialized.

Based on this latter text, one would conclude that the author must be Wen Rui'an, since *white cloak* is a symbol that is regularly invoked in works produced by Wen's Shenzhou Poetry Society. However, Wen Rui'an had long ago become irredeemably decadent . . .

Another sheet . . .

He found that nearly every document offered a different possibility, and every possibility appeared mutually contradictory. This discovery led him to fall into a deep reflection. After the girl left, he stood there in a cloud of mosquitoes, then picked up a branch and idly used it to brush away the tracks that ants had left on the ground. Before she departed, however, she offered the following words:

"By tomorrow, at the latest, you may know everything—regarding your so-called 'case.'"

He felt that he was getting closer and closer to solving the mystery, but at the same time the answer seemed to be receding further and further into the distance. After nightfall, he sat next to a lamp reflecting on what had transpired. A cold fog came in, and his ears were full of the sound of water. He felt somewhat restless, and opened his notebook to the equation: $M1 + M2 + M3 \ldots Mn, n_{\in} N_0$. The girl's image kept appearing in his mind's eye, her mysterious expression seeming to carry a sense of infinite "possibility." . . . This was autumn, and every rubber tree looked as though it were dead, as dried leaves piled high on the ground and there was an ominous feeling in the air. One day, after what felt like an eternity, he began to wonder how that man could have managed to stay here, alone, for several months? How could he have avoided going insane? The most difficult thing would have been the seemingly bottomless well of loneliness. He hoped that that boy would come and chat with him, but there was no sign of him. The lamp was burning brightly, but he couldn't make out anyone moving around beside it . . . or even shadows. The owls in the forest were hooting, and sounded quite deliberate. Occasionally, he heard the cry of a monkey, as if in a dream. A cool breeze blew out from the depths of the forest—it was actually bone-chillingly cold, and he guessed that everyone in the area must be busy gathering provisions. The moon suddenly peeked out from behind the clouds, and instantly illuminated the forest around where he was standing. The light had no warmth, and instead was but a chilly moonbeam.

The water sounded like the ebb and flow of the tide.

He suddenly noticed that the water really *was* receding, and for a moment he couldn't believe his own eyes. He pushed open the door and proceeded down the steps. He saw that there were just a few shallow pools of water on the ground below the stilt house, in each of which appeared a reflection of the moon. There were some small fish swimming around in them. When he looked up, he saw that there was a single-mast boat floating toward him. In the mire, he could vaguely make out piles of wood. The inside of the boat was wet, but he hopped into it without hesitation. Swaying with an oar, he floated over the mud out into the middle of the water. The water in front of him was jet black, and was surrounded by clumps of earth with trees and wild grass. The water got progressively colder, and the breeze had a slight chill. From near and far, he kept hearing what sounded like old wood splitting. Although it was actually the boat that was moving, it nevertheless seemed as though it were the entire area around him that was receding in both directions. When he turned around, he saw that the lamp from where he had come looked as though it were two or three *li* away. He felt this was not very promising and he had a sense of boundless terror in the face of the unknown, but he nevertheless kept moving forward. This time he perceived it correctly: the trees were in fact receding in both directions, and that soft splitting sound was the earth's crust. . . . Was this the sound the earth's surface makes when it splits open? He placed the oars flat on the water, as the boat continued floating toward its destination. The sound of insects and birds gradually fell silent. There was a thin layer of fog on the water, like a premonition of death.

For a long time, the small boat remained in the center of this lake with indeterminate borders, the water of which was pitch black. He was surrounded by silence. Waiting impatiently, he lay down on the floor of the boat. The moon was hanging low in the sky. It was milky white and appeared bigger and fatter than usual.

As he lowered his gaze, he suddenly saw a flash of light. He quickly sat up and looked upward, and saw that the entire surface of the lake appeared to be illuminated. Could it be that it was actually made of gold? He opened his eyes wider to try to make out what it was. The golden light was moving, and he followed it with his gaze to the side of the boat, where a golden fish was racing past. Where had all of these golden fish come from? How was it that no one had ever mentioned them? What *was* this place?

While he was in this state of surprise, the surface of the water suddenly dimmed, and the golden light faded.

He saw an enormous object consisting of mobile sheets of gold moving in a pattern as though links in a chain. Every segment was about a square yard in size and the golden object floated by under his boat like a submarine, though even after the longest time it still had not passed completely. It turned out to be an enormous fish, with resplendent scales like millennium-old artifacts that had just been unearthed, and which over time had endured a lot of suffering but had preserved their golden radiance. Perhaps he examined it too closely, but he eventually began to discern some inscriptions that seemed to have meaning, and which looked something like this:

The inscription was basically like this, though he couldn't remember it in more detail. This pattern on the back of the fish reminded him of the eight divination hexagrams, while the fish's movement left him in a daze. The inscription was dark gold in color, and was densely packed.

There was also a line of pictographic script, which looked like this:

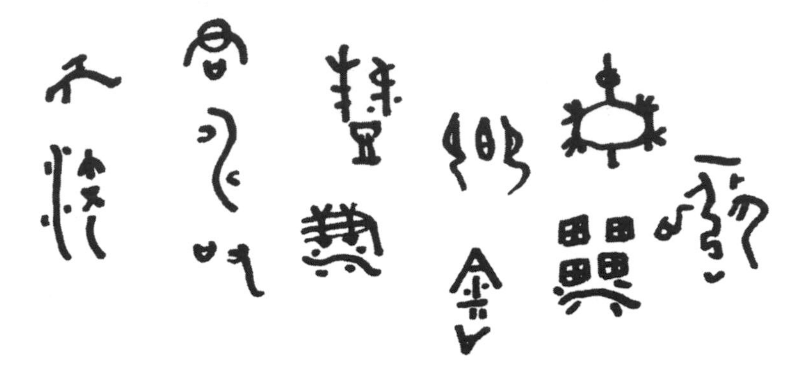

The sight of this latter script evoked in him a sense of historical nostalgia. It was as if a long manuscript written by a very ancient people were opening up before his very eyes. He couldn't help regretting that his education was so limited, and as a result he was unable to immediately make sense of these markings, or even translate them into conventional written text.

A deep sound reverberated through the darkness, and he suddenly felt as though his body were floating in midair. An enormous golden fish suddenly leapt out of the water and opened its mouth like a dragon, looking like it was about to swallow the moon. He felt a vague sense of "awakening."

After floating along for who knows how long, he finally returned to earth. Upon awakening he realized he was in a small room, and everything was as before. The ground below the stilt house was covered with water and his entire body was soaking wet. The sun was already high in the sky, and he hurried over to Ah Qing's house. Holding a rolled-up newspaper, she asked him what was wrong? He briefly recounted the previous night's events.

"It's said that a long time ago, a dragon fell into a nearby river," the girl said, as though recounting a story. "When I was young, I often ate the kind of fish you describe. The taste wasn't bad, very sweet. It also looked very appealing. But in recent years there haven't been any of them in the area—they've been fished to extinction. Do you believe in dragons?"

He neither nodded nor shook his head, and instead just stood there grinning stupidly.

"What about it? Have you found your 'answer' yet?"

He shook his head. She handed him the newspaper she was holding, and said,

"Take this back and read it. Don't linger here any longer—pack up your things and get going." Bird's Egg handed him a fragrant cempedak, and said he could eat it right away.

He opened the newspaper, and found a supplement labeled "Special Section on the Xiangqing Literature Prize." To his surprise, he saw that one of the essays was titled "The Disappearance of M," and the author was listed as "M". . . . The report noted that the real identity of the author was unknown.

The aroma from the cempedak filled the room, and he dug out the flesh and ate it.

When he compared the essay with his own unfinished manuscript, he discovered to his astonishment that they were nearly identical, while the places where they diverged involved merely minor embellishments. He suddenly felt his legs grow weak and abruptly sat down.

When I (uh, it's not me) . . . when *he* discussed that essay, he had an uncanny feeling that he had written it himself, while at the same time it was obviously mocking his writing. How could there be another author like this, who was able to penetrate into his thoughts and preemptively write his future, thereby forcibly removing him from this position of the "author"? This seemingly impossible conduct presented a profound challenge to his very "existence," implying that "I" could be completely obliterated. . . . And, who could that be? Who was it that was using M's name to replace *his own* account of M's disappearance? "It must be her," he thought. "It must be her, who is playing tricks."

The girl, with a sweet yet mischievous smile, suddenly appeared in his mind's eye. Was not this vision, which dominated his resting memory, some sort of secret omen? Or, to put it another way, once she appeared as a character in his memory, did not M's disappearance then become inevitable? Did that mean that *Kristmas* was a product of a collective authorship, like the novels *The Water Margin* and *Journey to the West*? . . .

How was it that it never occurred to him that M might perhaps not be a man, or even a woman, but rather a girl who was both the protagonist and the author? Was it therefore not surprising that the manuscript left behind by the missing author (whom perhaps we might call MX) was full of Yu Dafu's depressed lamentations? It finally occurred to him that M must be a compound entity, of which he himself was only one insignificant element. On a sheet of paper, he wrote,

"Perhaps after not too long someone will discover my own 'disappearance' (this is a structural necessity . . .)."

He lay down and read the final lines of "The Disappearance of M":

> As revealed by one of the members of the steering committee, the excitement of this appraisal was unprecedentedly interesting, because unfortunately the critics could not avoid becoming secondary characters in one of the work's own plotlines, even as the text anticipated the critical response that it itself would eventually receive. All of this speculation naturally contained a certain amount of error, and fortunately this was just a first draft. The host of the meeting, Chen Zhicheng, with a look of acute embarrassment, hollered for thirty-two seconds while grasping his enormous belly, until finally he lifted his beard and said:
>
> "Colleagues, I'm very sorry, that piece . . . I discussed this with Fu Chengde, and in order to avoid embarrassing you, we had originally intended to file this work as a classified document. In the end, however, we decided that if we were to have done so, it would have harmed the public perception of this literary prize and furthermore wouldn't have been fair to the author. How he chooses to write is his decision, and we have no right to interfere. We must respect the evaluation process, or otherwise there is no point in inviting you. Isn't that right? I'm sorry, Fu Chengde was only charged with weeding out works that were not submitted in the proper format. Perhaps we didn't communicate ourselves clearly. . . ."
>
> Chen was wearing a Western suit and Chuan (despite the heat) was wearing a traditional long gown, and was gazing down at the tape recorder. Sima Zhongyuan, who was also wearing a suit, said in a "soft and sincere" voice, as if he were telling a ghost story,
>
> "This was definitely written by a young person. Young people are mischievous, playful, and like to joke around. They are very different from people from our generation. Some of the things they write I simply can't understand, like much of what Zhang Dachun has written in recent years."

He turned to Zhang Dachun, who was wearing a batik shirt and appeared rather emotional, and added, "But just as there are many people in my generation who are still serving as gatekeepers, I don't know if there might be some mistake. I originally felt that this text was not realistic enough, and that it didn't reflect any actual reality. Later, I realized that it contained many "fringe" elements I couldn't understand. In a little while, I'll ask Prof. Chen to provide a detailed supplement."

Next, Lin Huanzhang spoke, "[*deleted, at Lin's request*]."

Zheng Mingli had combed her hair into a chignon, and was now wearing a very Chinese *qipao*. She pointed out one defect in the text after another, then added,

"This is a 'metafictional novel,' and readers in Malaysia will undoubtedly find it new and refreshing. Perhaps we should conduct a literary investigation. Based on the author's classification and the information he has provided, I suspect he probably studied in Taiwan." She surmised that the author had at least graduated from college. "Perhaps the work had been written by Zhang Guixing as a joke, although the work's style is not really his . . . [*remainder deleted, at Zheng's request*]."

After Zheng finished speaking, Zhang Dachun glanced over at Chen Huihua, sitting next to him, and the latter gestured for him to proceed. Zhang gazed out at the audience for a while with a froglike expression, and out of habit held his metal-rimmed glasses. Then he said in serious tone,

"I am very familiar with this writing style, which basically uses a fictional plotline to discuss a topic. The author's technique [*deleted, at Zhang's request*], and addresses a very serious issue: [*deleted, at Zhang's request*]. . . . [*deleted, at Zhang's request*]."

Next in line to speak was Chen Pengyu, who was also wearing a batik shirt. He began by offering some necessary supplements to what had already been said, analyzing one textual allusion to Malaysia after another. Because he himself was a poet, he was therefore most interested in whether or not the work had any poetic qualities, and therefore his decisions of what to accept or reject differed from those of the others. [*In order to prevent this text from becoming overly long, six hundred characters from Chen's speech have been omitted here, at his request. Readers are invited to consult the conference minutes on their own.*]

As was customary, after a heated debate they eventually reached an agreement on each item and the participants then tried to guess who the author was. Chen Pengyu was a popular suspect (on account of his deep familiarity with Mahua literature) and Chen Chengde was also a possibility. . . . Everyone turned to Chen, but he shook his head and said,

"It's not me. I couldn't have participated. And, furthermore, the tone is completely different from mine." So, who was the author? Chen Zhicheng took out a card, on which was written MN,K<NLOO

Finally, the conference moderator invited all of the critics to review and revise the portions of the conference transcript corresponding to their contributions—in order to bring fiction closer into alignment with reality, while at the same time bringing reality closer into alignment with fiction. Zhang Dachun, while reviewing the transcript, beamed with a *Great Liar*–like smile, such that the creases on either side of his mouth danced back and forth like a pair of carp. . . .

At that point an absurd situation presented itself: A group of Taiwan authors in the work were critiquing fictional characters who shared their name in a work by the same title, even as the fictional characters themselves were simultaneously critiquing a work by the same title. In the end, Zhang Dachun couldn't help but sigh:

"Don't you know, reality itself is actually so fictional."

It may be inferred that the author must have had a considerable influence on Zhang Dachun. Perhaps he personally knew all of the conference attendees, which is why he dared to include their names in his work. The basis for this inference may be found in the work's final two sentences:

> *This is a work of fiction, and any resemblance to reality is completely coincidental.*
>
> *Many thanks to all of the scholars and authors for attending the performance.*

dream and swine and aurora

WOO . . . KUNG KUNG KUNG KUNG . . . WOO! . . . A violent shaking woke her up. *Woo . . . kung kung kung kung . . . woo!* . . . The train crawled down the tracks squirming like a centipede underneath her bed. It gradually pulled away, then paused. The surrounding area returned to its former peaceful state, broken only by the sound of insects. The cock had not yet crowed. She was lying down, and wiped the tears from her eyes. Then, she turned to look at her unreliable alarm clock, which said it was four thirty-five. Was the clock slow . . . or fast? This clock had always followed the beat of its own drum—working when it wanted to, and stopping whenever it wished. It is up to you to decide whether or not to trust it, since the only standard for judging its accuracy was the clock itself. It must still be early, given that the cocks had not yet crowed. There was an oil lamp hanging from a column, and although the light was as tiny as a firefly, in the darkness it nevertheless shone brightly. In fact, it seemed that the light could even be turned down some, in order to conserve oil. . . . She gazed evenly at the top of the mosquito netting—her eyes squinting, her face painfully swollen, and her back limp. She decided to forget it and sleep some more. At this point she suddenly smelled a peculiar odor and felt a cold breeze coming in through the cracks in the boards as the smell assaulted her nostrils—the scent was sharp, ticklish, and familiar. She rubbed her nose . . . Ah, it was pig shit.

The first sound of crowing . . . the *kung kung kung kung* sound mercilessly severed her dream, leaving behind only an isolated strand flopping around in her wakened consciousness, like a gecko's severed tail flipping around in her mind. Clearly, the smell of pig shit had been brought by the dream, little by little. She closed her eyes and struggled to fall back to sleep, because otherwise a new day's work would be upon her, Buddha help her! She hadn't smelled the stench of pig shit for a long time, and it had also been several years since she raised pigs. But that dream. . . .

In the dream, she clearly saw Ah Xing, who appeared distressed and was leaning against a pole next to the pigsty railing, looking at those huge neutered pigs, who had their heads buried in the feed trough, blithely chomping away—a single-file line of course pig hair. "*Ah mu*, I want to go to Taiwan for college. All of my classmates have gone, and they all had worse grades than I did . . ." "Ah! Where would I find the money to pay for it? I'm lucky if I have enough for three solid meals a day. Go ask your father, and if he agrees so will I." (Didn't you graduate many years ago? Didn't you return home a long time ago? Didn't you earn your money in Sabah?) Suddenly, however, that face was transformed into Ah Cai's own, who also appeared extremely depressed. She stared as she—as she struggled to shovel the pig shit into a ditch. The sound of the shovel resounded again and again. The pigs seemed to eat incessantly. "Ah Cai, do you want to go to college? I said that if your grades were better than Ah Fa's, I would let you go—and if it turns out that we don't have enough money, I'll come up with some solution." (We'll think of something.)

This put me in a very difficult position, since I had to test poorly so as not to outperform my brother, but at the same time didn't want people to say that I was stupid. (Now I'm old, and can't raise pigs any longer.)

At this point, Ah Xing, with his single-fold eyelids, suddenly appeared in the pigpen. A pig that had already eaten its fill obsequiously lifted its back to present its buttocks. He grinned happily and laughed as he shook his feet with their black leather shoes.

Ah Cai shouted back, "Brother, these pigs are all yours. How is this possible, given that you have so many other brothers and sisters?" Ah Xing turned his head as though he were a puppet. "Why would it *not* be possible? *Ha ha ha ha ha ha.* Who told you two to wait so long before having children?"

The two faces gradually became reduplicated, and she couldn't help starting to cry. If you can't mock your own brother, then who else can you mock? The blurred face suddenly became clear, and it turned out to be her own daughter, Ah Yun. Ah Yun stared, with her bosomy cheeks and round eyes, and said, "Ma, you favor your sons over your daughters. I hadn't even finished second grade when you told me to come home to watch over my younger brothers and sisters, to feed them and clean up their piss and shit so that the boys might then go to college." (I had no choice! I had no choice! We have so many children, and when the girls grow up they had to marry into someone's else's family, but if boys don't get an education, they will have as difficult a life as your father. . . .) Her tears began to gush forth. At that point the train could be heard rumbling forward, coming straight at her. The train whistle sounded . . . and kept hooting loudly . . . The front of the train rushed up to her like an alarm clock, and she quickly jumped aside as the train rumbled past. The pig pen, which was made from thick tree trunks, was broken in half, and the fat pigs started running wild. The result was a scene like when they chase pigs for the slaughter. At the crucial moment, however, the pigs jumped up and, just as the train was approaching, they rushed into the field. My pigs! She wanted to call out to them, but discovered that those pigs didn't have names. . . .

She dozed quietly for a while, then heard the cock start crowing. She opened her eyes, and saw that it was four fifty. In the continuation of her dream it was still Ah Xing, who was speaking earnestly. After graduating and returning home, she now had double-fold eyelids, which made her appear very emotional. "Definitely, definitely, I'll definitely bring home any money I may earn. Give me five years . . . five years . . . and I'll build a two-story house for you and Ah Ba to live in. At that point neither of you will need to work. How about it? Could we hold out for another five years?" The cock crowed, whereupon she awoke and got up.

She unrolled her red blanket and sat up. She rubbed her eyes, moved her feet to the edge of the bed, opened the mosquito netting, then put on her slippers. She slowly got out of bed. A bone-chillingly cold draft entered through cracks in the floorboards, and she quickly got up and grabbed the dark purple sweater that was hanging from the post and put it on. In this dream there was a pungent stench of pig shit. . . . She yawned deeply and, looking in the mirror, she combed down her messy hair. As she did so, her eyes seemed to brighten. The stench of pig shit was still very strong. Her alarm clock began to ring.

She opened a cabinet and took out a red candle, then struck a match and lit it. She stared intently at the tightly closed wooden window. Many years earlier it had also been this sort of dawn, and this sort of scene. At the time, Ah Xing was still young, and every morning when she went out to harvest rubber she had to carry him, still half asleep, to the rubber tree grove. She would then erect some mosquito netting in an old shack with a roof made of sheet metal, so that he could continue sleeping soundly. Even if he woke up, he wouldn't make a fuss, and instead would practice his penmanship under the light from the oil lamp. A dog accompanied him. He was actually not at all afraid of the dark, and never gave others cause for concern. He invariably addressed his uncles and aunts very respectfully, and everyone always complimented him on his good behavior, and on New Year's they would never fail to give him a traditional red envelope stuffed with money. . . . She sighed, and left the bedroom.

"Hey, get up!" she called out, knocking the wall with her hand. She then listened, but there was no response. She knocked again. "Get up! The cock has already crowed. It's time to go harvest the rubber!" She then added, "You sleepy pig!"

She listened again, and the man inside produced a series of strange sounds, as if still asleep—*woo~woo~so sleepy!* "If you don't get up now, you needn't bother going to harvest the rubber. You are getting lazier by the day! Do I really need to wake up so early every morning to fix food for both of you?" "Huh, I'm getting up," the man responded wearily.

She slowly crossed the dark hall, as the darkness was pierced by light from the candle she was carrying. The tiny flame projected her shadow onto the wall as she proceeded forward. She stepped through the doorway, into the kitchen. On a round table there was an oil lamp, and both the lamp shade and its base were splattered with drops of wax. She pulled down the blackened upper half of the lamp shade, revealing a pile of scorched insect carcasses surrounding the lamp wick. She raised the candle she was holding and used it to light the lamp wick, and the room was immediately illuminated. Everything was in its correct place, as it had been before she went to bed. A cold draft continued blowing in through the floorboards.

Next to the stove, there was a waist-high brick stove, on which there was a wok, a kettle, and a pot, all sitting in a row. In the large area underneath, there were several neatly arranged piles of wood and kindling. The kitchen walls did not have any eaves, and above people's heads there was an opening to let out the smoke. It was through here that the stench of pig manure entered. Outside, it was clearly dawn in the dark forest. At the edge of the forest there was a train station, and trains would periodically pass by, virtually on the hour, running north to south. Holding a bowl, she removed the cover of the pot and dished out the leftover rice, which she then put aside. She then carried the pot over to the rice jug, where she got some rice. Propping one hand on her knee she stood up, whereupon her mind suddenly went blank. She rested for a few seconds, at which point she was able to proceed to the back door, reach out and get the lamp that was there, and place it under the table.

When she opened the door, a powerful gust of wind surged in and almost blew the door shut. She sighed (the stench of pig manure was still very strong), then pushed the door open and squeezed through. Outside, there was no moon or stars, and instead everything was as black as ink. Her hands were cupped around the candle flame. Several dogs came up to her, and looked like they wanted to affectionately jump up on her. "Get away! Blasted dogs!" She moved as though to kick them, and after a moment they finally left, jumping back into the darkness. The sky was dark, and it looked as though it were about to rain. She sighed, "If it rains, we won't be able to harvest any rubber. We've gotten so much rain recently . . ."

She proceeded over to the well, which had a rusted iron cover, a wooden board, and was surrounded on three sides by barbed wire. On the fourth side there was a pile of discarded wooden ties for people to stand on, and a small cement platform. She put down her pot and from beside the pile of ties she removed a paper tube. She put the half-severed candle on it and placed it on the cement; she then took the water bucket and lowered it into the pitch-black well. After the rope had descended for a while, she felt the bucket hit the surface of the water. Her hand trembling, she tilted the bucket slightly as it entered the water. She then straightened it again and pulled it back up, full of water, whereupon she proceeded to squat down next to the well to rinse the rice.

Remembering that her son needed to go to school, she once again began worrying about money. Every day was like a dream—quite unlike the past, when she was still young. Her eyes began to tear up, as her memories of the past and the present blurred into one another and she fell back into her dreams.

Before daybreak, Ah Xing began crying, his face pressed against that column in the kitchen. He said plaintively, "Pa told me to go to the bazaar to fetch some flour, saying, 'What use is it to study so much? It's not like you're going to become an official!'" She saw that the younger version of herself looked similarly hopeless. "If the two of us harvest rubber for an entire month, we earn only barely enough to buy food—and we can only afford to eat meat twice a month. What can I possibly do?" The house resonated with the child's sobs. "There are so many mouths to feed, what can I possibly do?" After washing the rice she poured the water into a wash basin, and then added another half-bucket of fresh water. She saw the younger version of herself and Ah Xing changing into their new clothes, and then riding their bicycles past row after row of trees. They boarded the bus, which proceeded down the windy asphalt road lined with tall trees. When they reached the door of someone's house, Ah Xing correctly determined that this was the house of one of his aunts or uncles. The owner would smile and serve them hot coffee or milo, as they chatted with one another: Is it raining? Ha ha, how is it that you have time to come visit us? Ha ha . . . Has Ah Xing graduated yet? Oh, oh! . . . Oh, ok . . . Are you are preparing for college? Ok, ok, you get such good grades, it would be a shame if you didn't go on to college . . . My kids don't study, they'd rather be laborers. . . . Huh? Ok, although we don't have much money, we can always raise three hundred or so. Don't mention it! After he graduates and starts earning a salary, you can gradually begin paying us back. . . . If one of our relatives goes to college, we all enjoy the glory . . . Ah Xing, after you become rich, you mustn't forget your relatives. . . . Don't mention it, don't mention it. Even if we don't have any money, we'll still give him a small red envelope for good luck. . . .

(She continued drawing water from the well.) So that's how it went from house to house, like climbing a vine to pluck melons. Afterward, Ah Xing, with his single-fold eyelids, left happily, and she accompanied him to the train station. When she turned around, she found a crowd of children waiting for her. She repeatedly exhorted them that those who are out working should send money home every month, and therefore those who are not interested in studying should go find work after finishing elementary school, since there's no need for girls to get so much education. . . . (She finished washing the rice and slowly took it back to the kitchen.) The *biyi babuy* pigsty was to be erected in a field, and she called out to her husband to come help her. Her husband was taking a nap and was annoyed when she woke him, cursing, "It's you who is going to go out and sell it, not me!" She therefore wiped away her sweat and erected the *biyi babuy*, putting up the posts and mixing cement as her face flushed bright red. . . .

She took out several sticks and stuck them in the oven, inserted some strands of rubber, then lit a fire. She piled on the kindling, as water from the pot dripped down. Countless angry versions of herself seemed to be bustling about inside the fire. One of these selves went into the rubber forest at dawn to harvest rubber while another went to feed the pigs, and yet another nursed a baby. In the afternoon, one of her selves went to help her husband make rubber sheets while another fed the pigs. In the depths of the forest, one of her selves picked yams and cut banana stalks, peeling the stalks and leaves from wild taros, then binding them together and tying them to the back of a bicycle. A little later, another of her selves was in the forest cutting timber and collecting kindling, while yet another was taking water to the pigs to help them cool off, peeling the yams, taros, and so forth, and putting them in the pot to cook. Rain or shine, several children followed her loyally, serving as her assistants. In the evening, one of her selves went to feed the pigs, another was in the kitchen cooking dinner, while yet another fetched water to cool off. One of her selves rode her bike through the forest, carrying a paint can inside a sack, and when she reached a residential area on the side of the asphalt road, she cut through an alley and began going door-to-door collecting swill—in sun, rain, or wind. Interspersed with these other figures was a younger version of herself, who shuttled back and forth through the dark forest wearing a black and white school uniform, under the light of the setting sun, and through wind and rain. Her increasingly elderly husband also appeared, and somewhere deep in the forest began cutting banana stalks. At night, he would stuff kindling under the stove while cooking slop for the pigs. He removed the lid from the pot and stirred vigorously, then ladled out something that looked like a chicken neck or duck foot, and fed it to the dogs. . . . She watched as her other self repeatedly biked through the forest, winding through the trees, up and down hills, carrying hot water thermoses to the hospital. Several days later, she would ride a taxi home with a newborn infant in her arms, while her husband would ride back to the hospital to fetch her bicycle. . . .

By this point the pot was already boiling over, and the kettle was beginning to whistle. She shifted her gaze to the dark forest, wondering why the cocks weren't crowing and why no one had gotten up after all this time. She also wondered whether she should start cooking some food. She then went up to the wall and once again began knocking, shouting "Wake up! Time for school!" No one answered. "Hey!" She knocked again, until finally someone mumbled something in response. "You sleepy pigs! Go wake up your father! He's slept so long he probably doesn't even remember his own name." She then went back to the stove.

She sat on a stool and began peeling potatoes. It seemed as though someone woke up, called out "Ma," then disappeared. Another woke up, called out "*Ah mu*," then vanished. He then appeared wearing a school uniform, then vanished again. The water boiled, and she got up and took the kindling out from under the pot. At this point, the stench of manure suddenly became even stronger. She couldn't help focusing harder, gazing into the forest as steam from the stove heated the side of her body. Even though it was foggy outside, she thought she could make out some white shadows moving around. There were many of them, and they covered an entire section of the rubber forest. She rubbed her eyes and looked again, but they were still there. Were they dogs? But if they were dogs, why weren't they barking? She felt somewhat uneasy, as though there were something slowly seeping out of her brain through her eyes, and was in a kind of conspiracy with the dawn. *Woo . . . kung kung kung kung . . . woo!* A train passed by, each car brightly illuminated, like a smiling mouth, or a centipede. Yes, they were pigs. So many pigs, each of them snorting away as they rooted around in the dirt with their noses. No wonder—no wonder the smell of pig shit hadn't gone away. Those pigs all looked up at her. It was hot, so very hot. *Dee dee da, da.* They jumped over to her. So many of them, during the temple festival they would feed the trodden feces to the dogs. Each pig began rushing toward her. . . .

"*Ah mu*," a girl's dainty voice called out to her. The candlelight came closer and closer until it nearly blinded her.

A girl wearing a white shirt and white skirt pulled aside the mosquito netting and stood next to the bed. As the girl called out to her, a smell of toothpaste emanated from her mouth, and by this point the stench of manure had finally begun to subside. "*Ah mu*. . . ." The train rumbled past.

Crap! She cried to herself, then quickly pulled off her blanket and got out of bed. She looked at her alarm clock. "Six o'clock!" she shouted in surprise.

"Shit! Today I'm the one who's the sleepy pig! I'm not even sure when I fell asleep . . ." While shouting, she quickly ran a comb through her hair. "Mingming, get up!" Feeling deeply confused, she threw on her jacket.

"Where is your father?" She went up to the door, as her daughter followed behind with a candle.

"He went to harvest rubber."

"Why is he so on the ball today? Did he wake up on his own?"

"He said that he dreamed you were telling him to wake up—and said that we should let you sleep some more."

"The sun is about to come up! I won't have enough time to cook for you . . ."

"I've already done it. I was woken up by the cock's crowing." They entered the kitchen.

(Her daughter had always been very well-behaved.)

"How is it that I didn't hear the sound of you cooking?"

"*Ah mu.*" A crowd of her children, all dressed in white, were standing around the dinner table, their mouths full of food. She examined each of their faces with a sense of uneasiness. Then she asked her daughter for some candlelight, saying, "You should go eat as well!" She pushed open the back door and walked toward the well—Mingming had come . . . She immediately entered that cave-like bathroom, placing the candle on the wax-covered wooden crossbeam. Wedged between the aluminum wall and the crossbeam was a row of multicolored toothbrushes. She picked out her own, took some water from her cup, squeezed some toothpaste (there was a strong smell of peppermint), then squatted in the doorway and proceeded to brush her teeth. The rooster crowed several times and black clouds appeared in the sky. By this point the smell of manure had completely disappeared, and had been replaced by a fresh smell of mist. In the dark forest an orange light was flashing—it moved sideways, stopped, then moved forward. . . . Everyone heading toward the forest would see this light, which was affixed to the men's foreheads and intermittently appeared in the distance as she was cooking, washing vegetables, brushing her teeth, and preparing coffee. She washed her face, and her eyes suddenly became very wet.

Even earlier, after a deity in the temple had predicted that she would have a hard life and would bring ill fortune to her mother, her parents had sent her several dozen *li* away to be adopted by another family with a different surname. She spent many years cooking, washing clothes, and handling childcare for this other family, and each day she always had to be the first to get up. One day, she was about to go rinse the rice when she opened the door and shined the flashlight outside, whereupon she saw two blinking orbs of light. Remembering what her elders had told her, she quickly slammed the door shut and shouted as she ran back inside, "Tiger!"

Everyone was immediately jolted awake and began shouting loudly while banging on pots and pans. Instantly, everyone in the village was struggling desperately to make a fearful ruckus. The tiger fled, but returned several days later and ate a piglet. . . . Occasionally the villagers might encounter a tiger when going down to the river to refresh themselves, and would be devoured.

She got up, and as usual massaged her waist and knees. She then turned around and went to the bathroom. She took several steps, whereupon that uncanny feeling returned, like mysterious bubbles coming up out of the marshy water. She looked, and noticed that the lights in the forest had disappeared. Could it be that they were now blocked by the trees? She watched for several more seconds, but they still didn't reappear. They had truly vanished. Was it because he had returned, or because . . . ? She couldn't help feeling anxious. Where were the dogs? Why were they nowhere to be seen? The smell of manure returned again, moist and pungent. She suddenly felt there was something soft and mushy on the sole of her sandals. She leaned over to look and, yes, wasn't that a black glob of pig feces? The moisture from the feces had soaked through the sole of her sandals under her toes, staining her feet black. She held up her candle and looked around, and saw that there was pig shit everywhere. The ground was covered with hoof prints, and the soil had been all rooted up by the pigs' snouts. The buckets, urns, flowerpots, and bricks . . . had all been overturned. She felt a deep chill, as her teeth started chattering. She turned around, and began striding back to the kitchen.

She pushed open the door and stared in shock: How could there be so many people? *Ai!?* Each face was familiar—they were all her own children. □□,□□, and □□, don't you need to be working? Why are you all wearing school uniforms? □□,□□,□□ . . . she felt as though her head was spinning. *Dee dee da, da . . . Woo woo . . . kung kung kung kung . . .*

woo . . . She opened her mouth wide and yawned—I'm so tired, I want to sleep some more, it's so cold, so cold, is it snowing, or is it . . .

"*Ah mu*," she languidly opened her eyes and kicked off her blanket. A train could be heard off in the distance.

"Ah Xing! You're back? When did you return? Why didn't you contact me sooner?" (It has already been several years since you returned, and every year you claim that there are no plane tickets.) She got up and sat on the edge of the bed. It was now five thirty-five. "I woke up before four. I wanted to sleep some more, but it was too late. I had to hurry and cook some food and wake up everyone else," she added. She got out of bed, got dressed, and quickly combed her hair. A cold draft blew in through cracks in the floorboards. It was only then that she suddenly noticed that her son was carrying a gray gunny sack, which seemed to be empty. "What are you carrying?" "In elementary school, I read the filial story of Zilu carrying the rice." (Oh, I remember you mentioning this.)

With large, black eyes, her son gently placed the sack in front of him, and as he untied the white string he explained, "I hear that the temple needs money. . . ." He couldn't manage to get the string untied. His forehead was covered in beads of sweat and he frowned as he struggled with the knot, but in the end he only succeeded in tightening it even more. He stomped his feet, muttering and cursing.

(He is still as stubborn as a mule.)

She took the sack, then brought over the oil lamp that was hanging from the rafter. Telling her son to hold the lamp, she leaned over and examined it, then used her long fingernails to untie the knot. Without even breaking a sweat, she undid the entire string (it was a shoelace from a sneaker . . .) and handed it back to Ah Xing. She then opened the sack and peered inside, and saw that it was full of green banknotes.

"*Wa!*" (You must agree to share this with your brothers and sisters.)

A sense of joy surged up through her body. "Did you rob a bank?" She smiled mischievously at Ah Xing, and Ah Xing grinned back. She suddenly felt that the things she was holding became a very moist *ah ah ah ah* . . . pig shit! . . . the bank notes were completely covered in pig shit! She examined the notes more closely, and saw that they were not printed with a portrait of the head of state, but rather with images of bananas and a pig's head. These were worth even less than weeds. What was this?! She angrily threw the banknotes back into the sack. At this point she heard something rooting around outside . . . *peng peng peng peng*, it kept knocking against the wall in different locations, and seemed like it might even break through. With a *thunk*, the window was pushed open, and a pig snout poked in, followed by an entire pig head, its chin resting on the windowsill and its ears twitching. A shadow flickered, and the pig scurried inside. It passed the bed and the table, and then lay down next to her son and facing her. The pig was soaking wet (was it raining outside?). It was about eight feet long, and when it shook itself, drops of water covered her face and body, and she turned to shield herself. Her son leaned over and slowly used that shoelace to tie the sack back up, then pulled it tight. His forehead was covered in sweat. He exhaled, picked up the sack, stepped over the pig, and said, "Zilu carries the rice . . ." (So I've heard!) Then he hopped over the pig, proceeded past the bed and table, and just as he was climbing out the window he turned around and, lifting a hand to his ear, said tenderly, "Bye-bye. . . ." Then, he disappeared into the rain. She stood there crying bitterly, her chest heaving. In front of her there was a thick white mist.

"*Ah!*" She woke up.

"*Ah mu*, don't get up." A young girl dressed in a white shirt and white skirt was standing by the bed.

"What time is it? How long did I sleep? The food . . ." Outside the window, the sun was shining brightly.

"No, . . . it's afternoon, and we're already back from school." (Afternoon? I never sleep in the afternoon, unless . . .)

"You were spitting blood and passed out." (Spitting blood? Passed out?)

The sunlight was so bright it hurt her eyes, so she began to squint. Next to her daughter there was an overweight woman whose smile and laugh was just like her own.

"Sister!" she called out happily. (Sister!) "When did you arrive?"

"I heard you weren't feeling well, so I came over." Her voice was very low, and it echoed slightly. (Sister, you always looked after me.)

"You must make sure not to work too hard. You just had surgery and should take it easy." (Surgery? Wasn't that years ago?)

"If you need money, I can lend you some." (Lending is not the same as giving, and if she were to offer to give it to me, I wouldn't accept it.) "*Ai*, you've truly had a hard life. Having given birth so many times, you've really messed up your body. After they are born you still have to raise them, and after you raise them you have to get them educated, and you will be burdened your whole life! Being a wife and working tirelessly like a dog . . ." (Sister!) She closed both eyes, feeling exhausted and completely unable to move.

Many years earlier, not long after she got married, her elder sister, from whom she had been separated since they were young, finally succeeded in tracking her down. From her elder brother she learned the surname of her new husband and the name of the street where they lived, which was several dozen *li* away, and then quickly went to look for her. First, her sister found the township, then the desired street. Next, she went door-to-door asking if anyone went by that surname, until she finally succeeded in finding this new bride who looked just like herself. The two sisters immediately recognized each other, acting as though they were each encountering a different version of themselves.

"Sis!" She opened her eyes again, but now there was no one at the head of the bed. A solitary lamp was sitting on the table. It was cold. The window was open, and the shutter was banging against the wall. The rain was pouring down, and her pillow, mosquito netting, and hair were all soaking wet. She closed the window, as a flash of lightning illuminated the sky and thunder could be heard from far away. The ground was wet, and there were footprints everywhere!

Someone had come. A row of wet footprints were visible in front of the bed. Who was it? Whoever it was had evidently been wearing sneakers. There was also a row of footprints left by someone wearing high heels—was it possible that these were from a pig? She felt very anxious. *Dee dee da, da.* It was now five forty. The house's aluminum roof was rattling, and the sound of the rain pounded in her ears. She put on her slippers, got dressed, and combed her hair. The light in the kitchen was on; someone had gotten up before her. There was the sound of someone cooking.

Upon entering the kitchen, she saw a girl dressed in white who was cooking vegetables. Several other girls also dressed in white were sitting around the table.

"Ah Cai!" Her son laughed. His face seemed thinner than before. She smiled calmly, but once she opened her mouth she found that she couldn't close it again. She had a silly grin on her face that she couldn't wipe off.

(Didn't you go to Taiwan? How is it that you're back already?)

(I hear you applied for a scholarship? *Ah mu* is very proud of you.)

(I've struggled my entire life, but what comforts me the most is that I've managed to raise several children who went on to college.)

(On this street, the most educated people are all from our family . . . among our relatives, it is the same . . . who would dare look down on us?)

"When did you return?"

"Yesterday evening." Her son laughed, then fell silent.

Then she noticed she was in an empty area in the middle of a rubber tree grove. Many of the trees had been cut down, leaving a bare circular area. In the trees' shadows, several fat pigs were lying around. There were white ones, black ones, and mottled ones, and all of them were staring at her. All with that defiant look of kids who have been spanked. The rubber tree grove was full of light and shadows, and a large group of women wearing work clothes walked over. Some were fat and some were thin, and their clothes were splattered with dark drops of rubber sap, banana sap, and taro juice. There was one sallow face after another. Some were neighbors who lived on the same street, while others were ones whom she had seen before or heard others mention, and whom she knew either by name or by sight. They leisurely walked forward between the pigs, covering the entire mountainside. They tracked pig shit into the house. None of them spoke and instead they all just stood there silently with their heads bowed. The mountainside was full of children with tattered clothes and bare feet—their faces, hands, feet, and bellies all covered in filth, such that they looked as though they had emerged from the legendary monkey mountain.

In the oval-shaped opening, there was a roadside performance in an open-air stilt stage, with a ceiling made from boards and leaves. The stage was erected in the blink of an eye, and they each placed horizontal banners and flag poles. A young man wearing a suit stood next to one of the flag poles, holding a piece of cloth that looked like a skirt. Women walked in from all directions, while men wearing black suits and dark sunglasses blew their whistles and directed the women to line up, as though they were elementary school kids. Each woman had a numbered bib on her chest: 15, 8, 12, 21, 7, 13 . . . Many of the numbers were repeated, leaving her befuddled.

"You've come too?" one of the women called out to her. "Yes." She replied without thinking. (Last time, when the government was stringing electrical lines, you didn't notify me? You even said, "I don't know whether you want this or not." I'd been waiting for decades for this, how could I not want it?)

"You're here," said No. 10, a woman with a gaunt face. (Even dirty water wants to fight me.)

She was bewildered and had no idea what was going on, or why so many people were there. Then she overhead someone whispering to someone else. Finally . . .

". . . I hear that they are going to award prizes! . . ."

". . . What prizes? . . ."

". . . Only those who have had seven will get one . . ."

". . . Did □□ come? She's not . . ."

". . . Yes, yes, she only qualifies if you count the one she's adopted. She's hasn't been able to have a son . . ."

". . . She almost ended up with a proverbial seven fairy daughters. *Ha ha . . .*"

"Shhh, they're here."

"Stand up! Silence!" the black suit–clad men shouted.

One black sedan after another rolled in from the north and from the south. Leading the way were eight enormous cars driven by large policemen wearing white hats and black sunglasses. They were escorted by a line of motorcycles, and there were also countless helicopters buzzing around in the sky. The doors of the two black sedans opened, and the black suit and black sunglasses-wearing men inside got out, crowding around someone. On the southern side, there was a man with slick black hair and thick lips, and who was wearing a white suit and sunglasses with black frames, while on the northern side there was a bald old man with white eyebrows and beard, wearing a traditional long gown and carrying a cane, who was a spitting image of those mobsters in the Hong Kong movies his son in high school was always telling him about. However, the strange thing is that the people on each side couldn't see each other. The elder and the younger men both climbed onto the stage as though they were each the leader, and both of them simultaneously broke into a radiant smile. One of them shouted in Chinese while the other shouted in Malay, "Stand silently, as we sing the national anthem!" Then, they each proceeded to broadcast their respective music and sing their respective national anthems.

When they finished, both leaders gave a speech. She could hear the speeches, but couldn't really make sense of what they meant: "Because overseas Chinese have contributed greatly to the revolution and helped the Republic of China in driving out the barbarians . . . countless people have donated money and sacrificed their lives . . . and therefore all these countless people who have helped all of us in so many ways . . . and even though today the communists have stolen the mainland and in recognition of the revolutionary mothers who have painstakingly developed new overseas branches to help us recover our former homeland, and therefore we are having this ceremony to award these revolutionary mothers, and therefore all of those mothers who have over seven offspring should be celebrated and rewarded in this vein."

"Bow three times to the portrait of the Father of our Nation!"

"First bow."

"Second bow."

"Third bow."

"The ritual performance is complete—now distribute the awards—"

"Mrs. Ma Chenluo, 12."

"Mrs. Li-Chen Yarang, 15."

At the same time, the leader on the other side was now speaking Chinese, and using the same tone of voice he said, "Malaysia has decided that in 2000 it will enter the community of advanced nations. To this end, it will first need to completely industrialize, for which it will need a population of about seven million. Rather than importing these additional people, it would be better to produce them ourselves. . . . In order to recognize the women who have made an extraordinary contribution to the nation's reproductive needs, we hereby award this 'Extraordinary Mother to a Population of Seven Million Award' to all mothers who have given birth to seven or more children, and for each additional child they will receive an additional thousand *yuan*. . . ."

Then, they began singing, as each of the women climbed up onto a different platform. She, however, was wearing only a pajama top and seemed embarrassed and deeply uncomfortable. For a long time . . .

"Mrs. Wang-Wu Yahao, 12." People on both sides simultaneously announced her name. She was startled by this, and stood there stunned. They announced her name a second time, but she still didn't respond, whereupon they announced her name a third time, and asked, "Is she not here?" Only then did she rush forward to the southern stage, while observing another woman rushing toward the northern stage.

Tightly gripping the railing, she proceeded forward in careful but firm steps. Her legs weak and her entire body cold, she advanced toward that great leader. Even in her dreams, she had never imagined that one day she would shake hands with such an esteemed figure. She bowed, her hands clasped in front of her, and accepted a bundle.

"Don't be afraid. Look at me," that person said in fluent Chinese.

"Your Chinese is better than my own," she said with sincere admiration. "I myself never went to school."

"Wow . . . a dozen!" Then the person awarding the award frowned and cleared his throat. "Stop raising pigs. You know that we don't eat pork. Besides, . . . we can't stand the smell of pig manure."

"But," she responded, "if I don't raise pigs, we won't have enough to eat, and furthermore . . . I won't have money to send my children to school. If I don't raise pigs, what would I raise?" She sounded rather forlorn.

"You could raise goats, cattle, rabbits, or even fish. Furthermore . . ." he smiled mischievously, "even if your children were to get an education, that wouldn't necessarily mean that they'll be able to find a job."

She stared in shock.

The smell of pig manure assaulted her nostrils.

All of the pigs in the yard began moving at once, and began circling the yard. She heard her son cursing, "It's not that the government has no money—they've taken it all to raise *pigs* . . ."

The smell of pig manure seeped in through every pore of her body, penetrating her lungs and heart. She had difficulty breathing, and everything became blurry. The pigs continued running around her one after another, becoming a blur of shadows. *Woo . . . kung kung kung kung . . . dee dee da, da . . .*

There was a strong smell of black coffee.

The lamp was flickering.

"*Ah mu*," a girl dressed in white called out, with peppermint breath. "What's wrong? Have a cup of coffee." "I feel dizzy," she replied weakly, her mouth moving as if on its own accord. "I haven't rinsed my mouth yet." "That's ok," the girl supported her while holding a cup of hot coffee.

"Ah Cai has returned, we should first . . ." She looked all around.

"No he hasn't . . . didn't he go to Taiwan?" The girl replied in confusion.

(She felt very dizzy.) "Your body feels very hot. . . ." (No, no. This, too, must be a dream. I can't stand it any more. I'm exhausted.) She closed her eyes.

"*Ah mu!*" (You can't fool me! I know this is a dream.) Tears streamed down her face.

"*Ah mu!*" (You can't fool me!)

"*Ah mu!*" (You can't!)

"*Ah mu!*" (Can't!) Her daughter shook her vigorously, as tears rolled down her face.

She abruptly opened her eyes and frowned. Her daughter was sitting on the edge of her bed, saying softly, "*Ah mu*, you are running a fever and have the chills. You must not be feeling well?" She didn't respond. She sighed deeply, then began breathing regularly.

"You've already cooked the rice and boiled the water, and I'll prepare some vegetables. You must have returned because you weren't feeling well, right?" her daughter said, as if to herself.

"We've eaten enough, and you need to go to school! It is dark outside, and I don't think it's necessary to go harvest rubber today. *Ah ba* is still sleeping."

At this point she noticed some light coming in through the cracks in the walls. Was it dark outside, or was it still light? The cocks were still crowing. Her head ached.

"Did you bring a raincoat?" "Yes."

"Did you come back this afternoon?" "No."

"Do you have money to buy something to eat?" "Yes."

"Be careful. When riding your bike, always look where you're going." "Ok."

She, however, couldn't help feeling rather bewildered, holding her head as she tried to speak but couldn't get any words out. Her daughter patted her on the back, and said, "Then sleep some more."

"Sis, why don't you leave? Let Mama sleep." A boy called out to her.

"Ah *mei*." Suddenly, she tightly gripped her daughter's shoulder, gazing at her intently. "Tell me the truth, am I dreaming now, or is this really happening?" Her hands were trembling, and the rain kept falling steadily.

Woo . . . kung kung kung kung . . . woo, woo, woo . . . dee dee da, da . . .

death in the south

Every time I arrive in a new place, I always have to leave something behind: some fingernail clippings, strands of hair, or bodily fluids—which is to say, my very flesh and soul. In my continual peregrinations, I gradually aged without realizing it, until eventually, after having lost too much, I die of languor.

YU DAFU, "THE TRAVELER"[1]

What else is in the travel bag? A poetry collection and a jug of wine.

YU DAFU, "FRAGMENTS"[2]

In the dark night, the skiff heads into the distance. The scenery of a refugee is always the most beautiful (with the people and wine complementing one another). A true poet always writes poetry in the face of death. As a result, extreme beauty is always stained in blood, and the desolation of death.

YU DAFU, "FRAGMENTARY NOTES"[3]

The sound of gunfire was ringing in my ears, and fires were flickering on the island's other coast. All of the territory in sight has fallen into the hands of the enemy. The boats full of refugees were silent, and with a melancholic longing for old China we are blown toward a nameless future. Who is sobbing in the darkness? Who is softly singing a mournful song?

YU DAFU, "IN DECLINE"[4]

In the delightful little town, the river is full of floating corpses.

YU DAFU, "FRAGMENTARY NOTES"[5]**5**

> I'm already fifty-four, and even if I were to die today, I would have already enjoyed half a normal life. Surviving in a chaotic world is easier said than done. You can never predict what will come, so having that in mind, I am writing my will.
>
> It has been a long time since I last wrote any fiction. Occasionally I have a flash of inspiration and jot something down, only to file it away and never do anything with it. I'm afraid that keeping these fragments is courting disaster, but it nevertheless seems a shame to throw them away. Instead, I bury them under a barren mountain, waiting for one who is destined to find them.
>
> YU DAFU, "LAST WILL AND TESTAMENT"[6]

IF YOU ARE A YU DAFU SCHOLAR or a devoted reader of his works, you will probably feel an uncanny sense of surprise upon reading the preceding quotes. And that is as it should be, because before being quoted here these texts had never been published in any form. That is to say, the texts' original published form is precisely that of being a quotation. In reality, however, this shouldn't be considered strange, given that any work that is published "posthumously" can be said to share this same fate.

Due to general writing conventions and my own fascination with quotes, below I will continue to quote heavily from these sorts of unpublished sources. Another thing I should address is why I don't simply publish the manuscripts for everyone to read for themselves. Couldn't this be seen as simply an attempt to lay claim to stolen property? I naturally have my difficulties, which are intimately related not only to my position (and specifically the social environment within which I currently find myself) but also to the process by which the manuscript appeared, together with my unusual perspective on the issue of "publication," and so forth, and I will elaborate on each of these issues in more detail below.

My more general reason for selecting and writing this text is because I have always been dissatisfied with the traditional explanations of how Yu Dafu died on September 17th 1945.[7] Recently, in fact, my skepticism was further reinforced by the work of a (so-called) scholar from Japan.

The news of Yu Dafu's death was originally announced on October 5th, 1945. As Hu Yuzhi recounts, on the evening of August 29, 1945,

> at some point after 8:00 someone knocked at the door, whereupon Yu Dafu walked over and exchanged a few words with the visitor. Then Yu

> returned to the living room and told everyone that something had come up and he needed to step out for a moment, but that he would return soon. He then left with the visitor, and was never seen again.[8]

The next day, less than twenty-four hours after Yu Dafu's apparent death, his local wife gave birth to their daughter. At the time, no one could have expected that Yu would disappear, his corpse never to be found. Therefore, after the news of his death (or disappearance) was released, his family, friends, colleagues, and readers excitedly discussed the matter, and simply didn't know what to think (most of them ended up not believing the news). Today, we permit ourselves to say that Yu Dafu is in fact "dead," since we assume that he couldn't possibly have survived up to the present day. At the time, however, everyone continued to hold out hope that Yu would eventually return, because from disappearance to death there needs to be additional evidence and additional conditions, one of which is obviously time.

For a long time following the publication of Hu Yuzhi's article, everyone waited for a "miracle": for Yu Dafu to return from the dead. Unfortunately, in 1970 a graduate student by the name of Suzuki Yamamoto working as a researcher at an institute at Japan's Osaka City University published a report titled "Yu Dafu's Death and Disappearance,"[9] in which he attempted to completely dismantle everyone's desire for Yu Dafu's return. In this report, Suzuki relied on testimony from some unnamed Japanese who had had close relations to Yu Dafu, and also met with an old Japanese man who had participated in Yu Dafu's "execution" (though, in order to protect the latter, Suzuki agreed to preserve his anonymity). From an academic and moral perspective, this decision to conceal his source's identity was completely understandable. Although most readers undoubtedly perceived Suzuki's "testimony" as equivalent to a symbolic "assassination" of Yu Dafu, given that he was able to preserve some useful documents, he nevertheless opened up a space for a potential reassessment of the received narrative.

Now, more than ten years later, another Japanese (and, once again, it was a Japanese!)—a professor of Asian history at Kyūshū University by the name of Hanmoto Shuichiro—published an article in the journal *Chinese Culture Quarterly* (no. 91), titled "Yu Dafu no shigo" [Yu Dafu's after-death], in which he announced that he had recently come across proof—in the form of two manuscript pages—that Yu Dafu had in fact survived his abduction and subsequent disappearance, and also that he had convincing evidence that the manuscript itself was genuine. This article dealt me an enormous blow, and I was certain if I didn't write about this then someone else (probably yet another Japanese devil) would probably do so instead. However, my academic training was truly deficient, and I was afraid that if I took this on I would end up approaching it as though it were a work of fiction (and I've also done the opposite). At the same time, however, I felt I could no longer afford to remain silent.

Hanmoto's "evidential research" was greeted by the academic world with considerable skepticism. Suzuki was particularly incensed, because for him Hanmoto's attitude was the ultimate humiliation. However, upon further inspection of the handwriting and the paper, those two manuscript pages were deemed to be "genuine." The problem, however, lay with their content.

One of the pages had only a few lines of writing, the contents of which appeared to be completely inconsequential:

> *The old man bowed his head and boarded the train. In the instant that he was about to board, there was a sound of gunfire. His limbs flailed out as a red stain appeared on his back, whereupon he immediately fell over backward. The air was full of the smell of gunpowder, but I could also detect the faint scent of late-blooming osmanthus blossoms.*[10]

As many commentators have pointed out, this passage was taken from Yu Dafu's famous essay, "Late-blooming Osmanthus Blossoms." That was originally a complete essay, and while Hanmoto did not speculate about what might have followed this excerpt, it was probably deliberately fabricated. At the same time, it may also be observed that this manuscript page didn't have a title and therefore shouldn't necessarily be viewed as a transmutation of the "Late-blooming" essay, and perhaps it may instead have been an entirely new creation.

The other page, meanwhile, was more significant:

> *In the sweltering evening, the room's sunlamp was very dark. The wooden door weakly swung open, and two guests wearing shorts and white T-shirts were sitting on stools next to the wall, looking sorrowful and silently smoking cigarettes. In the opening in the door screen, a young woman wearing*

a sarong was sitting on the ground and sobbing, hugging a wrinkled-faced infant to her breast.

It was already the seventh day since her husband's disappearance, and there still had been no news of him.

Everyone struggled to recall the face of the man who had knocked on the door that evening and then disappeared into the darkness. He looked Indonesian, but his appearance was so ordinary that it was almost impossible to remember. Afterwards, they had searched virtually every single house in each of the surrounding villages, but that extraordinarily ordinary face seemed to have mysteriously disappeared off the face of the earth.

Members of the Bukittinggi military police also joined the search, looking throughout Payakumbuh. Later, after everyone had begun to fear the worst, they carefully inspected every suspicious new digging in the area, every new grave, and every newly-deceased corpse. They continued the search until they finally departed, but without any results.

Little did they know, however, that even as everyone was plunging into despair over Yu Dafu's disappearance, he had in fact secretly returned. It was a moonless night, and his dog probably recognized him and therefore didn't bark. There was only the neighbor's parrot, which, perhaps in a fit of emotion, spat out a German phrase he had taught it . . . although it must be admitted that the bird's pronunciation was not very accurate.

He didn't correct the bird and instead, like a specter, gazed at the lights in the distant houses. Without even sighing, he merely stared intently, as if trying to memorize every tiny detail he may not have noticed before. Based merely on the distant silhouettes, he could make out who each person was, as if he were reading a text that he himself had written.

At one point, he tripped on an old tin can and rocked back and forth, almost stepping into a stagnant pool of water beside the road. He regained his balance, then gazed up at the unimaginably bright stars overhead, as though looking at the teary-eyed faces of soldiers who during the war had been heedless of their own lives, but after the war found themselves overcome with emotion. In every home, he saw the same teary-eyed faces.

It was in front of his own house, however, that he stood for the longest time. Under the cover of a banana tree, he reflected and, with a tender gaze, visually caressed his wife, her eyes swollen with tears as she stood there holding their newborn child. Although she was not particularly pretty and had not received much education, she was nevertheless young and wise.

She was his third wife, or "bodoh." Her youth was his remorse, and it was entirely on account of the war that they had gotten together in the first place. In addition to his public identity, his other identity was as her husband (although his two identities shared the same body), and this latter identity was also one that had come into existence purely because of the war. Given that he no longer had a reason to stick around now that the war had ended, he therefore had no choice but to quietly depart. He had to stage a conclusion that would convince everyone (like any structurally complete novel, he simply couldn't tolerate annoying surprises). In the end, therefore, he simply hardened his heart and didn't even wait around to name his child—this war orphan.

Instead, he departed, in the dark of night.[11]

On one hand, the article was written in a realistic mode, with the author clearly drawing on his historian's training. On the other hand, literary critics believe that literature permits all sorts of fictional conceits—and this is particularly true of novels. Even if it were to be demonstrated that this text was composed by Yu Dafu, this still wouldn't necessarily prove anything. The text would be even less significant if it couldn't be proven that Yu Dafu had written it. In the end, this sort of debate is fairly meaningless.[12]

After being attacked from all sides, the author of the article announced that his evidence had been obtained from the field, though he declined to elaborate further.[13] He did, however, concede that he had visited Indonesian Sumatra, where Yu Dafu had lived late in life, but everything else remained a riddle. Yes, it was all a riddle.

However, all riddles must necessarily have a rational solution.

As for the preceding passage, it was actually published in October of 1945 in the journal *Yuzhou Fang* under the title "The Death of a Poet and the Death of an Author" and under the name of Guo Dingtang, who was a minor poet but a good friend of Yu Dafu. Adopting a fictional perspective, the essay described the death of Xu Zhimo and Yu Dafu. For the romantic poet Xu Zhimo, the rainy night was undoubtedly full of poetic resonances, and was the most sublime manifestation of his aesthetic vision. For the fiction writer Yu Dafu, meanwhile, his "disappearance" was the best kind of death, since it was replete with uncertainty, undecidability, and sheer contingency. This was particularly true given that it occurred during wartime, which further reinforced the work's novelistic aesthetic, wherein the narrative becomes the subject. These two kinds of death correspond to two very different forms of aesthetic practice. Seen from this perspective, was this passage something Guo Dingtang actually said, or was it instead fabricated by someone else after the fact? Who, in fact, had provided Yu Dafu with this final "sequel"?

For me, the preceding "riddle" had a basis in lived experience, given that I myself had grown up in Payakumbuh.

The "foreign" land where Yu Dafu allegedly died, in other words, was actually my own homeland, and it was as a result of his death that our homeland's name, even against our wishes, ended up entering modern Chinese literary history and coming to occupy a key position in all subsequent Yu Dafu research. In the end, our beautiful hometown became a terrifying ghost town.

For us, however, Zhao Lian was more familiar than Yu Dafu. After Boss Zhao's disappearance, what everyone was searching for was actually Yu Dafu. Yu Dafu is a very powerful symbol, but it wasn't until after I entered the literary field that I gradually came to realize this. He wasn't actually a great writer, but given his training, talent, and experience, there is no reason why he didn't have the potential to become one—particularly in the literarily impoverished South, where compared with those cultural illiterates who are proud if they know even a handful of Chinese characters, he is effectively already a *Master*.

As someone with low self-esteem, I wouldn't dare to casually start writing, in order to avoid humiliating my illustrious predecessors. Yet I couldn't bear the thought that a little Japanese was casually trooping through my homeland, teasing out evidence relating to Yu Dafu's "disappearance" and using it to embark in a form of academic trading. However, all that I could contribute were some random memories and buried quotes (*ai, ai!*).

After Yu Dafu fled Singapore, he first went to Slat Panjang, then to Bengkalis Island and Padang Island, after which he returned to Peng Heling. Eventually he ended up in Payakumbuh, which was located 150 kilometers from Pekan Baru, in a charming little town in Minangkabau.

For an exiled author like himself, that was truly a "small town occupied by the enemy" (see Jin Ding, *Remembering Yu Dafu*, p. 27).

In his later years, my colleague at the time, Jin Ding, would emotionally unleash a stream of "if's," "had not's," "probably's," and "unfortunately's." He said,

> *If, on his way from Pekan Baru to Payakumbuh, Yu Dafu had not encountered that military truck approaching head-on, and if the long-distance truck Yu Dafu was riding had had some Indonesian passengers who were able to speak a few words of Japanese, and who could tell those occupying soldiers asking directions how to get to Pekan Baru, then would he have not subsequently encountered any legendary misfortune, to the point of ultimately being assassinated? Unfortunately, both the driver and the passengers all assumed that the Japanese had set up the roadblock in order to plunder passing cars, and so everyone dispersed. The only person left behind was Yu Dafu, who was offering the person directions.*
>
> (JIN DING, *REMEMBERING YU DAFU*, P. 24)

It was this unexpected development while fleeing—namely, a Japanese devil asking directions in Japanese—that ended up leading to Yu Dafu's final recorded moment from his life in exile. Because no one could understand the invader's language, the Japanese devils' collective pedigree naturally led their listeners to assume their utterance to be a death warning—which is why they all immediately scattered in all directions, leaving behind only Yu Dafu, who had studied in Japan for many years, and furthermore for a long time had been immersed in Japanese aesthetics and was able to write elegant Japanese. He was the only one who realized that the Japanese devil was merely asking directions.

He gave the Japanese soldier directions, but in the process also revealed his difference from everyone else. You could even say that, in giving the soldier directions, Yu Dafu was simultaneously orienting *himself* in a precisely opposite direction—a path that would never lead him home again.

During his subsequent career spanning multiple identities, Yu Dafu came to be perceived by the local Chinese as not only a spy but also a savior. He was not only a translator and friend of the Japanese devils but also a scholar of immense erudition. He was not only the owner of a local bar but also the husband of He Liyou. . . . Different people perceived him as having different identities, and out of their differing recollections it would be possible to compose a complex modernist novel.

Because my own supplementary postmodernist narration is soaked in personal memory, I can not avoid interweaving it with inconsequential personal narration, in order to insert the quotes and hearsay.

MY FAMILY LIVED ON THE OUTSKIRTS OF THE CITY, at the edge of the forest. Actually, this was also a very impoverished area, particularly during the war. To get from our house to Payakumbuh, it was necessary to traverse more than two *li* of wild mountain terrain. Therefore, by the time news arrived of things that had happened in the village, it had often already been transformed into "legend."

In the early wartime period, a stream of Chinese whose appearance and accent was quite unlike our own began pouring into our village. They both resembled and didn't resemble new immigrants, or Totoks. People of my father's generation called them "people of the Tang," or simply "Chinese," but they could be picked out of a crowd as easily as ducks in a flock of chickens.

"They've come from China," my father said. "They are all very educated."

It was around that time that Yu Dafu, operating under the name Zhao Lian, attracted attention upon being asked for directions.

In fact, you could even say that we *only* knew Zhao Lian, and had no knowledge whatsoever of Yu Dafu. Even years after Yu's "true identity" was revealed, many of us who were reluctantly imbricated with this story still persisted in calling him *Boss Zhao*. That is something we can verify from our own memories. Conversely, if you were to mention the name Yu Dafu, even in relation to something that immediately concerned us, it would still tend to carry a legendary quality. For us, the May Fourth romantic literatus Yu Dafu would always be someone we viewed as distant and inaccessible.

Many people who had lived under Japanese occupation later became the natural disseminators of the "legend of Zhao Lian." Perched on the edge of death, they saw that person translating for the Japanese. Having long since left China, they were still concerned that their Chinese pronunciation was "not standard," or even worse, that Boss Zhao's "rice pudding" Chinese would be as difficult to understand as Japanese. Instead, in his eyes, dulled from excessive smoking and drinking, they were able to find a crucial hint—which was that despite his yellow teeth and sunken cheeks, he nevertheless retained a certain scholarly air. As survivors, over the next several years they made an extraordinary effort to uphold his appearance, transforming their personal memories into familial or communal ones. They even regarded Boss Zhao as a stand-in for those survivors who had been sentenced to death but had not yet been executed. One man from my father's generation was one of those survivors, having been a secret agent for a guerilla force at the time.

As a result, my childhood memories, like those of many others my age, were full of the shadow and scent of this "Zhao Lian."

I only saw Zhao Lian twice before he disappeared, and both times it was merely from a distance when we happened to be in town. He was chatting with the Japanese, enveloped in a cloud of cigarette smoke so thick that I couldn't even make out his features.

Both times it was midday, under bright sunlight, when I was on my way home from the convenience store. His rice-colored shirt was extremely striking.

The evening before he disappeared, someone thought they saw him appear on that desolate road leading to my home. But the person couldn't be sure, because that was a moonless night and this path was as dark as a ghost town, as a result of which no one could make out his features. However, this rumor made Yu Dafu's disappearance seem even more mysterious. Many people interviewed that witness, hearing him describe over and over again that suspect testimony that has subsequently been translated into many different languages. A poor but honest Indonesian peasant (no one had ever bothered to ask him his name), the witness gradually aged as he repeated his story over and over again. Even though his life had not substantially improved, he was nevertheless constantly smiling, as though he had acquired a new faith. When with us, he would often recount the events of that evening, adding descriptions of the attitudes and the nationality of the various people who had come to interview him. Hanmoto came to see him, as did Suzuki.

If the attap hut of that Indonesian peasant by the name of Ah Sen marked the outer margin of this incident, then our house was located beyond that imaginary boundary line.

Beyond that boundary line, Lin Xun stepped into the desolate wilderness as though searching for an old friend he hadn't seen for many years. In the distance there was the sound of dogs barking, as the night fog hung low. He repeatedly came over to that grove of banana trees, sighing deeply.

Here the ground was slightly elevated, and there were no fires to be seen.

He turned around—and just as he was doing so, a spot of blue light shone from where his heart was. It was unmistakable, and for an instant it seemed to grow brighter, as though it had suddenly received additional fuel. There was not a trace of pain in his face, even as his buttons all fell off and dropped to the ground.

YU DAFU, "NIGHTFALL"[14]

Under the drizzling rain, Yu Jun once again went up to Chen Jinfeng's tomb. He felt a deep sense of loss and melancholia, which he carried on his shoulders like a rooster that had been defeated in a cockfight. He didn't bring an umbrella, and rain poured down his face. That afternoon, there wasn't anyone else to be seen in the cemetery. His thin and pale lips trembled slightly, as though he were trying to murmur something, but the sound of the rain nevertheless drowned out any sound.

There was a white expanse that extended in all directions, and Yu Jun stood in the same position for what seemed like an eternity. The young woman whose portrait was inlaid in the tombstone looked very youthful, and it was hard to imagine that she could have passed away so young. Yu Jun suddenly extended his emaciated and trembling hands and began caressing the portrait, as tears streamed down his own face and mixed with the rain. He sobbed:

"They all say that I'm useless, and I myself don't want to stay here any longer. Here, there are only ordinary and uninspiring people, together with a number of higher-ups! Jin Feng, I've decided to go to the South Seas, and although that is an uncivilized wilderness, there must be someone there who can use me! Once I go, however, it is quite possible that I will never return. . . . "

YU DAFU, "DECLINE"
(REVISED BASED ON THE ORIGINAL MANUSCRIPT)[15]

In order to avoid alarming the villagers, they didn't want to use guns for the execution. Therefore, decapitation was the only option. In response to aesthetic considerations, they stuffed a green pomegranate the size of an egg into his mouth, to prevent his cries from cutting through the quiet night, not to mention the peaceful atmosphere following the war. Using a culture of self-restraint possessed only by those who have been defeated in war, they transformed this secret location into a valuable and heroic performance site. Yu Jun suddenly smiled, but no one noticed, since the pomegranate wedged in his mouth stretched out his lips beyond where normally they would have been when he smiled. In the moment that he was painfully smiling, an icy cold hand forced his head down, and the instant before his face hit the ground he closed his eyes, to prevent sand from getting in them.

YU DAFU, "DECLINE"[16]

Decline, waning, terror, and death are the key motifs that characterize these fragments. What is particularly worth noting, however, is that the protagonists of several of the works Yu Dafu wrote before going south were selectively executed. But what does it mean when one uses a fragment to determine a work's completion?

These fragments are all undated, and therefore no one can be certain whether they were written while he was still alive or after his death. If the former, then were these fragments "anticipatory obituaries"? And if the latter . . . no, that was simply impossible . . .

Even in his dreams, he never imagined that his hand, so accustomed to holding a pen, might one day hold an executioner's sword. Upon realizing this, he started shivering and broke into a cold sweat. He felt that the samurai sword was simply too long and too heavy. Furthermore, the night was too dark and cold.

The Indonesian man knelt down, expressionless, his eyes covered by a white cloth and his hands bound together. His neck was stretched out, as though he were already exhausted. Two Japanese imperial soldiers stood to one side, holding his coattails. In Japanese, they ordered, "Do it!" His eyes staring straight ahead, he lifted his sword—his hands were still trembling, and he looked as though he could barely hold it up. Then he put it down and wiped his palms on his clothes. He lifted the sword again, and finally brought it down with a thunk, as the man's head was separated from his body.

Stunned, he stood to one side, his shoulders sagged. His body was bathed in cold sweat, as though he was grievously ill. A Japanese soldier took the samurai sword he was holding, then pushed the corpse into a hole they had already dug. The soldier quickly buried the corpse, then patted him on the shoulder and said, "Don't forget your promise." In pairs, they returned to the car and drove off.

He was left there alone, staring at that pool of blood as though he had lost his mind. Even after the car had disappeared from sight, he remained rooted in that same spot.

What is this all about?

When that Indonesian man, following orders, called him over, he probably never expected that he himself would be the one who would be killed. He had already been sentenced in their internal deliberations, and had been given a secret death sentence. The executioner, moreover, was his friend. Therefore, a transaction was established wherein he would trade his disappearance for his death, while the Indonesian man, as dictated by a secret directive, would have to die. In this way, he became an incidental executioner, in order to earn the status of a conspirator. On account of his guilt and his promise, he then had to disappear forever from the world, substituting one form of death for another.

YU DAFU, "CONCLUSION"[17]

This latter fragment raises the possibility of an "after-death," although that was a possibility that bore more resemblance to something out of a novel than to anything else. If that was the case, then you could say that he was dead but not gone. And it is only because he was a novelist that we dare say this. The conclusion of the war also brought about the conclusion of his disguise, and therefore "Zhao Lian" naturally ceased to exist.

At this point, I must add a supplement based on my experience.

That year, after everyone had accepted the notion that Yu Dafu had died and furthermore had called off their fruitless searches—by which point the daughter born after his disappearance was already three years old—I happened to stumble across some previously unknown secrets.

Apart from a handful of Indonesians, we didn't have any neighbors. Therefore, when I had nothing better to do I would explore that mysterious wilderness behind our house. Holding a bamboo pole, I would wander, alone, through the bushes and wild grass, between the earthen mounds. Especially after I had been punished by my parents, that was the only place I would go.

That day, I somehow forgot my parents' warnings and wandered into the depths of the forest. I kept going until darkness began to fall, at which point I began to feel afraid. By that point I had already picked a bag of wild fruit and another of wild fungus, and wanted to head back quickly before it got so dark that I would have trouble finding my way. As soon as I turned around, however, I discovered that there was a black dog lying in the grass to my left. The dog startled me, since I initially mistook it for a leopard. I stood there motionless for quite a while, but the dog didn't move either, and instead just stared at me with its two round eyes until I could hear my heart thumping in my chest. *How on earth could there possibly be a dog here?* At that point, I instinctively glanced toward the west, reasoning that if there was a dog its owner must also be close by. Indonesians didn't normally own dogs, though this particular dog didn't appear to be wild, and furthermore a wild dog wouldn't remain in the mountains all alone and instead would end up going to an inhabited area to find food. It was as if there were a single lamp ten *zhang* away, shining westward, but which was immediately extinguished at the sound of an alarm.

Not in the mood to investigate further, I walked around the dog and hurried away. By the time I got home it was already dark outside, and my family was furious. My father returned after I did, and proceeded to slap my face. It turned out he had gone to look for me, and must have lost his way. Because of this incident, I was grounded for a long time. Afterwards, however, I resolved to go searching again.

This time, I set out even earlier, and consequently I was able to proceed deeper into the wasteland. I found an old air-raid shelter, and just as I was stepping inside I suddenly noticed with alarm that behind me there was a flicker of someone's shadow. I quickly turned around, but all I saw were tree leaves waving back and forth as the sound of footsteps quickly receded. I immediately followed, but before I had proceeded more than a few steps, that black dog suddenly appeared, like a specter, and stood in front of me. This time the dog was not as polite as before, and instead was growling and baring its teeth. I therefore had no choice but to beat a quick retreat. When I returned to the entrance of the air-raid shelter, I was in the process of stepping inside when I suddenly smelled a foul odor. It was a steaming hot pile of shit. Holding my nose, I looked more closely and saw that, sure enough, it was human feces—just more herbivorous than usual and filled with specks of corn and persimmon.

I gingerly stepped over the shit and proceeded inside. I stopped where the light from outside ended, and all I saw were some old newspapers, a pile of candle stubs, together with several pieces of dirty, tattered clothing. So, there had in fact been someone here, but who could it have been? It was said that after Japan's defeat in the war, some Japanese soldiers hid in the forest and refused to come out and surrender. Could this place be theirs? I couldn't figure out why three vivid images of "Boss Zhao" suddenly appeared in my mind's eye. It occurred to me that no matter who the person was, now that the hiding place had been discovered it was unlikely that he would stick around. Perhaps that pile of shit was simply his way of bidding farewell—a tangible punctuation mark. Another thought was that perhaps someone was secretly spying on me, meaning that I must leave as quickly as possible. The latter possibility left me absolutely terrified. Remembering that phrase that parents often use to scare their children ("a stranger will grab you . . ."), I proceeded to beat a quick retreat.

I fell countless times, and while I did eventually manage to make it outside, my palms and face were all scratched up by the wild vines. I also didn't know why I remained afraid of that place, or why I continued having nightmares full of smoke and human shit, in which my pursuers would fly over the grass—their indistinct faces resembling either an Indonesian or Zhao Lian himself. I ran a high fever for two days, and my parents couldn't understand why, in my delirium, I would periodically shout out, "Boss Zhao," but they feared it was inauspicious.

Over the following years my life took many twists and turns, as I first went to school and then started a business. But given that all of that has no immediate bearing on the present account, there is no need to discuss it further. At one point, I ran into trouble as a result of a political incident (in which many Chinese were killed during a demonstration, whereupon several hundred thousand were repatriated to China while even more remained behind as undocumented aliens), as a result of which I ended up staying away from home for three decades. In the incident in question, Boss Zhao's wife was being repatriated to set an example for others. It was a most moving scene. The pier was filled with people coming to see her off, as those who could afford it brought her gold bars and other gifts and others simply came to bid farewell. They had all been the beneficiaries of Zhao Lian's kindness, and believed that the departure of his last survivor meant they would never have another chance to repay the debt they owed him. As they were leaving, their collective memories of Zhao Lian/Yu Dafu (who, here, are really inseparable from one another) were repeated over and over again. The death of the last of his survivors simultaneously signaled the death of Zhao Lian, in that there was no longer anyone left to wait for his return. The strange thing, however, was that precisely at that moment it seemed as though his "soul" had finally been liberated, and in this way it appeared that he had finally "returned."

He would sometimes appear as an old scraps collector, although by this point he was already very old and was not particularly distinctive, and furthermore for the preceding several decades had remained hidden in several nearby towns. He flatly denied it, but people could still easily recognize him—recognizing, for instance, that distinctive smell of tobacco. However, that mysterious veneration with which he was received was quickly replaced—and as for the tobacco smell, people discovered that the cigarette peddler was an even more likely suspect. An ever-increasing number of people came under suspicion, and it was from this that the true problem emerged. That is to say, it was only after his descendants departed that he finally realized how much they truly needed him.

For me, the most realistic testimony came from an ice cream peddler. He would often ride his bicycle from town to town, ringing his bell and selling ice cream. One dreary rainy day, he came across a village that had become a virtual ghost town after all of the Chinese were forced to leave, and in the drizzle he suddenly saw someone waving to him from the doorway of a small house on the side of the street. At first he just felt that the person looked somewhat familiar, so he peddled faster and his bicycle sliced through the wind. As he approached, he saw that that person was wearing floral pajama pants, wooden clogs, and had high cheekbones. The stranger ordered a chocolate ice cream cone, then invited the peddler to have a cigarette and come inside to get out of the rain. The peddler thought to himself, *This person must be inviting me in because he's lonely. . . .* That person chatted with him in broken Indonesian:

"Where are you from?"

"Payakumbuh."

"Oh."

He squinted, peering under the screen at the rain.

"The Chinese people who lived here have all left."

"It's by government decree. We also . . ."

"They've all left," that person repeated softly.

Based on the peddler's description, it appears that that person really did resemble "Yu Dafu." It's just that the peddler always felt strangely cold when sitting next to him. Perhaps this was because it was raining, or perhaps it was on account of their somber mood.

Later, I heard someone else describe how—on what had also been a rainy day—he saw someone who looked like *Tuan* ("the gentleman") standing in a banana forest trying to find shelter from the rain. That person wasn't smiling, and appeared as though something was weighing heavily on him.

It was as if, after all the Chinese left en masse, that person had secretly returned, for reasons known only to himself.

After it rained during the day, a chill pervaded the town that night. Shortly after nightfall, the town went to bed, to the sound of frogs croaking. The fog was very thick—so thick that the scene resembled a dreamscape. All of the houses had turned off their lights, and it was as if they never wanted to wake up. The night was so calm that even the dogs had lost their required vigilance. It was then that he secretly returned.

Trudging down the muddy road in his wooden clogs, the heels of his clogs clacked each time they hit the ground. He was wearing striped pajama pants, making him look like a sleepwalker, or a specter. His confused gaze urgently searched those empty houses, and his lips trembled as though he were trying to say something.

YU DAFU, A FRAGMENT[18]

Wen Pu gently opened the main door to the house, then felt around in the dark for a candle. He found one that was half burned down and was covered in ashes and dust. There were only three matches left in the matchbox, and he had to struggle for a while before he could manage to light one. All of the furniture had been taken away, with the only thing left behind being an empty milk crate that didn't even have the usual wooden board on top. There were also some ballpoint pens, but unfortunately they were all dried up. The floor was covered with books and magazines, which were all covered with a thick layer of dust. He moved very carefully to avoid disturbing those spiders in their webs, given that they were now the masters of this place. Eventually, his gaze came to rest on an oil-cloth umbrella lying

> *under the windowsill, and he reached out and picked it up. Several of the ribs were broken and, holding it, he turned around to leave, struggling to close the jammed door.*
>
> YU DAFU, "AT LAST"[19]

He succeeded in transforming a practice of perpetual return into a final departure. Therefore, I also cast aside some mundane affairs and returned once more to that desolate region.

That place was even harder to find than I had imagined. This time I was carrying a knife, following the path based on my memory and searching left and right. That place was still as desolate and undeveloped as before, and I used a machete to clear a path through the underbrush, searching for that air-raid shelter cave somewhere between the top and the bottom of the hill.

Eventually, I became completely lost.

I walked around aimlessly for a while until I eventually came across a row of thin banana trees in a grassy field, and it was only then that things began to take a turn for the better. Those trees were growing very close together, like a primitive door. I cut down several trees that were blocking my way, and behind them I found the cave I was looking for. I lit a torch, bent over and stepped inside, then took several steps forward. In a corner of the cave I discovered a pile of bones, and only with difficulty could I differentiate between those from a human and those from a dog—or perhaps they were from two humans, or two dogs.

I had found it.

The arrangement of the bones seemed to signify something. Inside the cave I found a depression, where I piled up some stones and buried the bones. In addition to a few empty wine bottles, tin cans, and tattered pieces of cloth, the cave also had several dozen bats hanging silently upside down from the ceiling. I looked around, but couldn't find anything else. I stared blankly for a while. Suddenly, my stomach started to throb with pain. I rushed outside and grabbed a few dried banana tree leafs, then squatted down and had an emergency release. At that moment when my spirit was relaxed, I suddenly remembered the pile of white human excrement I had seen when I arrived. I estimated that it must be located about one foot directly in front of me, so while continuing to defecate, I started digging around with the blade of my knife. After a while, I encountered a hard substance that was not stone. Even after pushing aside the dirt and rocks, I still couldn't tell what exactly it was. I quickly wiped my butt and proceeded to devote my full attention to unearthing that object. Eventually, I managed to uncover something that weighed one or two kilos, and was a foot long and half a foot wide.

I continued slicing with my knife until I eventually unearthed an object encased in multiple layers of a white substance. I struck it repeatedly, but couldn't crack it open. Eventually, I had no choice but to carry it home. There, I secretly dug several small holes in which I inserted candlewicks, and at night I lit it as though it were a candle. Although a lot of time had passed and the wax was now contaminated with impurities, it still burned well and would occasionally generate a dim, green flame. As the molten wax dripped down, I collected it in a tin bowl.

I kept watch over this object for three nights in a row, until I finally uncovered its internal core. It was dark brown, and looked as though it were wrapped in wax paper—like that from a wax paper umbrella. I turned it over and burned it again. After three days, most of the outer layer had melted off and I was able to cut away the remainder. After I cleaned it up, I saw that it was a large, and very light, package.

I opened it up to look inside, and found it to be full of paper with writing on it, with each sheet a different size. The documents included sheets from newspapers, cardboard, pages from books, ripped envelopes, pages from account books, toilet paper, Japanese-era paper money, candy wrappers, banana peels, and even durian peels . . . and the writing was in ink, charcoal, pen, chalk, or grease pen. . . . None of the sheets was signed, but the handwriting was very similar to that which appeared in a note Zhao / Yu wrote for buying wine, and which is now in my father's possession. As I was carefully reading these documents, that person quietly returned in the drizzle in the middle of the night.

In the windy night, his desolate shadow followed the breeze and was transformed into a solitary firefly, attempting to illuminate the final desolation of this uninhabited region. I had collected all of his writings that had been published either before or after his death—including works both by and about him—and piled them up in a corner of the cobweb-filled room. In the middle of the night I would occasionally wake up, as the shimmering fireflies kept watch over these desolate old pages.

Frantically copying his documents, I unconsciously transformed myself into the final reincarnation of his deceased spirit. As I penetrated deeper into the life revealed in and outside his writings, his style became so familiar to me that I could easily imitate it. It was as if I were able to read a vast amount of meaning from the margins of the text, as the unquenchable spirit of the deceased was projected onto the cycles of nature and the residue of memory.

One candle after another burned out, leaving the table full of melted wax, cigarette butts, crushed mosquitos, scraps of paper, crumpled up drafts, and piles of old books. . . . I slipped into a reverie and started sleepwalking through a valley of death.

One breezeless night, I was pondering a comma in one of the texts when, covered in sweat, I suddenly succeeded in finding my lost self.

The next day, when I melancholically went back there once again, I tried to find more clues, but instead discovered that the bones I had previously buried there had now disappeared without a trace. I searched through the foliage where I remembered having buried the bones, but could find no evidence of anything ever having been buried there. I looked around in confusion, and in the process stumbled onto a nearby cave. In the end, however, I found nothing. I couldn't even find the candles I had left behind. What was this all about?

At a corner in the road, I suddenly smelled the distinctive odor of tobacco, and I heard the sound of footsteps, whereupon I quickly went to hide behind a grove of banana trees.

"*Hakkakunojika!* Son of a bitch!"

I heard a strange shout, and saw a small Japanese man wearing a hat with a visor. He looked about thirty years old. His left foot was lifted up, and behind him were two Indonesians.

"How could someone have taken a shit here?" he asked one of the Indonesian men. "And furthermore, it's still warm!"

With a strange expression, he reflected for a moment . . . then slapped his forehead. Eventually, he smiled, as though he had stumbled onto a pile of gold. I saw him lean over and pick up several crumpled and yellowed pieces of paper, then held his nose and turned away. He opened the package and read it, then shouted, "It's this one, it's this one!"

I didn't dare try to confirm whether or not that Japanese devil was Mr. Hanmoto. As for myself, I just bitterly regretted that I didn't have enough room to include the remaining quotes. I was also wondering what kind of context I should provide for these quotes, in order to restore their original wholeness?

NOTES

1. "Fragments," p. 12. In order to prevent the loss of the original texts, I first used an octavo-sized notebook to preserve them in their original order, and furthermore added page numbers. I refer to these as "Fragments." If there was an original text, I have identified that text in the citation. Otherwise, all page numbers are for "Fragments."
2. P. 2.
3. P. 6.
4. P. 5.
5. P. 13.
6. P. 1.
7. This refers to a widely accepted theory. For instance, see Wong Yoon Wah's *Yu Dafu Collection* (Hongfan, 1984).
8. Ibid., p. 48.
9. Ibid.
10. "Fragments," p. 18.
11. "Fragments," p. 25.
12. See the essays in Kumoto Kenyu, ed., *On the Controversy Surrounding "Yu Dafu no shigo"* (Iwanami Shoten, 1992).
13. See the Hanmoto's interview with the press, included in ibid., Appendix 1.
14. *Fragmentary Notes*, p. 50.
15. *Fragmentary Notes*, p. 45.
16. *Fragmentary Notes*, p. 46.
17. *Fragmentary Notes*, pp. 47–50. (The original manuscript was written on the insides of a number of different coconut shells, with different page numbers corresponding to different shells.)
18. P. 7.
19. P. 10.

deep in the rubber forest

BY THE TIME I LEFT MY RUBBER FOREST HOME, it was already very late in the evening. The light of the lamps and the final rays of sunlight were proof of this.

As the car was winding its way from the house, I could not help looking back at everyone standing in the doorway to see me off. The lamp was burning furiously, making the array of tall and short people standing in the doorway resemble silhouettes, as dozens of rays of light shined out in all directions through cracks in the wall. In an instant, the last rays of sunlight were absorbed and broken down, whereupon my car slipped into the dark and boundless night. It was as if I were being driven into the night—as that vestigial image remained seared on my retina. As I proceeded deeper and deeper into the forest, that white light began to resemble a tiny lamp in the distance, its faint light casting a reflection of the night forest onto my retina. It resembled a firefly and, for a moment, the forest didn't seem quite so dark after all.

As I proceeded further and further away, at one point I turned around and saw that that "home" appeared as just a speck of light. Sitting there all alone, that was someone else's home. When I turned a corner, I noticed that in the forest under the light of the lamp an assortment of tiny ant-like figures were moving back and forth along the road, looking just like those primordial characters inscribed on oracle bones—assorted markings with indeterminate meanings.

After I rounded the corner, the road improved and the car turned on its brights and plunged into the dark night. When it slowed down again, the vestigial light was gradually absorbed by the dark night. In the end, fireflies provided the only real light in the dark forest.

The car proceeded steadily, but I was exhausted. I yawned several times in rapid succession and was so fatigued that I felt somewhat confused, as though I were skirting along the edge of a dream . . .

I opened the car window, so that the night breeze could blow on my face. I also took the opportunity to inhale this precious fresh air and savor the forest fragrance. The strange thing—and perhaps this was because I was overly eager—was that I also detected a faint odor of oolong tea. It was just like the trademark scent of that "Purple Vine" tea store that you often visit.

That was the autumn of 1992, when I was sent to Southeast Asia to work as a reporter. After the Manila Incident, I returned to Singapore, and during my final few days I planned to go to Kuala Lumpur to collect some information on the local Islamic party, on Chinese attitudes toward Kelantan's implementation of Islamic law, among other topics. Along the way, I planned to stop by Kuala Lumpur to visit some friends, and also go to Purple Vine for some Chinese tea.

I had come to Kuala Lumpur several times, and therefore found it very familiar. The atmosphere was quite congenial, and there were Chinese people everywhere. My friends there had all returned after going to Taiwan for college, and they were now scattered among a variety of NGOs: including sites of cultural clashes such as Chinese convention halls and Chinese high schools—as well as Chinese-funded Chinese-language newspapers (including the *Sin Chew Daily* and *Nanyang Business Daily*), and therefore they could frequently provide me with firsthand classified information. At the same time, my friends were themselves often my best objects of observation, as they would sip *tie guanyin* oolong tea imported from Mainland China while sitting in an old two-story building in a corner of the city. On a seat next to the wall, I quietly listened to their "Chinese" speech that carries Taiwanese inflections but is gradually acquiring more Malaysian characteristics—very distinctive!

The evening of October 9th, 1992, Wang Jun, the senior editor of the literary supplement of a certain Chinese newspaper, followed up on my recently published book *Southseas People* to discuss the distinctive path of a local Chinese author, which he found very perplexing. He knew I was very interested in culture, and had written quite a few articles on this topic (including my essay "Chinese Education in Malaysia," which was collected in *Southseas People*). However, I had never touched on literary phenomena—partially due to my lack of familiarity, and partially because I was concerned that if I did write something I wouldn't be able to find anywhere to publish it.

No matter what, however, I couldn't refuse to listen.

In the dim light of the teahouse, surrounded by the aroma of the tea, I sat on the wooden floor next to the wall and listened to Wang Jun's account.

This was the story of an author named Lin Cai. I knew this name and periodically would run across his essays in local newspaper literary supplements, though I never managed to finish any of them. I felt his essays lacked a certain quality that would make them attractive to readers. To put this another way, perhaps they suffered from a certain lack of "style." My impression was that he was a very ordinary writer, but perhaps I was being too rigid.

With a hoarse voice, Wang Jun proceeded to sketch out the story.

That author was living in seclusion deep in a rubber forest in the northern section of West Malaysia. Writing was his hobby, but it was also the core of his life. He spent his entire day supporting his family and eking out a meager living, and consequently it was only at night that he could find time to write. He made a point of writing every evening, and furthermore would always write at least a thousand characters. No matter what came up—be it a funeral, wedding, or illness—he would never miss his writing quota. He would rather risk offending someone rather than come up "empty" one night. Among his friends and family, this resulted in what we might call a "destruction of his reputation," as they sneeringly referred to him as "that writer." However, they naturally had no way of understanding how his behavior was related to his feelings about his special time, and specifically his conviction that "lost time can never be made up." He felt that:

> If something must occur within a certain span of time but doesn't, then it will never happen, and furthermore will never exist. Something that might take place at another time cannot be viewed as that which originally would have happened but didn't. (Lin Cai, "Dead Water," *Literary Age*, 9/12/1991)

As Wang Jun was retelling/supplementing this story, it seemed as though he were painstakingly climbing up the steps of an old, dilapidated tower, to the point that he even began panting at the end—that's how realistic it was. For me, however, there were some parts of what he said that could be debated. Given that something hasn't yet taken place, how can he at a later time say that it "should" have happened? This "should" can only be treated as a sort of "speculation." That sort of thing.

In any event, Lin Cai's literary output was extremely substantial. On average, he would produce about forty-five short stories a year (with each story being around five thousand characters long), which around here is extremely unusual. The more he wrote, the higher his publication rate became, and as a result Wang Jun—the senior editor who never turned down any of his submissions—gradually became a trusted friend whom he had never met. Since no one subjected Lin Cai's stories to critical analysis, Lin Cai would often insert a note to Wang Jun into each manuscript he submitted, which would say things like, "Mr. Editor, as an editor you naturally have the ability to engage in critique, and I therefore hope you might set aside some time to offer me some comments . . ." In this way, Lin Cai would express his desire for feedback, and to have someone enter into conversation with him about his works. His true hope was probably that he might find a soul mate. This made Wang Jun rather uncomfortable, and created a substantial burden for him, to the point that he ultimately had no choice but to respond with some critique, saying something like, "The predicament of Sister Zhen reminds one of that of the character Sister Xianglin in Lu Xun's story. She is an abject and oppressed figure . . . The author's unique perspective reveals the difficulties and anguish of the lives of the lower class. . . ."

Many years later, Wang Jun gradually began to realize that that kind of repeated request was actually a plea for help. This was particularly the case given that over the past couple of years Lin Cai's literary production had fallen off precipitously, to the point that eventually he virtually stopped writing altogether.

On October 5th, 1992, Wang Jun received Lin Cai's newest short story. The manuscript contained yet another short note, which read,

> Recently my thoughts have been in turmoil, making it very difficult for me to write. I am finding it increasingly difficult to control those words, which often seem to want to escape my pen. I have almost reached the point where I am unable to capture each word that I want to write. . . . I have also run into problems with respect to finding subject matter, since I

> have virtually exhausted all of my life experiences, and have already written about everything that I've heard or seen. As a result, I've been left almost completely dry. I feel like the stove in front of me, in which the kindling is already burned up and all that remains are ashes.
>
> Currently, the only thing before me is a sheet of white, cold ashes.

This, however, was merely Wang Jun's "translation" of the note. When I later saw the original document, I noticed that the writing appeared deeply diseased—distorted, contorted, and fragmented. Unless readers were very familiar with Lin Cai's handwriting, they would probably not be able to make heads or tails of what it said. I carefully copied several characters to serve as evidence:

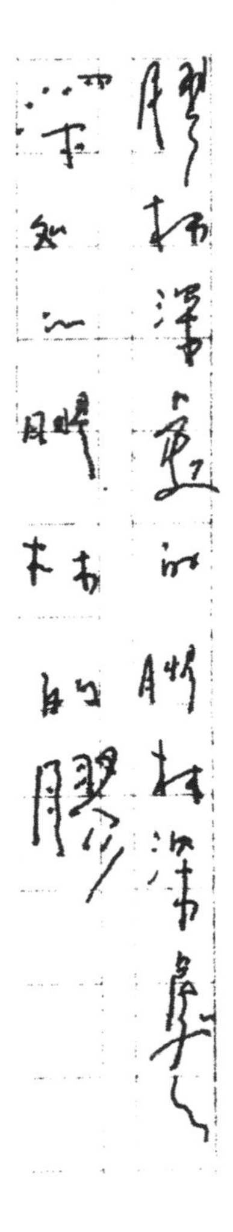

This fragmented and disjointed writing seemed to reveal his virtual collapse.

Wang Jun also mentioned that on September 6th he received another note from Lin Cai, which appeared helpless in its otherwise empty envelope. It read:

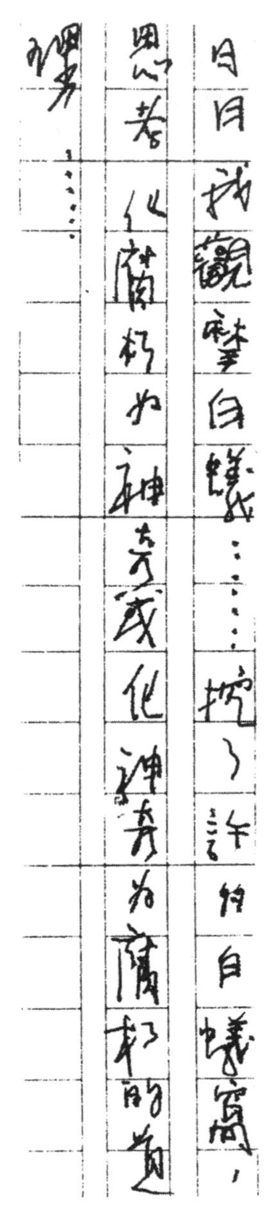

日日我觀察白蟻……挖了許多白蟻窩，
思若化腐朽為神奇或化神奇為腐朽的道
理……

This note consisted of just a few characters, but it was evident that he had struggled to direct his pen strokes toward a center. However, the strange thing was that that short note also included several "supplementary" elements, including a number of squashed mosquitos and dark bloodstains, a dried-up grain of cooked rice, together with fourteen live fire ants. As for the significance of these "supplementary elements," the note offered no additional explanation.

At this point, Wang Jun suddenly fell silent. He bowed his head, as that sheet of Chinese writing appeared to leave him increasingly depressed. After a while, a rasping sound once again began to emerge from his throat:

". . . uh . . . to tell the truth, he reminded me many times. Having been a literary supplement editor for so many years, sometimes I begin to wonder whether I have gone numb."

Wang Jun was never prone to saying much, much less giving emotional speeches. Therefore, I was astonished when he suddenly began acting like this. Given that we were drinking tea and not alcohol, he therefore should have been very clearheaded. He continued making a rasping sound:

". . . to tell the truth, I like to read articles that authors have written in their own handwriting, which I find much more interesting than printed ones. Perhaps this is an occupational malady.

"For others, printed characters may appear neater and more attractive. But for me, as an editor, my entire job involves interacting with writing (and particularly handwritten manuscripts). Once an article has been published, it seems as though it has lost something (its 'taste'). That kind of feeling is as awful as translation. Perhaps what is thereby lost is precisely the author's personality?

"A manuscript, after all, is something that the author has created stroke by stroke, line by line. It is an invaluable handcrafted artifact, and the more experimental a work is, the more this is the case . . ."

I examined him carefully. Even though we had known each other for years, at that moment I felt as though he were a stranger I had never seen before. After he returned ten years earlier, upon graduating from Taiwan University's Foreign Literatures Department he joined his current profession. He had previously been a rather well-known poet, and the assumption was that he had stopped writing because his job kept him too busy, but perhaps there were also other reasons?

The lenses of his eyeglasses were very thick, and in dim light they resembled a pair of white circles—that kind of opaque whiteness that also reflected your own image back to you. His eyes were hidden behind these lenses, and as you listened to his deep voice you would only see your own image reflected in his lenses.

". . . therefore, every time I read an author's manuscript, I always feel a strange throbbing. This is even more the case if the text is strange and remarkable. Often, it is not so much the article that moves me, but rather several specific Chinese characters in the manuscript, and specifically their mode of *representation*. I feel as though I can enter the author's heart through his or her handwriting."

His lips were slightly open, revealing his snowy-white teeth. He held his hands together, as he repeatedly brought his thumb and index finger together. I suddenly remembered that he was the odd senior editor who never accepted photocopies—and instead only accepted handwritten manuscripts.

". . . therefore, I feel I understand his problem. I can sympathize, but I can't solve it for him. This is precisely why I've felt so bad recently."

His discomfort was obvious in his movements. When he bowed his head, his black hair fell forward and covered his face in a dark shadow, reminding me of a forest in the middle of the night.

It was just like you, at that moment, racing through the endless dark forest. Under the light, the road opened up section by section, and just as quickly would be enveloped once again by the darkness. The trees lining the road were cold and strange, and the scenery was all identical. The differences that might have been apparent during the day were all blurred together at night. The road was endless—and in the darkness it seemed even longer.

My thoughts were tangled in knots.

I decided to act. The reasons I gave myself were: to use this local author in order to "understand the state of local Chinese culture in Malaysia," and to use his situation in order to "understand the hidden cultural conflict within Malaysian Chinese culture." This was very appropriate (at least for me), since writers are basically those who enable language and writing to mate. In this nation, where the Chinese language is perceived as fundamentally foreign, the pressure on authors is that much greater. Their "struggle" is enough to be read as an "allegory" . . .

The first step was collecting and interpreting the textual materials. Wang Jun was an enormous help in this regard—he seemed to view this as part of his job. These textual materials included literary works, interviews, author biographies, as well as (other people's) critiques of his works, and could be categorized as follows:

> *Literary Works*:
>
> Short stories: Nine hundred and twelve stories, totaling more than four and a half million characters. They were published in the *Sin Chew Daily*'s literary supplement, "Literary Ages," in *Nanyang Sian Pau*'s literary supplement, "Nanyang Literary Arts," in *Jiaofeng*, and other venues.
>
> Essays: Seven, all of which were published in the same newspapers listed above. They totaled twelve thousand characters.
>
> Poetry: One, published in *Jiaofeng*, issue 650, titled "Firefly, Mist."
>
> *Interview*: One, titled "An Eternal Writer: An Interview with Lin Cai," published in *Literary Ages*, 7/6/1989.
>
> *Criticism*:
>
> (1) La Mei (from Malaysia), "Lin Cai, 'The True Significance of the Population of Yamamura,' in *Nanyang Literary Arts*, 2/20/1979.
>
> (2) Lai Bairui (from China), "Typical Environment and Typical Characters: Reading Lin Cai's 'Brother Ah Shan and his Grocery Store,' *Jiaofeng*, issue 700.
>
> (3) Liu Jiangqiao (from the United States), "From Monotonal to Multitonal, from Monophonic to Polyphonic: 'Collapse of the Moon' and Lin Cai's Metamorphosis," *Literary Arts*, 9/30/1992.

The positions adopted in the first and second essays were rather similar, and basically emphasized the fact that Lin Cai's work "reflects reality," but the essays lacked any complex analysis. The third essay noted Lin Cai's "metamorphosis" (this would be evident to all readers with at least a passing familiarity with modernist literature), but it was actually a ridiculous mess, randomly copying Bahktin's theories to the point that it felt completely indigestible. After writing his entire life, Lin Cai finally managed to find three literary soul mates, though they didn't appear to really understand him. This demonstrated that he didn't have very much of a relationship with other local authors (which is possibly a result of the fact that he didn't write criticism), because otherwise he would at least have made some attempt at maintaining social niceties.

The interview, which was the only piece that exceeded the standard length for a typical short essay (which is to say, about 1,200 characters), contained standard information such as the subject's biography, when he started writing, his attitudes toward writing, and so forth, and also included an extremely important "response":

> *. . . writing has been my life-long pursuit, though neither my innate talents nor my subsequent accomplishments are much to speak of. My literary ability is probably not as good as that of Wen Rui'an, and as for my intellectual environment, I only completed primary school and therefore can't begin to compare with those who have university degrees. However, my strength lies in my grit and determination. Many others who are much more talented than I have already given up, while I continue writing. Although I don't have much education, I have enjoyed a very full life, and when it comes to writing my experience and determination are my two greatest assets. . . .*

His works were included in *Selected Works of Contemporary Mahua Literature: Fiction* and *Anthology of Mahua Realist Fiction (From the Postwar Period)*, both of which included his "Author Bio," which read as follows:

> Lin Cai, whose original name was Lin Acai, was born in 1939, in the Malaysian state of Perak. His family is originally from Yongchun, in Fujian province. Because of his family's financial difficulties, Lin Cai had to get a job immediately after finishing primary school, and ended up working as an apprentice in a bicycle shop, as a cashier in a grocery store, as a sanitation worker in a public square, and so forth. Because of his devotion to the literature, he continued studying on his own, and in 1958 he began submitting manuscripts to newspapers and periodicals. He was awarded the Writers' Association Literature Prize (1984), the Provincial Youth Literature Prize (1985), and so forth. His works have been anthologized in *Selected Works of Contemporary Mahua Literature*, though he doesn't yet

have a volume of his own collected works. He currently lives in reclusion in a rubber forest, and continues to write in his spare time.

Lin Cai has an understated literary style, but his works feature people from a wide range of occupations, including postal workers, sex workers, tin miners, grocery store owners, actors, rubber plantation workers, painters, ceramics makers, steel workers, ice-cream sellers, policemen, national legislators, teachers, principals, and others. Using a realistic approach, his fiction reflects the lives of people at all levels of society. He is one of our country's leading ethnically Chinese authors. (*Written in 1984*)

Drawing on new material, Lin Cai has a new fiction collection (*Deep in the Rubber Forest*, published by the Malaysian Chinese Culture Association, February, 1992). This collection features ten short stories, including one each from the 1950s, 1960s, and 1970, and another seven from the 1980s, but none from the 1990s. This was Lin Cai's first single-authored fiction collection, and the volume included a short preface that featured a very moving passage:

. . . I am a first-generation immigrant who was born and raised in the countryside. Because I had to quit school when I was young, I therefore cherish books and value educational opportunities. That was a tumultuous yet somber era, during which hot-blooded youth were squandering their lives. I had never been their "comrade," but I nevertheless took advantage of their reflected glory to read countless Chinese novels from the May Fourth era and the 1930s, which provided me with considerable inspiration. That was the only opportunity that I had, so I was always deeply grateful.

When I look back on my life, it seems I've never stopped writing, but don't have any regrets. With respect to the quality of my writing, I have nothing particular to report. With respect to the quantity of my writing, I was a pioneer, but a pioneer who was not worth mentioning. This cannot but be my greatest sorrow . . . (pp. 1–2)

I felt that I had seen similar sentiments elsewhere.

His 910 stories were all very similar in their language and literary technique, though they dealt with different subject matter. The biggest change occurred over the preceding two years—which is to say, in the stories "Passing Like Water" and "Flowing Clouds."

The remarkable thing was that of these 910 stories, there was not a single one that was written in the first person, and instead they all employed a third-person narrative voice. A first-person narrator didn't appear until these two most recent stories, which suggests that all of the others were written in a so-called "realistic" mode and feature a remarkable correspondence between their subject matter and political realities. From the arrival of Marxism to the arrests conducted under Operation Coldstore, it is possible to map out a series of direct cross-references between the stories and historical events. This made people suspect that Lin Cai may have been relying heavily on newspaper reports for inspiration. Something else worth noting is that virtually every single one of his stories revolves around the rubber forest, being set either in the forest or along its margins. From this, it is obvious that trees (and particularly rubber trees) are central metaphors in his works. Comparing his stories from the past several decades, it is apparent that the rubber forest became increasingly important. This was particularly true in the 1980s, when his works became full of green foliage. I therefore propose the following hypothesis: that during this period he was moving deeper and deeper into the rubber forest. The reason for this is very simple—the third-person narrators in his stories began appearing more and more lonely, and their tone became increasingly desolate. It was as if it was becoming more and more difficult for him to find "characters" on which to base his stories. This was especially evident in the late 1980s, with the characters in the several hundred works he composed during that period all appearing to have been adapted from ones featured in his earlier works. The plot and dialogue of these works also permeate one another. Perhaps he was simply unable to hold up under the strain of having to write so many stories under restrictive conditions, and as a result experienced a process of alienation.

After a thorough preparation, I brought a number of suspicions, hypotheses, and files to serve as reference material during our conversation. The only remaining question was how to get in touch with him.

Wang Jun helped me find Lin Cai's "mailing address," which was merely a P.O. box. Further investigation revealed that this was located in a large plantation in West Malaysia. We placed a telephone call, but the person who answered was a rather unfriendly middle-aged woman with an officious tone, who said, "You have the wrong number; there is no one here by that name," and hung up. Upon leaving the area covered in the district map, we relied on postal numbers and postal administration offices for clues. Our search area gradually narrowed, until suddenly my eyes lit up: *Porak*, it was in a rubber forest near the town of Porak. I had been there.

In late winter of 1989, I happened to pass through Penang, attracted by a piece of "society news" that was occurring there. A senior Chinese-language primary school teacher by the name of Zhang Zengshou had mysteriously disappeared, which almost precipitated a political crisis. . . .

Before we set out, Wang Jun suddenly began to appear uncomfortable and grew silent. He looked as though he had eaten something that hadn't gone well with him, and as a result he hadn't slept well. He appeared pale but firm, so I decided not to press the issue. Mine, therefore, was fated to be a very solitary journey.

I rented a car, ate a large breakfast that I would later regret (Indian roti + Indian tea), and at dawn on October 7, 1992, I left KL. At that point, the moon was still bright, but the stars were starting to fade.

It was still early morning when I arrived at the entrance to that plantation. On the road, I passed people riding scooters who had come out to harvest rubber—including Chinese, Malays, and Indians. Lin Cai must have belonged to one of these rubber-harvesting families. I followed the only available road, but passed countless paths leading in different directions. When I passed a worker settlement, the women and the elderly observed my bold plunge into the forest (particularly since it was so early in the morning), and felt anxious on my behalf. "Are you looking for that writer?" one asked, pointing me in the proper direction. I proceeded to the next meeting place, where they again gave me directions. This happened several more times, as I proceeded deeper and deeper into the forest. As I approached the end of the road, I came upon a solitary wooden shack. By that point it was already almost noon, and the writer and his wife were out harvesting rubber. I found them and told them who I was and why I had come. They were pleased and surprised, saying "You've come from Taiwan? What a rare treat!"

Lin Cai then asked, "Do they also know about me in Taiwan?"

I explained how I knew about him, and gave him several signed copies of my own work, including *Taiwan People*, *South Seas People*, and *Indian People*.

"Oh, so that's it. I'm sorry—why don't you come inside and sit for a while. I'll finish harvesting the rubber and prepare it, and then will come see you." He put the books I had given him on a table.

Given that they were busy at the moment, I suggested I could take a nap in my car and wait until they were done. As soon as I closed my eyes, I fell asleep in the quiet forest. After a long time, someone knocked on my car window.

He invited me to lunch. He had slaughtered a chicken and prepared a couple of dishes.

"Given that we live so deep in the forest, when our children went to high school they both lived in the school dormitory. They would return for vacation, and would often invite their friends to join them."

The room's furnishings were very rudimentary, with no decorations or ornaments. Each object (including bowls, plates, lamps, and baskets for collecting eggs) had an obvious use. We agreed to discuss "the matter" after the meal, over coffee.

"Ever since I was young, my family had always been very poor. I was the eldest, and even though I really liked school and received good grades, I nevertheless had to quit after finishing primary school. As you know, in poor families parents don't think about anything other than the assistance their children would be able to provide when they are older, particularly with tasks such as harvesting rubber, cutting grass, chopping kindling, carrying water, looking after their siblings, and so forth."

He exhaled a cloud of white smoke from his pipe.

"I felt it was deeply unfair. Why was it that so many other people could continue studying—even if they were getting poor grades—while I couldn't? I refused to accept this, but I couldn't really blame anyone. This was fate, and as the eldest son, I had to help my parents . . .

"Eventually I gritted my teeth and resolved to take action. I refused to believe that there was anything I couldn't accomplish. When I had the chance, I found some 'writings' to read." He sighed. "When I say 'writings,' I do mean anything with writing on it, including newspapers used to wrap pork, old cardboard boxes, the labels from tin cans, old books that have been stripped of their covers, old magazines, and so forth. As long as something had any 'writing' on it at all, I would read it. Whenever I encountered a Chinese character I didn't recognize I would jot it down in my notebook, until I learned it.

"I still have those notebooks—an entire box of them.

"On lunar New Year when I was fourteen, I took the money from my 'red envelope,' together with what little I had been able to save up, and bought myself a Chinese dictionary. Its title was *Large Dictionary of the Chinese Language*, though in reality it was actually not very large, and weighed only a pound or so. It was published in Hong Kong, and cost a dollar. That was the morning of the lunar New Year, and when the store clerk placed the dictionary in my hands, I became so excited that I started trembling uncontrollably, as though I were a thief who had just been caught. I nearly broke into tears right there in the store."

The dictionary was sitting on the table, and was wrapped in several layers of plastic covers. I gently leafed through it, and saw that inside there were many "patches" where the torn pages had been carefully mended. The pages had all turned yellow, and there was a faint odor of old wood. If I hadn't had the actual object in front of me, I would have suspected he was exaggerating.

"My parents and relatives all thought I was stupid for buying the dictionary, and would ask, 'What possible use is such a dictionary? You certainly can't eat it!' Other children used their New Year's money to buy firecrackers, watch a movie, or get something to eat or drink. But I didn't regret my decision."

Swirls of white smoke came from his mouth. His lips were not very thick, but their coloring was quite dark—almost black, like old pieces of rubber. His teeth were also discolored and crooked. His whiskers were quite long, and were interspersed with gray. His hairline was starting to recede, and his eyes were neither especially large nor particularly small. The area around his eyes was very wrinkled, and the whites of his eyes appeared muddy and bloodshot. His pupils, however, were quite bright, like an old well with a pile of leaves at the bottom.

He was wearing work clothes and his shirt was unbuttoned, exposing his chest, which was the color of a rubber tree. You could count his ribs, which resembled knife scars on the trunk of a rubber tree. He was wearing an old watch, which had streaks of dirt embedded in the crevices of the watchband. His shirt was splattered with drops of black rubber, and his long pants looked as though they themselves were made out of rubber.

"Eventually, I started working as an apprentice in a bicycle shop. I met several middle school students who would come to have their bicycles repaired. As we chatted, I would mention my self-study program, and they were very interested and invited me to attend a reading group. You know, in that era . . ."

"What kinds of things did you read?"

He smiled, and was quiet for a while.

"I rarely attended their discussions, because I simply wasn't used to reading with others. I felt that reading should be a very solitary act. You can probably imagine what kinds of books they were reading. . . . In the meeting hall there were many fictional works from that era, including works by Lu Xun, Ba Jin, Lao She, Mao Dun, Ding Ling, and others. This truly opened my eyes, and every night I would go there, find a well-lit corner of the room, and read those books word by word, and character by character. Whenever I encountered a word or character I didn't recognize, or a passage I would never have imagined, I could copy it down and slowly digest it. . . ."

"How long did you continue like this?"

"For about a year and a half. But then several of the key members of the reading group were seized by the authorities—and who would dare go again after that? The owner of the bicycle shop was afraid of trouble, and told me to get lost."

He squinted his eyes and exhaled a cloud of smoke.

"I therefore had no choice but to look for another job. I didn't immediately find anything—perhaps because people knew that I had attended the reading group—and I ultimately had no choice but to return to the rubber forest. At the time, I never anticipated I would continue harvesting rubber for virtually my entire life. . . ."

He showed me his right palm, and I saw that the area between the thumb and index finger was heavily calloused.

"At that point I resolved to set aside some time every day to read and write. Initially, I didn't have any books, so instead would just read from the dictionary and newspapers. . . . After several years, my dictionary began to fall apart from overuse. Later, after I managed to save up some money, I began going to the town's only book and stationary store to buy books. In this poor community, literary works were exceedingly rare, and even in the homes of the school's Chinese language and literature teachers there were barely any books. After buying several volumes, I, who was quite smelly from carrying rubber slabs and rubber tree fruit to the market, must have left a deep impression on the shop's owner, because eventually it got to the point that whenever a new book arrived, he would immediately send someone to notify me."

No wonder his house had so many books—box after box, and shelf after shelf, the pages all yellow and curled. When I opened one book at random, I saw that the pages had all been chewed up by worms.

"In the countryside, it is not easy to keep books in good condition." He sighed. "Several times, when I wasn't careful, an entire box could become infested with termites. Mice are an even bigger problem, since they chew up the pages. Cockroaches also leave droppings all over the books, and geckos lay eggs. As a result, if I went for more than a month or two without cleaning up, there would be problems—with ants of different sizes and habits all coming here to make their nests. Once, I even found a cobra, and it was only with great difficulty that I finally managed to get it out."

Boxes piled on boxes, and rows upon rows of shelves, all of which were made of wood. The ventilation holes under the boards were as wide as bricks.

He cleaned his pipe, added some more tobacco, then exhaled two more clouds of white smoke. He asked,

"Where were we?"

"Um, when did you start writing?" (That was a stupid question.)

"It was many years ago." He squinted. "I would often read essays in newspapers and literary supplements, and after a while my hand began to get itchy. So, I decided to try to write an essay of my own. Initially, I didn't want to tell anyone. I felt that writing was something very difficult and mysterious, and therefore I was exceedingly cautious. I would proceed character by character, word by word, writing everything very neatly. I was constantly afraid of missing a stroke or writing something incorrectly—and therefore it was only with considerable difficulty that I was able to finish a piece, even if it was only a few hundred characters long. Also, at that time I didn't know what drafting paper was, and instead wrote my entire essay on the back of an old calendar!" He laughed.

"I was excited for several days, after which I lost my confidence again. Given that there was no one I trusted whom I felt I could ask for advice, I had no choice but to keep this essay a secret. After that, I would write whenever I felt moved, ultimately completing more than a dozen pieces, all of which were based on my own experience. The more I wrote, however, the more unsettled I felt, until finally I gritted my teeth and sent out my manuscripts to a few literary supplements. For the next several days I was in a state of utter distraction, and don't know how many rubber trees I accidentally mangled while trying to harvest the rubber. After waiting for more than two weeks, one of my stories was finally published. I was ecstatic, and felt as though I were dreaming. I read the story from beginning to end, and then again from the end back to the beginning. I examined the title and the author's name. . . . Everything was printed very neatly, and for a moment I felt that life was full of meaning. Such a wondrous and mysterious thing, and it was my own doing! For several days, I felt truly 'great.'"

He grinned, with a hint of self-mockery.

"A few days later I received a short note from my editor, which offered a few words of encouragement and a recommendation: 'In the future, don't submit your manuscripts in primary school notebooks, but rather go to a stationary store and buy some real drafting paper . . .'

"The drafting paper was printed with a grid for writing characters, and each individual box was quite small, and at first I had a hard time getting used to it.

"I started out writing essays and personal reflections. After several years—initially, royalties were a very effective reward—I gradually became dissatisfied, and decided I wanted to have a piece of fiction published in a literary supplement. After groping around for several years, I began to look down upon some of the so-called authors whose work I would see in every issue of the newspaper, and became convinced that I could write something at least as good as theirs. So, I decided to give it a try, and naturally started by telling a story. I wrote down something I had heard, and sent it off—I remember it was a 'banana essence' story—and it ended up being published. Ha! It was at that point that I realized that perhaps I could become a writer. I had never imagined that it would be so easy."

As he said this, he didn't appear particularly proud or satisfied, and instead had a mysterious look of misery.

His expression abruptly cooled, and he became very serious. In a low and hoarse voice, he said,

"Maybe it all came too easily. Maybe these past few years it was simply too easy to get my work published. I once thought arrogantly that I would like to have my name included in literary histories. Especially after reading Fang Xiu's *Literary History of Postwar Mahua Literature* . . ." His gaze once again appeared vague. "I thought, even though it is true that I haven't read many books, I'd nevertheless like for college and doctoral students who want to study Mahua literature to have read my work. This desire was probably one of the key factors that drove me to want to write in the first place." A dog began barking impatiently.

"I found the essays by Fang Xiu and his colleagues very inspiring, and they helped me appreciate the degree to which literary works must reflect the spirit of the times. I practiced realism, as did those comrades who published their fiction in the newspapers. The realism that dominated the market at that time made me more self-confident, and I felt I had succeeded in finding a path into literary history."

At that moment his wife—that thin and hunched-over woman—quietly walked in and filled our cups with boiled water, then brought over a plate of sliced fruit, including yellow pears, star fruit, and jackfruit. The corners of her mouth puckered into a grin.

"I had subscriptions to two newspapers, and every afternoon I would ride my scooter to the grocery store to pick them up. I bought a thick scrapbook, and every day I would cut out all the important political and social news, and if it was an investigative report, I would excerpt it as well. I would then arrange these articles chronologically by incident, such as:

1985 / COLLECTIVIZATION INCIDENT

1987 / OPERATION COLDSTORE

1990 / THE INVASION OF TAIWANESE BUSINESS

"Afterwards, every afternoon I would find some time to go to a nearby coffee shop for a cup of coffee, and to secretly gauge the reactions of the lower class. Each night, I would grant identities to the characters in my fiction, giving them life, selecting settings, and creating fictional plots—in order to comprehensively represent contemporary reality."

He uttered the word *reality* very forcefully. He pronounced it with a falling tone—like all local Chinese, he spoke Mandarin with an excessive number of falling tones. It sounded as though he was squeezing fruit juice. He seemed a bit distracted, and those abstract "characters" fled from his mouth, spraying into the air as though on their own accord.

"For a long time, writing provided me with an oddly proud shroud. I thought to myself, of those who have graduated from high school or college, how many of them are now writers? And has any of them written more than I? Or, otherwise, they are writing fiction that is quite distanced from reality . . . I was convinced I was the only one who was writing for the sake of the people, and for literary history. Content was the most important thing, and my written language could be quite ordinary and didn't have to try to incorporate any novel techniques. All I needed was to make sure that everyone could understand what I wrote. After all, what was the point of making an effort to write something if no one could understand it?

"Every night, I would take my pen and sit down next to my lamp to work. The tranquility of the rubber forest left me relaxed and peaceful, and my writing flowed easily. It would gush forth, until I had met that day's quota. . . .

"My confidence never faltered."

However, his expression was very unstable, as though he had just endured a period of complete skepticism and had not yet reestablished his faith. He suddenly shut his eyes and, without any visible symptoms, leaned motionless against the wall, breathing rhythmically. There was a long silence.

On the side of the table next to the wall, there was a row of books, and on the table there were several piles of manuscripts and pens. I sat idly for a while, listening to the hens clucking to announce that they had just laid an egg. I didn't dare make any rash movements. Gradually, I was overcome with drowsiness. . . .

"Had it not been for the old man . . ."

As my head fell forward, I suddenly woke up from my nap and slammed on the brakes. My car had driven into a ravine, and my head was drenched in sweat. I let out a long sigh. The dark air was extremely cold, and I quickly rolled up the car window. Having to use the restroom, I got out of the car and relieved myself into the dark ravine. I shuddered with exhaustion, and my neck and shoulders were throbbing. I looked down at my watch—but saw that it had stopped. It seemed I had been going for a long time.

I wasn't sure what night this was. The sky was full of stars.

The moon was high in the western sky. It was as if I had been asleep for a long time, but that hardly seemed possible. It was even less possible that, after all this time, I still had not made it out of the rubber forest. Perhaps I had taken a wrong turn somewhere. I was surrounded by thick fog and, remembering Lin Cai's advice, quickly got back into the car.

"In the forest, there are often wild animals—including boars, pythons, tigers, bears, elephants . . ."

After a while, I reached a cemetery. The entire mountainside was covered with mounds of earth, and the air was filled with a strange smell. Several blue lights were flickering in the darkness. Were these will-o'-the-wisps, or fireflies? I turned around to look, but all I saw was an endless expanse of dark trees. The car proceeded forward and the car lights shone into the darkness, but they didn't leave behind any trace.

In a fit of wheezing, I struggled to open my eyes. The tape recorder began making a clicking sound, and I quickly reached out to change the cassette tape in order to conceal my lapse of attention. I must have fallen asleep! He, however, appeared not to have noticed, and it was the sound of his voice that had woken me. In my aural memory, however, there seemed to be a segment missing.

"An old newspaperman who had been retired for many years asked the bookstore owner to give me a message . . . I initially thought something had come up, but it turned out he simply wanted to give me some books. I went to his house, and when I arrived he saw me and told me that his children had all gone into business, and consequently all the books he had collected over the years would eventually get thrown out. So, he figured he might as well give them to someone who would appreciate them . . .

". . . I stared in amazement. Those books were already very old, and the pages had begun to turn yellow. Some of them were either ripped or had been chewed up by termites, and at that point he was still repairing them. There was hardly a single volume that was completely intact, but he treasured them nevertheless. He had used tape to carefully mend the ripped portions, and had picked out the parts that the termites had eaten and pasted the remainder onto sheets of vellum. None of the books had a title, but he said that it didn't matter, since they were all merely fragments. . . .

"Had I not met that old man, I would have probably kept writing like that for my entire life. What a terrifying thought!"

(Tell me about when you met.)

"He knew I was a writer. Moreover, he was possibly one of my most loyal fans, having read virtually everything I had ever published. He grinned when he saw me, and at the time I didn't realize he didn't have much longer to live. He said, 'Very good, young lad, you write very well.' It had already been more than twenty years since anyone called me a 'young lad.' 'Come, sit down,' he said. 'Let's chat.' He was very considerate. 'You are quite diligent,' he said, patting my shoulder. 'You just lack a solid foundation.' He added, 'A foundation is very important, because otherwise how can one develop into a big tree?'

"He explained the subtleties of Chinese writing, down to the level of individual strokes. He opened one of those books and showed me that mysterious seal script writing. He explained the relationship between objects and the forms of written characters, which made me tremble with excitement. That was the first time I received the shock of a dictionary. For me, those texts were all like books from heaven. He explained that the shape of a written character is critical, and consequently China will always emphasize calligraphy. The pronunciation of words is more varied, and need not be emphasized here. The meaning of a word is another critical point, and it is only through a reading of ancient books that one can master all of the various meanings of a word, and in this way can one's writing achieve distinction and avoid being merely a shallow record . . .

"He again showed me his life oeuvre, including calligraphic old-style poetry, random thoughts, and local anecdotes. In all, there were quite a few bundles. He brought them out, sighed, then put them away again.

"I asked him why he didn't publish them, to which he insisted that the time had already passed. When he originally composed these works he didn't show them to anyone. He simply wrote whenever the mood moved him, and his handwriting would differ depending on the moment, the circumstances, and his frame of mind. These different handwritings would reveal a different reality, which was impossible to duplicate. He didn't trust typesetting and printing, and particularly didn't trust simplified Chinese characters. He felt that printed characters were all alike, and were too inflexible and lacking in personality. Also, you can't discern the author's feelings or character from them. . . . Therefore, he preferred not have any readers at all."

I responded to his solemnity with more of the same.

"He gave me a lesson, and said, 'Chinese characters are not dead, but rather they are living beings with rich connotations. Based on my earlier works, even if those characters are not in fact paralyzed, they are at least asleep.'"

He laughed bitterly.

The shadows trembled gently. He raised his pipe to his mouth and inhaled a lungful of smoke.

"Those of us from that generation were all committed to writing in the vernacular. We followed Hu Shi and Lu Xun, and were convinced that literary Chinese was already a dead language that need not be read. However," he picked up one of the books, "the fact of the matter is that we were not able to read that kind of thing, much less write it. It occurred to me that perhaps what we were writing was too easy? Perhaps it was not 'difficult' enough? If something is too easy, that means that anyone can write it, so why should I? I reread everything I've written up until now, and as I did so I felt shivers run down my spine. I asked myself, did I really write this? Why did it have to be me? Couldn't it have been someone else? . . . I didn't have the guts to try confirm it . . ."

He picked up his pipe, but his hand was trembling uncontrollably.

"I felt as though I had been left empty, and didn't know what I should do. Should I start again from the beginning? I felt I was too old for that. In addition, if written characters were alive, how was I going to urge them on? How was I going to line them up? I knew I had run into trouble. That was the first time in many years that I had put down my pen and stopped writing altogether. Every time I tried to compose a character I felt it was mocking me—telling me to go back and study some more. I used to think I didn't care about anything, but now, looking back, I realize that was actually very difficult. In fact, it was already not even possible anymore. I frequently couldn't resist the urge to write characters incorrectly. . . . I would often stare blankly at an isolated character, which would come to resemble an ugly toad. I felt that it was gazing back at me even as I was staring down at it. The habit of writing that I had carefully cultivated over many years was instantly destroyed. Not only was I unable to maintain my usual thousand-character daily writing quota, on many days I couldn't even manage to compose a single line.

"Once, I permitted myself to write an entire page of miswritten characters, and after I finished I felt I was in agony. I sent off the manuscript, though ordinarily there would have been no possibility of its getting published. In the end, however, not only was the manuscript published but furthermore all of the characters were correct—it turned out that my editor had corrected them for me. This discovery left me depressed, but also made me sigh in relief. I began composing in traditional characters—laboriously writing them one stroke at a time. My brush was like a rubber-harvesting knife that had never been sharpened, and which was therefore unable to cut through the bark of the rubber trees. I found it even harder to accept the process of duplication—to accept the discrepancies that might arise between the original manuscript and the reprint. Accordingly, when I sent off my latest manuscript, I asked my editors not to typeset it and instead simply publish the handwritten text. In order to humor them, I deliberately used a black ballpoint pen, but never expected that they would do as I requested . . ."

"But wasn't that what you wanted . . . ?"

"Of course, that's what they said!" He interrupted me angrily.

After mentioning the old man who gave away his books, Lin Cai's temperament changed dramatically. He seemed to become somewhat perplexed and anxious, unsure what he should do next. I noticed that the hand with which he was holding his pipe was trembling violently. He wasn't able to speak as fluently as before, and instead seemed to stutter. Sometimes his mouth would remain open for a long time without making a sound, or else he would just utter a series of squeaks. His formerly sharp gaze became muddied.

"Was it that I suddenly lost my ability to write, or that I had never had it in the first place?"

He stared at me, as though attempting to verify something.

The entire time we were talking, there wasn't a word from his wife. There was, however, a lot of noise coming from her room, including the sound of an ax.

"You Taiwanese authors must not have this sort of problem? Is that not a nation of the Chinese people?"

I didn't know how to respond, and therefore simply offered some general remarks about the literary scene in Taiwan.

As he listened, his face appeared full of wrinkles. There was an awkward pause. The woman repeatedly chopped a board with an ax. Each time the ax fell, the board would split in half. She did this very fluidly.

"This land . . . living on this piece of land . . . what kind of guarantee can a piece of land give an author?"

He suddenly raised this question. I shrugged, then mustered the courage to discuss Taiwan's 1980s nativist literature debates with him, together with some of the topics that emerged during these debates, including sayings such as "without land, how could there be literature?"

He listened carefully. He was squinting and his wrinkles were trembling. After I finished, he bowed his head and pondered for a long time, periodically shaking his head.

"We need . . . an unusual ability . . . and only then would we be able to bring the two together. That sort of ability . . ."

He stared intently at his trembling right hand. His wife finished chopping the wood, and proceeded to pile it up. She put away her ax, then carried a hoe into the middle of the courtyard.

He fell silent for longer and longer intervals. Several times I wanted to leave, but upon seeing him that way I found myself unable to say anything. This was an unprecedented solitude. He needed a group of friends to read articles together, but money was very tight and he had no way of moving into the city. Given that he had no academic credentials, virtually the only job he could get that would allow him to work in the cultural field was as a newsboy—but that would not pay enough to support two people. Furthermore, he was no longer young, and it would be difficult for him to adapt to a new lifestyle.

In order to break through this impasse, and also to help raise his spirits, I began to tell him about my own experiences. From my interview on Taiwan nativism, to Seoul, the Tiananmen Square protests, Philippines under fire, South Africa, the Middle East . . . Once I started I found myself going on and on, touching on many minor figures, impressions, and other details not covered in the newspapers . . . such that his eyes lit up with delight.

"Ah . . . ah . . ." He repeatedly slapped his thigh in excitement.

"That's great! That's fantastic!"

. . .

In the blink of an eye, it was dusk and I decided that it was time to leave. He seemed a bit surprised.

"Won't you stay for dinner? . . . Perhaps tonight we could . . ."

I got up, but noticed that his wife had already slaughtered and plucked a chicken. She said, "Given that you have come all this way to visit, won't you join us for a meal before leaving?"

I therefore joined them for dinner, but was anxious to leave as soon as we finished.

I said, "We are deep in the rubber forest and I don't know the way, so I'm afraid I wouldn't be able to make it out at night."

He hoped I would stay overnight, but I lied and claimed I had already bought my plane ticket to fly back to Taipei the next morning, because I had some business to attend to.

I felt somewhat ashamed that I wasn't able to help him.

There were no cars behind us, nor did any approach from the other direction. On the side of the road there was a stone stele that appeared to have some writing on it, but which flashed by in the blink of an eye. The foliage of the rubber trees became increasingly dense—so dense you couldn't see the stars. The night was dark and full of thick fog, and consequently it was difficult to make out anything at all.

His old, bitter voice continued to echo in my ears:

"Every individual character seemed as heavy as an iron hammer."

His melancholy manuscript read:

I shouldn't only write about a transparent rubber forest.

. . . Only a symbolic forest is endlessly deep.

Death. . . .

I stared into space, then crumpled up the paper and burned up my manuscript. This used to be my most important means of writing, using fire, blood, sweat, and semen.

A symbolic forest, the edges of which were continually receding before your eyes.

"*Each individual character is a single rubber tree. My ultimate aspiration. . . .*"

As a dim light became visible in the distance, the car entered a small road and proceeded toward it, in order to confirm how lost you are in the night.

A dog barked.

"An illusory tree."

I slowed down. The rubber trees on the side of the road were dripping with white liquid, and the new knife wounds were overlaid onto the older scars. I knew I had entered a textual puzzle that he had created as he was drifting off to sleep—an endless muddy and bumpy path through the forest.

"At that point you will notice that everything in front of you is familiar."

That firelight continued to recede, as every tree continued to cry its original tears. The road in front of us was a messy tangle of footprints, all of which had been made by the same kind of shoe. That person who left the prints was already long gone, though on the trees he had left behind countless texts inscribed with his knife.

After a big turn, we finally left the forest. I spit out a mouthful of foul air.

The moon was bright but the stars were sparse.

After returning to Taipei, I composed an essay titled "Deep in the Rubber Forest, There Is Also Literature," and after sending off the manuscript I proceeded to Uruguay for an interview. The publisher sat on the manuscript for a long time, but eventually sent it back, saying, "Not newsworthy."

Half a year later, upon returning from a trip to Ecuador, I was surprised to find a letter from him:

> *. . . I left home with my wife to take care of some business, and upon returning I discovered to my surprise that all of my published books and unpublished manuscripts had all been eaten by termites. The building itself had been rebuilt. Was this fate? Dust to dust, ashes to ashes. . . . Against my will, I would have to move away.*
>
> *I decided to change career, save up some money, and open a bookstore in town. Buying and selling used books, dictionaries, periodicals, pens, drafting paper, and so forth. My children as well as the Malaysia Chinese*

Writers' Association all expressed their approval. I understand that in your esteemed country there is a famous author by the name of Yu Guangzong. I don't know if you know him or not? If you do, could you please ask him to write a couple of characters for my store sign? My store will be called "Chinese Writings"—Many of the Chinese here who open stationary shops use this name (or otherwise they call their store "Writings in Chinese" . . .).

With respect to my interview, when will it be published? Or is it already out? If it is available, could you send me a copy, to serve as a souvenir? We could ask Wang Jun, from the Sin Chew Daily, *to send it . . .*

fish bones

It was the twenty-fifth year of the Guangxu reign, when he was thirty-six, the same year that the oracle bone turtle shells were discovered in Dongyang.

LUO ZHENYU, "INTRODUCTION" TO *YIN RUINS*

Oracle bone inscriptions were discovered between the thirty-fifth and thirty-sixth years of the Guangxu reign of the Qing dynasty, in a small village twenty-five *li* to the northwest of the Zhangde township.

WANG GUOWEI, *GUANTANG JILIN*

Tortoise shells had already been discovered here thirty years earlier. These discoveries are not new. One year, a peasant was plowing his field and he saw several shells when turning over some soil. There were markings on them, which had been colored vermilion. . . . Because the peasants believed these to be dragon bones, they therefore ground them up and used them for medical purposes, for which they could charge large amounts of money. . . . The buyers would not be interested in the markings, and therefore would rub them off before selling the bones. The fragments that were either too small or had too many markings on them would all be thrown away into a dried-up well.

LUO ZHENCHANG, *RECORD OF A SEARCH FOR RUINS IN HUANYANG*

In ancient times, when Baoxi was king of all under heaven, he said that when facing upward they would observe celestial phenomena, and while facing downward they would observe terrestrial laws. . . . The markings on the tortoise begat lines, the Yellow River begat images, and the Luo River begat text, and the sages took advantage of them. Based on terrestrial laws and celestial phenomena, they would inscribe a divination. And based on these sorts of forms and patterns, the first texts were written.

DONG JIE, *TONGXI YIZHUAN*

The turtle was born in wild grass in the depths of the river.

CHU SHAOSUN (SUPPLEMENT), *RECORDS OF THE HISTORIAN*, "BIOGRAPHIES OF THE TURTLE-SHELL DIVINERS"

AROUND NOON ON A SEARINGLY HOT DAY, everything was silent. This was the time when all of the workers returned home to rest, and all that could be heard was the buzzing of gnats. In the depths of the marsh, birds were singing and toads were croaking, as large lizards crawled through the grass and monkeys leapt from tree to tree. The sunlight shimmering on the surface of the water was periodically shattered by the grass and leaves. There was the sound of steady footsteps treading on twigs and branches, as the man approached the riverbank. He was wearing tall boots, long pants, and a long-sleeve shirt. Even his neck and forehead were wrapped in a damp cloth. In his white-gloved hands, he was carrying a rod with which he would gently push aside the vegetation. Most of the stems and leaves were either as sharp as knives or else had pointy thorns, and if you weren't careful they would cut you and cause blood to start gushing out. The wind also contributed to the bushes' posture, as a dense network of razor-sharp leaves would sway forward. As soon as the man stepped forward his foot would immediately sink into the soft mud, and even through his thick boots he would feel an extraordinary chill. He would then extricate the foot that was stuck in the mud and take another step forward. The water became deeper and deeper, rising up to his pants leg, and then up to his waist. He eventually had no choice but to lean forward, grabbing the vegetation floating on the surface with one hand after the other, and in this way he half-crawled and half-swam up the river. As he approached, strange sounds emerged from the watery depths, produced either by toads or frogs, lizards of different sizes, or even common field turtles. Frequently, he would see the animals poke their heads out, look around, then quickly disappear back under the water.

Aimlessly following the river deeper and deeper into the forest, he eventually stopped stepping in soft mud and dense ink-black humus, and instead, using a combination of a doggy paddle, tortoise wade, frog kick, and so forth, he proceeded forward while continuing to hug the shoreline. After who knows how many twists and turns, he finally happened upon a beaver dam and its distant guards. Lizards as large as crocodiles were watching coldly, and the grass was full of messy birds' nests. . . . In one vertigo-inducing spot, he saw an unbelievable scene: a mountain of fist-sized turtle shells resembling discarded earthenware bowls—a veritable reptilian graveyard. There were also several giant tortoises half as big as he was, of the sort that you would only find in a primordial forest, slowly crawling back and forth. . . .

The younger brother sent a letter, which read:

> *. . . I've located my elder brother's remains. They have been submerged for so long that they are now covered in green moss. Our mother is devastated, reacting to the news as though brother had just passed away . . .*

Their mother was eighty-two years old and was born in the Year of the Dog. The elder brother was born in 1935 and disappeared in 1952, though it was not until 1992 that his death was officially confirmed.

As dusk gradually fell, the brilliant rays of sunlight were completely lacking in warmth. The golden rays shone down on the blue paper of the letter, which was written in a slanted script that appeared as though it had finally been released from years of imprisonment, leading him to fall back into an earlier time buried in the depths of his memory. The letter was being weighted down by a yellowish bone-like object. Eventually, there was no sunlight left, whereupon this unusually clear winter day disappeared altogether. The weather forecast reported that another cold front was approaching, and in the afternoon all of the joints in his body began to silently ache. Ah, those were unforgettable times! Did the appearance of these greenish bones mark the resolution for which their mother had been waiting for so many years? Now that the faith that had supported her for so long was finally destroyed by reality, would she be able to handle this depressing assault?

> *. . . For the past several days, mother has missed you more and more, and perhaps her grieving for her eldest son has extended to a longing for her second son, who has been away for so long. . . . Whenever you are free, perhaps you might return for a visit?*

It has now been many years since he last returned home. After living somewhere for a long time, one can't help but come to feel attached to the new place. Our lifestyle, friends and family, rhythms of daily existence, and even our basic livelihood are all determined by where we live. Consequently, we don't really have any more freedom than a tree growing in a courtyard; it is just harder for us to recognize how little freedom we really have.

Sitting across from the window of his study, he reclined in his oily black wicker chair. Regardless of whether the flowering tree in the courtyard was a cherry, peach, apricot, or pear tree, there is not one that is not withered and bare. When spring arrives, the blossoms always precede the budding new growth. Even though he, who was originally from the tropics, had already been living in that area for many years, he would nevertheless invariably find himself delighted by this sudden blooming of flowers in spring—just as he would be startled by this foreign land's bone-chillingly cold winters. The evergreen banyan tree in the courtyard covered half the sky, and through both the cold winter and the hot summer it invariably appeared mighty and illustrious. Underground, it probably claimed even more territory. One day, as he was leafing through some old documents in his study, he noticed that the tree's roots were beginning to poke out through the old stone-and-mortar floor. He had no idea when it was that their tiny yellow tendrils, like miniature antenna, began feeling their way toward the disintegrating shelves of old books. The library's walls and ceiling, which had not been repaired for years, had already begun to peel in many places as a result of the humidity. For several decades, he had repeatedly visited this library day and night, all year around, hunched over like a ghost, but he had never managed to see any new life within the walls. At the end of the day, under the light of the setting sun, specks of dust were floating around in the study, like a cloud of fog. There was a calligraphic scroll by Mr. Tai Jingchen, which contained the text of "Ode to Bygone Days" that he had copied over and over again in his final years, sorrowful and anxious, his calligraphy resembling the gnarled limb of an old banyan tree.

In the study, there were shelves upon shelves of books, the vast majority of which were old tomes, including the official dynastic histories, the thirteen classics and their commentaries, collections of writings by ancient philosophers, collections and translations of oracle bone inscriptions, ancient bronze inscriptions, the Zhen Song Tang collection of ancient law books, Wang Guowei's *Guantang jilin* collection, Guo Moruo's *Guo Dingtang* collection, the classic *Shuowen jiezi* dictionary, the *Jinwen gulin* etymological dictionary of ancient bronze inscriptions, the collected writings of the archaeologist Dong Zuobin . . . The tables and corners of the room were also full of assorted books and papers. In addition, there was also a computer, a printer, a water kettle, and a tea set. . . . Behind the glass book cases there were several seemingly authentic artifacts from China's stone age depicting images of legendary animals. There were several framed photos that were each slightly bigger than a fist, and contained yellowed black and white portraits of youthful and old couples, together with color portraits of entire families. . . . On the seven- to eight-foot-long desk, there was a black rotary telephone and a fist-sized turtle shell with the back and breast plate still connected. The underside of the shell was gray and the breast plate was yellow. Both sides of the top of the shell were inscribed with text that resembled a network of cracks, though there were no inscriptions on the back of the shell. He idly played with the shell in his palm, as though fiddling with a pair of old jade balls—opening the shell, closing it, then opening it again. The white ridges protruding from the back of the shell had begun to turn slightly yellow with age. The back of the shell featured a hidden pattern of images from the *Book of Changes*. The fading sunlight gradually wiped out this ancient splendor. In the corridor outside, the bronze bell commemorating the old school principal was tolling repeatedly. He called to say that he wouldn't be returning for dinner that night, explaining that he had to "stay up all night working on an essay, in order to meet a deadline."

Under the morning's first rays of sunlight, the last vestiges of the previous night's fog lingering among the trees began to burn off more quickly. The dense mist ebbed and flowed, as though the earth itself were breathing. When he woke up, he discovered that his brother was already gone. He wasn't sure when his brother had left, but did notice that his mattress was still warm. He pushed open the window, and the damp fog immediately poured in. His brother's tall, thin silhouette was barely discernible in the fog, as it gradually moved away among the expressionless tree trunks, heading in the direction of the sunrise. Why had he gotten up so early?

He had previously assumed that his brother got up early to help their parents harvest rubber, but one day he heard his brother rudely respond to their parents' request for assistance by saying, "I have more important things to do," whereupon their father responded with a terrifying roar, "What the hell do you mean by 'more important'? Do you not even want to live?" From that point on, their mother took every opportunity to entreat her son to set a good example, saying, ". . . you are the eldest, and we sent you to school so that you could serve as a model for your younger brother and sister. . . . In the future they will need to rely on you, so you mustn't stray down the wrong path." But the elder brother would either remain silent or would respond with typical youthful resentment, speaking with a very standard pronunciation that sounded as though he had learned it from a broadcaster with a Beijing accent, "If every parent thought the way you do, how could there be any hope for the nation or its people?" Accordingly, from his parents' depressed expressions he could intuit that his elder brother was doing something dangerous and of which their parents disapproved, which further piqued his own curiosity.

Once, as he was waking up, he dimly saw his brother shuffling some papers under the light of a lamp, looking as though he were deep in concentration. The mist was sucked in through the crack in the door by the light of the lamp, and after he closed his eyes again he heard the sound of the door shutting. On another occasion he tried to secretly follow his brother, but his brother stopped him and said, "You are still too young, but we can discuss it when you are older."

On that particular day, he found he could no longer control his curiosity, and therefore willed himself awake and followed his brother from a distance. He saw the sun rise over the horizon. First it resembled a yellow egg, then it crept higher and higher and burned away the mist. Eventually, his brother disappeared into that enormous field of tropical plants along the water's edge. He disappeared into a sheet of fog and water. After a little while, as the lingering fog began to seep into the dark corners of the room that had not been illuminated by the sun's rays, the sunlight suddenly changed color, as the rosy glow began to fade and the brilliant sunlight shone in all directions. In that instant just before the last of the mist burned away, he suddenly saw an indistinct figure flicker in and out of view. There was a series of loud explosions, like fireworks, mixed with the deep sound of running water and the high-pitched sound of screaming. It seemed as if the scene was taking place along the river's edge or in the middle of a swamp. He felt a terrifying scene was in the process of unfolding, and furthermore sensed that it directly concerned the elder brother with whom he shared a bed every night. He opened his eyes in horror, as he desperately pressed his back against a tree trunk. Apart from this, he didn't know what else he could do. Several dozen soldiers wearing red caps and green uniforms emerged from the mist, leaving their footsteps along the water's edge. Their faces, which looked as though they had been forged from iron, were full of murderous hatred, and each soldier had a rifle slung over his shoulder. Several of the soldiers were divided into pairs and, together, were dragging their victims by their feet. In all, they were pulling five blood-drenched corpses. At this point he didn't dare edge forward, and instead simply stood there staring in shock. He wasn't even sure whether or not he hoped he might be able to recognize amongst them that person who had recently disappeared into the mist. Eventually the soldiers noticed him, and one gestured for him to stop while another strode toward him furiously. The first soldier asked him several questions in a language he couldn't understand. He neither nodded nor shook his head, and instead he kept his back pressed tightly against the tree, as he slowly slid to the ground.

After his field of vision expanded somewhat, some people who lived or worked nearby came running over, staring in astonishment at the corpses by the riverside and the blood that covered the ground. The brothers' parents took the lead and rushed toward the corpses, turning them over one after the other. After anxiously inspecting each face they relaxed slightly, but eventually they saw him crouched under the tree, not even aware that he was being bitten by red fire ants. They immediately turned pale, and asked,

"What in the world are you doing here?"

". . ."

"Was that your brother?"

His mother swallowed her tears and quickly but efficiently used her scarf to brush away the fire ants covering his body, while his father lowered his head and mumbled a few questions to the soldiers. Eventually, with the assistance of others who helped translate, he learned that one of the corpses belonged to someone who had tried to flee under a hail of bullets. The sentries subsequently conducted a wide sweep of the area, but failed to find anything. Several of the other corpses belonged to his brother's classmates, all of whom were cadres in the local Communist Party Youth League. In the marsh, they found a dilapidated stilt house, and following this incident the house was torched and a nearby sampan was confiscated.

That year he had been about to enroll in elementary school, while his brother was about to move up to the third year of high school.

His brother was never seen or heard from again. His remains were never found either, and consequently in the official police records he was listed merely as "missing." The family had no way of obtaining a death certificate, and furthermore there remained a warrant out for his arrest. For a long time afterwards, plainclothes policemen would come virtually every year and ask his parents about his whereabouts.

By the time he reached his thirties, his youngest son was about a year older than his own elder brother had been when he last saw him. However, his elder brother, as a child of that earlier era, never had a chance to mature, grow old, or fulfill his ambitions. Instead, that youth, with a smile of satisfaction forever puckered at the corner of his lips and an arresting gaze, was never seen again. After martial law was lifted he himself continued his studies. There was a white flag in the school yard, and in front of the school entrance students were holding microphones and making speeches—all of which somehow gave him a feeling of tenderness. Perhaps, had it not been for what happened to his elder brother, he himself could almost be considered a son of that era as well.

In his sixth year of elementary school, on the school grounds everything was very calm but outside storm clouds were gathering. Almost every day they could see the corpses of youths who had been executed and put on display in the streets, virtually all of whom were overseas Chinese. Like afternoon showers, political demonstrations came one after another, featuring white cloth banners on which the ink was still wet, people waving little red books, soldiers screaming, and countless demonstrators scurrying through the streets. He had already grown accustomed to searching the faces of those youths—either alive or dead—but it wasn't until many years later that he realized that he was unconsciously hoping to be reunited with his elder brother. For many years he would repeatedly have the same dream, in which the outer edge of his bed would be warm to the touch. He would step through the door and try to scream, but no sound would come out. He would try to get out of bed, but would feel as though he had been beaten to the point that he was unable to move.

That was a tumultuous era. The British Empire, which famously called itself the empire on which the sun never set, finally began to confront its own sunset. East Asia's ancient dragon began to slough off its skin and take on new blood, and all of the Hua people who had been born and grown up in the South found their passions kindled, calling themselves sons and daughters of the Revolution, regarding their own blood as fuel for the revolution. Those who thought of themselves as youthful dragons thousands of *li* away from home believed that. That was an incendiary era. The elder brother's accident led his family to attempt to carefully safeguard the younger brother, exhorting and warning him again and again. Later they didn't hesitate to take out loans in order to send him far away, to Taiwan, so that he might escape this contemporary fervor.

The year he was in third grade, however, the government designated the rubber forest where his family lived to be a black zone and, like many of their neighbors, his family was forcibly relocated into a "new village" that the government created on the outskirts of town. The original buildings that had been there were burned down in order to eliminate the Malayan Communist Party's ability to move supplies and to prevent them from using this area as a secret base. Every morning, when each worker passed through the barbed wire-enclosed "new village" checkpoint to go work in the forest, they all had to submit to a rigorous search by the military to ensure that they were not carrying forbidden items (such as ammunition and leaflets) or an excessive amount of food. And upon their return, if they were found to be carrying any paper with writing on it they would run into considerable difficulty. During that period, Chinese writing was perceived as carrying a mysterious power, like a curse.

His elder brother, the year before he disappeared, had already taught him to recognize a few Chinese characters, including their family's surname, his own given name, the names of his parents and siblings, the words *South Seas* and *Singapore* that appear in large print in newspapers, and so forth. His brother would also frequently point to the word *China* in the large, blood-red newspaper headlines and ask him to learn that as well. His brother would solemnly tell him a story about a distant and ancient China—asking that, no matter what, upon growing up he must be proud of being a Chinese. His dream, like that of the other youth of that era, necessarily involved returning to that ancient mainland to visit the Great Wall, the Yangtze, the Yellow River, and the Great Plains, so that he might, as he put it, "inscribe his name on a stone from the fatherland." Therefore, for many years he was convinced that his elder brother had secretly returned to his Chinese fatherland. He innocently believed that in that seemingly bottomless marsh there might be a secret passage to the Yangtze or the Yellow River. His elder brother resembled a young dragon, soaring home. Nevertheless, the divine China of which his brother dreamed was one he had never seen, and furthermore was one he had never even thought of visiting. After the lifting of martial law in Taiwan, his wife, children, in-laws, and workmates all traveled to Taiwan several times, but he simply sat there silently, enveloped in his own sorrow. Although he was keenly interested in Chinese antiques, and made the study of old Chinese cultural symbols his lifelong vocation, whenever he received invitations from universities on the other side of the strait or from colleagues writing under their own name (including invitations to attend conferences, give lectures, or engage in other forms of collaboration), he would invariably ignore them. On the other hand, he would purchase large quantities of academic books imported from Mainland China though semi-open routes. The furthest abroad he ventured was to Hong Kong, where he would attend conferences, buy books, and purchase some antiques—though the only things he truly loved were stone artifacts ostensibly from the Neolithic era, together with simple Xia and Shang dynasty flaking tools used for making stone and jade artifacts. This was a result not of political considerations but rather of a set of more deep-rooted sensibilities.

China, Oh China! This was the dying curse of his elder brother and of so many other youth of that era!

In the darkness, he fell into a contemplative silence. For many years, there were countless things he had not been able to bring himself to consider. Day after day, he spent much of his time "gaining new insights from old material"—which is to say, rereading the classics—and carefully comparing the commentaries and editions from different historical periods, with a focus on the pre-Qin period, and repeatedly browsing, parsing, and copying ancient writings that he didn't fully understand.

He would read domestic and foreign articles, together with academic journals from both sides of the strait. He would take notes on the key concepts and write down his thoughts, and occasionally would give a lecture or other commentary, or teach a class for college or graduate students. Students would come and go, as one class graduated and a new one enrolled, and this cycle would continue on and on. In the blink of an eye, their four years of college would be over. He would often encounter other students from Malaysia, virtually all of whom regarded him as a "fellow national," but his attitude toward them was neither particularly warm nor terribly cold. He didn't single these students out, as did some professors with problematic attitudes, but neither did he invite them over to his house for every holiday, as did some overly friendly professors. Even his own wife couldn't tolerate the detached manner with which he treated these students from Malaysia, and repeatedly complained, "Don't you remember how your own teachers treated you when you were a student?" But he wouldn't say a word in response, and instead appeared as though he were lost in thought. After a while, people stopped trying to encourage him, and he himself seemed to have no intention of changing. Occasionally he would encounter a particularly hardworking student for whom he would consider making an exception, but in the end the dispassionate attitude he had cultivated for so long would make it impossible for him to take that first step. Soon, they too would graduate, and he would watch as they returned to their homeland, never to contact him again. More than once his fellow nationals would ask him, "Why don't you return? Why don't you make more of a contribution where you are most needed?" He would always respond first with a long pause, after which he would whisper, "I *can't* go back. How could I ever go back?" Regardless of what the other person said, he would merely continue shaking his head, and at most would add, "Although tortoises originate from the South Seas region, these tortoise shells come from China's Central Plains. You have to kill a tortoise to get its shell, so how can it ever return to its origins?" After he repeated this remark over and over at several graduation ceremonies, it eventually spread far and wide, to the point that new students would ask him this question merely in order to verify if the rumors were correct. He eventually came to realize this, and consequently learned to keep silent. The student group for Malaysian students in Taiwan frequently invited him come lecture or participate in their thesis defenses, but he would never agree to do so. The university, high school, the Association of Malaysians in Taiwan, the association of overseas students in Taiwan, and other organizations would all invite him to participate in conferences on topics such as "The Future of Mahua Literature," "Chinese Culture and Malaysian Chinese Society," "Malaysian Chinese Culture in the Twenty-first Century," and so forth, but he couldn't even trouble himself to write back to decline their invitations. He would rarely even go back to his family home, returning only about a dozen times over the preceding several decades. Each time he did return, particularly in later years, he would regard his parents and siblings as though they were pieces of driftwood floating in opposite directions. They would only manage to exchange a few remarks with them about household matters, and otherwise would have nothing to talk about.

"How is your health?"

"Good."

"Do you have enough money?"

"Yes."

He would rely on his wife to relay all of the details about his life, and also to keep him updated on his family's affairs.

After living abroad for many years, he had come to adopt a practice of prudent self-preservation. He came to inhabit a world that, although sealed off, was nevertheless at least "safe." He had no ambition, and neither curried favor nor offended anyone. Instead, he merely remained silent, and would curtly decline the countless dinner and banquet invitations he received. He would turn down all of these invitations, regardless of whether they were from the state, party elders, senior faculty, colleagues, classmates, or students. . . . To help make sense of his withdrawal, his acquaintances had known for some time that he couldn't tolerate alcohol, even beer; that he was so terrified of his wife that if she were to claim that the earth was flat, he wouldn't dare contend it was round; that he was extremely sensitive to politics, and would respectfully keep his distance from anything outside of the formal requirements of his job, whether it be related to environmentalism, or petitioning a student in danger of veering into radicalism not to quit his studies. He knew that to live in this world no one can avoid excessive criticism, and this is especially true of someone trying to eke out a living in a narrow and sealed-off environment, with books and texts as his only companions. Everyone's back is carved with other people's insults: "Bookworm," "bookshelf," "silverfish," "South Seas tortoise," and so forth. The act of holding a turtle shell had already become his distinctive trademark. After continually slouching for a long time, he had become slightly hunchbacked, and after staring at dust- and parasite-covered books for a long time, he had become nearsighted. He developed heavy bags under his eyes and a hypnotic voice. He could not help but feel he was a prematurely aged tortoise. It was as if he had never been young, and instead had been born old and depressed, dragging out an ignoble existence in a tumultuous world. It was as if he had already become part of the dark musty corners of this ancient dilapidated structure that was formerly built in a European style in the Japanese imperial period, when it was known as the Taipei Imperial University—as though he were a parasite dwelling in the dark recesses of this ancient structure.

In the pitch-black night, the Fu Sinian bell tolled. The spectral figure of the old school principal emerged for a walk. Countless humanities scholars who retreated to Taiwan with the Nationalist government spent the remainder of their lives in this dark building. When they arrived during a period of tumult, they were approximately the same age as he was now. They belonged to a great era, and to a greater or a lesser extent they were all infected with the spirit of their age. It was as if traditional learning provided the basis for their contemporary sense of superiority, and when one hears their teachings, one can only stare in astonishment. This was not entirely due to their northern and southern regional accents, but rather was because of that nearly limitless memory—from the late Qing, the Republican period when they came of age, and back through the Ming, Yuan, Song, and even the Wei, Jin, and Northern and Southern dynasties, as well as the Han, Qin, Zhou, and Shang dynasties—all of this knowledge becomes the stuff of anecdotes in which one becomes immersed like a storyteller, describing historical figures and historical events as if they were unfolding before one's very eyes. They are all seers, and when they teach it is as if they are offering a simplified ritual ceremony and performance. As a result of his South Seas identity, these old professors gave him special attention and would frequently recount historical events from that period. Not only would he frequently have tea and share meals with the professors, go to their homes for class, and listen to their lessons, the professors would also frequently chat with him and supplement the gaps in his learning. As a result, he distinctly recalled their voice and appearance, as well as their parental warmth. After they passed away one after another, all of this faded away, ghostlike, to haunt these dilapidated buildings at night. Every evening, he would be virtually the last one to leave, not departing until he heard the janitors shutting the doors and windows. After everyone else had already gone to bed, he would find himself the only person left in this monastery, with ghosts for company. His footsteps echoed through the long hallway in this solitary night. The roots of the banyan tree grew through crevices in the road.

Actually, what he did there at night was one of his secrets. On several occasions, an old janitor from Hunan would ask him what he was cooking in the middle of the night, why it had such an odd smell, and whether he was baking or boiling something. Occasionally, some colleagues who were returning late would also complain that late at night there was a strange smell on the school grounds, as a result of which he didn't dare carry out his experiment too frequently.

While watching the turtles in the Drunk Moon Pond climb over one another in an attempt to sun themselves many winter mornings or evenings, he would quickly grab one and hide it in the laboratory. Then, in the middle of the night, he would secretly carry out his "experiment."

This experiment was actually not all that complicated. First, he would light a stick of incense and use it to burn a turtle's tail. The instant the turtle stuck its head out of its shell, he would slice it off, followed by its legs and tail, and finally he would pry open the skin between the upper and lower halves of the shell. Sometimes he would merely carve out the animal's intestines (so that the residual fecal matter would not cause problems), after which he would place it in the oven and bake it. Within ten minutes he would hear a distinct *puk* sound—an ancient turtle language. Other times, he would place the turtle in an electric steamer and cook it, after which he would enjoy some turtle soup. His primary objective, however, was not the soup itself but rather the turtle's shell. After he finished eating, he would wash the shell, dry it, and then leave it out for several days. Afterwards, he would carve out the scales and smooth the shell's ridged surface. Then, he would cut the shell into two halves and use different grades of sandpaper to smooth it until it was as shiny as a piece of jade. Next, he would use a diamond bit to drill a hole in each shell in the same location, so as to be able to string them together, whereupon he would drill a shallow hole in the surface, to scorch them. In this way, he would enjoy this secret pleasure of eating turtle flesh in the middle of the night like an addict listening to the turtle language, and making a private divination in order to test out this mysterious method. He would carve a message in oracle bone script, seeking to re-create an ancient experience. . . .

It was bitter cold, and furthermore it was pouring rain outside.

After being stationed in New Town for several years, residing in a metal-covered wooden house not unlike those found in the rubber forest, he ultimately settled down in the margins of the town. The year he finished primary school, the nation was liberated—to the delight of one people and the sorrow of another. Overnight, China became a foreign country. All first-generation immigrants spent their days in a state of terror, even as the country's youth seethed with excitement. Afraid that his generation would be unable to read Chinese, his parents sent him to a Chinese middle school, even though the school was seething with revolutionary fervor.

Among the upperclassmen, he would frequently notice the look of excitement he remembered having seen on his brother's face, and he could virtually feel their temperature rising. His classmates were all very articulate, and were particularly good at giving speeches. They would frequently engage in collective activities, and you could observe a strong collective action even when they were merely selecting a class representative or attending a basketball game. A reading group frequently invited him to join them, but he would always come up with excuses not to go. When he was in the second year of middle school, a classmate nicknamed Long White Mountain solicitously extended him a hand—not only helping him with his schoolwork but also drawing on his collective resources in order to help him obtain the school's only work-study position in light of his economically precarious family background. Naturally, the classmate invited him to attend their reading group—sometimes they would organize excursions, campfire gatherings, hikes, birthday parties, Duanwu and Mid-Autumn Festival banquets, as well as any other events you could possibly imagine. To spare their feelings, he would only attend those functions having to do with Mahua culture or literature, for the sole purpose of borrowing a few books—since he didn't own any himself and even the school library didn't have very many volumes.

He had no idea where his classmates obtained their publications, which included novels, essays, and poetry by Lu Xun, Hu Feng, Ba Jin, Mao Dun, Guo Moruo, among others. He read them all. Based on these reading materials, his classmate White Mountain would patiently explain to him the principles of peasant rebellions and class struggle, and would relate the Chinese people's difficult history dating back to the Opium Wars. Pointing to the color photographs on the covers of various newspapers, his classmates would teach him to recognize contemporary China's political leaders—one yellow face after another. There were aerial photographs of the Great Wall, stretching out over the Chinese landscape like an ancient dragon, of the setting sun shining down over the Yellow River, together with the Yangtze's Three Gorges, and he and his classmates would emotionally sing "folk songs" as military songs, responding to each as though they were shots of adrenaline. Imitating a certain someone's intonation and gestures, he would intone,

"The Chinese people have stood up!"

They covered the Long March, American imperialism, Chinese coolies, and revolutionary youth. With this, White Mountain proceeded to give him a lesson in modern history, attempting to endow him with a sense of historical destiny, an awareness of historical depth, and an appreciation of his position within a system of abstract ideals. He was quiet and rather skeptical, but nevertheless got into the habit of following the stories that were being reported in the news each day, including the various criticisms of Li Guanghui and Chen Zhenlu. However, he seemed somewhat closed off and unwilling to respond as quickly as his classmates demanded. He was never able to join in their discussions and debates, and whenever he was asked a question he would invariably respond with a long silence. One day, White Mountain sighed and said, "perhaps you are simply destined not to be a child of this era." It was not until many years later that he finally understood that what White Mountain meant was that he was doomed to be left behind by history, but at the time, when he realized that the organization was going to give up trying to recruit him, he gave a sigh of relief.

This sense of organized fervor began to cool off, and he was able to retreat from public view. White Mountain, however, didn't lose interest in him, and instead merely settled for not forcing him to do things that he wasn't prepared to do. White Mountain didn't forget to indoctrinate him with a sense of nationalism and an abstract sense of historical materialism. On another occasion, White Mountain also sighed (perhaps because he saw him reading a book too intently), and uttered the latter half of the phrase "perhaps you are simply destined not to be a child of this era," which was "though your elder brother was a revolutionary to the core!" This statement made him immediately lose his customary calm demeanor. He turned pale and began to tremble as he gripped White Mountain's shirt and spit out a question word by word, "Did . . . you . . . know . . . my . . . brother?" White Mountain shook his head and said, "Calm down," then added, "we all knew of him."

"Where . . . is he now?"

White Mountain once again shook his head. "We spent a long time looking for him, but couldn't find any clues. He never again established contact with the organization."

He let go of White Mountain's shirt and apologized. Then he abruptly sat down, and was quiet for a long time.

He distinctly remembered that at the time they were at the top of a hill. They were on the grounds of a Chinese elementary school, under a tall acacia tree. Yellow leaves were piled up all around, and blood-red acacia buds were scattered all over the ground. From there, one could see almost three-quarters of the town. In the evening, all of the households in the "new village" would go out to the quiet, yellow street, and occasionally a car would slowly drive through. In front of the houses there were faint shadows of human figures, ditches, palm trees—like a scene out of an old photograph.

"Is my brother dead?"

He heard a chilly voice emerge from his throat. It sounded as though that voice did not even belong to him, but rather belonged to his adolescent Adam's apple itself. No one answered him, as the sound of his voice dissipated into the empty fissures between different eras.

On the eve of White Mountain's graduation from middle school, a group of comrades roughly his own age were arrested and imprisoned due to their involvement in some case, after which they were forced into exile. Some of them were voluntarily returned to China, and were never heard from again. After he himself subsequently went abroad, he never told anyone about these experiences (not even his wife, during their many years of marriage). During that era when he felt such an acute sense of insecurity, he was able to avoid many problems by simply locking up his memory.

Until his wife finally visited his family's hometown, even her knowledge of that part of his past was exceedingly limited. She originally believed he was his family's eldest son, and it wasn't until one day when she inadvertently noticed that a letter from his family referred to him as "second brother" that she finally realized that the situation was actually more complicated. His explanation, however, was quite simple: "My brother died unexpectedly when he was in the third year of high school." She only knew that in his family's hometown, there was that small building in the "new village," but as for his leftist leanings when he was growing up, he never uttered a word, instead maintaining a strict taboo about this aspect of his past.

In his heart, he always regarded White Mountain as his elder brother's extension and substitute, and he had a considerable influence on his life.

One day when they were in high school, White Mountain gave him a fragment of a book—which, in fact, consisted of merely a few sheets. In those termite-eaten pages, he read for the first time about Shang dynasty oracle bone inscriptions, including a brief description of their discovery, characteristics, quantity, and so forth. White Mountain remarked, "Great discoveries like the Shang dynasty oracle bones, the Dunhuang manuscripts, and dinosaur fossils were all made in our ancestral land during a period of extreme instability and crisis, and most of the artifacts were subsequently confiscated by foreign imperialists." Regardless of the current political situation, these records left him completely mystified.

In these fragmentary pages, there was a passage discussing the autumn of 1929, when researchers from the Academia Sinica unearthed four tortoise shells from what is now Xiaotun village at Anyang, in Henan province. Mr. Dong Zuobin subsequently dubbed these the "four tortoise shells." When scholars consulted a tortoise taxonomy compiled by Mr. Gray from the British Museum, they confirmed that these shell fragments came from the same species of giant tortoise that is indigenous to the Malaysian peninsula but which has never been native to China. In other words, the shells had very likely been offered as a tribute from the distant South Seas region. But this was three or four thousand years ago!

This discovery left him extremely excited, though he himself could not say why precisely he reacted as he did. Thanks to this serendipitous finding, several years later he found himself in study room #5 of Taiwan University's Chinese Literature department examining black oracle bone inscription rubbings and dark red oracle bone fragments, and he suddenly felt an irrepressible sense of euphoria. Of the oracle bones that had been excavated and exposed to the elements and the ravages of war, these few that survived intact were dispersed throughout an ancient and oddly-shaped region. On some of these fragments you could clearly see the delicate ancient inscriptions—be they partial or complete, deciphered or still undeciphered.

In the dark, he gently caressed the hand-carved inscriptions on the shell's surface with his thumb, as though he were an avid gambler selecting a card. He had an intimate familiarity with the texture of these symbols, and they often made him recall, despite himself, that disquieting dream he would often have when he was young, whenever he got nervous.

That dream was originally based on an actual event. One day when he was in high school, a family who had moved back home to the rubber forest was attacked in the early morning, and a boy about his age, whom he knew well, was shot to death and his bed was drenched in blood. After hearing the news, he rushed to the scene, where the corpse was still lying in its original position. The shooter had pried open the boy's window and shot him more than dozen times through the mosquito netting, killing him instantly. Based on the techniques used, it was apparent that this assassination must have been committed by a communist activist who subsequently fled into the forest, and the deceased must have been viewed as a traitor or informant. However, most ordinary observers would have regarded the deceased as an uncompromised communist activist. This incident left everyone completely mystified.

That night, he had an erotic dream in which he cuddled with a young and tender partner until dawn. Lying on a mist-covered wooden bed at the edge of a forest, he nervously removed his companion's clothes. In the moonlight, his companion looked as pale as a fish. He reached out to caress that mysterious region between her legs, but was terrified by the cold sensation he felt—it turned out what he had touched was a testicle. He looked more carefully at his companion, whose gaze was directed toward some indeterminate point in the darkness, and saw that he resembled those who had been killed, but also bore an uncanny likeness to his brother, who had disappeared many years earlier. When he awoke, he removed the tortoise shell he had hidden in his bureau and, without thinking, placed it over his erect penis. In this way he was able to reach an unprecedented orgasm, as white semen spurted from his own swollen red "turtle head."

Later, that orgasm he experienced at the interstices of dream and wakefulness became a source of irrepressible desire. Although sometimes in his dreams he would feel a warm sticky feeling, he imagined it was freshly laid egg surrounded by chicken droppings.

. . . I never expected my elder brother would have remained buried in the marsh all this time. According to the calculations of the experts, he must have died about forty years ago, not long after that attack. He wasn't the only survivor, and neither was he the only one to flee. Perhaps he died because he lost too much blood in the attack, or perhaps he survived for another several days after being shot (since so much time has elapsed, it was impossible to determine the precise time of death). The problem was that under these sorts of conditions, someone with an untreated wound would eventually be claimed by either the mosquitos or the ants. Moreover, what would he have eaten while in hiding? Why didn't he come out to seek help? Did he know he would eventually die no matter what? Why did the military never find him, even after sending several dozen soldiers to conduct a thorough search? If the county government hadn't decided to raze that area to build new houses, who knows for how many more years my brother's bones would have remained hidden in the water!

Our father and mother were both devastated. They had always hoped that sooner or later my brother might have managed to escape to China, gotten married and had a child, perhaps even become a minor official, and sooner or later would suddenly return to visit them. After his disappearance, our parents went for several days unable to eat or even say a word. But I think they understood better than anyone that it was most likely that he had in fact died in the depths of the marsh, because if he had in fact managed to escape why he would not have made an attempt to contact them after all this time? Mother told me many years ago that he didn't want to implicate his family. . . .

. . . Judging from the distribution of the bones, my brother's corpse must have been devoured by wild animals, fish, and insects. Some of the bones had been dragged away by river otters to make a nest, others remained buried in the mud for years, while the remainder had disappeared without a trace (this was particularly true of the small bones from his fingers and toes). Most of the bones were broken and fragmentary, and the strangest thing was that his skull was mixed in with a pile of tortoise shells that had been brought in from who knows where. I've never heard of turtles being able to shed their shells, and these looked like they were all shells left behind by very old turtles. Why were they here? They looked as though they had been collected by some animal. Remarkably, the spine and breast bones were still intact, though the leg and neck bones had come apart. As for the spine and breast bones, they had been submerged for so long that at first glance they looked like the bones of a large fish, albeit appearing somewhat warped.

. . . Although mother's eyesight was not very good, she nevertheless insisted on helping clean the bones. She spent an entire day carefully scrubbing them, while exhorting us to be very careful and not use too coarse of a brush. After having been exposed to the elements for so many years, the bones had become quite fragile. The ones that were buried underground had turned dark red, while the ones that were underwater were light green, and no amount of scrubbing could get them clean. . . .

The police report was promptly released, but consisted of only a few short lines of text.

When he closed his eyes, he could still hear the wind and rain. By this point it was already late at night, and downstairs the sound of the old school workers' doors slamming shut echoed in the darkness. The sound of the bell tolling resonated loudly, and the old principal once again came out of his graveyard and gestured toward the dark corners of the campus, where various pairs of students were having secret rendezvous while in each classroom professors and graduate students were hard at work. Only the sound of the wind and rain remained as before.

With the thumb and index finger of his right hand, he held the paperweight. It and those turtle shells became precious treasures that never left his side. Apart from his wife, family, and coworkers, over the preceding several decades there had been many others who had curiously asked him what this was, to which he would invariably reply, "It's a fish bone." If they pursued the matter further, he would concede that it was a souvenir he had brought back from the South Seas, explaining, "It is a vertebra from a species of large tropical fish. After the rain forests began to be cut down, one rarely sees such a large specimen anymore." Sometimes he would add wistfully, ". . . it is a good luck charm my mother sent me." He would lie to everyone about this.

Following his elder brother's disappearance, what also became submerged in the depths of that marsh was his own irrepressible adolescent desires. He continued waiting for the right moment—waiting for his family to relax their supervision over him, for the dark region to be cleaned up, for everyone's memories to fade, and for his own body to mature. After this long wait, he remained as calm as a seer, and before he knew it eight years had passed. Lacking any intellectual preparation whatsoever, he entered adolescence. As his bones lengthened, he developed a kind of silent roughness. His light brown facial fuzz turned black, his Adam's apple began to protrude, his voice deepened, and part of his body came to resemble a reanimated beast. His impulsiveness and the restless changes in his body echoed one another.

In the years that followed, he made numerous attempts to enter the marsh alone. On several occasions he almost drowned, but eventually he learned to float in the deep and muddy water. Sometimes, because he did not prepare fully enough, he was almost discovered. For instance, the sharp leaves would cut his hands, feet, and face, producing a patchwork of open wounds and leaving him with no choice but to lie and say that he had participated in a scouting expedition. His clothes would get muddy, and consequently before returning home he'd have no choice but to wash them outside and dry them in the sun. He found each trip more stimulating than the last, and he felt as though he were on his way to a romantic rendezvous with a mysterious partner. Eventually, he learned to prepare a spare set of old clothing, a face mask, and boots; and although he was not able to secure a small boat, as his brother had, but with some courage he was still able to proceed deep into the marsh.

Each time he advanced deeper and deeper, growing ever bolder. The amount of time he spent in the marsh also steadily increased. Eventually, it reached the point that after he entered that dark and icy cold water, he would strip off his clothes and swim naked. After a long, long time, he would ejaculate.

On that most unusual occasion, he proceeded deeper than he ever had before, because he was pursuing a large tortoise. He entered an area that he had never explored, which was separated from the water by thick vegetation. There was a lot of bamboo, windy paths, and sunlight. As he pushed aside the tall grass that was blocking his sight, he was momentarily blinded by the bright light. Next, standing in the middle of the black water filled with white silver grass and green algae, he noticed a protruding white bone—a breast bone that was oriented upwards. When he saw it more clearly he was able to confirm that it was in fact part of a human skeleton, with all of the bones almost completely buried in the muddy soil. The skull's mouth was open, and the teeth were all neatly arrayed. Withered grass was poking up through the holes in the ribs, and both legs were lying outside the water. He swam over, knelt down next to the skeleton, and gently caressed it. The bones were shallowly buried, but because over time roots had grown through them, they were now impossible to move. He felt an odd shiver, and with a trembling hand he caressed the bones, as the sun shone down on his back and sweat poured down his body. He laughed and cried, and repeatedly exclaimed, "So, this is where you were." In a surge of emotion, he became determined to take the entire skeleton back with him, whereupon he unconsciously poked his fingers into the ground and rooted around in the soil where the skeleton was buried. The pain in his back combined with the sweat pouring down his face gradually dampened his emotion. He returned to the water, and began considering how to resolve this unexpected situation. His initial conclusion was that he definitely wouldn't be able to take the entire skeleton because it would create an enormous scandal, and he would never be able to explain why he had gone there in the first place. At the very least, he wanted to take all of the vertebrae, but he recognized that although they were arranged in a beautiful configuration, they would nevertheless be difficult to collect. Alternatively, he could take the skull, which was even more beautiful, though it might create many problems. Eventually, he decided to take some small but well-preserved appendages. Perhaps a finger or bone from the palm? Perhaps a toe, or bone from the foot? Or how about . . . ? He eventually decided on a vertebra from directly behind the throat. The problem, however, was that this would mean he would need to separate the skull from the rest of the body. As he was using sticks and stones to extract the bone, he realized with surprise that he didn't feel any sorrow, and instead was thrumming with excitement. He also recognized that he would never again return to this location.

As he was about to leave, he noticed, in the grass not far from the skeleton, a pile of palm-sized turtle shells, some of which had obviously been burned. In the grass there was also some deadwood and charcoal. He quickly grabbed one of the shells, turned around, and proceeded to ejaculate on the skeleton. Then he left.

In the cool, dark night, the skeleton seemed to give off a faint glow. Carrying these two souvenirs and with a burning desire in his heart, he left his hometown, as though the statute of limitations on his search had not yet expired.

It seemed like it was not long before that he had been leafing through a copy of *Asian Weekly* and came across a report of how the local government had released a statement about a case from the earlier colonial period, declaring that "The statute of limitations on the search will never expire."

The rain began to fall even harder, and the temperature dropped precipitously. The phone began to ring. He still didn't want to return home. Nevertheless, the sound of his footsteps preceded him, as they echoed up and down the lone hallway. The door slammed shut behind him.

allah's will

In the name of the merciful and gracious Allah:
Say, "O, Unbelievers! I do not worship what you worship, nor are you worshippers of what I worship. I will not worship what you worship, nor will you worship what I worship. You have your religion, and I have mine."

THE QUR'AN, SURA 109 (THE UNBELIEVERS)

(*Originally written in Malay*)

I AM VERY AWARE OF THE FACT that if the following story were to be revealed to the world, it would surely precipitate a grave crisis.

It would have dire consequences not only for my wife, children, grandchildren, and many other descendants with whom I've already lost touch, but also for my "most cherished friend," the island where I live, my country, as well as my fellow countrymen.

This is a very complicated matter, and I hardly know even where to begin. My thoughts are very confused—especially given that I haven't written in Chinese for over thirty years and there are therefore a lot of Chinese characters I've forgotten how to write (I often either add or leave out strokes, mistake one character for another, remember the character only vaguely, or only know its pronunciation . . .). But if I can't write a certain character, I refuse to transliterate it into Malay, and instead prefer to use another Chinese character with a similar pronunciation. Given that I've already breached the contract that I signed on pain of death (and which I will describe below), I might as well go ahead and break it completely.

If this confession ends up being destroyed in a disaster (either natural or man-made) or being locked away in a classified archive for political reasons, then that will simply have been Allah's will. If, on the other hand, this confession some day ends up being revealed to the world, I'm certain that by that point I will no longer be alive. I therefore would like to take this opportunity to express my utmost gratitude and heartfelt apologies to my most cherished friend and benefactor (I regret I can't reveal his name). I am very grateful to him for having granted me these past thirty years of life, and sincerely apologize for having broken our agreement. And if it turns out that in doing so I have created trouble for my wife and children, I also ask their forgiveness and hope that they will be able to find it in their hearts to forgive an old man who for much of his life has remained imprisoned on this remote island. For many years now, there hasn't been a single moment when I didn't yearn to write something in Chinese. These past two years, perhaps because of a marked acceleration in the aging process, I've felt a growing urge to write. I eventually decided that if I don't write now, I may never again have the opportunity.

Although my fingers tremble as I try to hold a pen, they are nevertheless still as strong as a craftsman's, and in this way I have proceeded to create a record for myself. Outside, a light drizzle symbolizing happiness is falling.

When was it that I arrived on this island? I remember very clearly: It was October 2 of 1957. Why do I remember this date so clearly? Because that was originally the day I was to be executed. Several friends and I had been arrested on September 10 for possessing firearms, and on September 15 we were all convicted of conspiracy and treason, whereupon we were asked to offer "a reason why we shouldn't be executed." After hearing the sentence, these five dear friends initially turned pale, but then—perhaps because of their youth—they all looked at each other and laughed. Even as they put on a show of being at ease, however, hidden within their laughter there was a hint of torture-induced terror, as if they had all experienced this before. They felt as though they could see their own fresh red blood about to spurt into the air. Their smiles revealed a hint of confusion, obliviousness, and loss of control.

The hardest thing to endure, however, was the need to bid farewell to our families. This was not a simply a question of being filial, since before deciding to follow this path we had already discussed our decision with our peers countless times, and had agreed that revolution always requires that people shed blood. We had, therefore, already made the hardest decision. The difficulty was that this had all been carried out behind the backs of my parents—who trusted me to study and do the right thing—and therefore you could say that I had betrayed their confidence. Their disappointed gaze left me speechless. According to an old proverb, "A good man does not become a soldier, and a good piece of iron does not become a nail." My parents, who merely wished to have healthy children and to be able to live in peace, could not possibly comprehend our actions and our attitudes. At the time, we all believed our blood was red ink used to display the intaglio inscribed on that giant square seal of our era.

My parents' faces were wrinkled and their hair had turned gray overnight. I suspect they had barely slept since I was arrested. My younger sister was about five or so at the time, and didn't know what to do. She ended up bringing me some lightning bugs, but since it was daytime when she arrived the insects were therefore all asleep. She said quietly, "There are many more in the mosquito netting."

To my surprise, my most cherished friend also came to pay me a final visit. By that point he had already managed, thanks to his royal bloodline and his intelligence, to attain a very high position, though in political terms we were mutually opposed. In his eyes, I had betrayed not only this young nation but also his imperial house, his race, the trust he had granted me over so many years, together with our former friendship. That day, he was neatly dressed, was sporting a well-groomed mustache, and, apart from the furious expression on his face, looked just like a high-ranking official.

As soon as he saw me, he immediately pointed and began cursing angrily,

"You bastard! You pig! Pig! Bastard! Chinese pig! You fat bastard!

"How did I let you down? How *did* I let you down? Why did you need to go and do this sort of suicidal thing?!"

Shouting in Malay interspersed with English, he stamped his feet, pounded the table, and breathed loudly. "Damn it, damn it! I should just let them execute you." He kept repeating the same thing over and over again. From his hitherto unseen fury and the way he shouted until he was hoarse, it was clear he was extremely attentive to our friendship. I couldn't help but feel heartbroken.

After about ten minutes or so his rage began to subside. Seeing me standing there silently with my head bowed, he gestured with bloodshot eyes at my parents and sister who were kneeling at my side and shouted,

"Did you ever think about *them*? You pig!"

From the moment my cherished friend appeared, my parents and sister had been kneeling there, kowtowing to him and begging for his assistance:

"As long as they don't execute him, they can detain him for as long as they want . . ."

"The two of you have been playmates since you were boys . . ."

"Little sister, ask *Tuan* ("the gentleman") for *tolong* ("assistance") . . ."

My cherished friend quickly helped my mother to her feet, but when he reached out to do the same for my father, my mother immediately knelt back down and again began kowtowing and begging him for help. As a result, my friend found himself very busy, repeatedly helping up my parents one after the other. In the end he had no choice but to call over the guards and have them forcibly lift my parents to their feet. In an exasperated tone, he exclaimed, "Your son committed a crime that is punishable by death. What do you expect me to do? It's not as though he is . . ."

Eventually the room grew quiet, as my parents cradled their swollen and bruised foreheads.

My cherished friend bowed his head and pondered for a while, then ordered the guards to lead my family away, explaining that he wanted to "speak to me alone." He took out his sunglasses, idly wiped them, and put them on.

After regaining his composure, he once again displayed his aristocratic restraint and detachment. He asked softly,

"Do you have any final requests?"

I laughed awkwardly for a couple of seconds, then gazed intently at the reflection of my own wan and sallow face visible in the lenses of his sunglasses.

"Do you still regard me as a friend?"

He didn't respond, and instead stroked the gold rims of his glasses.

"This request is perhaps somewhat extreme. . . . Please don't punish our entire race simply on account of our activities."

He repeatedly snorted.

". . . If you have a chance, please continue to help my family . . . . . ."

He continued to stroke the rims of his glasses.

"And for yourself?" he asked hoarsely.

"I'd say, you can help by having me cremated. I don't want my body to be devoured by worms after I die. . . ." I said, half-joking.

"May you live long and prosper," I added, with a laugh.

He sat quietly for a while, then removed his sunglasses and handed them to me, indicating that I should put them on. Patting his stomach, he stood up and quickly strode away without glancing back. The sound of his footsteps continued to echo for what seemed like an eternity.

On the morning of October 2, before the cocks had begun to crow, we were woken by the sound of the Qur'an being recited. I tried to leave the sunglasses with the prison warden but he didn't dare accept them, afraid it would be inauspicious to take something from someone who was almost dead. Instead, he urged me to return them to my most cherished friend. I cursorily washed my face and combed my hair, relieved myself, then proceeded to eat my final meal of rice with curry chicken.

It was drizzling when I was led to the execution ground, where I was blindfolded and my hands were tied to a pole.

The executioner read aloud our sentence, and confirmed each of our names.

The firing squad took their positions. The sound of them loading their guns was bright and clear.

One, two, three. There was a loud retort, whereupon I immediately passed out.

When I regained consciousness, I couldn't see a thing and all I could hear was the sound of water. For a long while I couldn't tell what was going on. I thought that I was dreaming—a postmortem dream.

The blindfold over my eyes was still blocking my sight, and I felt very cold.

Eventually I tore off the blindfold, then touched my chest and discovered that there was no trace of a wound.

I crawled up from the hold of a boat, and found that we were facing a storm and the entire boat was shaking. This turned out to be a dilapidated fishing boat with a loud outboard motor. An official-looking man wearing a grayish-blue khaki uniform and dark sunglasses said with a hint of a smile, "Good afternoon." Next to him were two soldiers armed with rifles.

I looked around, but all I saw was open ocean and cloudy skies.

An official—I always called him *Tuan*—who would meet with me every month for the next twenty years until he retired, took several sheets of paper out of his leather satchel, on which were written several rows of densely-packed characters. He handed me the papers, and said, "Look these over, then sign here, here, and here." He took out a fat fountain pen and pointed at several blanks.

The clauses were extremely detailed, but I found that the most important were the following:

> *(1) In order to avoid execution, from this point on you must assume a new identity and live in a new place, and furthermore you must accept all of the arrangements that have been made for you. We hereby rename you* Munshi Abdullah.
>
> *(2) You must not have any contact whatsoever with your friends and relatives from before your arrest—regardless of what might happen and irrespective of how the world may have changed in the interim.*
>
> *(3) If in the future you should have another wife and children, you must never reveal to them your true history. The relevant authorities will provide you with an appropriate and usable past, which you must commit to memory. Your former identity will be permanently discarded, and you must treat your former self as though he were already dead.*
>
> *(4) You must never again use or teach Chinese. You must not speak Chinese, even to yourself.*
>
> *(5) You must immediately convert to Islam. You must find a wife on this island and have a child, and help reclaim land for cultivation.*
>
> *(6) Unless the island sinks under the waves, or the relevant authorities come up with different arrangements, you must never leave this island for the rest of your life.*
>
> . . .

This contract came in two copies, the only salient difference between them being that one was written in the second-person while the other was written in the first-person. The remaining minor differences were all the result of adjustments made to reflect the pronominal changes. The contract fluttered in the cool breeze.

After carefully reading both copies, I stared intently at the final blank awaiting my signature. My thoughts were in turmoil, as I realized that I would never again be able to see anyone I had known before, and wouldn't even be able to let my parents know that I was still alive. I would have to make a clean break with my past and adopt an identity that is "not me." How could this possibly be of any interest to anyone?

"Do you need to think about it some more?" Tuan asked coldly. Referring to my cherished friend, he added, "'Tuan' told me to tell you that we could send someone to take your ashes to your parents this evening."

"Of course, you don't *have* to sign it." He pointed to the soldiers standing behind him. "We'd be happy to take responsibility for sending your corpse over to the island for burial."

I felt an acute sense of anguish. By signing this document, wouldn't I be betraying those comrades who had already been executed, as well as those who had managed to survive? My mind went blank. It eventually occurred to me that as long as I could live another day there would still be hope and, therefore, with a trembling hand, I signed the contract. I glanced down, and saw that I had signed with a chaotic mass of Chinese characters.

I handed both copies of the contract back to Tuan, who looked them over and snorted loudly. He then carefully stored them in his satchel.

From this point on, I would no longer be myself, and instead would become someone else. I would be a completely different person.

Tuan gave me a new ID card. The picture was the file photo, taken when I went to prison, of me wearing striped prison garb. The fingerprint was also the one that had been taken at that time. Tuan urged me to store the ID card carefully. There was also that pair of sunglasses.

Referring to my cherished friend, he said, "'Tuan' is very generous. He said he once agreed to give you an island, and despite the fact that you have done such an unforgivable thing he has nevertheless kept his promise. Although the island where he is sending you currently has a village chief, you will become its new leader." He vigorously pounded me on the shoulder. "Forget the past, and become a new person. Don't disappoint 'Tuan' again."

It was actually a long time ago that my cherished friend had originally agreed to give me an island. But how old were we then? Probably only seven or eight. . . .

Initially, no one realized he had royal blood. When he was young, perhaps because his mother had been a concubine, he had been sent to our village—to live, fish, climb trees, catch birds, pick rambutans, and swim in the stream with the other village children. Perhaps it was fate, but for some reason we ended up getting along very well and shared our bounty. Once, he exclaimed,

"If one day I were to become *raja* ("royalty"), what would you like for me to grant you?"

"How about a small island?" I replied casually.

"Why?" He sounded somewhat surprised. "Don't all of you people of the Tang ("Chinese") like large, open lands with old-wood forests, which you can chop down for lumber? What use would a tiny little island be for you?" I shook my head, and struggled to come up with an explanation.

"My parents came from an island in southern China."

I still remember how, when I turned his question back against him, his expression suddenly became quite severe, and he responded angrily,

"That's simply not possible." He furiously shook his head, repeating, "How could that be possible?"

"But, 'if . . .' "

"If that were the case, then I would demand that you return the island to me."

He clinched his fist and ground his teeth, and shook his fist at my chest, saying angrily, "This land is *our* land!"

He added, "You shouldn't ever joke like this again."

This island was not entirely nameless. Like any other island, as long as someone lives there, it will inevitably have a name. Tuan, however, insisted that it didn't appear on any map and, indeed, I couldn't find it on the maps my son subsequently brought back from the peninsula. Later,

I would learn from the people living there that the island was located in the South China Sea, and was probably positioned somewhere along the outer periphery of the territory controlled by my cherished friend. The island was known as *Pulau Jelaga*, which means "island of black smoke." According to the elders, the island got its name from the fact that for centuries its highest peak had emitted black smoke, presumably on account of its being a live volcano. Given that it had been more than a century since it last produced any smoke, though, people were now willing to come and live here.

The island was not very large, measuring only a few square kilometers, and most of the residents lived along the western coast. When I first arrived, there were only fifty or sixty households, who all belonged to a primitive Malay people popularly known as the *Orang Laut*, or "sea people." As their name suggests, these people had long lived off the sea, continually moving from one island to another. Yet, regardless of how much they moved, they would never relocate to the mainland nor could they ever allow themselves to become too attached to any particular island. Instead, they always had to keep moving, following the seasons and the local conditions. They have a very different attitude toward land than do people from China.

The fishermen's villages were located in the redwood forests along the coast, and the houses were built in an architectural style known as stilt houses, such that during the rainy season the area beneath them would often be covered in seawater. The boats—which were typically made by hand—were not large and could hold a dozen or so passengers. Most of them had a sail made from ox hide or fish skin. It was typically the strong and healthy men who went out to sea, while the elderly, the infirm, and the women stayed behind to repair the boats, mend the fish nets, and sun-dry the fish, shrimp, and crabs. Between October and March, however, the northeastern winds would make it impossible to go out to sea, and therefore everyone would remain in the village, living off the provisions they had stored up during the dry season and leading an austere existence that was nevertheless full of laughter, as they passed the time retelling popular stories.

When I arrived on the island, the rainy season had just begun. There was no welcome ceremony of any sort, and instead Tuan simply introduced me to the villagers and asked the village chief to provide me with somewhere to stay. As Tuan was summarizing "my" life, I clearly heard some of the women laughingly chant, "*Orang cina! Orang cina!*" ["Chinaman, Chinaman"]. Tuan explained that I was not actually a Chinaman, but rather I just resembled one because I had been raised by a Chinese family since I was a child. That was also why I had never been circumcised and had never converted to Islam. Because I had previously eaten a lot of pork, I had therefore voluntarily come to this island to start over, serve the masses, and become a new person.

In front of everyone, Tuan asked the village chief and the local priest to schedule a circumcision ceremony for me, and also to quickly arrange a wedding. He then announced my "responsibilities":

> *To serve as a model for the island dwellers, and specifically:*
> *(1) To grow rice in the island's wetlands.*
> *(2) To grow vegetables, fruits, and other foods in the island's arable soil.*
> *(3) To raise poultry and livestock, though not pigs.*

Tuan also stressed that I was an "official" who had been sent by the owner of this island and of this area of ocean.

The circumcision ceremony was performed two days later. The absurdity of holding this sort of ceremony for someone my age became a running joke for everyone on the island—particularly the unmarried women, who laughed so hard they rolled around on the ground.

There was no anesthetic, and instead I just drank some coconut wine. I washed the area in question, and then the village chief took out a small knife (similar to the one that my father used to castrate pigs) and, while grasping tightly with one hand, he lowered his other hand with a nimble motion. After an instant of searing pain, the operation was complete. The wound was then covered with cut tobacco, ashes, and some other blood-clotting agent made from a variety of different materials. The smell was reminiscent of the folk remedies that my father used to use after castrating pigs.

Before and after the operation, and even as it was proceeding, I kept remembering what my parents had taught me: Chinese are Chinese and foreigners are foreigners, and although they can play together and study together, Chinese cannot become foreigners and neither can foreigners become Chinese—unless, that is, a foreigner is raised by a Chinese family as one of their own, or a Chinese is adopted as a child by a foreigner's family. In short, "You are what you eat."

"Once you enter a foreign community, there will be no turning back. You will never again be able to worship your own ancestors."

This was my mother's warning.

My wound healed much more slowly than it normally would have, and ultimately it took more than half a month for it to close up. During that period, I ran a high fever for several days and, delirious, I dreamed many confused and multicolored dreams. I'm not sure what I dreamed about, but what I do know is that I didn't dream of either Karl Marx or Chairman Mao. In that patchwork of dreams and the flickering light of the fireflies, what gave me the deepest impression was a dream that I had over and over again—in which I had been seized by my former comrades, several of whom had bullet holes that were still spurting blood, and with a look of fury they demanded to know why I had betrayed my ideology, my comrades, and my people. I tried to respond, but my throat was burning such that I couldn't utter a sound. Blood was spurting everywhere—covering the sky and the earth. My comrades tied me to a tree trunk, stripped off my shirt, and ripped off my pants, whereupon each of them pulled out a shiny knife. Someone shouted, "Let's castrate this fucking traitor!" Several powerful hands forcibly held down my frantically moving arms and legs, as a blade was jabbed up to my crotch and my entire body began to convulse in agony. I suddenly felt a coolness on my chest, at which point I finally managed to calm down.

Later, I learned that it was the island's blind, three-footed shaman who placed his palm, which had saved the lives of so many others, on my chest.

"He's eaten too much foul pig flesh, and therefore Allah has given him a more severe trial than He has given others," the shaman announced.

"We must use the island's methods, and in the name of the water spirit help him cross this difficult juncture."

After I regained consciousness, I nervously examined whether I might have lost something down there as a result of infection.

Within a week of the operation, I was able to wander around the island with a parasol and a pair of sunglasses, my genitals wrapped in cotton gauze. I attempted to collect my thoughts and make plans for the future.

There were many wild coconut trees, banana trees, palm trees, sour wildfruit trees, and breadfruit trees on the island. There were also monkeys, lizards, and countless species of wild birds. This, though, is not the focus of this essay, and therefore there is no need to discuss it in more detail.

After a couple more weeks—by which point I had already abandoned my former conception of time—Tuan caught a ride on a military vessel and brought over some simple farming tools such as hoes, shovels, hammers, plows, and saws. He also brought fruit tree saplings, vegetable seeds, and rice sprouts, as well as chicks, ducklings, goslings, turkey chicks, calves, and lambs. He even brought two boxes of English-language farming manuals. He left two soldiers to serve as my assistants, but also to keep tabs on me. They wouldn't leave for another ten months.

Before Tuan departed, he remarked,

"This is actually an excellent arrangement. You Chinese are truly able to 'develop.'"

I'm not sure why, but when I heard this I felt a vague sense of discomfort, which remains etched in my heart to this very day. As if it wasn't enough that he didn't permit me to be Chinese, why did he have to add salt to my wounds? Maybe it was unintentional, but over the next several years he made many similar slips of the tongue. Perhaps *you Chinese* was an expression that he had already grown accustomed to using. It wasn't until much later that he seemed to have a startled realization of what he was saying, and repeatedly apologized for using this expression.

I understood my cherished friend's intention: he hoped he could use me to help improve the living conditions of these island-dwellers, while simultaneously taking this opportunity to mock my advocacy of a "proletarian revolution" and of "serving the weak." From swords to plowshares, I was forced to return once more to the beginning, shifting from one kind of operation to another and from one kind of praxis to another. In that sort of rainy season, all we would be able to grow would probably be rice, tarot, and water lilies.

Under the logic that "to labor is the essence of being human," I exhausted myself clearing the existing vegetation, planning out the drainage and irrigation systems, establishing a location where we could recycle night soil (thereby permitting the locals to reform their practice of "defecating into the water supply"), together with a myriad of other tasks. But I couldn't stop recalling my previous life. I often tried to use my exhaustion to force myself to forget the past and instead face the unknowable future. Apart from the times when I had to stop working because it was raining so hard I couldn't even see my hand in front of my own face, I continued putting all of my efforts into my work, even on days that it was cloudy or drizzling.

But then, there were also my dreams, in which I would see myself either returning home and being reunited with my parents, or studying, singing opposition songs, and engaging in secret operations with my comrades. Otherwise, I would dream of returning to my childhood and my cherished friend. . . . In my dreams, I almost always lived in the past. This was particularly true during my first decade on the island, while during my second decade I threw myself wholeheartedly into life here, and over this final decade I once began yearning for old dreams I experienced when I first arrived.

Almost every year, I would write a letter imploring my cherished friend to tell my parents that I was still alive, that I was safe, and that I now had a family and children. Even if we weren't permitted to see each other, as long as they could know that I was still alive, they would be able maintain hope.

Either these entreaties would sink, unanswered, like a stone in the ocean, or else I would receive a document with two lines of crab-like writing, saying,

"Don't forget your oath! Stop making presumptuous requests."

The letter would arrive with a square provincial seal, and after I finished reading it Tuan would confiscate and burn it.

Sometimes I suspected that my cherished friend didn't even take the opportunity to read the full text of my requests, and instead would simply have his secretary summarize them for him. It would undoubtedly have enormous political repercussions if it were to be revealed to the media that I (someone who had been sentenced to death!) was still alive, and although my cherished friend enjoyed a high position it would nevertheless be difficult even for him to avoid being implicated. Tuan repeatedly urged me, "Forget it, living this way is actually not bad at all." Referring to my cherished friend, he said, "Think of 'Tuan,' and also think of yourself. If this were to be publically known, it would create problems for him, and you would once again be sentenced to death.

Think of your wife and children." He would even speculate, "If you could demonstrate that you have been completely reformed, perhaps some day 'Tuan' may permit you to see your former family again."

After more than three decades, however, I had virtually given up hope.

Within half a year, my model vegetable garden and fruit orchard had begun to take shape, the chicks, ducklings, and goslings had grown up and begun laying eggs, and even *their* chicks had grown up and begun laying eggs . . . The lambs had also grown up. In April, at the end of the dry season and the beginning of the fishing season, the village chief arranged a marriage for me. You could basically say that it was a case of my marrying into his family, as my wife was to be his own sixteen-year-old daughter, Mina. Dark-skinned and rather short and squat, Mina was not particularly attractive, though she did have a decent temperament and, unlike so many other women, didn't have a habit of laughing for no reason.

My most cherished friend sent a betrothal gift consisting of two oxen and three sheep, and we hired a villager with passable culinary skills to slaughter and cook them with curry, distributing the food to the entire village. That evening, bowing in what I imagined to be the direction of my hometown, I silently told my parents and ancestors, *I am truly an unfilial son and grandson. . . .*

I gave a pair of sunglasses to the shaman who helped me through my most difficult period—and while the other residents of the island regarded this gift as inauspicious, the shaman instead viewed the glasses as a sacred object, since after putting them on he was able to gaze directly at unimaginably bright light. Actually, it was through him that I finally encountered Allah. The shaman solemnly indicated, "He may be found in all visible light, from starlight to candlelight." But that is another story, for which we don't have time here.

Whenever I see the lights of fireflies, I can't help but feel a deep sense of sorrow, and this all seems like it was just yesterday.

After the model garden began taking shape, I started distributing its produce to the villagers, as we had agreed. I proceeded from house to house, allocating provisions based roughly on the number of members of each household. Apart from tending my own parcel of land, I also had to assume the role of supervisor and director of the island's agriculture. Looking at today's flourishing crops, it is hard to appreciate the difficulties we originally had in clearing the land for cultivation. The most difficult thing, however, involved changing the islanders' age-old habits of living off the sea. In the past, during the rainy season or when there was a shortage of fish, the islanders would take up piracy and loot commercial ships that had come close to shore to avoid a storm. For the islanders, this was like the fishing harvest—it was a result of "Allah's will." As for my own exile (my God! I still remember that heartrending word!), for them this too was a function of "Allah's will."

One year, I invented an exceedingly sour fish soup (using large quantities of sour wildfruit), which was very well received by the islanders. I self-mockingly dubbed the soup *liufang*, meaning "exile," and consequently from that point on the word *exile*, on our island, became the name of a kind of soup.

In the past, we would have to take our fishing harvest to barter with the residents of other islands for all of the mainland foods that, unlike wildfruits and coconuts, we couldn't pick on our own island for free. The initial function of the model garden, therefore, was that it permitted the islanders to engage in a local bartering system with me, wherein they would use the prices they had agreed upon with the residents of the other islands (though, in practice, given that they didn't use money, they therefore didn't really understand the concept of what a price was, and instead usually used weight or volume as a standard). The result was that, using the produce from only two *mu* of arable land, I was able to acquire enough fish to last me half a year. This attracted the interest of some of the islanders, who were receptive to my suggestions. As a result, within three years I was able to open a green field in the non-brackish soil in the center of the island. It was not until many years later that I belatedly learned from an old newspaper that at some point the government had also instituted a similar regulation on the peninsula, which I think was some sort of "land cultivation plan" in the New Economic Policy.

We concluded this first stage of the plan after only three years, and in addition to giving me a small parcel of land to provide for my basic livelihood Tuan also brought news of my most cherished friend's new arrangements for me—namely, that I was to teach the local children. Beginning with the most basic ABC's, the curriculum also included mathematics, geography, history, citizenship, science, art, and other standard elementary school subjects. The textbooks, homework booklets, stationery, blackboards, chalk, and other supplies would all be provided. My cherished friend also sent me a dictionary and a set of reference books. The children's "tuition" would be paid in fish, shrimp, or cowrie shells.

Tuan read aloud the letter from my cherished friend:

> *I hear that your land cultivation efforts have been quite successful. If every Chinese were like you, our country wouldn't have any racial tensions. I opened an account for you at the national bank, which your children can use when they decide to go to college or start a business. For the time being, we will handle the deposits for you.*
>
> *I'm giving you a new assignment: to build an elementary school on Black Smoke Island, for which you will be both the teacher and the principal. If you need anything, you can simply ask your "guardian." I hope that in the near future some of the island's youngsters will be able to pass the national entrance exams, permitting them to attend an elementary school in West Malaysia. This would, of course, include your own children. . . .*

After he finished reading, Tuan lit a cigarette and then used the same match to burn the letter. At that time, my eldest son, Aci, was two years old.

I therefore became a teacher, and remain one to this day. Sometimes I can't help but reflect ruefully that my cherished friend really did know how to "make use of rubbish." Although most of the children on the island like to horse around and rarely apply themselves, for each of the past several years between one and three of them have managed to test into one of the middle schools in West Malaysia, including all seventeen of the children I fathered with Mina. In another letter that was subsequently burned to ashes, my cherished friend complimented me, saying, "This is truly a victory for our national pedagogy."

When my eldest son was about to leave the island, I had a sudden urge to encourage him to find an opportunity to go visit my hometown and see how my parents were doing. In my heart, I must have had an inexplicable desire to let my parents see this boy who, though he was darker and shorter than I, nevertheless bore a distinct resemblance to me and was, in fact, their own grandson.

In the end, though, I couldn't bring myself to utter a word.

Even last month, when my youngest daughter Ana left the island, I still found myself unable to do anything other than silently grind my teeth.

I knew that I continued to be observed.

Later, Aci and my other children told me that after they arrived in West Malaysia, the school had made very satisfactory arrangements for them, while the fellowships they received from the provincial government and the provincial sultan permitted them to live quite comfortably, "particularly when compared to those Indians, Malays, and Chinese from the countryside." They were asked whether their parents had requested that they bring anything back for them, and their activities were also carefully monitored, "which was no different from how the minister's children were treated."

To tell the truth, at one point I had in fact considered asking them to bring me back a Chinese-language newspaper, or any book written in Chinese. Fortunately, I hadn't dared to open my mouth.

I once submitted a request for a Chinese-language Buddhist sutra, but Tuan instead brought over an Arabic-language edition of the Qur'an. On the title page there was my cherished friend's grandiose signature, together with a line of carefully-written text: "Never forget Allah's will."

I always remembered his promise: "In the event of the slightest transgression, we will instantly revoke your pardon."

I couldn't even attend my own children's graduations. Instead, my "guardian" also served as their collective guardian, and in this way he represented me.

By this point four of my children have gotten married, but I still have not been able to leave the island. I have repeatedly requested permission, but was always turned down. Were it not for the fact that my guardian was attending the weddings in my place, I would have invited the parents of my future sons- and daughters-in-law to come to this island to visit.

Even my wife couldn't understand this, much less forgive it. More than anyone, she yearned to be able to personally attend her children's weddings. Every time that she, speaking on behalf of our children, said something like, "What's wrong with leaving the island for a few days? It's not like you were born here," or "Didn't you originally come here from elsewhere?" her comments would rend my heart, plunging me into a fit of depression that would last for several days. However, my family would simply assume I was sulking. No one was capable of understanding my feeling of loneliness and isolation—no one, that is, other than "them," and Allah.

But what choice did I have, other than to silently endure this?

Similar things happened again and again. I recognized quite clearly that my children felt alienated as a result of their inability to forgive me, to the point that they might begin doubting their father's love. Every letter politely declining their requests always contained the same unstated sentiment: "Perhaps some day you may be able to understand—but I fear you never will."

Eventually, some of thoughtful people on the island began searching for explanations for my "isolation" and "coldness," speculating that perhaps it was "because I had been raised by Chinese." This was particularly true of those who believed in shamanism and refused to believe in Islam.

Almost by accident, those people ended up stumbling on the correct explanation—only they didn't realize why or in what way they were right. Nevertheless, it remained true that they had managed to guess correctly.

Once, because of this, I stood in front of the Black Smoke Elementary School, weeping inconsolably.

A Chinese . . . But *what is* a Chinese?

For thirty years, I haven't spoken Chinese, haven't written Chinese, and haven't read Chinese. Instead, I have spoken Malay, taught Malay, have abstained from pork, have eaten Malay food, married a Malay wife, and had Malay children. Yet, that Chinese flame in my heart hasn't been extinguished. Why is this?

I often wondered why *couldn't* I become completely Malay, given that I was no longer able to be completely Chinese?

Was it because of that unerasable past?

As I was growing up, the fires of revolution were burning bright.

My cherished friend and I gradually went from being playmates to following our separate paths, as he embraced his own language and ethnicity, and I did the same. Upon entering adolescence, however, I fell into a state of anxious patriotism. Like all of the hot-blooded youth of that era, I was confident that I was an extraordinary individual destined for greatness.

A dragon cannot be confined to a small pond, and this particular dragon's scales were forged with the crucible of this era.

Language, ethnicity, and culture. The stipulation that "Chinese will be one of the nation's official languages" was one of the conditions on which Malaya was granted its independence, and furthermore was a condition on which there could be absolutely no compromise. During the ensuing political discussions, however, this condition was eventually dropped. Having already shed its blood, how could the dragon retain its soul? At that time, we were all filled with righteous indignation.

As educated youth forced to come of age prematurely, we decided to launch a revolution that was probably doomed from the start, but which we nevertheless had no choice but to launch. This resulted in a series of secret assassinations of Chinese traitors, turncoats, collaborators, foreign Sinophobes, as well as British imperial officials who had sold out Chinese interests.

Once, before one of our secret activities, my cherished friend invited me to a game of soccer, and I even helped his team score its two winning goals. (After middle school, the imperial pastime of soccer became the only bridge connecting us.) The next day, I was arrested before having a chance to participate in the secret activity, and given the circumstances it was a miracle that I wasn't simply executed on the spot. Perhaps the police had already figured everything out?

Did that soccer game save my life?

Apart from playing soccer, virtually all we did in those days was discuss the fate of the nation, frequently arguing until we were all red in the face. I gradually came to realize my friend's "royal" status, and given the resulting disparity in our social status I had no choice but to let him angrily lecture me.

"Which of you Chinese didn't come from somewhere else? And yet you have the gall to fight about this and that. Do you want to become our masters? Isn't this completely beyond the pale?"

"If we weren't so magnanimous, we could have sent you all back to China long ago!" he shouted fervently.

Yes, I thought, if the famous Ming dynasty Chinese navigator Zheng He had had any foresight at the time, I presumably wouldn't be in this situation today. The Chinese have repeatedly missed their opportunity, and perhaps this is because they are all castrated?

Or perhaps we did seize the right opportunity, but were just born in the wrong era?

I knew why my most cherished friend rescued me—it was in order to carry out an experiment that on the surface seemed innocent but which in reality was actually quite cruel. You could think of it as a sort of cultural blood transfusion. I often wondered why I had decided to live on, rather than committing suicide by jumping into the sea—was this simply because I was afraid to die, or was it to preserve a figurative "flame," to engage in a final struggle? Was it because I was curious about the "experiment" itself? But now, I simply felt a strange sense of dread.

I dreaded dying. I dreaded learning under what name I would be buried. But what I dreaded most of all was the possibility that, to avoid a future lifetime of trouble for my children, I might ultimately decide to be buried as a Malay. If I reached that point, I would have to concede defeat.

Meanwhile, my other self continued to stubbornly resist.

Recently, I looked for some stones on which to carve an inscription.

It would be too obvious if I were to carve actual Chinese characters, because they would immediately be recognized, leading to enormous problems.

It occurred to me that ancient Chinese characters were all pictographs, but I hadn't learned ancient seal script and consequently could only imagine what it might have looked like. It would certainly not be a violation of our agreement if I were to carve some made-up designs or figures.

First, I inscribed a lopsided pig—my zodiac birth sign.

After writing a period, I proceeded with my name. . . . I carved an ox together with several copper coins and the sort of cowrie shells that the islanders occasionally collect along the seashore. My surname is *Liu*, which rhymes with *niu* ["ox"], and my given name is *Cai*, which is homophonous with the *cai* ["wealth"] that many parents dream their children will one day obtain. More specifically, my given name was inspired by the fact that just before I was born my father happened to find some coins in the courtyard. Mina asked me what I was drawing, and I suggested she try to guess. After going through the names of several dozen different sea creatures (to each of which I responded in the negative), the field of possible choices narrowed considerably. I offered her an additional hint, at which point she finally guessed correctly, "ox," together with another animal that can't even be found on this island: "pig."

"But why does the ox have leaves growing from its horns?"

I explained that the leaves were meant to commemorate my contributions to the island's agriculture. Then, I requested that after my death she place these stones in front of my tombstone. I took out a broken stele that I had found while preparing soil for plowing. It only had two fragmentary characters left on it: [illegible]. I couldn't confirm whether or not these were in fact the characters I suspected them to be. I stressed to her that, come what may, she had to inscribe the stele fragment with the same signs as I had carved on the stone, and then leave it face-up. I explained, "Those are some shrubs and grass."

Actually, in the process of preparing soil for cultivation I had also unearthed several bone fragments and shards of a porcelain bowl, in addition to that broken stele. The scribblings on the stele indicated that on this island there had previously been Chinese people living, eating, shitting, and burying their dead. I searched everywhere for the other parts of the stele and urged the islanders to help keep an eye out for it, but to no avail.

I collected all of the porcelain shards I had been able to find, carefully washed and dried them, then called upon everyone in my family to help me study them, but still we couldn't reconstitute them into a complete bowl. Everywhere there were critical missing pieces.

After having discovered these apparent traces of earlier Chinese inhabitants, I asked the village elders about the history of Chinese on the island.

"Actually, for the past several centuries Chinese merchant ships would frequently pass through this area. There was nothing they didn't have and nothing they didn't want—from the most valuable gold, silver, and rhinoceros horns, to women and potable well water. Like the Portuguese, they were interested in everything. . . . Like us, some of these Chinese were pirates. According to legend, there are two kinds of Chinese: one kind wore a queue and the other didn't. The first Chinese our ancestors encountered didn't wear a queue. They were just like you, except that their bodies were covered in terrifying tattoos."

"'Just like me? . . .'"

All of the village elders, including my father-in-law, immediately broke into wide grins, revealing their black, jagged teeth.

"Don't worry, we don't mean anything by that. For us, all living things have the same value. Even seaweed, rocks, and the wind have a soul."

I once requested permission to go out to sea, to visit other islands.

The elders discussed this for quite some time before finally granting my request. At the same time, they warned me, "Whatever you do, you mustn't let 'Tuan' know we let you go out to sea. He has repeatedly stressed that, in accordance with Allah's will, we mustn't permit you to leave the island."

It turned out, however, that "going out to sea" merely meant visiting another nearby island, since they still wouldn't permit me to proceed any further. The reason they gave was that "the elders say that at sea there are malevolent spirits constantly summoning you." I couldn't find any trace of any Chinese, though once I did see a Malaysian navy vessel patrolling nearby.

After I had been on the island for about a decade, we began to see many boats full of terrified refugees, like a mass of ants crowded onto a floating leaf during a flood. These refugees were, without a doubt, Chinese. I was shocked into silence, assuming that there must have been some horrible crisis in my homeland, while at the same time frantically scanning the faces of the refugees to see if there were any that I recognized. They never had a chance to come ashore, however, and instead were quickly transferred to local navy vessels and taken away, after which they disappeared without a trace. All of this happened very quickly, with the refugees leaving almost as soon as they appeared.

Later, Tuan consoled me, saying, "Don't worry, those were not Chinese from our country. They were from Vietnam."

Without any television, radio, or even newspapers, I was like an idiot, knowing absolutely nothing about what was going on in the rest of the world. I repeatedly protested but eventually learned to be cooperative, and would periodically send Tuan some chicken, duck, dried fish, and cowrie shells. Whenever he came to visit, I would spend the entire day fishing and swimming with him, so that this business trip would feel like a vacation.

We didn't even hesitate to use his visit as an excuse to declare a school public holiday.

Tuan, in turn, would bring me eye-opening copies of the old Malay newspaper *Berita Harian* [Daily news], and continued doing so until a few years ago the authorities finally lifted my "news prohibition" (though, needless to say, even then I was still restricted to reading Malay-language newspapers). At the very least, though, I was able to have a general idea of what was going on in the world. The clearly-printed dates on the newspapers permitted me—stuck here on this island without calendars, clocks, or watches, and where work and rest schedules are determined by natural rhythms—to once again experience the precision of time. Meanwhile, I frequently saw news reports about my most cherished friend.

I read each news report twice, and the second time I would attempt to translate it into Chinese in my head, though I frequently found I couldn't come up with the appropriate words. Heavens, I urgently need a Chinese dictionary, even if it is merely the kind used by elementary school students.

It has already taken virtually all of my free time during this rainy season to write this much.

On several occasions, my wife became suspicious upon seeing me sitting upright on the ground and, with a trembling hand, struggling to write one square-shaped character after another. She feared I was possessed. Confronted with her uncomfortable, solicitous, and skeptical gaze, I had no choice but to try to reassure her, explaining, "I am praying for rain." Given that it had not rained for more than six months, our crops had suffered critical damage and we had even had to beg Tuan to bring us drinking water from the peninsula. In light of our crop failures and reduced fishing harvest, the islanders would have all starved to death had they not received emergency provisions from the peninsula. In his letter, Tuan reported that the peninsula was also experiencing sorrow and misery: "All of Borneo is in flames." It was no wonder, therefore, that for the preceding half year the island has been enveloped in a cloud of smoke, of which we could never find the source. At the time, the islanders used a variety of different methods to pray for rain. For about half a month, we prayed and recited the scripture. When that didn't yield results, we dug up a legend of a fire spirit sacrifice that used to be practiced on the island but which was thought to have been long forgotten. At one point I even secretly sacrificed to my memory of the sea dragon king. All we received for our efforts, however, was merely ashes. One day, I saw the sky filled with layer upon layer of thick clouds, and suddenly it began to rain. It was precisely at that point, meanwhile, that the island again once began to emit black smoke.

Let me pray for the island's well-being
Because the dry season is getting longer and longer, and rainy days are becoming fewer and fewer
Our crops will suffer serious harm
More and more young people are leaving the island, applying to attend school in town, and to look for work in the city
They rarely return, and their children and grandchildren will never again set foot here
In their children's and grandchildren's childhood, there will be no island, no tides, no ocean, and no island rainy season
Not to mention listening respectfully to the ocean's sonorous roar
They will never again chant the "The Song of the Fishermen," which has been passed down from generation to generation.
For many years now I have faithfully performed my prayers five times a day
But now the island is once again emitting black smoke
I hope that the fire gods will not be angry again.
And that the rain may return
In accordance with Allah's will.

I caressed my wife and stared intently at the words on the page, instantly "translating" them into her language. I recited them in a cadence familiar to her, like a lullaby. The document, however, was too long, and by the time I had read a few pages she had already virtually fallen asleep.

"We're both old now." She laughed with embarrassment. Her gaze returned to the words on the page. "What kind of writing is this?"

"A kind of prayer. I learned it as a child."

"Is this Chinese writing?" She laughed, making her appear younger and more charming.

"Huh?" I stared at her in astonishment. "Uh, no. They just look similar."

I made an effort to collect myself. "Why would you think that?"

"Everyone knows you grew up in a Chinese household."

I lightly caressed her body—that body that I had helped fatten up each time after she gave birth, in accordance with our Chinese customs. When I first learned she was pregnant, I, based on my own memory of Chinese postpartum customs, proceeded to raise thirty or forty chickens and planted several plots of ginger. I asked my "guardian" to go to a Chinese store and help me purchase a box of sesame oil, twenty *jin* of glutinous rice, several clumps of fungus, some yeast, and a jar of pickled vegetables. First, I tried to use my mother's recipe to brew some rice wine, and after several unsuccessful attempts (which ended up yielding nothing but vinegar) I finally achieved success. Our traditional Chinese custom of eating sesame chicken and avoiding cold water following childbirth were quite different from the islanders' native customs. Within a week of giving birth, for instance, the local women would once again be bathing in cold water, doing housework, engaging in strenuous activity, and carrying heavy objects—leading them to age prematurely.

Not long after our eldest son was born, my cherished friend sent someone to bring us a present—a soccer ball decorated with the design of the state flag, a *kris* [sword], together with a line of crab-like writing: "Congratulations on bearing a son on the island."

However, I repeatedly declined his offer that he name my child—which could be seen as my most minimal token gesture of resistance.

After the birth of each of my children, I would help arrange for my wife's month of postpartum recuperation, and as a result she became healthily plump.

My cherished friend never forgot to send a present.

Once it was a pony. Once it was a sampan. Another time it was a fig tree.

As one birth followed another, I became scared out of my wits. After the birth of my third child, I requested that Tuan send me some form of birth control, only to have this request treated as a joke. "The number of children you have will be determined by Allah's will." In the blink of an eye, I found that I, following Allah's will, had enough sons to field an entire soccer team. After having followed the island's custom of planting a coconut tree following the birth of each child, our house was soon surrounded by a veritable forest. Were it not for the fact that life on this island was very simple, I can't imagine how I could possibly have afforded to raise so many children.

With each new birth, I felt a combination of excitement and dread. How could I be responsible for so many new lives?

My cherished friend continued sending presents. Chopsticks, lanterns, moon cakes, commemorative gold coins, national flags . . . Once he sent a string of firecrackers, another time it was a light green jade pendant, and yet another it was a chess set.

I simply couldn't curb my libido, particularly during the rainy season and on nights when there was a high tide and a full moon. Consequently, I couldn't control the neverending birth of new life.

My fat and sleepy wife dozed off and started to snore softly, like a field that had been overly cultivated. . . .

I could hear the sound of someone nearby reciting the Qur'an. As a teacher, and under the orders of my cherished friend, I had designed and constructed the island's largest mosque. However, it had never occurred to me to want to travel to Mecca—for the simple reason Mecca is not located on this island. Some of those who were able to make the Hajj to Mecca using government subsidies (the subsidies were initiated about fifteen years ago, with five fellowships every year) liked to joke and, behind my back, call me "the unbeliever." Every year, my adopted name would appear on the list of fellowship recipients, but Tuan would always privately stress to me, "You must find a reason to decline the fellowship—and furthermore you yourself must accept that fictional reason as though it were real." He explained, "It's not possible for your name *not* to appear on the list, given that you are a teacher. But you also can't accept the fellowship, because this is also an important test."

Yes, whether it be in terms of religion or pedagogy, I was truly this island's teacher. At the same time, however, I was, and could only be, an unbeliever. My cherished friend was perhaps afraid that I had some sort of devilish ability that would allow me to get close to Allah, thereby becoming a true believer. That was my trump card, so I couldn't help but admire my friend's cleverness—in confiscating all of my gambling money, he left me with no alternative but to linger on in this world, continuing my path to salvation while wearing a black Muslim *songkok* cap.

It often seemed as though the only way I could prove I still existed was by repeatedly getting my wife pregnant. I once dreamt of collecting more wives and concubines, but in the end that was merely an empty fantasy. Furthermore, my offspring would ultimately all be children of the island and not really my own, and even if they should eventually succeed in leaving the island they would only be coddled citizens, and not Chinese ethnics like myself accustomed to a life of hardship.

Sometimes I couldn't help but curse, "Let this island sink beneath the sea! Let the volcano erupt again!" In the end, however, I find myself overcome with remorse for having these thoughts. What blame, after all, does everyone else on this island have, given that this is ultimately my own private anger?

But now, even as this rain for which everyone was yearning has finally arrived, the island has also begun emitting one cloud of ominous black smoke after another. Is this because my curse has finally been realized?

Before the rainy season concludes, should I burn up this cursed document, in order to bring to an end this painful lineage?

What, in the end, is the punishment that I deserve?

monkey butts, fire, and dangerous things

The aborigines here have not yet evolved into humans.

CHARLES DARWIN, *VOYAGE OF THE BEAGLE*

I HAVE ALREADY COME MANY TIMES TO THIS ISLAND, where countless drifters have begun to put down roots. I have also written quite a few essays about it. After all, this is a place where Chinese live. Although this particular trip, like the others, was by invitation, it nevertheless turned out to be far more portentous than the others. This is because this time I was invited by *Elder*. Perhaps, though, you might wonder, "Who is Elder?" On this island, however, this is a question that simply need not be asked—the same way that you wouldn't go to that other island across the water and inquire "Who is Agong?" Elder's invitation made me feel as flattered as though I had received an invitation from Agong himself. Elder is, after all, *our hero*. And in the present (post-1949) era, apart from those long-haired, eagle-hunting "heroic figures who continue gazing back at the former dynasty," Elder is virtually the only hero we have left. When it comes to height, he is not only taller than comrade Xiaoping by I don't know how many inches, he is even taller than many foreign premiers and prime ministers. For the past several decades, he is unique in having been able to travel back and forth across the Taiwan Strait, playing golf and swimming nude with leaders from both sides. From the way I am rambling on, you can surely guess how excited and overcome with emotion I am. How different this is from the tone of my popular essays!

As I was saying, virtually all of my previous trips were at the invitation of cultural organizations, and they typically involved lectures, roundtables, art camps, or new book signings. As everyone knows (and if you don't, that means you must be backward), several of my collections of essays about Chinese culture have sold very well here (of course, it is not only here that they have sold well, and you could even say they have sold well "throughout the Chinese world")—though to tell the truth I am actually quite skeptical about whether or not the residents of those thorny islands who buy my books can really understand them (I discretely referred to this problem in my essays "The Chinese Condition" and "Here Everything Is Very Peaceful"). In addition, I sometimes come for a short-term teaching position at the university (salaries here are high and easy to obtain—Long Live Evil Capitalism!). In fact, I have already come four times for this purpose (it is never a problem to return home). My classes are naturally all about classical Chinese culture (which we used to call the "Four Olds," but now it is known as the "Great Flowing Out" of national treasure) and furthermore I have received very good evaluations (for the past several years they have been struggling to establish high-level Chinese culture on this pathetic island, having already set up a few short-lived research institutes and hired a handful of professors of traditional culture on limited contracts, but in the end these initiatives all turned out to be as fleeting as castles made of sand), but basically you could say that the courses are all pure cultural exchange.

Why, then, did Elder invite me? (*Aiya!* I can't contain my excitement—this is not at all like the restrained, deep, and mature me you typically see in my essays.) It turns out he had an extremely important memoir he wanted to publish, and couldn't resist adding a few extraneous words. Who on this island is more qualified than he to write a memoir? Or, to put this another way, if he doesn't write a memoir, who else would dare to? Wouldn't they be afraid of being imprisoned? (*Aiya!* I'm afraid I may have misspoken!)

Given that before coming to the island I had first gone to Hong Kong to earn some Hong Kong dollars and then proceeded to Taiwan to earn some New Taiwan dollars, and only then did I receive the invitation and fly over here (perhaps there are some Singapore dollars to earned here?), by the time I arrived it was therefore already rather late. Based on what I had observed during my journey, sales of Elder's memoir seemed to be as hot as a bun just out of the oven on a summer afternoon. In every bookstore there were tall stacks of the volume, and the people lining up to buy it included quite a few Indians and Malays. Moreover, even among the yellow-skinned customers, there were several who didn't look like fellow Chinese—including some ginseng-like Koreans and daikon-like Japanese (the older generation of Chinese on the island call the latter "Japanese ghosts"), not to mention all sorts of Westerners. Seeing these long lines of customers always made me think of the sound of money clinking. It turns out that that was the day the publisher had released the autographed edition of the memoir, which Elder had spent so much time signing that his hands and feet had started trembling. It was said that there were Chinese, English, and Malay editions of the memoir—and it was likely that after he was promoted to the status of National Father, the number of editions would increase even more.

Less than half an hour after calling Elder from the airport, I was hustled through the special priority line at security and brought to him. Although this wasn't the first time I saw him, I nevertheless found myself as excited as a young girl meeting her pop idol, to the point that I even suffered some embarrassing physical responses, such as having a persistent urge to relieve myself. . . .

Elder was sitting in his modest office, his face as red and shiny as though he had just swallowed a large vitality-enhancing pill, though his gaze remained as keen as that of a bird of prey perched on a cliff. The only change from before was that his gray hair had begun to thin, revealing a little more of his red scalp. He warmly addressed me by my first name, and I hurriedly presented him with a copy of my one-kilo essay collection, which had just gone on sale. While shaking his hand I noticed that, like the previous time I saw him, his hand was trembling slightly. The rumors must be true—he must have indeed "signed so many volumes that his hand trembled."

"There is something very important that I need to ask of you." He placed a light-colored wooden box on my still-trembling legs, and said, "This is a gift. Open it up and take a look."

On a resplendent gold memorial disk, there was his beautiful English signature, together with several words that were so tiny you could barely make them out: "Not for sale." This was truly a "collector's dream" (to borrow a specialized phrase)—given that it is precisely things that are not for sale that always fetch the highest price.

"I deliberately left this one aside for you. I hope you like it."

"It is a great honor to work for Elder, and to receive such a magnificent gift is . . ." I was so nervous that I began to stutter. He gestured authoritatively, cutting me off, then said seriously,

"I want to ask that you serve as my plenipotentiary representative, and take a copy of my autographed memoir to give to someone. And if that person asks you to bring something back to me, then you should of course do so."

Elder briefly explained that that person was "someone from a former era" and was rather old-fashioned, but added that when Elder was young that person had been his most powerful rival, and one of the few who could inspire his fear and respect. Of course, that person was eventually vanquished, and you can well imagine the result: "Even now, he is not willing to admit defeat. It's as if he wants to compete with me to see who will live the longest." There was a chapter in Elder's memoir about that person, but Elder explained that "since I have so many important things to keep track of these days I don't have time to keep a diary, and therefore often have to rely on news reports to help aid my memory. As a result, it is almost inevitable that some things will end up getting garbled or left out altogether. That person, however, finds himself in precisely the opposite situation. These past several decades he had nothing but spare time on his hands, and, besides, the newspapers would never mention him." Elder laughed, and added, "I hear he has written about countless things that are surely of no consequence, and in this respect we never impeded him. We always treated him quite humanely, supplying him with all the pens and paper he wanted." Elder held out his hands and added fluidly, "You're from China, and therefore you must be very familiar with this sort of situation. After someone has been defeated and their life becomes less free than that of others, their thoughts will often become increasingly extreme. Even before that person became *buang pulau*, he was already rather antisocial. He must have written some antisocial things, and in the process very likely destroyed the favorable system we had so arduously established. Last year we caught some so-called "new horses," and last month we finally forced into bankruptcy an anti-Party activist who had a tendency to run off at the mouth. As your

Chairman Mao once said, one should on no account go lightly on one's enemies. You also know that today's youth have never experienced suffering. They complain incessantly about one thing or another and take for granted everything we ourselves struggled so hard to achieve. They don't even ask what kind of lives people in other countries lead. After all, how much *do* those people in other countries make each month? They are all desperate to come over here to earn some money. In their view, things here are as good as they are in America. If you become infected by this sort of groundless assumption, it will be difficult to find an antidote. Furthermore, what will they do after these inconsequential things get published? Don't you agree?"

Elder suddenly grew more animated, saying, "Even though I am already retired, I'm still as active as ever. You Chinese are busy relearning capitalism, but you don't have any experience and consequently are likely to be bullied by white foreigners. You need our help, and over the past several years I have offered many opinions. Furthermore, political leaders on both sides of the Taiwan Strait are too young and inexperienced. Even though that long-chinned Japanese who recently stepped down in Taiwan was no longer young, he nevertheless refused to see himself as lightweight and instead liked to throw his weight around. I don't know when it was that that person used his *laide* (lighter) to burn my ear, but even today one of my ears is still black. If you don't believe me, you can compare it to the other one. On such a small island, though, who is he going to fight? Besides, if fighting *were* to break out, this little sweet potato island of ours would be crushed by your elephantine China. These sorts of things all make me anxious. And then, there was also that premier who worked in industry and to whom I handed over my seat. . . ."

Upon hearing this, I suddenly became very concerned for my safety. Wouldn't having all of this classified information make my journey even more treacherous? I partially stood up and grasped the arms of my chair with both hands. In this awkward posture, I said in a plaintive, mosquito-like voice, "Elder, I . . ."

Elder was an intelligent person, and immediately understood my concerns.

"I apologize, I shouldn't ramble on like this. I'm getting old. This is how things stand: You are Chinese, and moreover are a man of culture.

That person will definitely want to see you, and I have no doubt that the two of you will have a lot to talk about. Furthermore, that person is even more worth writing about than those other people you always discuss in your essays. Only, I should warn you, *You must be very careful what you write about. Our laws here are very strict.*" Elder's expression became quite terrifying, as he frowned sternly. I suddenly felt as though I had fallen onto a hornet's nest—as though I had mysteriously been tied up inside a hemp sack and tossed into the ocean.

Elder then promised to give me a surprise.

I think this must have been the most difficult stop on my journey of culture.

The next day, a Friday, I learned that the surprise Elder had agreed to give me was to have me dropped out of an airplane.

This was an old World War II plane that had been confiscated from the Japanese. It shook violently and, of course, emitted vast quantities of black smoke. Following Elder's special arrangement, they helped me pack my parachute and also gave me an instruction manual written in English. The soldier who pried up my fingers and pushed me out of the plane said in a toneless Chinese, "There is nothing we can do. Whose fault is it that we have a China complex?"

Fortunately, this was a very developed country, and the parachute drop was impressively accurate. Upon reaching a prearranged altitude, the parachute deployed automatically. I saw my feet plummeting toward an island covered in olive trees. Unfortunately, one of my Italian patent leather shoes slipped off, plunging into the deep blue sea.

Before I had a chance to react, I found myself dangling from the branch of an olive tree.

I couldn't climb up or down, and only after I had shouted for a long time did I finally hear a whistling sound, as a monkey raced up the tree and helped cut some of the lines holding me in place, thereby permitting me to laboriously climb down. Then, the monkey disappeared like a puff of smoke.

After a little while, I noticed a frail middle-aged man or woman sitting calmly in a rattan chair outside a hut reading a newspaper.

In falling from the tree I had scraped my palms, and there was a burning sensation inside my pants—presumably indicating that I had suffered an embarrassing physical reaction. Fortunately, though, I had managed to keep my backpack on. I limped over to where the person was sitting.

When I arrived, the person was still seated—his hands opened to about the width of a newspaper and his legs were crossed. He was wearing a Chinese tunic suit and a pair of Western pants, both of which were old and tattered. He wasn't wearing any socks, though his leather shoes were very shiny and it was clear he put considerable effort into maintaining them. His hands and face were as black as his shoes, and at first glance you might have assumed he was Malay. The lenses of his glasses were very thick, and he had an aquiline nose and an unusually long chin. His dense hair was obviously oiled, leaving it as black and shiny as seaweed. His facial hair, on the other hand, was quite sparse, though impressively long. He was concentrating intensely, and even after I walked up to him he still didn't respond. For a moment I suspected he might be deaf, or perhaps even a wax statue. I walked around behind him, to see what he was studying so intently.

"Look," he suddenly exclaimed. "To think that there could be even *this* sort of thing." He pointed at a government announcement in the paper:

> *In order to preserve the quality of our future countrymen, the most intelligent men of our nation, together with the future fathers of our county, have decided—following a painful process of deliberation—to sacrifice the individual and, under risk of death, donate their last drops of precious semen.*
>
> *Those families willing to help improve the quality of the race are welcome to come to a family planning clinic to pick up a form and make a formal petition (those women whose husbands are sterile will have priority). The basic requirement for petitioning is nationality (all applicants must bring their national ID card; permanent residents may not apply). Married women are not restricted by race or class (though they must first have their husbands sign a letter of consent; those husbands who sign this letter of consent will receive many legal subsidies; please see the* National Bloodline Improvement Handbook *for details; this requirement does not apply to women with advanced degrees or those with high salaries).*
>
> *Given that the individual in question is very old, our medical experts feel that this will be a once-in-a-lifetime opportunity. Those who miss this chance will regret it forever.*

All applicants will receive a beautiful souvenir.

Those who become pregnant will receive a certificate of bloodline purity, and the government will, free of charge, draw up their life plan.

"This is not surprising; it is actually an announcement that appeared several years ago."

"Yes, they only give me old newspapers," my new companion replied sadly. He immediately recovered his spirits, however, and added, "What a rare delight to have a guest! Over the past forty years, he has only sent me five visitors. Two of them, however, had their brains smashed against the stones and a third fell into the ocean and became shark bait, though I still use and treasure their shoes. You are only the second visitor who has managed to make it here alive. Last time, the Japanese visitor broke his foot. May I ask your name?"

We each introduced ourselves and chatted for a while. He told me he had originally been the plenipotentiary of the Malayan Communist Party on Lion Island [Singapore], but that it had been a long time since he had used his real name—and given that he never saw his name in those old newspapers, he therefore had already nearly forgotten it. However, just as typical Communist Party members from that era all had several nicknames or pseudonyms for their safety and in order to ensure greater freedom of movement, he similarly had a memorable nickname, which was *Laide* ("Lighter"). He emphasized, however, that if I needed to mention his name in one of my essays, I should simply refer to him as *the plenipotentiary*, since he had come to prefer this Japanese-sounding nickname.

He used a stone mortar and pestle to grind the wild coffee beans that he had grown himself on that island, while lamenting the news about deceased fellow soldiers he had read about in the old newspapers. "They surrendered one after the other. One went to London to peddle sanitary napkins, another went to an American Chinatown to hawk toilet paper, another went to Taipei to hustle potency pills, while yet another went to Beijing to sell condoms. None of them enjoyed any real success, and certainly not better than mine—serving as *plenipotentiary* here on this island. Here, I am as great as a president."

He suddenly grinned, like a flash of lightning in a cloudless sky. It was clear that he'd gone for so long without smiling that he had almost forgotten how, and consequently when he did so now he appeared rather terrifying. Furthermore, he was exceedingly thin, and after he smiled it took the wrinkles in his face a long time to smooth out again.

"What ultimately came of that matter?" he asked excitedly.

"What matter?" I had been just about to carry out my formal business and give him an autographed copy of Elder's memoir.

"What other matter is there? That advertisement about sperm donations."

I myself wasn't entirely clear what had eventually come of it. Probably it was treated as classified information. I could, however, describe to him the circumstances under which Elder and I first met, which was probably around the time that the advertisement initially appeared. At the time, I had been at one of the large Chinese-language bookstores on the island-nation signing books until my foot trembled, when suddenly two mysterious men wearing black suits and dark sunglasses positioned themselves on either side of me and whispered in my ear, "Come with us, there is someone important who wants to see you."

In no time at all I found myself in a place for having afternoon tea with Elder, who was sipping his Darjeeling tea and breathing heavily. His face was red and his head was completely soaked with sweat. Two doctors and a nurse were anxiously attending him. They were holding a white metal box, a large needle, a stethoscope, and a blood pressure cuff, and would periodically come measure his pulse and blood pressure. The bald doctor appeared to be very senior, and I could hear him quietly advising Elder (from his accent I could tell he was from Beijing), "Sir, I really think we should stop; your health is critical. We can't extract any more, since we're already drawing blood. If we continue, I'm afraid we might kill you. As for the remainder, can't we ask your son to sub in for you?" Before the doctor had a chance to finish, I heard Elder bellow, "How would that be possible? How can I cheat my countrymen? Keep trying, until you've succeeded in extracting the mother lode."

When the plenipotentiary heard this, he couldn't help but burst out laughing.

At the time, I had observed this scene in confusion, baffled as to why I had been brought here to watch something that by all rights clearly shouldn't be seen. By that point the pot of red tea had been drunk and refilled so many times that all that was left was clear water (Elder had always been very frugal). Only then did he reappear, looking utterly exhausted. He tapped me on the shoulder with his limp hand, asking in a voice so soft I could barely hear him, "What do you think? Isn't this more worth recording than those Japanese devils' tombstones?" He was referring to my essay "Here, Everything Is Very Peaceful," which I had composed after visiting several of the island's Japanese tombstones.

"Here, everything really *is* very peaceful. So much so that you would be hard-pressed to even hear someone fart. So, did you write about it?"

"I'm still considering. According to my theory . . ."

"Don't start with your theories. At least he gave himself a reason to air-drop you onto those stones." The plenipotentiary removed his glasses, the lenses of which had been ground down from the bottoms of a couple of wine bottles, and placed them on the stone table, revealing thick dark bags under his eyes. He said, "Wearing glasses makes me look a bit more intellectual. Mother-##, here I don't even have any toilet paper to wipe my own ass; where am I going to find real glasses? Stop beating around the bush. Why did that old dog drop you here to find me?"

By this point the coffee he was brewing in a clay can had come to boil, and it was actually quite fragrant.

He poured half of a coconut shell and passed it to me. I brought it to my lips and found that it was even tarter than a lemon!

I grabbed my backpack and handed him an autographed copy of my critically-acclaimed and best-selling essay collection, together with the copy of Elder's memoir. He accepted them, snorted, and began nervously leafing through the memoir. Upon reaching a certain page, he suddenly became very agitated and his entire body began to tremble. As he gazed out at the hazy water and sky, I grabbed the memoir, which was titled *This Time and That Time*, and looked at the page that had made him so upset.

Secret Meeting with the Plenipotentiary Representative of the Malayan Communist Party

I walked out of the office and went to the location where we had decided to meet. As we had agreed, I looked for a thin overseas Chinese wearing a white shirt, with a communist haircut, glasses with thick black frames,

> *and skin so dark it looked like an ink stone. In fact, he was standing furtively under an olive tree, pretending to read a newspaper. We used our local dialect to ask about each other's parents (which was our agreed-upon password), and then I followed him to a dark, solitary location. He kept his head bowed while glancing around furtively, as though he wanted to engage in some shady business that he didn't want anyone to see.*
>
> *His body reeked of insect repellent, so mosquitoes didn't dare bother us. He told me he was the plenipotentiary of the Malayan Communist Party, and that for a long time he had been very eager to meet with me—to see if there was any possibility that we might collaborate. He suddenly took out a piece of jet black metal and pointed it at me. Thinking it was a gun and that he was going to execute me right then and there, I immediately dove behind a nearby trash can. I heard a loud* bang, *saw a flash of light in the corner of his mouth, then smelled the familiar scent of tobacco. Without pausing to tend to my head, which I had hit on my way down, I sheepishly crawled out from behind the trash can. He smiled coldly as he handed me the object, saying, "Don't worry, it's only a* lighter." *Even though we were standing in a dark area, you could still see that the gun-shaped object was exquisitely made, and was definitely the work of a master craftsman. I held it, estimating it must have weighed at least a kilo. Even though I was a member of the capitalist class, most of the people with whom I had associated over the previous several decades were high-ranking officials and even royalty who traveled from country to country as honored guests, and I had therefore seen more fancy lighters than I could count (I often received lighters from friends overseas, though I myself neither smoke nor collect lighters). I couldn't, however, remember ever having seen such a fascinating artifact. After I inspected the lighter and returned it to him, he again smiled coldly and said, "Can you believe it? This is actually a real gun, and furthermore it's loaded."*

The odd thing was that that section of the memoir consisted of only a single page, and furthermore was unusually short. All of the other sections ran for at least seven or eight pages, but this one felt as though it had been left unfinished.

I wanted to tell him that my own essays were actually better written than these, but decided that under the circumstances it would be better not to say anything. Who knew whether he might have violent tendencies? There seemed to be no women on the island, and what if he were to try to vent to his pent-up desire by forcing himself upon me? (I, after all, am but a frail intellectual.) I might never again be able to walk like a normal man. How would I live with myself? It was better to let him continue staring off into space. I braced myself and took a sip from that cup of the world's worst-tasting coffee, which had the consistency of Indian *shorba*. When I finished, he still hadn't moved, so I decided to go for a stroll, to gather material for my next essay. It was always important to take advantage of an opportunity to explore a new scene. This was the key to a successful essay, and furthermore when writing the background you could always add some extra details—because, after all, you get paid by the word.

This island is truly desolate, and therefore would be an excellent place to do someone in. It has weeds and coconut trees, stones and sand, a freshwater stream, together with many monkeys and wild bananas. The coast is covered in large stones, and there isn't even a beach. If there were a dog to wag its tail, the island would feel more welcoming, but even that was lacking. Later, this person explained that everything on the island had been air-dropped from planes, but dogs couldn't be safely dropped. On the other hand, cans of dog food *could* easily be air-dropped, so they would periodically deliver some expired cans donated by foreign charitable organizations in order to help "supplement his nutrition." He had to be responsible for his own food and daily necessities, remarking, "So don't think I have any leisure time; I'm actually as busy as a primitive." It was impossible to grow rice on the island, and consequently it had been decades since he had had a chance to taste any. Every time he remembered this, he would become so nostalgic that tears would stream down his face. Nothing you could say could make him stop, and he would cry to the point that he needed to guzzle water to rehydrate himself. Therefore, if you wanted to see him cry, all you had to do was talk about eating rice. His clothing situation was similar, given that all he had were items that had been discarded by monkeys in the zoo. "Do you know that, in some respects, they are even more frugal than the Communist Party?"

This place didn't even make you want to take a walk, much less interact with your environment.

Besides, I was only wearing one shoe.

Therefore, after walking around for just a few minutes I quickly returned to his side.

A female monkey was picking his hair for nits, as he attentively read my collected essays.

"I know why he told you to come," he suddenly looked up and said, as he pushed the monkey away.

"Come with me." He pushed aside the thatched door and invited me into his dark hut. Inside was a bed made from dried coconut leafs, which was blackened by soot and covered with dried blood and the carcasses of countless squashed mosquitoes. Obviously there were a lot of mosquitoes here at night. The walls were plastered with layer upon layer of old newspapers, containing old news that was almost as moving as bulletin board announcements. He explained that on this island there was no glue, and therefore he had to take a kind of seaweed and grind it to a pulp, such that it became "even more resilient than glue, and smelled like the sea." There was a mountain of dried-up ballpoint pens in the corner of the hut, and it turned out that there were also several-foot-high piles of papers that looked as though they had Chinese characters crawling all over them. I wondered, Couldn't he use these sheets of paper to wipe his butt? The only item on the stone table was a thick volume that was so worn that the cover was falling off. I opened it at random and saw that the page had been half-devoured by termites. Many of the characters had been partially eaten, and quite a few of the phrases were incomplete. Several of the definitions were fragmented, and in general the text was so mangled that trying to read it was like the proverbial blind men feeling an elephant. Whenever I turned a page dust would fly up, as the deformed characters danced in the air.

However, you could still make out that this was an old edition of the classic Chinese dictionary *Sea of Words*.

"Be careful, don't use so much force!" he bellowed at me. "Apart from dropping some old newspapers every few years for me to use to wipe my ass, those imperialists' greatest act of compassion was permitting me to have *this*. They said that all of the other books were poisonous and could harm my 'rectification,' so whenever I'm bored I read this instead. This is my wife, and my bible."

The ray of light streaming in illuminated the scene in front of me: a dark, cave-like dwelling with light shining as though through a thick lens, illuminating the thin silhouette of a resolutely idealistic revolutionary romantic who had been exiled for longer than Nelson Mandela or Shih Ming-teh. He pushed open the large, flat cover of the well-worn copy of the *Sea of Words*, and it looked as though he had tears in his eyes (this final detail could only be made out by adjusting one's perspective). The indistinct background looked as though it were a several-foot-high stack of paper, and you could imagine it consisted of neatly-arranged pages from classic works. The background music emanating from a tape player had a raspy sound, covering up a muffled and unclear version of "March of the Volunteers." Isn't this a ready-made symbol? Ah, ah, ah, my soul is inspired!

"They haven't treated you badly, giving you so much paper and so many pens."

He snorted.

"This is my compensation. They periodically air-drop some horribly rendered Chinese document that some bastard has translated, and ask me to polish it. Sometimes it is a wretched essay written by some wretched author that they want me to correct, while other times it is a draft of some error-filled essay that he himself wrote. For every essay that is eventually published, they make a wire transfer to my private bank account, and this is what I've managed to accumulate after much scrimping and saving. But I still need to sign a contract affirming that these documents only belong to me while they are here on this island, and that as soon as they leave the island they are automatically transferred to the government. I might as well tell you a huge secret—that memoir you brought with you is actually one of the works I wrote. It was originally called *This One and That One*."

I couldn't help but cry out *Ah!* At that moment I stepped on something with my shoeless foot and got poked. It turned out to be a sharp fish bone, and blood started gushing out of my dirty sock. He quickly helped me remove the sock, expertly grabbing a fistful of dirt from under the bed and rubbed it on the wound. As he was doing this, I noticed that the ground beneath the bed was actually covered with fish bones, some of which were as large as those in *The Old Man and the Sea*.

"A lot has been excised from that volume you brought me—so much, in fact, that it now resembles a mere novel. All of the nonfictional portions have been removed," he muttered to himself. "I should have known that there was something wrong with that Japanese Sinologist they sent over last time. He said he was on some accident-prone Taiwan airline when the plane developed problems in mid-flight and he happened to land here on this island. And to think that I even invited that bastard to have several slices of sashimi made from fish that I had smashed to death on the rocks! But after I asked him to take this book when he left, he sold me out." As he got excited, his pants noticeably began to protrude.

"How did that Japanese man leave?" I asked carefully. I certainly didn't want to spend the rest of my life here with this dangerous madman who didn't even have any underwear.

"One morning I woke up, and he was gone. At the time, I had no idea how he managed to leave. Later, I learned from old newspapers that he had been kidnapped by Philippine rangers, though I find this implausible. As far as I know, it is impossible to leave this island. The shore is covered with rocks, and even a little sampan wouldn't be able to approach. I should have known that that Japanese man was a fraud—I should have been able to tell from the way he held his nose while eating the sashimi."

(But couldn't it simply have been that the dead fish you gave him was already spoiled?)

"I never expected he would turn out to be a spy." He sighed heavily.

He started rummaging around, and came up with a dark brown wooden box. He removed the top and let me peer inside. The box was filled with rolls of paper covered with writing. He then closed the box again and said, "This is made from driftwood that has been soaked in saltwater, and is therefore resistant to termites. There was another box that was as large as a child's coffin, but the Japanese man took it with him. This island is full of termites, and consequently there is almost nowhere you can safely store paper. If I'm not careful, most of what I write ends up getting eaten. Some nights when I'm writing under the lamp, I can hear the termites munching away . . ."

We returned to his stone table, and he solemnly passed me the wooden box.

"You can give this to your hero. This is what I was able to preserve from *This One and That One*. This portion is historical. However, what is past is past, and it is already not important. This is my most recent response to my old enemies. As for your essays, you can leave them here for me to use to wipe my ass."

In the sorrowful evening light, he began to hum an old communist song that even I had never heard before, while picking nits from a female monkey nestled between his legs. Gesturing at the group of monkeys happily playing in the trees that covered the landscape, he said, "Among those monkeys, there are probably several that carry my bloodline." Tears started streaming down his face.

Those monkeys covering the mountainside seemed to be lost in thought, and their expression *did* bear an uncanny resemblance to his.

This is the ineffable sorrow of a defeated revolutionary.

The sky gradually grew dark.

Our dinner consisted of half-ripe bananas that the female monkeys had painstakingly collected for us, together with the foul-smelling dried fish he himself had stored. We drank a soup that was so sour it made our eyes water and our noses run.

We lit a small fire, as the plenipotentiary representative waved and said, "If there is anything else, we can discuss it tomorrow." He then took the female monkeys into the thatched hut and began emitting some hoarse screeching sounds that he must have thought were bold and valiant while the female monkeys squealed continuously. The sound was unspeakably vulgar.

After a while, as the fire began to burn down and I was wondering whether I would need to spend the night out here, a small monkey came and led me in the dark down a long stone path. The path twisted back and forth, sometimes going uphill and sometimes going downhill. The fire next to the hut gradually faded from view, and I felt as though I were entering another world.

After leading me up to a dark and damp cave hidden behind a large stone, the little monkey turned and disappeared into the night.

There was a sharp yet familiar smell—the rancid stench of human sweat. In the dark, I fumbled around for something with which to light a fire. I wondered whether I should make my way back to where I had come from to find materials for a fire, but was afraid of getting lost. The cave seemed wide and deep, but I figured there must be some reason why the monkey had brought me here—perhaps it knew a way off this island? After a while, once my eyes had begun to grow accustomed to the darkness, I saw a white object, like an elevated platform, near the cliff. I discovered a lighter there—and not only one, but rather a whole pile of them, like a small mountain! I tried one lighter after another, but they all appeared to be empty. I kept trying until my head was covered in sweat, which dripped down into my eyes. There must have been several hundred lighters there, and just as I was about to give up and start rubbing sticks together, I finally managed to generate a tiny flame. I carefully protected it, and used it to light the coconut oil left over in the coconut shells sitting on the platform.

A light breeze was blowing from the other side of the cave.

Under the light I could see that there were actually several thousand discarded lighters. They were all standard plastic lighters, but many of them already had their tops rusted away.

On the wall there was a faint picture of what appeared to be a dragon boat, which looked as though it had been drawn with coconut oil and ashes. It was sketched very awkwardly, and was vastly inferior to even the primitive cave drawings that I had seen elsewhere. Standing on the boat's prow there was a man with one shoulder raised and the other lowered, in the standard pose of heroes in propaganda images from communist countries—and with lines symbolizing rays of sunlight radiating from the tip of his index finger. The boat was full of people who appeared to be trying to row it. Needless to say, this was a standard image of "the masses," while the painting's open spaces were full of countless figures representing "the People."

As the night wore on, I couldn't resist reading the documents in the box:

Secret files from Malaya's Communist Period

(1) Plenipotentiary—that's me.

(2) Laite ("Lighter"), *Huaite* ("White"), *also known as Hoang Thieu Dong, Huang Nalu, Lao Wu, Li Tek, Yalie, Huang Jinyu, Huang a Nhac.*

Lighter was one of the most legendary, controversial, and terrifying leaders from Malaya's communist period. His reputation was heightened by the uncertainties concerning his family background. Although he was reincarnated with a different name and among a group of Chinese speaking a different dialect, files in other languages (including English imperial files, Japanese files, Malaysian national files, together with the University of Singapore's prewar Malayan-Chinese files) all assume that he is not ethnically Chinese, though they lack any convincing evidence to substantiate this. In addition to being fluent in Mandarin, Lighter was also proficient in Min Nan, Cantonese, Hakka, as well as several South Seas dialects. He was also fluent in Malay, and his skin was as dark as that of an ethnic Malay—though dark skin is also not unusual among Chinese (including the black-skinned people discussed below). Furthermore, Lighter ate pork and was particularly fond of pig trotters, which in and of itself should be enough to prove he was not Malay. Some people suspected he was Vietnamese, given that Malaysian Chinese who are able to speak Vietnamese are exceedingly rare, and furthermore in addition to English he also knew some rudimentary French—though his French sounded like a crow with a bad cold.

His reputation was further enhanced by his claim that he was the plenipotentiary sent to Singapore and Malaya to represent the third world (though we have not been able to find any evidence to support this), who quickly earned the trust and support of those impassioned young people and consequently was elevated to the position of a leader of the Malayan Communist Party. This proves that this person is extremely smart and resourceful. However, some suspect he was originally a mere dock worker who happened to know a lot of languages, and who managed to infiltrate the Malayan Communist Party after being caught up in a revolutionary fervor. Around 1942, after being sold out by a comrade within the Party, he fell into the hands of the Taiseikaku organization of Japanese special agents. In the end, however, he was not executed, and instead miraculously managed to use this opportunity to become a Taiseikaku secret agent and started systematically selling out his comrades in the Malayan Communist Party (particularly those high-ranking cadres with real influence, especially those who were also members of the Chinese Communist Party)—arranging for Taiseikaku to arrest and execute them one after the other, while eliminating all of those who might challenge his authority. Even more miraculously, he collaborated with Taiseikaku to train two "Malayan communist turncoats" who would later become widely accepted, and in the process effectively took himself out of the equation. When the Japanese army surrendered in 1945, even Taiseikaku suspected he had simultaneously become a secret agent of the British military.

After World War II, Lighter disappeared somewhere in Singapore, after which his name vanished from all official documents. There was a rumor that he had been killed and eaten by some young Malayan communists, and another that he had been arrested by some government office, as a result of which all of his false identities had been erased—and without an identity, he simply disappeared like a drop of water in the ocean.

As for how Lighter got his nickname, the legend is that he had an almost fanatical obsession with lighters. Quite a few Malayan communist survivors attest to this point in their memoirs, and virtually all of them mention how, when lighting a cigarette, he would often produce a shiny gold square lighter with a picture of a sickle on one side and a profile of Lenin on the other, which would emit a sharp screech when lit and was as heavy as a bullet. He referred to this lighter as a "Gift from Comrade Stalin" or a "Gift from Comrade Ho Chi Minh." But there were some people who heard from comrades who they feared had later been assassinated that they had seen him use a Japanese agent's lighter with a Japanese flag and a red stone in place of the rising sun.

(3) Ke Ping, also known as Gao Keping.

*Having surrendered after being arrested by the Japanese in 1940, Ke Ping was absorbed as a secret agent, organizing a "Syonan [*Singapore*] group" to support Japan and resist British imperialism. This fervent anti-Japanese patriot surrendered, and in 1945 he disappeared without a trace. It is believed he was either murdered by Malayan communists aware of his background, or else he changed his name and went into commerce—using the large amounts of money and gold that he had received from the Japanese to develop an impressive reputation within this Pacific golden age, perhaps even becoming a postwar leader of overseas Chinese.*

(4) Xiao He, also known as Ah He, OOpe, OOtuer, Ta He, Bak Zue, and OOkazen.

Regardless of whether you consult the Taiseikaku "Secret records of the extermination of overseas Chinese in Syonan" or the official files from England, Malaysia, or Singapore, you will inevitably find many people going by Xiao He *or other pseudonyms that, like* Xiao He, *invoke the concept of blackness [*he/hei means "black"*]. It is worth noting, however, that there may be some slight redundancies in the various* He's *appearing in these documents, and we can't rule out the possibility that Xiao He himself also appeared in these documents under other pseudonyms. From this fact it can be observed that* Xiao He *is a term of address of which many* *revolutionaries at the time were quite fond. In reality, it must have been the case that, in the course of pursuing revolutionary activities, virtually everyone in this tropical region, irrespective of their race, eventually became black from the sun.*

Many of the He's *mentioned in these various files ended up dying of unnatural causes.*

(5) Xiao Luo, also known as Xiao Lu and Chen Peiqing.

(6) Siu Cheng, also known as Zhang Chuangqing, Zhang Fengyun, Ah Soo, Lin Wen, and White Mountain Lingyun.

(7) Chen Ping

(8) Huang Liu Mao Niu Yang

(9) *Gua* c/o

(10) # & * ♀

AN ODD, REPEATED SOUND WOKE ME UP, whereupon I belatedly realized that I wasn't sure when precisely I had fallen asleep. It was at this point that I noticed that the sound was coming from a distant location. Everything was jet black. However, there was a slight breeze blowing in from an area where there was a small fire. The flame flickered in the distance, but for me, standing here in the dark, it functioned as a lamp.

At that point it must have been high tide, and the water in the cave was already up to my knees. Feeling around in the dark, I picked up the wooden box and waded through the water toward the light.

Feeling as though I'd just made my way down a long, slippery intestine, I was assailed by a sour and acrid stench. After walking until I felt like I was about to be digested into a ball of shit, I finally reached the exit.

With a strong breeze blowing in my face, I saw up on a high stage a bright fire that illuminated the entire area. Next to the fire there was a tall flagpole, at the top of which a flag was flapping furiously in the wind, though the image on the flag remained indistinct. Between the fire and the flagpole, there was a man who was dancing about while roaring what sounded like a passionate oratory at the top of his lungs. I couldn't understand what he was saying, but occasionally could make out a few phrases in Mandarin or various southern Chinese dialects. When cursing British imperialism, he used English. When cursing Japanese devils, he used Japanese. When speaking of "my friend Stalin," he used Russian. There were also some strange sounds that I couldn't identify as belonging to any particular language, and I couldn't entirely rule out the possibility that they might correspond to an extraterrestrial tongue. Although I couldn't, due to my limited linguistic abilities, make out what he was rambling on about, his posture during this performance was nevertheless very familiar—it resembled Hitler, but also Mao Zedong. It appeared as though he wasn't wearing any clothing, and below him there was a mass of shadows of short figures.

The latter turned out to be an enthusiastically cheering audience, whose voices rose and fell following his hand gestures. This made him look like an orchestral conductor. Even though the audience was standing in neat rows, you could tell from their posture that they weren't human—not to mention the fact that their shadows all had curly tails.

I struggled to make out the performer's face, and kept trying to figure out a way to approach him. The closer I got, the more I saw that his face was unnaturally pale, as though it had been painted white.

The fluttering flag was also larger than I expected. It consisted of multihued patches, and seemed to have words written along the top.

Just as I was about to climb down from the stage, a hand suddenly reached out of the darkness and grabbed me, pushing me back into the shadows. The hand covered my mouth, then someone whispered into my ear in a foul-smelling and mangled-toned Chinese, "Whatever you do, don't shout." The speaker appeared to be a large monkey, but then it removed the mask covering its head, revealing the face of a Japanese devil. Pulling me aside, he asked, "Who are you, and why are you here? Don't you know it's very dangerous?" He introduced himself, saying his name was Yamamoto Gojuuichi, and that he was a researcher at the Japan-Asia Economics Research Institute, with a specialization in the history of the Malayan communist movement. He said he had already published many fruits of his research, but that it was only with great difficulty that he had finally managed to track down news of one of the most mysterious survivors of Malaya's communist movement. For many years he had repeatedly applied to the relevant country before finally receiving permission to come and do field work. “But I never expected that they would then abandon me,” he added. I saw that he walked with a slight limp, as though he had suffered a significant injury.

We squatted under a large stone, and he produced a cigarette and offered it to me. It turned out he even had a lighter. “I made a careful preliminary examination and discovered that these are very useful, so I brought several.”

It had probably been quite some time since he had spoken to anyone, and in a mangled-toned Chinese, he told me his bizarre story. “I think that old chap has already gone mad.” He exhaled. “During the day he is like a man, and acts as though he has lost the will to live. At night, though, he becomes animated and begins performing speeches and policy announcements. It has been almost half a year since I came here, and I’ve seen these sorts of performances every night. Initially, I would carefully record them with my tape recorder, but now . . .” He exhaled a mouthful of cigarette smoke.

“He just performs speeches?”

“Exactly. Do you see what it says on that flag?”

He pointed toward the flag fluttering in the wind.

“It’s too dark for me to see,” I said.

“It says, South. Seas. People’s. Republic.” He read out the text word-by-word, for emphasis.

“It’s a national flag? For this worthless little rocky island?”

“That’s right. For someone who is insane, it’s all the same. I even found a map in his doghouse of a hut. It was extraordinary—his “South Seas” includes not only Vietnam and South Korea, but also Guangdong, Fujian, Hainan Island, Taiwan, Southeast Asia, and even Australia. Is that large enough for you? He even regards himself as the national father of his People’s Republic.” The Japanese man took out another cigarette, and pressed it to the butt of the old one. “I originally wanted to interview this national father, but at night he becomes extremely dangerous.” He frowned and laughed bitterly.

“Can’t you interview him during the day?”

“It is only at night that he truly comes into his own. During the day, he is only a pathetic exile. I tell you . . . ,” he assumed a mysterious expression, “. . . the daytime version of him has absolutely no recollection of what he does at night. During the day he writes, but at night he performs.

He probably regards his nightlife as a mere dream. The nighttime version of him, meanwhile, doesn't seem to be aware of the existence of the pathetic daytime version. This nighttime madman calls himself *Hitam* (*meaning* "*black*"). And furthermore, each of the two figures operates in a different territory, with each claiming a different half of the island. Therefore, I needed to adjust my persona. My daytime work as a historical investigator concluded long ago, which means I can't reappear in that guise. My nighttime work, meanwhile, consists of an extremely challenging anthropological observation, for which I needed to play the part of a monkey—and it had to be a female monkey—in order to approach him."

"This kind of research does sound very difficult."

To my surprise, he suddenly became rather melancholic.

"Look at this disguise. It took me an enormous amount of effort to obtain it. It was originally the hide of one of the male monkeys he skinned in order to make an example for the others. But I had to disguise myself as a female monkey, you know, because he simply won't tolerate male ones. Based on my investigations, over the past several decades he has either skinned all of the male monkeys that were here or driven them to the center of the island. Like a king of the apes, he has claimed all of the females for himself. I don't know if it is on account of his having consumed too many monkey testes, but for some reason those female monkeys allow him to do them like a male monkey would—though I suspect that when the females are in heat, the real male monkeys must somehow sneak out and do them behind his back (*I've also encountered this . . .*), because otherwise how could the island possibly have so many baby monkeys? They couldn't really *all* be his offspring, could they?" This voluble Japanese monkey rambled on and on. "In order to disguise myself as a female monkey, I painstakingly collected the scent from *that* area from many female monkeys and rubbed it on my own butt, and then put on this unbearably hot monkey hide. But to be defenseless like this is actually very dangerous, you know." He suddenly began to sob. "One night he seized me, and I didn't dare tell him that I was actually a human—and moreover was a man—and consequently he . . . ," he once again began to tear up, ". . . he grabbed me by the neck and, heedless of the consequences, proceeded to enter me from behind and unloaded his wad into me. The mother-fucking wild stag! The hemorrhoids I brought with me from Japan exploded, to the point I was bleeding copiously from my butt. He fucking left me in such a state that for three days I could neither stand nor sit. To this day, it even hurts when I fart. I'm very concerned that this will have irreversible consequences."

"That's horrible. However . . . ," I ventured a reasonable doubt about his story, ". . . is it really possible that he can't tell the difference between a monkey butt and a Japanese one?"

"I think this is something we must ask Darwin," he replied with the seriousness of a scholar. "Afterwards, however, I didn't dare get too close to him, since I was afraid that if he were to discover that my butt was slicker than a monkey's he might grow fond of it and then castrate me, to keep me as . . ." He had a terrified expression.

After a pause, he shook his head and abruptly changed the subject. "Do you know what that is made from?" Pointing to the flag, he smiled, revealing his teeth. "It is stitched together from all the men's underwear he saved up and couldn't bring himself to wear. They are all very florid and colorful, as is the style in the tropics."

The one-man show was still continuing. After finishing two cigarettes, Yamamoto didn't take a third. Instead, he squatted there in the dark, rambling on while explaining to me, like a tourist guide, the scene that was unfolding in front of us. One segment was from "A Speech from the Seventh Meeting of the United Nations," another was "An Announcement to the General Assembly of the Twenty-Seventh Congress of Third World Nations," another was "An Announcement to the General Assembly at the Tenth Congress of Non-Aligned Nations," and yet another was "A Speech by a Member of the Standing Committee at the Thirtieth Congress of the Chinese Communist Party" . . .

Yamamoto explained that during the day the madman reads old newspapers, while at night he imagines he is personally attending the historical events he has just read about.

The night continued to grow darker. Suddenly, we heard the low sound of a lullaby-like song, "*Communism, the faith of our Party . . .*"

"My god, this is . . ."

"The national anthem of the People's Republic of the South Seas."

"Come with me," he said. He glanced meaningfully at the wooden box I was carrying. "There are a lot of things in my den I'd like to show you."

Leading me along a dark path, he rambled continuously as we proceeded forward. Although he walked very slowly with open thighs and a raised butt, he nevertheless continued enthusiastically discussing his research. He said that despite the fact that he had paid an incalculable price for this field research (including the loss of his anal virginity), he had nevertheless made several groundbreaking discoveries, which would allow him to rewrite existing histories of South Seas Chinese communities, and particularly many aspects relating to the Malayan Communist Party. Moreover, this island's unique conditions had allowed him to make enormous advances in his methodology, permitting him to extend anthropological techniques from humans to sentient nonhumans, and specifically to monkeys. During this period he learned not only the language of the monkeys on this island but also their indigenous knowledge and abilities (he tried to approach issues from their perspective, and to master their mode of thinking).

We continued to climb higher and higher, and by the time we arrived at the cave where he said he had hidden many of his secrets, both of us were completely covered in sweat. "During the day I hide out here and sleep, and at night I wake up and go about my business."

He calmly pulled aside the rattan curtain that served as his door. We had barely taken three steps inside when, as he was still talking, we suddenly heard the sound of a lighter coming from the dark interior of the room. The lighter created a tunnel of light, and in the instant that the scene was illuminated it resembled a realistic photograph: a naked man sitting in the dark recesses of the cave—his face painted white like an aborigine, and his entire body tattooed with the outline of a Western suit. On his chest there were four enormous buttons, and from his crotch a monocle-wearing serpent rose up proudly. He had one foot extended into the darkness, making it appear as though he was missing one of his black leather shoes. Yamamoto Gojuuichi quickly put his monkey mask back on, then began emitting loud cries like a female monkey. He turned around and, with his hands on the ground and his butt in the air, he crawled backward toward where the naked man was sitting.

supplication

¥Ãx:¥Z¥Xªº¦³¤@Ó¦a¤è¦³«nªº¿ù¦r:"§Aªºµ²»y¨Ï§ÚÌ³h§x"À³°µ"§Aªºµ²¾l¨Ï§ÚÌ³h§x",¬Oª½±µ¦^À³«Ø°ê³Ì
¶}©lªº¤@«¤¤ªº¸Ü:"¤èx¨º¤@¥N¬O¨S¦³¿iªk¤F,¥u· Q»\´Ã½x©w«eºâºâ¥LÌªº¥¿±µ²¾l".³o! ;Ó¦a¤è§A¤§«e¦
³¬dÃÒ,˚O±o§Ú¤]´¿½T»{.¯NÓ¤H¥ß³õ¨Ó»¡,§Ú¹ê¦b¤£Ä@· N¨£¨i«¦^°¨µØ¤å¾Çªº§x¹Ò,¨º¥i¯à¬O»{ÃÑ½xª
º°ÝÃD»· ¤j©ó¤HÃþ¾Çªº.³Ìªñ¤´¬Ý¨i°¨µØ¤å¾Â¤W¤@¨ÇµL²á½§²Lªº½Í½! ;x©Î¤ÏÀ³,Ë¤& pound;¥²³¨
º¨Ç¤H¤£ªø¶i,¦U¦Û°µ¦n¥÷¤ºªº¨Æ§a,¤Ï¥¿¨i³Ì«á¤j®a¹ï¥²¶· ±¹ï¾ú¥vªºµô¨M.¥t¤@¤è±¤}¥i¥H²M· ¡ªº¬Ý¨
ì¦b¤Ö¼ÆªB¤Íªº§V¤O¤U¤@¦~¨Ó°¨µØ¤å¾Çµû½xªºº¥ÁÍ¦¨¼ô,¨º¬O»á¥O¤H¦w¼¢ªº.¥[ªo.! ÀA¾ð

slow boat to china

Syahadan maka diberi oleh Tuan Bonham tiga pucuk surat berpalut kuning, sepucuk depada Raja Bendahara, dan sepucuk kepada Raja temenggung, dan sepucuk depada Yang Dipertuan Kelantan.

KISAH PELAYARAN ABDULLAH KE KELANTAN

THE WIND WAS BLOWING HARD and the sun was high in the sky, as rays of sunlight gently penetrated the dense forest canopy. The startlingly thick smell of coffee announced to everyone that it was time for afternoon tea. The coffee shop, which was wedged between two enormous durian trees, was quickly filled with customers hailing from all over, each of whom sat in their accustomed seat. Leaning lazily to one side, they would read the newspaper. They were all men, and from the marks on their clothes you could easily guess their line of work. Some were splattered with paint, others with dust, oil, and drops of rubber. Some looked as though they had just crawled out of the mud, while others appeared as though they had just climbed down from a tree. . . . With their feet up, they gulped down their fried noodles, red bean buns, and other dishes, as they debated, in a cacophony of different accents, the issues of the day. Subtle political differences would occasionally erupt into red-faced disputes, and while these arguments involved customers of all ages, they were quickly quelled by the elders, or else the customers' bosses would summon them back to work. After tea, everyone would scatter in mere minutes.

On the other side of the shop, as usual, a group of children was sitting around a shadowy old man who was telling them a story.

Next to the coffee shop, in the shadow of the claw-like canopy of the hundred-foot-tall durian trees, the elderly man who was as thin as an old-time rickshaw puller was leaning lazily against the tree trunk, idly fanning himself with a melon-rind hat. He was wearing dusty black cloth shoes, and his hair was as white as a scallion. He was holding a bamboo pipe, and periodically would take a puff, as a trickle of white smoke seeped out of the wrinkled corners of his mouth. No matter how warm the weather was, he would always wrap himself in that faded silk gown that the young men mockingly called a "funeral shroud"—which he never washed and as a result was completely covered in sweat stains. Some of the more uncouth youngsters would secretly describe him as someone who had just "crawled out of a grave." Because he was so hot, he would open his front collar, revealing the veins throbbing under his mottled skin.

No one was certain exactly how old he was, but it seemed as though he, like those durian trees, had always been there—and indeed had *only* been there. The youngsters and children particularly felt this way. All they knew was that he seemed to be very familiar with events relating to the Xuantong Emperor and the first emperor of the Ming, Zhu Yuanzhang. He must have lived in old China for a while, but one day must have somehow drifted over to this peninsula, where he apparently got stranded and was unable to return home. Some of the elders in the village dimly recalled how, in the old days, many towns and cities once had this sort of old man. In the new Chinese villages and the Malay *kampungs*, these men would pick a piece of unoccupied land (as long as no one came to drive them away, a piece of land was considered unoccupied), on which they would use some old boards and metal sheeting to build a small hut. They would then cobble together a bed and proceed to live there. This particular old man must have had some education, and could recite old Chinese poetry. He also knew a thing or two about geography and astronomy, and would pass his days helping country folk with their weddings and funerals, selecting auspicious names for newborns, and assessing the *fengshui* of prospective grave mounds. On the lunar New Year he would compose several Spring Festival couplets, and sometimes would inscribe a shop sign for a newly-opened store. His handwriting was strong and vigorous, and his written characters were neat and uniform. Sometimes he would even help take sick people's pulse, and write them prescriptions for health supplements. The money in the thin "red envelopes" he periodically received was enough for him to lead a simple life, and even occasionally enjoy some opium.

In that era, it was very rare for anyone to be able to read and, aside from the Chinese teacher in the town's sole primary school, this old man was probably the most literate person around—indeed, he may even have been more educated than the teacher, since he could read classic texts, and furthermore came from China. Perhaps it was on account of his dress and appearance that some elder Chinese would call him "Mr. Tangshan," though others, because they resented all of the crazy stories he would tell, would call him an "old bookworm" behind his back. Meanwhile, the Malays would all call him *Orang Cina*. No one, at any rate, had any interest in his real name. No one ever asked him what it was, and consequently no one knew. Even the Malay bureaucrat who came to conduct a census survey declined to include the old man in the count of local Chinese—a number that, at that time, was extremely sensitive.

Most of the time the old man was idle with nothing to do, but he liked to hang out with the local children. He would tell them stories about the origin of the world, beginning with how Pan Gu opened the sky and split the earth, how Xihe made the sun rise and set, and how Kuafu chased the sun, and of the three-eyed god Erlang. . . . Myth and historical narratives would intermix freely in his story, as he drew on characters from classic novels like *Investiture of the Gods*, *The Water Margin*, *Journey to the West*, and *Romance of Three Kingdoms*. He would recite from memory one story cycle after another, and in this way was able to capture the children's attention.

The stories he was most fond of recounting were the tales of Zheng He sailing the Western Seas, including how durians, the king of fruits, originated from Zheng He's habit of squatting beneath a tree to defecate—and depending on the consistency of the feces (for instance, whether he was diarrheic or constipated), they would develop into different kinds of durians. Needless to say, the children were very fond of this sort of familiar story. The elders would often remark on how Zheng He actually left behind his valuable ship somewhere, perhaps in some hidden harbor in the north, and on the eve of the annual Duanwu Festival it would periodically set out and slowly make its way toward Tangshan—which is to say, to China. The boat would take three or five years to arrive at its destination—Beijing. Then, it would return to the same harbor and wait for more passengers to board. Because the boat was already very old, it was therefore extremely slow, and each round-trip would take more than a decade. Consequently, if you were to miss the boat, "then you won't ever have another chance to board, even after you grow up." Every time the old Chinese man reached this point in his story, he would lower his voice, take a couple of steps toward where the children were sitting, exhale some foul-smelling breath, and announce solemnly, "The boat only accepts children under thirteen." The old Chinaman would then jab at his chest with his black finger and add, "It has no interest in old men like me!" He would dejectedly shake his head and sigh, then slowly walk away.

After listening to the story, the children would disperse. It is possible that some of them went home to ask their parents for evidence, though no one ever really believed that the old man's stories had any truth to them. However, one of the children, a schoolboy named Tie Niu, *did* believe the stories, and every time he ran into the old Chinaman he would invariably ask a volley of questions about the slow boat, including when and where it anchored, whether it was necessary to purchase tickets, which route it would take, among countless other details. These questions were so specific that the old Chinaman would often have to invent answers on the spot. He would stammer out his responses, pointing to the railroad tracks, the river, and the red clay road that connected the town to the outside road, and simply make things up. He would confirm the direction the boat would take—if he was facing in the direction of the rising sun, it would be to his left, or if he were facing in the direction of the setting sun, it would be to his right. Eventually, it got to the point where if Tie Niu was present, the old Chinaman wouldn't dare even mention anything concerning Zheng He and his slow boat.

It is said that once, when Tie Niu was three, his father went to Daba to chop some trees, but because he was too "iron-toothed"—which is to say, stubborn—a log ended up falling on him and crushing him. Later, for financial reasons, the family had to sell the two rice fields that Tie Niu's father had bequeathed them, leaving them only the water buffalo that had been Tie Niu's constant companion ever since he learned to walk, and which the family had originally used to help plow the fields. Even though the family continued to live in the same ancestral hall as before, the widow's mood nevertheless changed dramatically, and her relationship with the townspeople became unusually acerbic. She would frequently get into violent arguments with neighbors over inconsequential issues, and invariably felt that people wanted to take advantage of her simply because she was a widow. Every time she purchased something, she would always take it home and weigh it several times using her own scale, but it just happened that her scale was calibrated differently from theirs. She would often chase a villager's dog that tried to eat her chickens, and once she even followed the dog home to where it was hiding beneath its owner's bed. She then took a stick and beat the animal until the area beneath the bed was covered in dog urine and dog feces. Upon leaving, she made a point of taking one of the family's chickens that was roosting on its nest or a rooster that was unable to get away in time, and furthermore kicked over one of the family's flowerpots. There were countless things like this. Naturally, she didn't neglect to curse and beat her only son. After he started primary school, she kept close watch over him and expected him to be first in his class in every subject. It even seemed as though she hoped that he would go on to pass the civil service exams (everyone in the village whispered this kind of thing behind her back). On her wall, there were several dozen reed switches of different lengths, but like other kids his age, Tie Niu liked to fool around. Furthermore, he lived up to his name, which literally means "iron ox," and was not afraid of being beaten. But his home was extremely dilapidated, and there was no way for it to contain him. The more he went out, the more his mother would beat him; and the more she beat him, the more he would go out. She beat him so much that he began to suspect that he had been abandoned and picked up as an infant—a suspicion that was reinforced when she cursed "that damned *fanzai* midwife!" As for his father, all Tie Niu's mother would say was that he had "gone to China to sell pickled eggs," leaving Tie Niu with countless unanswered questions. Given that his family was very poor, he would frequently have to eat pickled eggs, which would always make him think of his father in China. But he couldn't ask why his father didn't simply go into town to sell the eggs, and why instead he had to go all the way to China. Tie Niu's mother was very strict with him, and there were countless things he was not allowed to talk about. As a result, he wasn't able to obtain any confirmation of the old man's story about the slow boat, but in any case he wanted very much to believe it. He remembered how his father had been fond of taking him out to fish, catch birds, and so forth. He suspected that if only he could find a way to board that slow boat, he would be able to find his father in China selling pickled duck eggs.

In the season when durians ripened, the second afternoon after Tie Niu left home, the old storyteller was telling tales about "Black Whirlwind" Li Kui's awesome hammers, when a fist-sized durian that had been chewed off by a squirrel fell from a branch more than a hundred feet high and landed on his head. Without uttering a word, he returned to China to sell pickled eggs. When the other children who were there listening to him saw that he had been exploded by a durian, they were so terrified that their necks shrunk by a few inches, and they all had diarrhea for more than a month afterwards.

On that particular day, Iron Tooth's widow got up at dawn as usual, and after lighting some candles and an oil lamp she cooked some breakfast. Taking the lamp, she then went out with the other village women to harvest rubber. Tie Niu's daily chore was to take their ox out to graze every morning after sunrise, but on this day after waking up he proceeded to pack all of his clothes and then followed the river northwards and out of the village. He had not given any indication of his plans before departing, and therefore when his mother returned home at noon and noticed that the breakfast she had prepared had been eaten but her son was not home, she initially assumed he had gone into the village to play marbles or listen to stories with other kids, or else had gone down to the river to fish. Unconcerned, she proceeded to cook lunch, wash some clothes, chop some wood, sweep up some leaves in front of the house, then prepared to wait for him to return, whereupon she was determined to teach him a lesson. It was not until dusk began to fall and Tie Niu still hadn't appeared that she finally began to feel anxious, and proceeded to go to all the places where he liked to play. She asked everyone she saw, but they all reported that on that particular day they hadn't seen any trace of him. Everyone found this rather odd, and they all assumed that little Tie Niu—who was as stout as an ox and seemingly impervious to the wind and the sun—must have fallen sick.

At this point, Iron Tooth's widow panicked and collapsed in the middle of the street. She opened her mouth, but for the longest time was unable to get any words out. Instead, she kept mouthing her deceased husband's nickname, "My dear departed Iron Tooth . . ." Everyone had often observed her furiously pursuing her son, switch in hand, but up to this point no one had ever seen this fierce woman openly sobbing, her tears splattering to the ground.

After the longest time, she finally managed to regain her composure and begged everyone crowded around to help her search for her son—to see if he had fallen into a ditch, been kidnapped, or perhaps encountered a snake or something.

After a while, Tie Niu's companions reported back to say that they had checked all the places where he would usually go to catch fighting fish, tiger fish, and leopard fish, secretly pick mangosteens and rambutans, dig up sweet potatoes, and so forth, but had found no trace of him. As Iron Tooth's widow was jumping around anxiously like a grasshopper, a villager suddenly asked, "What about your ox? Is your ox still there?" It was only then that she realized that not only was her son Tie Niu missing, so was that obstinate water buffalo that had been her son's constant companion. A little while later, a considerate neighbor reported that an old Malay man who lived next to the river thought he saw, at the crack of dawn, a boy riding an ox and laughing happily as he proceeded northward. That was her only clue.

The widow's eyes flashed, and she immediately got up and proceeded to borrow a bicycle from a neighbor—the village head owned the village's only motorcycle, but she was terrified of the noise this saw-like machine made—and rushed toward the riverbank.

The dirt path along the riverbank functioned as a road, but actually it was full of irregularly-shaped footprints, as a result of having been walked over by countless people and oxen on rainy days when the ground was wet—with the irregular shapes of the footprints reflecting not only the different weights of the bodies supported by those feet but also the soil's varying degrees of firmness on different days. This kind of road did not lend itself at all to being ridden on, and the bicycle literally hopped along it, to the point that her intestines got all tied up in knots. Eventually, she reached an area where there were piles of cow manure everywhere. The piles looked very fresh, and she was secretly pleased as she thought to herself, You damned kid, you brought me all the way out here, but I've finally tracked you down! At the same time, however, she recognized that this was a path that was used primarily by oxen, and therefore it was to be expected that there would be manure nearby. Indeed, what would have been unusual would have been if there had been no manure at all. As she proceeded forward, she asked everyone she encountered—most of whom were Malays who enjoyed living along the riverbank—and some of them reported having seen her son, while others said that they didn't know anything. As she went further along, however, she saw fewer and fewer people, and eventually she reached a point where she no longer saw anyone at all.

Before she knew it, the sun had begun to set and the manure on the side of the path became increasingly scarce. She was covered in sweat, parched, and bone-tired. At this point she had just reached a cool area, where the air was full of bird calls and monkey screeches. In front of her there was a primitive forest, and the only hint of the path was some slightly tilted grass. She looked back, and saw that she was indeed a long way from the village. She got off the bicycle and proceeded on foot toward the riverbank, but just as she was about to scoop up some water with her hands to drink, she suddenly noticed that the riverbank was full of hoof prints and manure, some of which seemed to have been left by an ox. There were also some foul-smelling feces left by some meat-eating animal, together with paw prints from some sort of large cat. Upon seeing this, she immediately began to wail.

When the other villagers caught up to her and saw this scene, they turned pale and were stunned into silence. Upon seeing so many people, Iron Tooth's widow began weeping loudly while crying, "My miserable fate, my miserable fate! My unfortunate son, and I, your unfortunate mother!" She then collapsed, and a group of men had no choice but to half-drag and half-carry her home.

It turned out that the old water buffalo had slowly ambled forward while grazing. It had continued walking until the sun was about to come up, but had not yet gotten very far. At this rate, even if it had continued walking until the sun set behind the mountains, it would not have gone more than a few *li*. By the time they reached this edge of the forest, the sun was already up. When the ox lowered its head to graze, Tie Niu suddenly heard a soft whispering sound. He listened carefully, and it turned out that the sound was coming from several wild piglets that were eating on the riverbank, and who were being watched by a snorting and not particularly friendly female boar. After a while, the boar sounded an alarm, and the piglets all started yelping in unison. He felt the ox's hair grow erect, and its muscles seemed unusually taut. He and the ox both turned around.

It turned out to be an indescribably large tiger, and the ground around it was splattered with drops of water from when it shook its head. Saliva was dripping from its mouth, and it was panting slightly. A thick fog surrounded it on all sides, but he could make out the tiger's black stripes and its blindingly golden fur. Suddenly, everything became very still.

And then, just as quickly, the world seemed to come alive again. Tie Niu heard the piglets' terrified squeals, followed by an enormous roar that appeared to come from the sky. He lowered his head and gripped the ox's horns with all his might. They rushed forward, as the wind blew past his ears and leaves and branches brushed his hair and back. Ignoring the tumult behind them, the ox ran into the forest, not caring whether or not there was a path to follow. All Tie Niu was aware of was the ox galloping forward at a terrifying speed, but fortunately his body remained anchored securely on the animal's back. He was like a gecko, suctioned tightly to the ox's back, though the spare clothing, water bottle, and packet of crackers he had brought with him were all stripped away by some tree branch or another.

He had no idea whether the terrified ox, which was now running for its life, actually believed that the tiger was still pursuing them. At any rate, they covered several dozen *li* in the blink of an eye, and continued running until the ox was foaming in the mouth and could barely stand. When they finally stopped, both the ox and the boy were so exhausted that they immediately fell asleep.

It was only after Tie Niu dreamed that he was being eaten by a tiger and entered its intestines full of ants, that he finally woke up and discovered that he was in fact lying on an anthill. His entire body—including even his groin—was covered in fire ants. He quickly got up and began shouting and frantically hopping about. It was quite a while before he was finally able to get the ants out of his hair. At this point, he suddenly remembered the tiger. He immediately looked around, but all he saw was the ox calmly grazing several feet away. It was only then that he was able to relax a bit, and it was also only then that he suddenly realized that he was quite famished. However, the packet of biscuits that he had brought with him had been lost in the flight. He was also thirsty and had no choice but to scoop some water out of a ditch with his hands. The water in the ditch was so clear that he could easily see the bottom, where there were tiny fish swimming around. He took off his clothes and waded into the freezing water, and proceeded to wash himself from head to toe. It was only then that he noticed that the wounds he had received from the branches and leaves began to sting.

He wrung his clothes and squeezed out all of the water that he could, then put them back on.

Not far from where they had stopped, there were some railroad tracks. At that point, he remembered a dream he had once had about a train, in which he, his father, and the ox were all riding the train together. The ox took up an entire car all by itself. His father was dressed very nicely, with a white dress shirt and white dress pants. In real life, Tie Niu had never seen his father dressed so elegantly. The hair gel combed into his hair made it appear jet black. He looked quite young, and displayed a row of white teeth when he smiled. His face was full of sunlight, as though he were on his way to an exciting banquet. His father warmly lifted him up with one hand, but the hand turned out to be ice cold, with water dripping from his fingertips.

Tie Niu suddenly remembered the father who appeared in the wedding photo on his mother's table. But in contrast to the image of his father that Tie Niu preserved in his memory, in real life his father had always been as dark as a mud fish.

A train spit black smoke as it slowly proceeded northward. Golden rays of sunlight shone in through the window, as a field of tall grass shimmered in the sunlight. Tie Niu's original plan had been to follow the railroad tracks, but his ox would always go berserk when the trains passed so close to them. He had originally planned to sneak aboard a train, but in the end couldn't bring himself to leave the ox behind, since he knew his mother would have taken advantage of the opportunity to sell the animal for slaughter. This is something she had long wanted to do, and he would either stare at her in fury, throw a tantrum, and then climb to the top of the tallest tree he could find and refuse to come down, or else he would go down to the marsh area and bury himself in the ground until the only thing that was showing was his head. Once, he used a candle to burn a hole in the wooden outhouse, so that a cool breeze could blow on his butt while he was taking a shit. When he didn't have anything else to do, he would whisper into the ox's ear, and he actually talked more to the ox than he did to his own mother—though no one had any idea what it was he said.

By this time, the sun had gone down to the point that it was even lower than the grass in the fields.

He looked around, and noticed that not far away there was a small wooden stilt house. Therefore, he mounted the ox and slowly made his way over to the structure. He smelled the scent of roasted sweet potatoes, which made his mouth water. As he approached, he heard a dog barking, as a little dog with tiger-like markings rushed over. The ox snorted anxiously, so he tied it to the trunk of a thin tree, then crouched over and, speaking in a soft whisper, went over to try to calm the dog. After a little while, the small dog began licking his warm face and enthusiastically wagging its tail.

Next to the railroad tracks there was a small field with tapioca, sweet potatoes, papaya, taro, and wild bitter melon. A topless old man wearing short, wide-crotched pants was sitting next to a fire that was producing lots of smoke. He was expressionless, and appeared to be quite old. His skin was dark brown, like a sweet potato that had just been pulled out of the ground. He resembled a Chinaman, but also a mountain aborigine. Seeing that Tie Niu's mouth was watering, the man silently took two sweet potatoes from the fire and handed them to him. Tie Niu, ignoring how hot they were, immediately proceeded to peel them, and in no time at all was chewing on the inside of the burnt potato skin. Seeing this, the old man handed him two more potatoes. Afterwards, Tie Niu discretely asked for some water, then found somewhere to go to sleep. For his basic needs, he used the handful of Malay words that he had learned, including *makan* (to eat), *air* (water), *tidur* (to sleep). During the remainder of his journey he mostly relied on this handful of key words.

Periodically, a train would pass by, running along the rusted tracks, producing a loud roar.

The fire was covered with a layer of mud, but it continued burning all night as smoke poured out from benerath the floor.

Tie Niu and the old man both slept on the ground.

Tie Niu dreamed he was sleeping on the deck of a ship, which was rocking back and forth in the waves. The ship's sail was taller than a tree and the mast was covered in leaves, as the ship sailed toward that ancient nation the monkey had extracted from the center of a stone. The boat was full of monkeys, which were all jumping around and making a huge uproar. However, he didn't see his ox, which was nowhere to be found. Suddenly feeling very melancholy, he proceeded to wake up, then rolled over and went back to sleep.

He dreamed his mother was furiously pursuing him on her kitchen broomstick. His ox was rushing forward as fast as a train riding on the tracks, and even had fire in its eyes.

In this way, he was pursued all night.

The sun had just come out, and as soon as Tie Niu got up, he saw that the old man had wrapped several baked sweet potatoes in a banana leaf and tied it up with a piece of straw thatch. The old man also handed him an old aluminum kettle full of warm water. Following a path beside the railroad tracks, the old man led Tie Niu and his ox forward in the warm early dawn fog.

In this way he departed, riding barefoot on the ox's back.

They passed one Malay *kampung* after another. The ox ambled forward very slowly, and frequently stopped to graze. Soon, Tie Niu had consumed all of his provisions, and became increasingly famished. He therefore mustered the courage to go up to a Malay woman selling rice boxes and ask her for something to eat. Or he would go up to one of the women laughing happily in front of the stilt houses and ask her for something.

When passing through a Chinese town, he would continue like this, but mostly he begged at stores selling food. In this way, he would obtain a meat bun, some chicken with rice, a bottle of water—none of these was very difficult to obtain. Occasionally he would encounter someone who would curiously ask him where he was from and where he was going, but he remembered his mother's warning that he not talk to strangers, and therefore he would merely smile and act as though he hadn't understood.

Under a tree next to a river, a silver-haired old man was gripped by a loud man with an ugly face, who was shouting at him. The old man exclaimed something in a high-pitched voice, and then proceeded to vomit, and in the process produced some even more unpleasant noises. He vom-

ited up one fish after another, and it was hard to believe that his stomach was able to hold so many fish! Finally, he vomited up a red object that looked as though it were covered in blood. The old man picked it up and mumbled something as he handed it to the man with the ugly face, who then leaned his head back and proceeded to swallow the object. He extended his arms like a rooster spreading its wings, then picked up a large stone. Next, he uprooted a large tree, as the old man quickly devoured the various fish he had just spit up. Finally, gazing forward with his red eyes, he dove into the water.

That day Tie Niu, riding his ox, arrived in a village. Next to the houses along the side of the road, the trees were filled with the red rambutans he was so fond of eating. He had never seen a sight like this before, and found it thousands of times more beautiful than a field of China roses. Immediately his mouth began to water. This was obviously a Malay village, and the roof of each stilt house resembled a boat about to take flight—appearing even more vivid than he had imagined from people's descriptions. He would frequently see sarong-wearing Malay men and women sitting outside enjoying the cool air and eating rambutans, or sweeping up the leaves next to their house. There were also countless chickens strolling around everywhere.

The number of rice paddies also increased. Previously, he had only heard his elders discuss the paddies from which rice came, but had never seen one with his own eyes. In the fields there were also many oxen. He guessed the oxen were being used to plow the fields, and found that they looked just like the illustrations in his textbooks.

Those days, the sun always shined bright, but he kept his body shielded under the shade of his straw hat. His ox was so hot he would always make a beeline toward wherever there was water to drink. Usually this would be a ditch with either clear or murky water, but sometimes it would be a river, or even an overgrown well. Sometimes he would have to frantically rein the ox in and fiercely wave his stick, but other times he would simply follow the ox down to the water, where he would then remove his clothes and go for a swim. In the process, he would almost forget where he was heading, and often they would walk all day without advancing more than a few *li*.

At night, he would often sleep in huts that had been left behind by migrant laborers, but sometimes he would simply use a covered walkway. Other times he would sleep in a tree, if it happened to have a bed-like space where he could lie down. He occasionally would sleep in a small temple erected to Tudi Gong, the God of the Earth, or in multicolored Chinese temples, Indian temples, abandoned houses, and even tombs.

He seemed to have completely forgotten his mother, who was still urgently searching for him high and low. She later repeatedly returned to the scene of the struggle, carefully inspecting the various prints that had been left behind. She found several of Tie Niu's "remains," including assorted pieces of clothing, a flattened water bottle, a bag with two dollars, together with an array of hoof prints from the ox and the pack of wild boars. However, unlike other tiger attacks, she didn't see any physical traces of the tiger itself—such as hair, crushed bones, ripped clothing, and so forth. Therefore, she continued to grasp a glimmer of hope, although a famously pessimistic observer threw cold water on her hopes by suggesting that "maybe the tiger took him back to her lair to feed to her cubs."

The further north Tie Niu proceeded, the more tense the atmosphere seemed to become. Everywhere he went, be it a village or a town, everything appeared to be unusually tumultuous. He saw more and more people, who filled the streets. Sometimes they were Chinese holding white signs with red characters written on them. They were always led by someone holding a loudspeaker who was shouting something that Tie Niu couldn't understand, and who would be followed by a long line of people, three-wheeled carts, or small lorries. Sometimes the people would be Malay troops wearing white headbands. They would also have loudspeakers and would be shouting as they waved their fists in the air. The number of police also increased, and everywhere officers with faces blackened by the sun could be seen marching back and forth, and they would whistle at Tie Niu and his ox. The number of tumultuous gatherings also increased steadily, taking place in Chinese temples and Malay mosques, as well as marketplaces and coffee shops, in schools and even under trees. On electrical poles, electrical lines, walls, tree trunks, and stones on the side of the road . . . there were posters with pictures of an ox head and a scale, or of a series of men's faces that he had never seen before. The ground was also covered with sheets of paper that had been blown off by the wind.

He had a disconcerting feeling that something was amiss. It was as if something were slowly moving.

Could it be that the boat had already left?

The strong man was strolling around while dragging two stones that were even larger than he was.

In an Indian village, all of the trees were flowering, and everywhere there was a strong Indian scent.

He passed through a small town, where the fields were full of papayas. In front of every house there were piles and piles of red and green papayas, and we won't even mention what the orchards looked like. Everyone in the town was dressed differently from people elsewhere. They were all wearing dark blue, with the men in gowns and the women in wide dresses. Several women gave him large papayas, and one household consisting only of women insisted that he stay with them for several days. The mother was so kind that he almost began calling her "mother," just like her own daughters. The vegetable plates and meat and papaya dishes she prepared were so tasty that he almost wanted to stay behind—he imagined that helping them pick papayas would be the perfect life.

At the same time, however, he was afraid he would be late for the boat, and therefore was anxious to set off again as soon as possible. When they asked him where he planned to go, he hesitated for several days, but eventually whispered the truth to the youngest daughter, saying, "Don't tell anyone, but I'm going to China. There is a boat waiting to take me." He promised that if he ever passed by there again, he would definitely drop by to pay them a visit.

The daughters' mother helped him peel one more rambutan, packed several sets of clean clothes and crackers, together with an oil cloth umbrella, then tied everything up into a bundle and slung it over the ox's back. She even bought him a pair of rubber shoes. As he was about to leave, she urged him, "No matter where you go, you mustn't forget to return to see your mother." She then handed him a large red papaya, and even after he had left the family far behind his tears continued to pour down onto the fruit he was holding in his hands.

Tie Niu felt he had suddenly grown taller.

There were mountains on both sides and the sound of rapid hoof beats, as someone rode up quickly on a horse. The person was like a bride in olden times—dressed completely in red and wearing a red veil. The horse and its rider quickly rushed past, but then suddenly there was a loud sound and the rider tumbled off the horse. Several topless men shouted and rushed out from the darkness where they had been hiding. One of them picked up a knife and proceeded to slice off the head of the person who had fallen from the horse, who turned out to be a heavily bearded old man. Shouting and hopping around in delight, they proceeded to run away. The headless man lay in a pool of blood, as countless ants crowded around.

The mood became increasingly odd. The townspeople were all out in the streets shouting, their eyes red with excitement. The entire town seemed to be made of paper, shreds of paper blew everywhere. There were police everywhere.

There was a train full of soldiers wearing green uniforms.

When young men from the Malay villages saw him, they would often stare suspiciously, as though he were a thief. Sometimes they even seemed as though they were about to come over and beat him. He was terrified.

One evening, he entered a village and saw everyone rushing outside while trying to fish something out of their throats. Their mouths were wide open, but no sound came out. They gesticulated wildly for a long time as they endeavored to extract something from each other's throats, which they then angrily threw down. As night fell, the wind began to die down. He rooted around on the ground in the dark to see what they had thrown, and they turned out to be fish bones.

The sound of sutra chanting at the local mosque was different from other places and sounded very hoarse. There were even some portions where there were no words at all, and instead just a dry rasping sound.

Sometimes he could smell the sea, and several times he even reached the coast, but all he saw was a handful of small fishing boats, some waves, or people playing on the beach.

There was a tall dike, and a small boy stuck his finger into a hole that had formed in it. When asked what he was doing, the boy replied, "I can feel the ocean."

Wasn't it that he was afraid everyone would be inundated and drown . . . ?

He remembered what the old man had whispered into his ear:

"That's right, there's no need to worry. They may come for you, and they may recognize you. This is not a boat that just anyone can board. You must be fated to do so. But there really is a boat there."

He dreamed his father brought out two large urns of pickled eggs. His father's body, face, and the outside of the urn were all covered with yellow clay. His father smiled at him, as he carefully peeled the pickled duck egg he was holding. When he finished, however, it turned out that there was nothing inside, and there were just a few strands of human hair, which were disgustingly stuck together with a white viscous substance of some sort.

He could hear a nest of sparrows quietly discussing whether to move to a new home.

Several times he went through a dccp forcst, and was terrified of encountering another tiger. Fortunately, all he saw were elephants, wild boars, baboons, lizards, cobras, turtles, crabs, and a host of other animals that he had never heard of and had never eaten.

At night, the villages were full of fires. Periodically, someone or something would approach him with an angry expression and stare at him fiercely, while his ox would also snort and stare back.

Once, a young man with no eyebrows suddenly punched him. The young man was originally going to do more, but was restrained by his companions.

That night, neither he nor his ox got any sleep. He caressed his cheek, which was burning hot, and couldn't help bursting into tears. He had walked very far.

By this point, his provisions were almost exhausted. Like his ox, he drank fresh water, picked fresh fruit when he could, and ate fresh grass, but he felt increasingly dizzy and lethargic.

When the cock crowed, he dreamed that the man dressed in a yellow dragon-patterned gown quickly walked up to him and said, "You're almost there." But when that person ran away, his feet became stuck in the earth, such that the further he ran the shorter his legs got, to the point that by the end all that was left was a head with a head running all by itself, with a long queue dragging behind like a tail.

Under the light of a torch, a group of masked young Malay men lifted up a shining sword, and repeatedly shouted, "*Orang Cina*, Marxist-Leninist *Cina*! c/o * ✳ ♀ ♂ !"

Two Malay men with ugly faces were staring fiercely at each other. They looked as though they had been doing so for so long that their eyes were all red and swollen. Each man was holding a shiny metal sword that was curved like a snake. Their feet were soaking wet, though it was not clear whether this was from sweat or from urine. Quite a few people were standing around them, from a safe distance.

Suddenly, the two men rushed toward each other, each of them slicing at the other with his curved sword. Then they both stopped and returned to their original positions. Like cocks in a cockfight, they tilted their heads to the side and looked around.

*After a while, they both rushed forward again, as though they had each seen some money they could grab. Once again, they both swung their swords wildly. Suddenly, there was a sharp cry, and it turned out that one of the men had somehow managed to slice open his own abdomen and was howling in pain. Just before he fell silent, he bellowed, "Devil (*hantu-ah*)!," whereupon the other man quickly looked around in all directions. Suddenly, everyone gathered around them erupted in delight, then rushed forward and lifted him up, shouting* "Jiwa, jiwa!"

Tie Niu woke up in a *tua pekong* temple under a tall and sturdy jackfruit tree. He was awakened by a loud sound of drumming and fireworks. The ox was startled and yanked at the tree to which it was tied, knocking down one jackfruit after another. Tie Niu couldn't remember when precisely he had arrived. The town was full of people, and all of the young people, both men and women, were hollering and running in the streets. People kept lighting firecrackers, as though it were New Year's. They also were performing lion dances, dragon dances, and shouting, "We won!" Some people had loudspeakers, and repeatedly shouted.

As soon as Tie Niu untied the ox's rope, the ox immediately ran away. It ran into the forest, and he had to struggle to coax it to return to the main road.

They passed a road overgrown with wild grass. It was dusk, and everything was very peaceful.

Under the golden sunlight, he reached a place unlike any he had ever seen before. There were no trees, the road was very wide, and the strange thing was that there were no cars. There were people lying everywhere, without moving. They were lying in bright red pools, and their bodies were also dyed red. There was smoke coming from some of the houses, and periodically someone would dash from one side of the street to the other, pursued by a man whose face was wrapped in cloth and who was holding a sword in his right hand. Both of them would be shouting strange things or emitting a long scream. Someone was pounding on the door or knocking on the window, and somewhere a woman and her children were crying. Disheveled people were all pursuing one another.

The cars by the side of the road had all been crushed. The windows had all been shattered, and the ground was covered in broken glass. As the ox slowly walked forward, it made a lot of noise stepping on the glass. There was one matchbox-like building after another, entire rows of them, and they were all adorned with national flags and other flags with an ox head and a scale. The police, red-capped soldiers, and a large crowd of people all rushed out. There was the sound of fireworks, whereupon several people cried out and fell to the ground. The soldiers faced the people running in the streets, and regardless of whether the people were running in the front or the back of the crowd, they were all seized together. However, it seemed as though no one was interested in Tie Niu and his ox.

The strong man also appeared to be mingling with the others. He didn't seem to know what to do, but was nevertheless telling everyone that he really was extremely strong. He lifted up a stone larger than himself and walked back and forth through the crowd. Every now and then he would put it down, look around, but seem to decide he had placed it in the wrong spot, so he would lift it up again and continue wandering around.

The ox didn't stop walking, and appeared to have gotten accustomed to the sound of the fireworks.

They slowly proceeded through a marketplace. There were even more red-capped soldiers, and even more people lying on the ground, piled awkwardly one atop another, resembling an overturned statue of a crowd of people. The blood was even redder and brighter than the setting sun.

He had no idea that just as he was passing through, an electrical shutter had blinked in the distance, capturing him, his ox, and the blood-red sunset in the background. There was the sound of thunder coming from nearby.

Night quickly fell, and the land, which had been parched for so long, was suddenly inundated by a thunderstorm. Tie Niu and his ox suddenly paused—perhaps they wanted to get wet, to wash away the sweat and heat. A strong wind blew loudly, and it was raining startlingly hard. Sheet after sheet of rain pelted down on their heads and blanching the night white. It was as if the entire land was floating away.

The water rose quickly, and soon it reached the ox's knees. The ox waded through the water, which quickly reached the animal's back. As the ox proceeded forward, Tie Niu, who was faint with hunger, was swept off its back.

The rain finally stopped, and Tie Niu had a vague sensation that a strong hand was lifting up him up from where he had been lying. The hand tossed him forward and he smashed up against something. There was a strong stench of blood. Then some more things were piled up, and some of them smashed near him. One of them pinned his lower body, and he struggled to open his eyes but simply wasn't able to. Then he heard the loud sound of a truck ignition turning on. He wanted to call out to his ox, but found that he couldn't utter a sound.

When the truck proceeded forward, he fell back asleep and dreamed that the strong man was carrying his ox and was walking over from a considerable distance.

After a while—he had no idea how long—he woke up again. All he could see were the stars shining brightly. There wasn't a trace of a cloud in the sky. Two towering columns supported a pair of gray wings, on which he could dimly make out the character (唐) *Tang*, as in Tangshan. He noticed that the location where he was lying was shaking, and he could hear the sound of water gushing past. He struggled to extricate himself from the various objects that were lying on his body, and eventually managed to crawl out from under them. It was only then that he discovered, with a shock, that he was already on an enormous boat—a boat so huge that he couldn't even see the front or rear. Under the starlight, he could dimly discern that the deck was covered with motionless bodies haphazardly piled on one another.

Was this the boat, he asked himself. And what about my ox? Both the sea and the sky appeared boundless and indistinct. He crawled over the corpses, trying to make his way out of this pile of bodies. But even after crawling for what seemed like forever, and even after he reached the boat's bow, he still couldn't avoid touching the other bodies lying around him. Then he saw the boat's helmsman, who looked extremely thin and appeared uncannily familiar, and he suddenly heard his own voice ask, "Is this the boat to China?" The other person turned around, and Tie Niu saw that his head was full of spikes, like a durian. All of a sudden, Tie Niu passed out.

As the truck was carrying him away, all he could hear was the sound of crows squawking. There was also a bone-piercingly cold wind. Later, when he reached the mouth of a river, there was a ceaseless sound of crows. When he opened his eyes, he saw that the sky was brilliant gold and red. It was dusk, and the trees were covered with black crows flying about. He got up, and slowly made his way toward the river. On the water's surface, there were countless pouch-like objects floating, and the crows were repeatedly landing and taking off from them. The cold wind had a thick fishy smell, and it turned out that the ocean was not far ahead.

By the time he reached the harbor, the wind had grown stronger and colder. By this point the sky was also darker, although the crows continued to circle overhead as before. Suddenly, he saw it. Or, perhaps it would be more accurate to say that he *felt* he saw it. Although the boat appeared to have been submerged for a long time, it was nevertheless still possible to discern its enormity, which made the entire harbor resemble a graveyard. The boat was wedged in the harbor and was leaning to one side, its masts either tilted or broken, reaching up into the sky like a skeleton hand. The sails were faded to the point that it was impossible to determine what their original colors had been. On some of the patches of fabric it was still possible to make out vestigial traces of Chinese characters, as the fabric swayed back and forth in the wind. As the wind blew the boat's skeletal remains, it produced an enormous roar. The top of the boat was covered with a dense row of crows, which resembled black dots, producing a sense of endless sorrow. He felt as though everything were spinning, as his head throbbed in pain. It was as if that mass of buried people had suddenly sliced off his head and carried it away.

A Malay man driving his truck back to his hometown took Tie Niu—who felt as though his head had already been separated from his body—home with him. The man's home was in an isolated village with a lot of large Malays. Afterwards, Tie Niu settled down there, adopted by a poor and elderly Malay couple. The couple, who were childless, viewed his arrival as a gift from Allah. One afternoon, he, expressionless, was taken to be circumcised and converted to Islam. He was also given a new name: Abdullah.

Of course, he had no way of knowing that several months after he was given his new name, his ox finally made its way, alone, back to the location from which they had originally set out. There, the leaves from the rubber trees had already fallen, but there was no one there waiting to greet the ox. The ox also had no way of knowing that Iron Tooth's widow was no longer home, she having left long ago to go search for her son. All the villagers, however, were convinced that Tie Niu had already become reduced to a pile of tiger droppings.

Not long after that, a news article began circulating through countless Chinese villages in the region: At the top of the article there was a color photograph with a crimson background and piles of corpses and indistinct statues of martyrs, while in the foreground there was an ox with a small child riding on its back. The child had just turned his head, and the setting sun was casting its golden rays on his face. Circling around over his head there were several crows or pigeons, casting their indistinct shadows on the ground. In the midst of all this, there were signs that appeared to have traces of actual blood, and which read: *The May 13th Riots*.

The elderly couple lived next to the river. They had an old sampan and a tilting stilt house, and made a living from fishing and going into the mountains to collect wild plants that they would then sell to the villagers. Not long after Tie Niu joined them, he received a small government-issued mottled ox and several chicks that were constantly clucking. But after changing his name to Abdullah, he proceeded to live here in the shadows, receiving some food or financial assistance from kind villagers. When he was clear-headed, he would sometimes go down to the river to fish, but nearly every evening he would appear at that same harbor with the crows circling overhead, staring at the sunken boat with his head tilted to the side, sometimes even drooling. In general, however, he was virtually silent.

The boat, which had been stuck in mud for who knows how long, appeared enormous—almost half as big as an entire village. Apart from the mast, the only part of the boat that emerged from the water was a portion of the stern—but even that was as large as a small settlement. No one from the village was willing to go to the boat to fish, and children never swam nearby. As a result, the area around it was always very quiet, as though ever since ancient times the location had been viewed as inauspicious.

One day, he suddenly saw a white tiger lying on the stern of the boat. Or it would be sniffing around, as though looking for something, but then would emit a dry roar. It was so large that whenever it made the slightest movement the entire boat seemed to rock back and forth. Whenever it was there, the crows all kept a safe distance, and therefore whenever the villagers saw the crows retreat to the red tree marshland on the other side of the river, they would tell each other, "The king has returned to watch his boat," or, "The Chinese general has returned." As a result, from dawn until dusk, someone would always secretly watch the tiger, as though it were a friend who was solitary and difficult to entertain. They said that the tiger had returned almost every year for the past hundred years. It would always stay on the boat for several days, as docile as a cat, and would never venture into the village and threaten people or livestock. Some said that the tiger looked like it was getting older and older, and its coat appeared to be getting whiter and whiter. Some even claimed that originally it was not white but rather bright orange, but as it aged its coat became increasingly pale. If it got any older, even its black stripes were likely to fade away, in which case it really would become a big white cat. They said that, previously, the guard had been a great white whale.

However, no one mentioned when this boat first appeared there. It was as if it had always belonged to this abandoned harbor.

One day, the tiger disappeared again, and the crows once again returned to keep watch over the abandoned boat.

One day after he had already grown up, a cloud of dust heralded the arrival of many trucks driving over from the city, bringing cranes and many complicated and strange machines. They spent many days pulling and digging and lifting, until they finally succeeded in dismantling the ancient boat and bringing it to shore. The trucks then had to make several dozen trips before they were able to cart it away. It was said that they planned to transport the boat to a museum in the old city. Tie Niu, meanwhile, followed the last truck out, finally leaving the village where he had lived for so many years. The government tried to recruit many people in the village who were in a similar situation to help excavate artifacts for the museum, but virtually all of the villagers declined. He, however, acted as if he had been suddenly awakened and actively participated in the excavation efforts, and before departing he took all of the money he had earned and left it with the foster parents who had taken him in.

It turned out that the government had decided to clean up this once-glorious harbor in order to build a modern pier, so that the backward villages in the area might thereby be able to enjoy the pace of modern life. However, throughout the entire process, the villagers could not help but feel grief-stricken, and during that particular period they seemed to become even more depressed than usual. Finally, an old man muttered, "This means that the king won't return next year." When the tiger had showed up the previous year, its coat was already as white as snow, and even the mark on its forehead, symbolizing prestige, had faded. Now all that remained were a few black dots over its tail. Afterwards, someone saw a pair of cats, one white and the other black, that had somehow crossed the water to go play on the boat. They appeared rather large to be cats, but were nevertheless obviously still cats. Some women pointed to them playing and catching mice on the ship, and remarked that they looked as comfortable as angels.

When his former coworker, a Chinese foreman, dropped Tie Niu off at another harbor, he lovingly sent him a long, sharp copper nail that was said to have come from that ancient boat, but which didn't look like it belonged to a boat as much as it looked as though "it had been pulled out of a coffin." He held the nail in his hand, and estimated that it must have weighed about three pounds.

One day many years later, when he was drifting aimlessly from one island to another, he found himself on a small island, and was so thirsty that he started devouring some rambutans, but he started to choke and suddenly passed out, falling into a patch of weeds. When he woke up after an indeterminate amount of time, his consciousness abruptly returned to that evening many years earlier, as if the intervening years had suddenly evaporated. He felt he was surrounded by dense fog and didn't know where he was, or even who he was.

He struggled to open his eyes, and amidst the sound of water he heard someone say in Min Nan dialect, "He's finally woken up." There were three short middle-aged Chinese men and another thin, dark-skinned man who was wearing a brightly-colored *baju melayu*, had a thin mustache between his mouth and nose, large eyes, and looked Indian. When he exhaled, his mouth resembled a duck's, and he appeared as though he didn't want to interact with anyone. One of the Chinese introduced him, saying, "This is our chief, the famous Munshi Abdullah. We just traveled through Kelantan, and are now heading back to Singapore."

supplement

. . . I am but a fetishist of corpses.

YU DAFU, "SINKING"

IN THE SEVERAL MONTHS BEFORE WE SET OUT, the television and newspapers would periodically post reports on local anti-Chinese policies. While we found these developments somewhat worrisome, we ultimately did not put much stock in them, given that the region in question was far away—so far away, in fact, that it felt as though it were even more distant than the United States. And, furthermore, even had we been inclined to worry about this, it was already too late to do any good, given that now it appeared everything was already right before us.

This was the second day we were stuck in our hotel room. This was a small three-star hotel located at the end of an alley that reeked of urine. It was a four-story building, but had only a handful of rooms and was filled with the stench left behind by countless people who had stayed there over the years. Our room was warm and damp, and full of mysterious yellow stains. The hotel manager was a local Chinese—the sort of thin man in his fifties who is often seen in the area. After purchasing several cans of crackers and white rice tea, he sniffed the politically volatile air and decided to close his doors and stop admitting new guests for several days until the storm had passed. He even shut the outer iron gate and proceeded to cower with his family in a small sitting room in the back of the hotel, listening to the radio. His wife looked very worried as she sat in front of the sewing machine staring off into space. He urged us not to go outside if we could possibly avoid it, and said anxiously, "Those cursed hooligans are incapable of recognizing anyone.

"Regardless of whether they perceive you are to be a Chinese or a foreigner, they will still beat you like a dead dog. They couldn't care less whether you are from Taiwan or China."

The day we arrived, things already didn't feel right even as we made our way from the airport to the hotel, and there was a burning odor in the air. In the once-bustling streets, the doors of virtually all of the shops were now tightly shut. Some of the shops bore obvious traces of having been burned, while others had had their windows shattered. Everything was almost unnervingly animated. The pitch-black pedestrians shouted and white banners with unfamiliar phrases written in blood-red letters flapped in the wind. The slogans were written in a language we didn't understand, and all that we could make out were a handful of words such as *Suharto*, *Cina*, and *China*. As soon as we got into the taxi, we were immediately asked, "Why have you come here at this time? Are you from Taiwan? Have you been sent by a television station?" As our dark-skinned Chinese taxi driver translated for us, we learned that the white banners were adorned with slogans such as "Hang Suharto," "Chinese should go back to China," "Suharto must step down," and "Expel the Chinese." Initially, Xiao Lin exclaimed happily, "The Chinese here are able to speak Taiwanese!" Upon hearing these translations, however, he immediately became as white as a sheet and muttered, "How is it that the situation here is so different from what we read about in the newspapers back home? Didn't they say everything was very calm here?" The driver sighed and replied, "The rich all fled long ago, going to Singapore, Malaysia, Australia, Hong Kong, the United States . . . or anywhere, really. Over the past few days, it is not only the local Chinese who have left but also the Japanese and the red-haired foreigners. The only people still arriving are Taiwanese like yourselves." Xiao Chen was fairly quiet, as he brought out his V8 lens and began taking some pictures. I urged him to remember that this was not our assignment, and that we hadn't brought many blank tapes. The driver sighed again, and said, "If it weren't for the fact that business has been bad, I myself wouldn't even have come out today to try to earn some money."

"Our money has all been taken by the Italians. The Indonesian rupiah is on the verge of becoming as worthless as these banana notes from the period of Japanese occupation."

The Indonesian rupiah had already fallen into a tailspin. We exchanged U.S. dollars on the black market for two large bags of rupiah notes. In so doing, however, we ran the risk that the money would become further devalued to the point of being worth less than the paper it was printed on, but we didn't dare carry our dollars around for fear of making ourselves a target of attack.

Following the address we had been given, we found the specified three-star hotel. The people at the reception desk told us that Takatsu had gone out early that morning, but given that he hadn't taken his things with him they assumed he should be back by nighttime. We decided to get a room, but had no idea why Takatsu had picked such a mediocre hotel. After a couple of days he still hadn't shown up, or even called. The hotel manager was worried that he might have been mistaken for a local Chinese and killed, but when we asked to see what he had in his room, the manager declined, explaining, "We have our rules here."

We tried to contact the local trade office, but no one answered.

We then called Taipei for advice, telling them the dangerous state in which we found ourselves, but Director Lei replied calmly, "Given that you are already there, why don't you simply wait a while and see what happens? It would look bad if you were to come back empty-handed."

We had come for a "supplement."

We were working on a set of biopics of Chinese authors, of which the first series, titled "From the May Fourth to the Nineteen Thirties," had already been completed and released. Sales had not been great, but they also hadn't been too bad. At any rate, the films were intended for instructional use, and despite the fact that at the time native consciousness in Taiwan was surging, there was nevertheless still a basic level of market interest in authors from Mainland China. It was unfortunate that it was not possible to find professional commentaries on the series, and the only review so far was one that questioned, from a cinematic perspective, why the producers had chosen to use this sort of documentary format to try to capture the lives of the authors, and asked whether, from a technical perspective, it should therefore be considered a failure: "*With this series of biopics of Chinese authors, if you just use an approach grounded on a theory of reflection, are you not thereby limiting yourself to these sorts of surface characteristics of the authors' lives? But wouldn't a more artistic approach permit the authors' lives to be revealed more accurately, thereby making it possible to more closely approximate the biographical form itself?*" These were nevertheless merely lofty sentiments, and were difficult to realize in practice. With respect to the biopic on Yu Dafu, titled *The Sigh of a Cipher*, a critic had written that, "The section on his period of exile and subsequent disappearance appears to be too cursory." Given that even experts cannot confirm the location of Yu Dafu's grave, however, what were amateurs like us supposed to do? In the same series, there were a number of intractable technical blind spots that were hard to overcome, but these cannot be understood by people outside the industry.

One evening the preceding month, the director suddenly received a long distance call from Takatsu Suzuki, who identified himself as a Yu Dafu expert (it was unclear where he was calling from). In a hesitant and halting Japanese-accented Chinese, Takatsu offered a few polite words, "Mr. Lei? I saw your *The Sigh of a Cipher*, which I admired very much." Then the director heard some surprising news. "With respect to Yu Dufu's fi·nal disappearance, I have news of an astonishing dis·covery. I can't explain this over the phone, and instead I need you to come visit me in per·son. Please bring your video equipment with you, and I gua·rantee you won't be disappointed. At the very least, you will be able to add an exciting new conclusion to *Sigh of a Ci·pher*. I can serve as your guide." He left a contact number, together with the address and room number of his hotel in Jakarta, then specified, "Things are very chaotic at the moment, but I'll de·finitely be here for another week and you can find me after seven each eve·ning. After that, it's hard to say where I'll be."

After receiving this telephone call, the chief editor contacted several key members of the production group to discuss the matter. First, in order to justify a group of us traveling so far, they had to confirm that this report was in fact credible. The more troublesome thing was that by this point they had already begun filming the second round of biopics for the series—of which one film had already been completed and edited, two others were in postproduction, and a fourth was ready to be filmed—and therefore it would not be easy for them to get away. We communicated several times over the phone, and although Takatsu repeatedly reassured them regarding his new information, he was nevertheless very reluctant to reveal any details at that time. As a result, we were left in a state of considerable frustration. Many of our colleagues suspected that this Takatsu fellow might be a fraud, and they therefore wanted to contact some Japanese Sinologists they knew to see if they could confirm his claims. From several scholars who had previously studied in Japan and were now based at different universities, they obtained the same information (though, of course, there were also many people who simply answered "I don't know"), and confirmed not only that this person existed but also that, of the post–Suzuki Masao generation, he was one who had invested the most in studying Yu Dafu, diligently doing fieldwork and investigating lacuna in previous studies.

Our production team decided unanimously that this was worth looking into, and if it turned out to be truly of value then we quite likely could—and even *should*—add a "supplement" to our original Yu Dafu biopic. In practical terms, however, the funds for the first series had already been exhausted, and therefore we might have to use some of the funds allocated for the second series on local authors. What was even more troublesome was that at this point the production team was unlikely to assign much manpower to work on this, because otherwise other ongoing projects might be delayed and the financing of the project might be similarly affected. Given that we had neither the manpower nor the resources to pursue this matter, it was decided after another round of discussions that I should take a small group to investigate. Since I had participated in the planning of the overall project and had contributed directly to *Sigh of a Cipher*, I had a rather deep understanding of the subject and consequently wouldn't have the sorts of limitations that an outsider might have. At the time, I had also followed the production team to Singapore and Indonesia to do fieldwork, and was not unfamiliar with the local conditions and should be able to handle any problems that might come up. I took two new recruits, Xiao Lin and Xiao Chen, who did not join the team until work on the second series on local authors had begun. Lin and Chen had some relevant experience, but were still in training. Their primary advantage, however, was their energy and their curiosity. If they weren't available to continue working on the actual series, accordingly, it wouldn't affect the progress of the project. Finances were tight, and even the plane tickets had to be obtained from China Airlines through unofficial channels. As for equipment, we only took two V8 camcorders, two miniature recorders, one rather good Nikon camera, together with an assortment of accessories.

"At any rate, we are only filming a supplement, so shouldn't we be done in about five days or so?" Whatever Director Lei says, goes.

But what if Takatsu never showed up? What would we do then?

Trapped here, we felt extremely dejected. Apart from the hotel owner and the small group of other guests who still remained, we also chatted with the handful of other Chinese who lived nearby and had snuck into the hotel through the backdoor. I heard them exchange secret information and sigh in frustration. "There is chaos everywhere." I heard this plaintive phrase repeatedly. "Maybe things will turn out as miserably as they did back in the 1930s." An old man sighed, "I've changed my given name, lost my family name, and don't even know how to write Chinese characters anymore. I no longer have any opportunity to read Chinese newspapers or Chinese books. Newspaper offices and guild halls have all been shut down, as have all Chinese schools. You won't even find any Chinese names on tombstones. The authorities, however, are still not satisfied. Is it wrong to earn money just to put food on the table? They say that the Chinese are vampires who take others' money, that they are not industrious, and that they beg for every meal." He looked genuinely exasperated. Virtually everyone mentioned how they heard that overseas Chinese women were being assaulted. "Things are just as they had been under the Japanese devils." "Things are just like they were in the thirties." A white-haired man in his seventies exclaimed, "I've already prepared some sticks, and if they come for me, I'll fight them to the death!" "Burnings and riots, beatings and rapes. These are horrible times, and on top of that there are those uprisings. Truly. . . ."

We crouched down in the terrace peering out in all directions, but all we could see were dark-skinned youths hauling bag after bag of merchandise out of shops with shattered windows, as though no one were around. They were smiling broadly, like guests enjoying a banquet. They were most interested in targeting those shops stocked with merchandise that could be easily carried away. There was dark smoke in the distance, and fires were burning all around us. Agitators repeatedly tossed Molotov cocktails, several of which nearly hit the building where we were staying. The streets were full of youth with bad intentions roaming around, frequently kicking down doors and rushing in. Terrified, we huddled inside our hotel.

Xiao Chen shot several rolls of blank tape. Even though I warned him that the tape could be of use and repeatedly urged him to stop, he refused to put away his camera. Instead, he switched equipment and began shooting stills. His explanation was not without merit: "I can take these back with me and sell them to a magazine, where they will almost certainly fetch a very high price." I still warned him that he should economize. Xiao Lin said that mobs beat up people based on their own assessment of who they were, but that normally they wouldn't bother people from Taiwan. Knowing that visitors from Taiwan brought money to the region, the locals didn't despise them the way they did the local Chinese. Therefore, the hotel owner borrowed some red paint and cardboard, and helped us write *Taiwan* or *Taiwanese* on the backs of our shirts. Tired of simply sitting around and doing nothing, he also recommended to the Chinese locals who entered the hotel, "Avoid trouble, and everyone speak Taiwanese and help each other."

The following night, a short man appeared at the back door. He was wearing a white shirt with the word *Japanese* written in uneven red letters. The hotel owner said, "This is Takatsu." When the hotel owner photographed his face, Takatsu appeared very discomfited. He kept wiping sweat from his face and apologized, while exclaiming, "Danger! Danger!" He shook his head and said that he had risked his life running around, but in the end had been unable to rent a boat: "No one will to go out to sea at this time, which is truly trou·blesome. Fortunately, I even·tually found someone to rent to me." By this point, his entire body was soaked in sweat. He added, "Come with me. There is something in·teresting to see. We'll discuss everything else later."

Following Takatsu and his shirt with the word *Japanese* in blood-red letters on the back, we proceeded up three flights of stairs. He unlocked a door, turned on the light, then pulled a heavy suitcase out from under the bed. He entered his combination, whereupon the lid sprang open. Inside, there were bundles upon bundles of grass-green bills in astonishingly large denominations, including 1,000, 5,000, and even 1,000,000 notes. These denominations were so large they didn't even resemble bills, but rather lottery tickets or ghost money to be burned at funerals. "Do you know what this is?" He picked up a bundle and handed it to me. Xiao Lin responded, "They aren't counterfeit, are they?" Takatsu replied happily, "You could say that they are, but you could also say that they aren't." "Look carefully at the image on the bills." It was a bunch of bananas. "Look more care·fully. What is on the front?" I leaned in to look, and discovered with surprise that it was a dense mesh of ant-like writing. It resembled Chinese running script, but at the same time looked very odd. "It's Japanese," Xiao Lin exclaimed in surprise. "That's right, it's Japanese," Takatsu replied even more happily. "Could it possibly be . . ." I opened my mouth, as a thought suddenly popped into my head. "That's right," Takatsu immediately replied. "I've already investigated. It is as you guessed, it is the 'Dream Fantasia' mentioned in his bio·graphy." He lifted his head high. Was it for this that he had summoned us to come all the way here? So that he could display his satisfaction in the middle of a war zone?

Within a couple of minutes Xiao Lin and Xiao Cheng had set up the equipment, and were ready to begin taping.

"How did you obtain these?" I asked in surprise.

"I should start from the be·ginning. These are from the World War II period, when Japanese troops controlled Southeast Asia. The bills issued locally were not backed by gold. To put it simply, they were almost completely worth·less and furthermore were poorly printed, but they were nevertheless used by locals as tokens of exchange with their own exchange value. The locals called these *banana notes*. Since no·thing could be traded after Japan's defeat, the vast majority of the locals treated these bills as mere scrap paper and burned them. As a result, not very many sur·vived." The camera focused on him, as a dim light shone down.

"I have a relative who trades in old bank·notes, and I've long been interested in ones from Asia. Once, I happened to notice that there was some wri·ting on a couple of his old banana notes." As Takatsu was saying this, he took out his notebook, in which there was a million-yen bill, on which there were in fact several uneven lines of writing. He read aloud his translation. "Where should I start?"

"I study Yu Dafu, and am therefore very fa·miliar with his handwriting. Moreover, I also sent a sample to a crime lab at Tokyo Univer·sity, and they found that it had an eighty percent match with Yu Dafu's own handwriting."

"This discovery is simply too impor·tant." Takatsu could not conceal his delight. "Upon tracing the origin of the banknotes, we discovered that they ori·ginated from Indonesia. We requested some documents from merchants who import old banknotes, and I immediately came here. We've had a very signi·ficant result." He vigorously patted the suitcase. "I bustled around and visited more than twenty collector's shops around the country, and vir·tually every single one of them had some of these banknotes. Given that the notes all had writing on them and furthermore the print quality was very poor, they were therefore deemed to be of little value. Most people had simply depo·sited them in a warehouse, though some were supersti·tious and proceeded to burn them. It should still be po·ssible to find a few more." He kept shaking his head regretfully. "For us in Japan, these are all inva·luable cultural resources."

He continued, "I looked through them and found that although they are not complete, these banknotes ne·vertheless contain text for at least four novels. I inve·stigated this for a long time, and finally got to the bottom of it. Tomo·rrow morning I will go look into it."

Outside, the sound of fighting continued. There was the whistling of bullets, low shouts, and an occasional scream.

I asked him what he was going to do with all these banknotes, and he said that he had originally planned to send them to the Japanese embassy and have one of the embassy officials take them out of the country. Ordinary citizens would probably not be able to get out with such a large suitcase full of banknotes (even though they were all now expired), which furthermore all had writing on them. Customs officials would not necessarily be able to differentiate between Japanese and Chinese script, and consequently they could very well create difficulties for the travelers. But given that the current situation is so chaotic and the embassy is so far away, one would almost certainly run into trouble trying to travel with such a large quantity of banknotes. Under the circumstances, being able to reach the embassy might well end up the least of one's worries, given that there is the very real possibility that one could even get killed on the way. He therefore requested that we help provide cover for him afterwards.

Over the course of the night, Takatsu generously permitted us to look through and photograph some of the sections he had already translated. I notified Taipei of our discovery, and they said, "Go ahead and look into this, and record anything useful. In any event, everything is already passed." They also added, "Don't worry—we've already taken out a large insurance policy on you."

Where should I begin?

Facing the same sort of lake water day after day, my path is endless, and even though there may be a slight variation in the seasons, ultimately there is not that much difference between them. I don't know how long I've been imprisoned on this island, but based on the changes in the seasons and the constellations, it is entirely possible that I have been here for less than a decade. I feel, however, as though it has been an eternity, probably because my routine has been so monotonous.

This is an island full of the fragrance of wild grass.

Representatives from the mountains and from the peninsula did everything they could to help me with everyday tasks. I traded with the islanders for some chicks and ducklings, and began raising them in this virtually uninhabited land.

Neither of the two men was over thirty, and they could be considered as belonging to the next generation. I repeatedly pleaded with them to ask their supervisors why they needed to keep a superfluous person like myself imprisoned on this isolated and desolate island, given that the war was already over? Their response, however, was firm, as they reaffirmed their earlier position: The original orders handed down by the Ministry of Information were that I be secretly executed and buried in some remote location like a dog. In fact, I would have already been killed and buried, had it not been for the fact that a high official at the time loved literature and was supportive of literary talent, and therefore suggested that I be "imprisoned on a remote island, and allowed to continue writing." Once, after having a drink (a fruit drink that we brewed ourselves), one of the mountain leaders revealed that all of the people who had originally been involved in the case had already passed away, and consequently the original command had become but a "vestigial order." They now had no alternative but to carry it out, and there is no option of annulling or revising it.

That is to say, I will grow old here, and eventually I will be buried here.

Apart from preemptively storing up a significant quantity of food (including rice and canned goods), there was also a large amount of cut-up paper, printing ink, ink sticks, writing brushes, and a hand-cranked printer. When they didn't have anything better to do, apart from coming to give medical attention to the people on the island (the local shamans were at a loss as to how to treat some of the more difficult diseases), the leader from the peninsula liked to bind those blank sheets of paper into various volumes, and they particularly liked to use butterfly binding and whirlwind binding. He would often say, "As soon as you finish writing, I'll help you bind it. I'll bind it in whatever manner you wish." He would say this very sincerely, adding, "You should write something, in order to give me the opportunity to publish something meaningful."

"First you lock me up and then expect me to write? My ability to write has long since been destroyed. Furthermore, I have aged to the point that I can no longer feel romantic."

"Mr. Sato said, if you experience adversity, this may offer you some inspiration, thereby helping you find the 'symbol' you are seeking."

Many spices were grown on the island, including lilac, cassia, nutmeg, and black pepper. Some of the cassia trees were more than a hundred years old. Every couple of weeks a ship would arrive to collect the spices and deliver some staples such as tea, rice, oil, and salt. Two "hired hands" looked very nervous, and wouldn't allow me to approach the ship, but one of them was responsible for taking me to the mouth of the river to fish for devil rays.

In this area, there was an extremely large number of devil rays, though the local aborigines regarded them as taboo (this is because devil rays have tails, and it is said that the locals don't eat anything that is "covered"). This kind of fish cannot be used for sashimi, but it can be dipped in curry, wrapped in banana leafs, then baked and eaten. The result is very fragrant, and we usually eat the entire thing, including skin and bones. My two bodyguards also came to love this island's cuisine (here, there is a crooked line of commentary: "it is truly delicious.").

I was feeling bored and depressed. Apart from fishing for devil rays, diving, digging for clams, and catching crabs, on rainy days I particularly liked to use that hand-cranked printer and, as though I were pressing sugar cane, would print a number of banana bills of different denominations and distribute them to the island's naked children in exchange for some wild fruits, stones, seashells, or tree leaves. I also taught the children to use these civilized objects to make paper boats, airplanes, frogs, and so forth, and some people quickly learned how to make origami cranes.

Finally, one day they convinced me to accept the job of watching over the lighthouse each night and lighting the lamp every evening. This was an extremely important task, and I could have fun being a "great helmsman." I would spend each night alone. I could see further than before, and in the distance could discern fishing boats and ferries. Against the dark sea, there are countless points of light, like a myriad of stars in the sky. This was conducive to quiet reflection.

The condition for being given this position was that I had to write something, for better or worse, in order to make them feel better, so that at least there would be an "accomplishment."

There is no direction, there is no shape, and it is not clear where the endpoint is.

I never did discover where they hid their guns.

I miss my family like crazy. They must assume I'm already dead?

As in the past, just before nightfall I climbed up the lighthouse to add oil to the lamp. Each time, it was the same scene and the same sentiment, and I experienced the same lack of inspiration. I had already done everything I could. I continued copying out more than a hundred Tang poems. Using the brush, ink, and paper I had made myself, I copied the poems. I planned to copy more than two thousand old and recent poems, more than three hundred old and recent essays, together with countless pre-Qin works. Over the years, I copied the original text of Goethe's Faust, Milton's Paradise Lost, Dante's Divine Comedy, and the Old Testament, among other works. In this way, I managed to bring a modicum of civilization to this desolate island. However, my two bodyguards did not appear very satisfied, and whenever they saw me happily working away they would grumble, "This is not literary creation. In fact, it's not even as good as translation. Whenever you have a chance to go abroad, you can purchase all of these texts in a single trip, so what is the use of wasting your time like this?"

That beautiful girl who was bursting with curiosity came up to the lighthouse to find me. Is this not true happiness?

As the rainy season approached, the situation was not ideal. My circumstances seemed to have been discovered. This was frustrating. The indigenous peoples were all Muslim, which was a considerable inconvenience. But, no matter what, I had to endure it.

I was locked up for ten days. If the islanders who held power had not shown up, I fear I would have ended up losing more than that piece of foreskin. I had never expected that, even at my advanced age, I could still manage to get that girl pregnant. It was likely some lover—perhaps her cousin—who was responsible. I suspected that those two Japanese also had something to do with it. Who told me to be unable to resist temptation? It is also no wonder that all of the women on this island are excellent specimens, plump and voluptuous, with the young ones being particularly passionate.

In order to avoid being castrated and killed by the men on the island, I had no choice but to marry the girl. I paid a betrothal gift of two oxen and three sheep, which I charged to Mr. Sato, and before the wedding I had to be circumcised. At that point I was already more than fifty years old. . . .

One morning, when the populace and the police were all still asleep, as the sound of chanted prayers was coming from the mosque, we boarded a taxi that had been recommended by the owner of the hotel. Avoiding major roads, we sought out small back roads, and also made a point of skirting the cemeteries of the Dutch, Indonesians, Chinese, and Japanese. "Areas where people are buried are not safe," our driver said. In this way, we quickly reached the desolate outskirts of the city. "Aren't we going to Payakumbuh?" I asked Takatsu. That was where Yu Dafu had disappeared. He shook his head. "We're pro·ceeding even further. Several stores that buy and sell old banknotes all provided the same information, saying that it should be on an island." After a while, the car turned into a fruit orchard. Up ahead there was a white, three-story Western-style house, and we stopped in front of the thick wall around the building's perimeter. It turned out that this island had been bought by an over-the-hill and corrupt Taiwanese legislator who was pursuing the Southern Expansion Policy a bit too enthusiastically and wanted to develop the island into a tourist site. There were private armed security guards patrolling the perimeter, and whoever wanted to enter had to seek his permission. But given they were from the same province and furthermore both worked in media, this naturally wouldn't be a problem. But there was still an important condition—which was that we couldn't spend the night on the island.

"Those old banknotes are ones that he re·moved from the island, as though they were mere scrap paper." In the car, Takatsu added, "He assumed it was paper that one would burn for the dead. What do you call that?"

"Ghost money."

"I heard that some people came onto the island without permi·ssion, and were shot and killed? These sorts of spices are extremely valuable, and therefore the island is usually not open to outsiders."

At dawn, he said, "We will need to go see someone. And in a while I'll need your help with something." Takatsu gestured for us to get out of the car, and said, "You are all from the same re·gion, so it is easier for you to speak to each other."

We encountered an iron door that could stop a tank. Takatsu rang the doorbell, and they immediately heard someone's heavy footsteps and someone's depressed sobs. Lights inside and outside suddenly came on, including ones along the wall, over the pond, on the rockery, on the stones, on the trees, and in the car. On the second floor terrace, many people suddenly turned around to look, trying to avoid being seen. We shouted out the message that Takatsu had helped us prepare, "Mr. Zeng, we are your compatriots from Taiwan." The person watching us took out his binoculars, while holding a black rifle in his other hand and looking around in all directions. We proceeded to an illuminated area so that he could see us clearly, lifting our hands to show that we were unarmed.

Eventually someone came down and opened the side door for us. He was wearing a green camouflage shirt and had a protruding belly. So, *this* was him. We all recognized him as one of the representatives from the previous session of the legislature. He was darker than he had been before, and while in the legislature he had been better known for his fisticuffs than for his actual debating skills. He was very much admired by his brothers, but then retreated into anonymity under the Southern Expansion Policy. Gripping a rifle, he peered out and said, "Come in." He vigorously waved us in, then asked to see our Taiwan ID and passport, both of which he inspected carefully. He said, "Sorry, sorry, so, we are both from the same region, and are friends who work on cultural matters. Ha ha, things are really too chaotic here. Even Liem Sioe Liong cannot keep things under control. If you are not careful, you'll die a horrible death. Please come in and sit down."

There was a black helicopter on the grass in front of the building, and it also had the word *Taiwan* printed on it in large letters. We politely declined his invitation, then explained why we had come. "Don't film me!" He suddenly lifted his rifle and shouted at Xiao Chen, who was so startled that he almost dropped his V8 camera. "*Sorry, sorry.* I'm too touchy. I apologize, but you really can't film here." He vigorously patted Xiao Chen's shoulder, using a gesture he had perfected while out canvassing for votes.

"That is only a small island for growing spices, which I purchased not long ago. I can call up the *Jaga* ("the guard") and explain the situation, and everything will be *OK*. However, there is no way to use the helicopter to take you there. This is . . ."

"We've rented a boat."

Takatsu let out a sigh of relief.

"However, and I apologize for this, but you definitely cannot spend the night there. It would not be convenient. I'm sure you understand."

In the period just before daybreak, the fishing boat belonging to the old Indonesian man floated for a long time in the open sea. Takatsu was very animated, and he rambled on and on. I think he was very excited by the thought that he would soon be promoted to associate professor.

The filming of our supplement continued.

The ocean was covered in fog, reminding us of the Singaporean television series, *The Awakening*. The South Seas region was traditionally regarded by Chinese as a malaria area.

By the time we arrived it was already late in the day. The boat ride had taken us four or five hours. Fortunately, it got dark late here, and we still had several hours of daylight left. The old fisherman told us that this island was called *Tongkak* (meaning "crutches") because it was long and narrow with a hook at one end, like a crutch. For ages, it had been used to grow spices, including clove, cinnamon, nutmeg, and black pepper, and it was also a nesting ground for countless species of wild birds. Two Chinese men with hunting rifles, who looked like public officials, were standing on the wharf carefully inspecting us, but after we explained why we were there, they let us pass. Many children ran over from the shell-covered beach, or otherwise continued playing in the crystal clear water with beautiful women wearing tight skirts. Although the distant fog made this island lose some of its brilliant coloration and the air was filled with the smell of smoke, it nevertheless gave the region a misty quality.

Takatsu quickly found a white-haired old man on crutches who was said to be the owner of the island, and who immediately proceeded to spurt out a string of Japanese phrases. Takatsu nodded to us, then followed the old man over to a weed-covered area. They walked around a fairly tall hill, behind which there was another forest. Takatsu said, "These are all cassia trees." In the shadows cast by the trees, there was a densely packed array of bamboo-shaped sticks stuck in the ground. The old man gestured with his crutch at a faded stick in the middle and said something, which Takatsu translated: "Mr. Ibrahim was bu·ried here, and according to Muslim custom, his head is o·riented toward Mecca."

After converting to Islam, he had been given the name Ibrahim. He was known for his erudition, and therefore many of the islanders called him *Rasul* (meaning "seer").

The sunlight shone down through the forest, and because it was misty it appeared dusky. The forest was bare except for the smell of burning, the scent of cassia, and an array of wooden boards. None of the boards had names written on them, and instead they only had a code: *C15001*. When you approached, you could distinctly smell the scent of cinnamon. "He died at the age of eighty," Takatsu translated. "It has been more than twen·ty years since he passed away."

"This is the tombstone of a mountain leader." The old man gestured at another wooden board. "He eventually converted to Islam, and ten years ago he finally went to meet Allah."

"Then you are . . ."

"I am from the peninsula. I also converted to Islam, and my name is now Abdullah." Upon saying this, he turned around and walked away.

Takatsu first translated this into fluent Japanese, then repeated it again in stuttering Chinese, looking as though he were speaking to himself.

He slowly led us to the thatched hut where Yu Dafu had lived when he was here. It was truly a hut—only about eighty square yards. Only the columns were rather unusual, being made from trunks of cassia trees, and from them there hung a sign with the words *Thatched Hut of Trials and Hardships* in faded Chinese characters. The ground was full of depressions left behind by footsteps long ago. Sitting inside the dark room were two women, who were taking turns blowing into the stove. The old man from the peninsula greeted them, and said a few words in Indonesian. The two women laughed in response, revealing gap-toothed smiles, though they were only about sixty years old. In a corner of the room there was a small machine that looked like a rusted sugar cane presser. "That is the banana-bill printing machine he used at the time," Takatsu explained.

"After converting to Islam, Rasul quickly married four wives. The other two are now pro·bably swimming with the fishes. Collectively, they had twenty-four children, eight of whom were born in ra·pid succession in the first few years after Rasul returned to the Kingdom of Hea·ven. After growing up, all of the children went to live in the city, and now they are probably all partici·pating in revolutionary protests to try and topple the dictator."

We leafed through several bark- and leather-bound volumes in a wooden cabinet against the wall. Each page was seeped in the pleasant odor of old tobacco leaves and were written in the scripts of various different languages, including German, French, Dutch, and Indonesian. They are bound together with animal tendons.

"There are another several hundred volumes that Rasul copied from ancient Chinese texts. But after they were burned up during that difficult period, he was heartbroken. After this, he never again wrote in Chinese, nor was he permitted to do so. He never wrote again."

Takatsu led us along the coast up to the lighthouse up on the promontory. We climbed the stairs, step after heavy step, until we finally reached the top of the lighthouse. He had white, wispy hair, and his body was bent with rickets. Leaning his crutch against the wall, he took out a mirrored platter in the middle of which there was a dried-up oil lamp. He carefully lifted the lamp's lid and, with trembling hands, filled it with oil, then struck a match and lit it.

White light immediately poured forth, shining into the mist over the ocean.

"I, like Rasul, like this work very much."

He then led us to an even steeper promontory. As the sky darkened, the remaining rays of sunlight appeared even more intense, at which point we reached the base of the cliff.

"Every day for the past few years, unless it was raining heavily, Rasul would always climb up there."

All alone, he would stare out toward his homeland to the north. The old man said that at one point Rasul told him that he missed his wife back in Fuyang. Particularly during his final few days, he was keenly aware that she was back home missing him day after day and year after year, always waiting for him to push open their door like he used to. "I let Ah Qin down," he said, leaning on his crutch, his white hair waving in the wind and tears streaming down his face.

"When Rasul later returned, it seemed rather strange. One day, after a heavy rain, a new stone statue of a human figure appeared at the top of the promontory."

Under the sun's rays, the statue cast a thin, dark shadow with many curves and edges."

"The islanders subsequently came to call this a gazing woman stone."

Eventually, the stone sank into the evening mist.

(In the mist, the scene begins to fade, whereupon the music at the end of the work begins to sound. . . .)

There was the light of the flashlight being turned on. Then there was the sound of shouting, which was coming from those dark-skinned men carrying guns. They approached, shouting for us to get into the boat, on which there was a bright light. Some islanders generously sent us a few cinnamon-scented baked fowl to take back to our boat.

Takatsu suddenly appeared to think of something, and in a loud voice he asked the old man a question. The man immediately shook his head, whereupon Takatsu opened his eyes wide in confusion. The boat continued forward.

"What's wrong?"

"How could they . . . no, it's simply not po·ssible.

"He says that the island's banana notes are already all . . ."

After returning to the ship, our colleagues from the work unit were so exhausted they immediately fell asleep. Only the heartbroken Takatsu remained awake, softly singing a melancholy Japanese song. Then, amidst the soft lapping of the waves, we suddenly heard the sharp sound of a motor. Everyone abruptly woke up and saw motorboats rapidly approaching from all directions. Everyone appeared shocked, and had no idea what was happening. The old Indonesian man looked even more terrified, as though all of the blood had been drained from his face. His lips trembled as he tried to mumble something unintelligible. We felt that the old man must certainly know what was happening. As Takatsu heard what the man was saying, he became even more distraught. We didn't even have time to think, much less respond to what was happening. By this point we were already surrounded by five speedboats, and the old Indonesian man brought our own boat to a stop. Standing on every boat there was a thin, young man with a familiar face and a dark complexion, wearing a snakeskin vest and holding a heavy gun. One of the young men, who appeared to be the leader, exchanged a few words with the old fisherman, then waved to him. At this point all of the motorboats departed in the same direction, with the fishing boat following behind.

"What's going on?" someone asked.

"They're pirates," Takatsu replied solemnly, in a low voice.

The fog gradually grew denser and denser, to the point that eventually all they could hear was each other's shouts. Apart from the fog itself, they couldn't see anything at all.

A series of dark shadows periodically appeared in front of us, only to recede again. These shadows turned out to be an island. This kind of occurrence became more and more common, indicating that we were entering an unusually dense archipelago. If the motorboats had not been leading the way, we almost certainly would have crashed into one of the barriers between the islands and the reefs.

After a long while, the fishing boat finally pulled up to a rudimentary wharf. By this point it was already the middle of the night. Given that there was fog everywhere, and furthermore it was pitch black outside, we therefore couldn't see a thing. A man holding a rifle indicated that we should leave our film equipment on shore, and shortly afterwards a refined-looking young man wearing a white Chinese T-shirt and black leather shoes came over and greeted us. It turned out he spoke fluent Hakka. Despite having a dark complexion, he was unmistakably of Chinese descent. Impeccably polite, he first apologized for using such a rude way of bringing us there, and added that because the local elder was aware that we had come under such dangerous circumstances, he was therefore very eager to see us. That was all. Because of time constraints, they hadn't been able to offer a more complete explanation, and for this he offered his apologies. He then led us to a small building to rest, and had someone bring over some tea and sweets. With an expression of reluctant obligation, he asked that we hand over all of our film equipment so that they could temporarily keep it for us. After he had carefully made an inventory, he excused himself, saying,

"Why don't you get some sleep? The elder is already resting. But he wants to meet with you first thing tomorrow morning."

After the day's events, we were frightened, exhausted, and hungry. We proceeded to devour all of the tapioca, durian, and coconut pudding we had been brought, and refilled the pot of Chinese tea three times. We devoured it all, and then went to bed.

The sound of the ocean could be heard throughout the night. It was truly a dark sweet sleep. At the break of dawn, the alarm sounded. Everyone woke up and was told, "Please come have some congee."

We were enveloped in fog, though it wasn't clear whether this was vestigial fog from the night before or a new morning fog.

Xiao Lin had already gotten up and taken a charcoal pencil and paper outside to make a sketch. He said softly, "Last night while I was sleeping, I thought I heard the old man repeatedly reciting a poem. Then, he recited, *Often I sit below the flowers and play my flute, as the Milky Way and the celestial Red Wall stretch out into the distance. It seems as though this constellation is different from before. Several years passed like several nights, but 'tis a pity that the wine in my cup has never been drained.*"

Xiao Lin revealed a charcoal sketch of a thin man wearing a long gown and hovering, ghost-like, under a new moon. The figure was holding a jug of wine in one hand and a paper fan in the other. The surface of the half-open fan was covered in a poem written in characters like autumn earthworms.

The air was bitterly cold.

On the beach there was a tall stilt house, below which there was the shadow of either a motorboat or a sampan. In the corridor of the stilt house, there were shadows of people carrying guns walking back and forth, and the heavy sound of their footsteps echoed throughout the night.

The old fisherman was in the stilt house waiting for us.

We were taken inland, but didn't get very far. There was a basin surrounded on all sides by steep cliffs, and after passing through this filter the sound of the tide became muted, and the sea breeze also became very soft. Walking along a stone path that had clearly been laid out with great care, we were led by the same young person from the previous night. He was carrying a yellow lamp, and as his thin and swaying shadow cut through the early morning fog, he led us forward as though in a dream.

After a while, a light appeared before us, as an array of hanging lamps lit up a large courtyard house. Outside there was a ceremonial archway, and the lamps illuminated the inscription at the top of the archway, which read, in vigorous characters, **Hall of the Two Equals**.

We entered one room one after another, and saw many people already sitting in the bright hall. At first glance, it appeared as though we had entered a film set for an old costume drama. The atmosphere was very solemn and respectful, and none of us dared to utter a word. All of the men and women were neatly attired in traditional Chinese clothing, and the order in which they were sitting was evidently determined by their age or status. In the two palace chairs there sat a man and a woman who were so thin they resembled a pair of dried-up raisins. The man was sitting on the left and the woman on the right, and they both had hair that had gone completely gray. The man was wearing a dark gray long gown and had an odd expression (perhaps he was not yet fully awake) as he sat half-shrunken in his chair, while the woman was wearing a sparkling *qipao*, had bright eyes and hair tied up in a bun. You could see at a glance that they belonged to a different era. Their silhouettes looked as though they had been sketched—with the man's having been drawn with a thin-tipped pen and the woman having been drawn with a course one, and from these portraits you could guess the rough difference in their respective ages. Nevertheless, from the vast number of wrinkles that reduced their eyes to narrow slits, plastered their nose, and collapsed their mouth, it appeared as though they were both over a hundred. The entire hall was full of the scent of cinnamon, as though they had just entered an old pharmacy.

The people who were standing were dark-skinned and were wearing simple clothing, and from their expression and their posture you could tell that they were probably servants. They were rushing forward with steaming congee.

The young man who had led us there came forward and bowed, saying, "I have brought them."

The guests were invited to sit down and eat, whereupon the old woman began singing in Hakka, in a voice so shrill that it made our teeth numb.

A group of people was invited to sit down. They were so silent that all you could hear was the soft sound of them sipping their congee.

The congee was very thick, and aside from this everyone only had half of a pickled egg and a small plate of pickled vegetables. We all shared the same side dishes, and quickly devoured the entire pot.

Moving extremely slowly, the two old people brought the congee up to their mouths one spoonful at a time. Only after we finished eating did we notice that, other than ourselves, everyone else in the room was eating very slowly and deliberately, and furthermore they were doing so in absolute silence.

Several cocks started crowing frantically, as though afraid they would be boiled alive.

After they finally finished eating, the old woman lifted her hand, whereupon two men came in carrying two large leather suitcases, and quickly proceeded to open them. Takutsu looked shocked and stammered, "My . . . suit . . . cases." They removed the contents of the suitcases and spread them out on the floor. They first put all of the wads of banana notes to one side, whereupon Takatsu lunged forward, but was immediately restrained by two men and pulled to one side. They carefully sorted the contents of the suitcase, including Takatsu's notebook, camera, tape recorder, and so forth, and laid them out next to the banana notes. Each article of clothing was carefully searched, and eventually even his coat and the suitcase itself were cut open with a sharp knife, and inside there turned out to be additional banana notes. Evidently, Takatsu had anticipated there might be problems, but had been determined to take back some evidence. Upon seeing this scene, Takatsu's expression became as coarse as the floorboards. Then he himself was strip-searched, and his clothing was carefully examined. They found two more bills.

The worst was yet to come. The old man and woman looked at one another, whereupon the old man nodded and said something in a soft voice. His speech was so distorted that it sounded like Japanese.

Those banana notes and notebooks were taken to a room for drying grain, where a fire was lit and everything was unceremoniously burned up. Inside, Takatsu began sneezing and wailing.

They carefully watched the fire, as though they were burning silver and gold paper to pay tribute to the gods. Only after everything had been burned to a crisp did they finally return to the sitting room.

By this point Takatsu was still completely naked—it appeared that even his rectal cavity had been searched—and was taken to a side room to get dressed.

Several people who appeared to be servants brought out a television and a video player, and proceeded to broadcast the contents of our camcorder. We initially assumed that they were going to show a short report (though we naturally never anticipated that they would have such advanced equipment!), but what they broadcast turned out to be the as-yet unedited "Supplement" that we ourselves had been filming on this trip.

The old lady took the remote control, and pressed (selected?) "Play."

The tape quickly fast-forwarded to the end:

A ray of sunlight was shining down, the color of dark tea.

A soft sigh was suddenly heard coming from the ground beneath the wooden plaque, which rustled the tree leafs.

The old lady snorted a couple of times, and then gently asked the old man, who was watching very attentively, "What do you think?"

"It's OK." The old man nodded. "The atmosphere isn't bad."

"Then let's leave it at that," the old lady said. "When we have time, we can come back to take a look."

She clapped her hands, and a servant removed the videotape. She said that they would help us take our video equipment back to the boat. All of our negatives and blank tapes were removed. Seeing this, we all became very anxious. Wouldn't this mean that our entire trip would have been for nothing? But after having seen what happened to Takatsu, none of use dared do anything rash.

Suddenly Xiao Chen, who by this point was beside himself with anxiety, rushed forward and started begging the old man, saying, "This is for a Taiwanese nonprofit cultural program. It is not a commercial product. It is only for the purpose of making a historical record. . . ."

At this point we only heard the old lady say coldly, in her oddly accented Chinese that sounded almost like an opera singer performing on stage,

"You're lucky we haven't fed you to the sharks. Why don't you go ask around and see who else has returned alive after falling into my grasp. If it weren't for my trying to give him some face . . ."

Looking as though he were about to laugh, the old man glanced at us.

Then we were taken to a side room and subjected to a thorough search, in which everything but our rectal cavities was carefully examined.

And, sure enough, they found several additional banana notes we had taken from Takatsu to keep as souvenirs.

At this point the sun had not yet come up. After we had had a chance to get cleaned up, the old man and several servants invited us to accompany him to his library in a corner of the courtyard for tea. Or, as he put it, "Have some tea and apologize."

The library was filled with old books in many different languages, but we don't need to discuss that here. There were also several hanging scrolls that were shaking so much that it was difficult to read their inscriptions. A strong scent of cinnamon permeated everything.

"I can't see very well anymore, so I simply did this for show. At my age, I no longer have many needs. But when I smell this scent, I am content," he said faintly.

He further explained that at the break of dawn all of the young people would have to go sell fish. Everyone had to make a living. After the harvest season, they all became proper businessmen, and had a major presence on the peninsula. Naturally, smuggling contraband was not an extraordinarily illegal activity. Life here was not easy, and if the military police were to change their clothes they would become pirates. "Therefore, we need some basic provisions to protect ourselves."

At this point he switched to a heavily accented Chinese. He spoke with a slow drawl, like those educated old men from the mainland whom you often see in Taiwan.

He said that he had never expected to encounter the famous widow pirate. "Even in her sixties, she still gave me two sons. She is really a remarkable woman."

He then proceeded to ask us many questions about our program and the contemporary cultural scene on both sides of the Taiwan Strait, together with the fate of various figures from the May Fourth generation.

We carefully answered all of his questions, speaking with him for quite a while.

He was initially very focused, and periodically would break into tears. But eventually his head began to droop. When we turned to Zhou Zuoren's essay "Old Age Is a Disgrace," he began to moan, "Brother Qiming!" and weakly shook his head. In this long declaration, the name of one dead person after another came up, and the statement turned out not to have anything to do with anyone alive. After a while, someone couldn't resist asking, in a stammering voice, "Ex . . . excuse me, sir, could it be that you are Yu . . . Yu Dafu?" They finally succeeded in spitting out this name. After a pause, the old man raised his head, with apparent difficulty. His eyes turned out to be completely bloodshot. He slowly but firmly shook his head. In a soft but clear voice, he replied, "My surname is not Yu, it is Do—as in the phrase, 'shake your head, just as I do.'" (Even as his mouth was moving, I somehow seemed to hear another sound, like gears shifting: "I am the famous pirate, Scarlet Phoenix.")

As he was saying this, he slowly lowered his head, to the point that it was resting on his chest. He began to snore, and even drool.

A brawny servant appeared and promptly wheeled him away in his chair.

We, however, were left with countless questions.

That terrifying old lady appeared again, and warned us that after we went back we couldn't say a word about what we had seen. Then, she informed us that we were free to leave, and furthermore insisted on giving each of us two live lobsters, saying that this was to compensate us for our losses.

Takatsu, appearing as depressed as though he had just been castrated, received two large crabs, and as soon as the boat left the wharf he ate them raw.

After we were escorted back to Surabaya, it took us three days before we were able to finish eating those hard-shelled fellows.

Several months later, as Indonesia plunged deeper and deeper into chaos, we had already returned to Taiwan and were once again engrossed in our own work. One day we unexpectedly received a letter from some Japanese university. The letter was from Takatsu, and it was written in a very excited tone.

Dear Taiwan friends,

Do you still remember me? I am Takatsu, from Japan.

What happened last time left me deeply depressed. But now I once again have good news to share with you. As you are well aware, Indonesia is even more unstable now than before, and countless Chinese graves have been dug up. This is particularly true of the graves of the rich, since you Chinese like to use expensive wooden coffins and also like to bury valuables with your deceased. If you unearth one of these coffins, dump the corpse out, then clean it up, you can usually sell the coffin for a very high price. Some of these coffins are used to make dining tables, chairs, cabinets, and even beds. This has all been covered in the news, so I assume you must already know about it.

But this is not why I'm writing you now. I'm ashamed to say, if it had not been for these disinterments, I would never have come into possession of this precious object. That's right—I managed to get it. Do you remember that spice island? His brother's corpse was dug up by someone, but after spending a considerable amount of money (at least enough to purchase an entire island in Indonesia) and bullets, I was finally able to purchase it from various Chinese pharmacies, and furthermore successfully shipped it to the collection of the □□ Museum. If you don't see it with your own eyes, you won't believe it. The corpse was far better preserved than a mummy or those figures from the Han tombs in Mawangdui. Although it was somewhat dried up, like a preserved duck, it was nevertheless essentially perfect and was very fragrant—smelling strongly of cinnamon, star anise, and black pepper. The mere sight of it was enough to make your mouth water. Would you be interested in coming over to take a look? I regret to say I can't take a picture and send it to you; the museum stipulates that you must come and see it in person, as a gesture of respect for the author.

Unfortunately, the corpse's most precious "three jewels" were missing. They must have been removed by some merchant trafficking in Chinese medicinal products. It was possible that they had not yet been consumed, and there is a rumor that one of these "jewels" might still be in Indonesia. I have asked some local Chinese to continue searching, and told them to spare no expense in getting it back. It was also possible, however, they had ended up in your Taiwan. In the black market among Chinese doctors it would be worth over ten million of yuan. The central "treasure" probably ended up in the hands of a merchant on your beloved fatherland, though someone in the know has revealed that it is instead in the hands of a woman known as the "Demon of Black Mountain," who has been in hiding in America for many, many years, and who is now even older than the Empress Dowager Cixi was at the time of her death. This Demon of Black Mountain has apparently drilled two holes in the artifact and fashioned it into a pipe, and spends her days sucking on it, in a trance. Everyone who smells the smoke that comes out says that if the goddess were to sniff it, she would immediately sink into depravity.

inscribed backs

Legend has it that once, after his prayers, Viye Tunra took a branch and whipped himself on the back three times, and said, "If you are more calm and peaceful, and stop struggling, I will help you find the way."

GUAN LIYE, *AL-RASHAH*

1

INITIALLY, this had been merely an accidental discovery that Mr. Yur, a "coolie expert" in the history department of a local university, made in the course of his research. Mr. Yur had spent over three decades investigating early nineteenth-century patterns of Chinese transnational migration, and his research had already yielded rich results. His representative works include *A Typology of Coolies* (doctoral dissertation, London, 1969), *Interactions Between Chinese Coolies: Struggle and Cooperation* (Taiwan: Academia Sinica, 1975), and *Coolies and Aborigines: 1900–1941* (University of Australia, 1978), all of which are regarded in the field as must-read classics. Once, he was on the riverside with a coolie with whom he had developed a close friendship after having interviewed him for a long time. They were singing (he still remembers it was a song called "Ah, South Seas," from the War of Resistance), and the coolie was crooning sorrowfully out of key (because he couldn't read or speak standard Chinese, and only knew a local dialect, he therefore had no choice but to memorize the lyrics): "Ah, South Seas, you are my beautiful homeland." When the elderly coolie took a towel and started vigorously rubbing his back, Mr. Yur suddenly noticed several dark blue

Chinese characters on his shoulder. Initially, Mr. Yur thought these marks were merely moles or scars, but when he looked more carefully (even as his curiosity aroused the coolie's resistance), he saw that they were in fact a line of characters written so closely that they almost ran together. Each character, moreover, had a subtle mistake and was either missing a stroke or had an extra stroke. The text seemed to say, "Ah, South Seas, you are my mother's homeland" (Mr. Yur remarked with a laugh that, to use a linguistic term, this was but a process of verifying a transcription). The character for *land* had too many strokes, to the point that it appeared to be merely a dark blue blob. Mr. Yur could tell that the characters had been inscribed with a needle, like a tattoo. Upon noticing that Mr. Yur was staring intently at his back, the old coolie became visibly distressed, as if someone were staring at his private parts. He quickly put on his shirt and refused to answer any questions (such as who did this, and why?). And while the coolie remained outwardly friendly, his manner grew noticeably colder. From the coolie's reaction, Mr. Yur sensed that these tattooed characters must be subject to some sort of taboo, perhaps having to do with religious (or superstitious) belief, but more likely they had to do with some secret society. As everyone knows, in contemporary Chinese society tattoos had already become virtually an exclusive symbol of membership in a secret society. Those, however, are typically tattoos of tigers, dragons, flowers, the demon Zhong Kui, or of big-breasted women. These tattoos rarely include much writing, and instead typically feature the name of the man's beloved. Mr. Yur joked that he remembered that the mother of the Southern Song general Yue Fei had tattooed the words *Serve the Country with Utmost Loyalty* on her son's back, and in one of Jin Yong's martial arts novels the disciple Chen Xuanfeng, who secretly learned the "Nine Yin White Bone Claw" technique, has the *Nine Yin Sutra* tattooed on his belly. Mr. Yur also recalled an old joke about how a male patient was visiting the doctor, and while the doctor looked down and saw a tattoo that said "a flow," his pretty nurse looked down and saw instead the phrase "a spring river easterly flows." Or how several years earlier there was a rumor that when communists caught men visiting prostitutes, they would tattoo the word *whoremonger* on the men's cheeks.

If this had been merely an isolated incident, he would not have felt that there was any value in pursuing an investigation. But over the following two decades, he indirectly obtained various pieces of corroborating evidence.

Of course, this was not yet another tall tale. He had a relative, a Dr. Tiao, who had spent a long term working as a doctor in the former Straits Settlements. Dr. Tiao was a practitioner of traditional Chinese medicine who could treat virtually anything, and Mr. Yur mentioned this case to him. Dr. Tiao laughed and replied that in the several decades he had been practicing medicine, he had indeed encountered "quite a few" patients with tattoos, many of whom were coolies. Unfortunately, he couldn't recall the content of any of the tattoos he had seen. "These are secrets that belong to the patients," he declared solemnly. "And, furthermore, those sorts of patients are generally very uneasy, and are not willing to let a doctor examine their back." Therefore, it had never occurred to him to look closely at the tattoos, to the point that he would deliberately avert his gaze when he happened to glimpse one. When asked to try to recall what they were, he pondered for a while but eventually shook his head. All he could remember was that one of the tattoos was quite large, covering the patient's entire back like a swarm of ants. Maybe it was an essay or the sort of poem that in ancient times people would sometimes carve on the blades of their swords, but all of the characters looked like they were miswritten. He requested the patient's information, but his request was denied on a technicality. Dr. Tiao, accordingly, did not create a file for the patient. Mr. Yur asked him whether he could recall any of his colleagues having mentioned similar cases, and Dr. Tiao pondered for a while but again shook his head and said that he couldn't think of any. "We all have great respect for our patients' privacy," he emphasized. Dr. Tiao couldn't understand, however, why those coolies had Chinese characters tattooed on their backs, given that virtually every single one of the coolies was illiterate. In fact, they couldn't even write their own names, and when filling out any form of documentation (either official or private), they had no choice but to use a thumbprint in lieu of a signature. Why, then, would they be tattooed with text that they themselves had no ability to read? Who had done this? And why? What was the function and purpose of these tattoos? Were they a charm for avoiding evil spirits? I had never heard of such a thing. Dr. Tiao suggested that perhaps the tattoos were part of a classification system used by the company that had originally sold the coolies as children, the same way that it is still popular among Malaysian Chinese who raise pigs to brand their farm's code on the pig's back. Mr. Yur, who was an expert on coolies, weakly protested, "But, we have no proof . . ." But even Mr. Yur recognized that the questions Dr. Tiao had raised were precisely ones that he himself had long been pondering.

Mr. Yur asked Dr. Tiao to notify him if either he or any of his colleagues ran across any similar cases in the future, but for several years there had been no news of any new discoveries. At the time, Dr. Tiao had added an important caveat: "Even if that clan were to still exist, by now they would be so old that they wouldn't need a doctor anymore, since they would already have almost all died out."

One year while Mr. Yur was out doing some sightseeing after having come to Taiwan for a conference, he encountered a scene that left him completely stunned. Sitting in the shade under some trees by a temple, a group of slightly overweight and gray-haired old men were chatting and fanning themselves. Each of them had a tattoo clearly inscribed on his arm, which said things like, "Oppose Communism and Restore the Nation," "Long Live the Three People's Principles," "Great Neutrality" [on the left arm] / "Perfect Uprightness" [on the right arm], "Accept Death" [on the left arm] / "Like Homecoming" [on the right arm], "Counter-attack" [on the left arm] . . . Each of these men seemed completely at ease, and they displayed their tattoos without the slightest concern that anyone might care what they said. Initially, Mr. Yur thought that this must be the meeting of some secret society, but when he asked his Taiwan companions he learned that this was actually a very common scene, and that the men were all former soldiers who had retreated to Taiwan from the mainland. During the Korean War, captured POWs were forcibly tattooed, and they later got corresponding tattoos in the same location to demonstrate their determination and loyalty. The result was indeed a label, but it simultaneously functioned as a political slogan. Mr. Yur's friend, who was studying Taiwan history, asked, "Are you interested in them? This is a very simple phenomenon, and there is really nothing worth investigating there."

Later, at a banquet with some fellow academics, a scholar specializing in Shang dynasty oracle bones heard about Mr. Yur's fascination with these tattoos, and remarked with a mischievous smile, "This sounds like it is even harder to investigate than our oracle bone inscriptions. The texts we study are all engraved on shell and bone—although they were merely turtle shells or ox scapula, and not actual human bones—and therefore they can be preserved for quite a long time. Furthermore, after the oracle bones were buried, they were protected by the soil. But your object of study is inscribed on human skin, which is easily damaged. It's not even possible to take a rubbing of it." He laughed bitterly.

In the interim, Mr. Yur looked up virtually all of the relevant books and articles on the subject—including studies by Victor Parcell, who had done the most in-depth work on new Malaysian Chinese communities during the colonial period and on Chinese secret societies—but was unable to find any relevant records.

Sometimes he would think that somewhere there must be a lead of some sort. At the very least there must some clues regarding the men's families? He repeatedly submitted oral history proposals to the National History Archives, but invariably received the same response: "This proposed project is completely unbelievable, and lacks any discernible research value."

Many years later, when he was working on other "valuable" projects that he had no choice but to complete (because if he didn't, they would impact his annual appraisal, and might even affect his chances of promotion), he had virtually forgotten all about that incident. Even his coolie friend, whose tattoos were the only ones he had been able to see with his own eyes, and Dr. Tiao, who was his sole witness, had both passed away without his knowledge.

This all changed following that unexpected incident. The incident in question occurred not long after he was reminded by his school that "he had reached the age of mandatory retirement." Just when it seemed as though he had completely forgotten about those texts, they suddenly found him again.

Once when he was abroad, a car accident happened to send him to the hospital. He wasn't sure how long he was unconscious, but was eventually woken by a bubbling sound, as if from an endless river. Before he was able to figure out where he was or what had happened to him, or even where he had been injured (he had a throbbing pain, but couldn't determine its precise source), he turned his head and saw that in the bed next to his a withered body was lying motionless, like a bronze statue. The figure's head appeared very small, like a desiccated fruit. The sunlight shining in through the leaves and the glass window was still burning hot. He noticed with a start that the skin containing those bones was covered with blue markings that appeared to undulate like ocean waves under the room's intricate lighting. He fumbled around for his glasses and, after finding them on the bedside table, he put them on. Finding that the scene in front of him was blurry, he realized that his glasses were missing a lens. Yes, the markings were indeed Chinese characters. He wanted to immediately copy them down, but couldn't find a pen and paper and therefore had no choice but to try as hard as he could to commit the text to memory. At the time it didn't occur to him that he could have asked the nurse for a pen and paper. Eventually, perhaps because he was concentrating so hard, he passed out. After a while, he was violently shaken awake again, and an overweight Malay woman asked him coldly, "Do you remember your name? And your home phone number?" He sat up with a start, but noticed that the bed next to his was now empty. "Where did that old man go?" Mr. Yur asked in a soft voice. "First answer my questions." The nurse refused to give ground. He therefore had no choice but to cooperate, and only then was he given the answer he wanted: "He was just taken away to be cremated. Like you, he was picked up from the street, but since he had no known relatives the government therefore had no choice but to cover his expenses."

Mr. Yur was extremely disappointed, and desperately searched his memory for that text, which seemed to have gotten shredded. In the end, he was only able to recall a single sentence:

On that long, hot September afternoon, that was oppressively sweltering. . . .

But he couldn't be certain whether that even one sentence was correct. That was what he remembered hearing through his right ear, while in his left ear there echoed the sound of a different sentence:

"I, in exchange for my own, now appear on everyone's back."

Who would write such a hyperbolic phrase on someone's back? It was almost like something he had recently read in a novel. He instinctively reached for his glasses, but discovered that now both of the lenses were missing.

That happened to be September, and it was still as sweltering as the weather described in that sentence tattooed on the man's back. Perhaps for that reason, during the two months that Mr. Yur stayed at that courtyard, those two sentences continued to echo in his head. They quickly reverted back to pure speech, to the point that he lost all recollection of the original written characters. A low rumbling sound resonated between his ears like a curse, and for a long time he was unable to make out any other sound, and everyone around him complained that he always spoke in a cold and disinterested manner. Gradually, he also began to feel that the people around him were treating him coldly in response. It became virtually impossible for him to teach his regular seminars, because all he would do would be to lower his head and listen to the sound in his ears. Eventually he went to see an ENT doctor, who told him that his ears looked completely normal, adding, "You should be able to hear anything you want to." After a while, he had no choice but to request early retirement, on the grounds that "he needed long-term recuperation in order to address the lapses in concentration he was experiencing as a result of PTSD following the car accident."

The following year, during Taiwan's Southern Expansion Policy, Southeast Asia became a hot new area of academic study, and given that Mr. Yur had been working in a related field, he was therefore invited by some academic institution to serve as an advisor and oversee some research projects. It was as a result of this that we had the opportunity to participate in this remarkable search.

Mr. Yur's original plan was to find some sort of cover. For instance, he came up with a proposal to investigate "a life history of Chinese coolies in the nineteenth-century Straits Settlements: including their disease, medical treatment, and recovery." This three-year project was designed to prevent him from encountering again that kind of "utterly absurd" criticism on the pretext that he was using a New Historicist approach. Embedded within his stated proposal was his original plan, but it wasn't until the project had advanced to a certain point, and he and the other youthful participants had established a certain amount of familiarity with one another, that he finally began to relate the entire story to us in an emotional and nostalgic tone. He casually mentioned his "personal request," and asked that we make every effort to keep it a secret from the funding agency. He hoped to use a large-scale fabricated background (what he calls a "maritime resource") to investigate, to see whether or not it was possible to have the object of his search "float to the surface."

"I think it might already be too late, and we may now be even less likely to encounter any survivors than if we were investigating a critically endangered species." Mr. Yur sighed, adding, "This is how things always turn out. Twenty years ago this might still have been possible, but eventually you reach the point where history fades into legend."

What followed was three years of formal investigation. After a meticulous division of labor and preparation, Mr. Yur was responsible for participating in the group discussions at each stage, and for adjusting the project's ensuing implementation. The project proceeded like a well-oiled machine, and his plan was that during the latter stages the project committee would be granted a considerable amount of autonomy. Eventually, apart from participating in postmortem discussions and directing the writing of the final report, Mr. Yur was able to virtually disappear. The eighteen team members were divided into various groups, each of which was given a different set of responsibilities. They traveled to the former Straits Settlements of Singapore, Malacca, and Penang, where they conducted broad and meticulous field research. They visited old Chinese medical clinics, brothels, restaurants, coffin stores, barber shops, Chinese cemeteries, guildhalls for various different villages, towns, and cities, together with retirement communities, mental asylums, and so forth . . . visiting every location where, based on available records, they could determine there lived residents who were ninety years old or over. This historically unprecedented investigation (into the former Straits Settlements and the history of overseas Chinese, though of course it would have been ideal if they could have extended this to cover the entire Southeast Asian region) yielded impressive results, which vastly exceeded those of the Jiyi Academy's classic study, "Mapo: A Displaced Chinatown." With respect to the establishment and transformation of the former Straits Settlements and the public spaces where overseas Chinese would go in the course of their daily lives (comparable to their private lives within the home), this investigation yielded an impressively thorough description that even included descriptions at the level of individual streets and alleys. This, therefore, lent itself to the possibility of enacting a re-creation (or an imaginary re-creation) of this social history.

Consider, for instance, Mr. Chen, from the Kampung Kling neighborhood of Malacca. He was born in 1900 on Hainan Island, and in 1917 he went to take shelter with a relative who worked in a hair salon. After 1940 he opened his own small family-owned hair salon in Kampung Kling, and from that point forward his life history was basically finalized. Every morning he or his wife would take turns going to a bazaar half a mile away to buy vegetables and some breakfast. After eating breakfast, they would open their hair salon for business punctually at nine o'clock in morning, and would then close at eight in the evening. At three each afternoon he would go to the Xin Mingji coffee shop on the same street for afternoon tea and to chat with some old friends. Each Monday he would take the day off, and would also observe all the major holidays. For recreation, he would play mahjong either in the parlor by the riverside half a mile away or in the Hainan guildhall on the second floor of the South Seas by the Guanyin Temple. There were two temples that he would frequent, with one being the Guanyin Temple and the other being the Temple of the God of the Land on the other side of town. There were also two brothels that he would occasionally visit, with one being a Chinese brothel behind the bazaar and the other being an Indian brothel on Queen Street. When he got sick, he would go buy medicine and see a doctor either at the Taisheng Chinese pharmacy on Shaw Road two blocks over, or at the Longsheng Hall clinic another block over. . . . If someone didn't have children or family property, then at the age of fifty-one he might be sent to a retirement home on Elephant Road, a mile away. And if he died, he would definitely be buried in a Chinese cemetery three miles away. And if he did have children and family property . . . One of Mr. Yur's research assistants was a video game whiz, and was able to use a series of hypotheticals to plot out an entire "Straits Chinese" life history game. Under the categories specified by these different variables (such as family ancestry, occupation, and residence), it seemed possible to cover all of the possible individual transfigurations of a hypothetical subject.

The result, meanwhile, was that they accumulated enough raw data to write a "History of everyday life of the new immigrants to the Straits Settlements from the nineteenth to the twentieth century." Despite searching the entire old colony based on Mr. Yur's instructions, they failed to come up with any useful leads. And even if he carefully questioned the old Chinese medical doctors, they usually only shook their head or softly said, "I have no recollection." This kind of result was extremely disappointing, but Mr. Yur nevertheless made an effort to remain positive and said optimistically, "Look more carefully. It should always be possible to find something." Then he mumbled to himself, "I'm afraid that they're all dead. Or perhaps they have gone somewhere else? Perhaps to the township government? Or perhaps he is in a coffin? From ashes to ashes, and dust to dust . . ."

From Mr. Yur's appearance, you could see that he had suddenly aged considerably. He had a depressed air he simply couldn't conceal.

By this point, his project was reaching its conclusion.

We suddenly received a notification, however, that Mr. Yur had been seriously injured in a car accident, and was now in a coma.

We continued our investigations and began tabulating our results. This, at any rate, was all work that had been arranged ahead of time.

Until all the work was concluded, there weren't any extra funds for us to go visit him. Furthermore, we weren't even his relatives.

2

When we first saw the person, we were instantly seduced by the sight of his back.

That was an ordinary beach without many visitors, and he was sitting there facing the South China Sea. He was listening to the sound of the waves lapping up on the beach, and appeared to be lost in thought, as though he had fallen into a reverie as deep as the ocean. Although the weather was quite chilly, his shirt was unbuttoned and his collar was blowing in the breeze. He seemed unusually tall for an Asian man, and had a thin neck and an elongated head like those sorts of pears you often find at the market. His limbs were unusually long, to the point that even when he was seated he couldn't help attracting my gaze. From a distance, it was like character strokes that had been drawn out of line. He had a standard buzz cut, and his hair had gone completely gray—the sort of dry white that results from having all traces of color thoroughly washed out over the years. He must have been at least my grandparents' age, and perhaps even older. In any event, he belonged to an earlier generation.

By this point it was already monsoon season, and the wind blowing in over the sea was suffocatingly strong. You could barely hear what other people were saying, and even your own words would be blown away the second they left your mouth. For several days in a row, we would go take a walk after lunch, in an attempt to soothe our sorrow. Occasionally, someone would come down to stroll along the beach, but usually all we could see was the person's shadow. He would typically maintain the same posture and sit in the same place, staring out to sea as if the entire ocean belonged to him. We speculated that, for him, we were probably also objects of curiosity—just as he was for us. At the same time, however, we recognized that it was also quite possible that he wasn't even aware of our existence. We considered coming up with an excuse to go over to him, just to see what he looked like, yet we felt an unusual sense of solemnity when confronted with his intense gaze. As described above, even the sea itself seemed to be claimed by his gaze. We felt that his gaze belonged to an age that was not our own—we were shocked by this realization, and ultimately had no choice but to sneak around behind him, to reach the office we had rented located at the other end of the long beach.

One evening after dinner we returned to that location, but he had already left. Feeling bored, we went to the place where he had "rested his butt" (to use my companion's expression) and took turns placing our own rear ends in that same spot. We found this very amusing. When it was my companion's turn, however, I discovered with surprise that when he sat there, he appeared very short and shabby. You could also imagine his desolation.

Eventually, one day the wind blew his clothes in a way that revealed his back, and we were astonished to notice a slightly discolored region, though at first we couldn't tell whether it was a scar, a mole, or a birthmark. Or perhaps it was some form of writing? We didn't dare approach too closely, so we had no choice but to gaze at it intently from afar. Unable to confirm what it was, we quietly prayed for help, like poor misers searching for a dollar-sign in the sky. We hoped that it was an index, but were afraid that, on account of this, we would lose track of him. Not only could we hardly resist the temptation to uncover his back to take a look, we also wanted to follow him, to see where he lived and what he did. What was his story? Why was he always coming out here alone to gaze out at the sea?

One day, however, we didn't stop with idle speculation, and instead one of my companions went up and pulled away the man's clothes to look at his back. Even though he only managed to get a quick peek, it was clear that the markings on the man's back were neither scars nor moles nor birthmarks, but rather they were written characters. In fact, there were many, many characters, including countless 毎, 母, 水, and 毋 characters, and even a 海, suggesting that all of the other characters were derived from this final one, which means "sea."

The man immediately sat up and, in a way that seemed to belie his age, dashed away without even looking back. Everything happened so fast that we initially didn't have a chance to react—particularly given that we had never imagined he would be able to run away so quickly. Up to that point, however, he was our only useful clue and therefore we had no choice but to pursue him, despite the fact that he had a substantial head start on us. In the blink of an eye, he ran through the windbreak trees into the old street, whereupon he turned a corner and disappeared without a trace.

We were astonished and disappointed to see him disappear before our very eyes. We tried asking people in the streets and in local shops, but everyone gave us the cold shoulder. Eventually we had no choice but to return to the seaside to see if we could find any clues. Perhaps he might have left something behind as he was fleeing.

We searched everywhere for a long time.

There was no one around, but in the windbreak trees there was a pushcart. Perhaps this was his.

We each looked for a large stone to hide behind, and then held our positions.

We stayed there until nightfall. That evening—and this is embarrassing to admit—we were apprehended by a group of police on night patrol. We then spent the night at the station, where we were firmly reprimanded. Furthermore, after having been exposed to the ocean breeze all night, we started sneezing uncontrollably. For the next several days both of us suffered from bad colds, leaving us unable to do even simple work. Furthermore, we both had a series of bizarre dreams, in which we saw someone's back inscribed with Chinese characters and covered in blood. Because of all the blood, however, we could only see the knife marks but couldn't make out the actual characters, or even whether they were characters at all. Perhaps they were just meaningless marks—random cuts and scars—including stab wounds, oblique cuts, horizontal slices, and tears. Markings of dislocation.

The eighteen members of our group who had been dispersed among the former Straits Settlements all reunited in Lion City, all of whom had pursued clues we had provided when we were sick—proceeding from Singapore's Chinatown to Geylang Serai, Little India, Quinn Street, Telok Ayer, the Singapore riverbank, Tanjong Pagar, Kongkoan St. . . . We searched everywhere, but to no avail. At that point, some of us began to speculate that perhaps we had interpreted the clues incorrectly, or maybe we dreamed them up in a moment of delirium.

After nearly half a month of searching, everyone's own work began to be delayed on account of this, and some even began to feel that Mr. Yur's instructions had been inconsistent. Even though Mr. Yur was himself a local, he had nevertheless been unable to find any useful clues even after decades of searching, and therefore others felt there was no need for them to go to such an effort trying to track down a rumor. Furthermore, Mr. Yur himself was only being kept alive by a respirator, and it was unclear whether or not he would ever recover consciousness. As a result, the group was soon disbanded.

The situation in the Taiwan Straits became very tense, as the young president was suddenly afflicted by a mysterious illness. First he lost his voice, then he became bedridden, and finally he lapsed into a state of delirium. A month later he was relieved of command, on the grounds that he was "no longer able to carry out the responsibilities of the office," and was temporarily replaced by his vice president. As everyone had expected, the vice president—who was known as the female Hunchback of Notre Dame on account of her distinctive laugh—immediately proceeded to declare independence. In this way, Taiwan's democratic republic was reborn.

Because they were concerned for their families and their country, the members of the investigation team had to quickly wrap up what they were working on and hurry home. After a few days of hesitation, even the younger men, who were worried they might be sent to the front, eventually decided to fly back, reasoning, "if we are going to die, we should die together," and "for better or worse, we should fly back and discuss the situation with our family." Here, meanwhile, it was announced that they would relax existing restrictions on immigration. The senior minister returned to Beijing, calling for both sides to calm down. Furthermore, from the moment the president fell ill, vast amounts of capital and labor began flowing out of the island to different regions around the world. The majority of the people who departed were industrialists and politicians, as well as scholars at the nation's most elite research institutes. The stock exchange was completely paralyzed. A week after the Hunchback took office, the amount of out-migration had increased by ten percent. Apart from repeatedly calling upon the United States to send an aircraft carrier to the Taiwan Straits to help maintain regional stability, the Hunchback openly criticized the people leaving the country, calling them "traitors" and "national criminals," and telling them that if they left now they shouldn't even think about returning. She asked, "What are you afraid of? That country on the other side of the Straits is still so backward that if we were to fight, we would not necessarily find ourselves at a disadvantage." At the same time, she considered closing down the airport.

The clouds of war were dense, and the threat level remained high. The unconscious Mr. Yur was picked up by some worried relatives.

One afternoon, I went for a walk alone.

That shadowy figure returned as well, this time with a pushcart. I hid behind the camouflage net until late afternoon, waiting for him to leave.

He suddenly stood up, turned around, then strode away. After a while, he went behind a shady evergreen tree, where he grabbed that pushcart and quickly strode away without even glancing around. I didn't have a chance to see his face clearly, and therefore had no choice but to continue following him.

Soon, he turned into an old street, proceeding under the shade of the trees on either side. On either side of the street there were some ancient buildings, including Indian incense shops, Chinese or Malay coffee shops, cold beverage stores, hair parlors, stationery shops, grocery stores, Hainanese chicken and rice restaurants, and so forth . . . appearing like a market town that had formed out of a society of recent immigrants. Occasionally, acquaintances would shout him a greeting, but I couldn't really make out what they were saying. Were their greetings getting drowned out by the sound of my own footsteps, or was my hearing failing? We quickly ran away, and just as quickly we stopped again. We found ourselves at the door of a house adorned with countless flowerpots, a few of which had been placed in the cart, and which contained fragrant orchids, blooming chrysanthemums, and foreign begonias. . . . He proceeded a ways down the street, then stopped at another shop to buy something. Then, he sprinted forward, running like a man half his age. He sprinted down several old streets, and cut through several back alleys that we hadn't realized had survived the city's inexorable process of development. As we passed foul-smelling ditches and deeply stained walls, old telephone poles, and hopeless-looking shops, the sound of radios playing music and old songs in different languages could be heard through the windows. His expressionless face was perhaps a reflection of the depressing underside of the community's apparent prosperity. The cart's wheels came rumbling toward us.

The air temperature shifted abruptly. First it cooled off, as we entered a shady alley, whereupon it warmed up again and our field of vision expanded. A sheet of sunlight shined directly onto the bright stone street. The man's footsteps began to slow down, as did the sound of the cart wheels. Then the sound stopped altogether. He continued walking forward in virtual silence, his shoulders sagging very, very low, to the point that his head and neck also began to droop, as he appeared to shrink down to the point of resembling a loyal servant. I hadn't expected that this was how he would reach his destination. I suddenly found myself following too closely, not concealing myself at all. Even if I had wanted to hide, it was probably too late. On one side there was the old city wall and on the other side there were the backs of futuristic skyscrapers, the windows of which reflected sheet upon sheet of golden light. Time seemed to freeze, as though I had suddenly stepped into a different kind of temporality. The smell of fresh flowers surged forth.

Of the bougainvillea on display under the eaves of the buildings, there were three kinds, and they were all facing the sunlight. It was very dark under the eaves, and there were countless flowerpots hanging there. Below, there was layer upon layer of fragrant herbs, including lavender, thyme, sage, clove, and black pepper . . . together with hydrangea and cloudflowers, while the branches and buds on the ground included orchids of different colors, cacti of assorted sizes, and water lilies in large cisterns of clear water.

A faint woman's voice—which sounded as though it were emanating from the darkest depths of the night, and yet at the same time was unusually clear—could be heard coming from the dark shadows beneath the eves: "You've returned." Because she was backlit, he initially couldn't see her clearly and could only roughly make out her position. Then, in a flurry of blue and white, she retreated back into the darker shadows of the doorway.

"Why don't you invite your guest to come inside and have afternoon tea?" That drawled and slightly high-pitched voice slowly made its way out.

By this point I was so close I should have been able to make out her face. She, however, respectfully bowed her head and remained in the shadows, while at the same time reaching out her remarkable hand and gesturing for me to come inside.

I stepped across the threshold. Inside was an ordinary home, and on either side of the door there was a pair of wooden bookcases with glass doors. The bookcases were packed with books with very old spines, some of which were peeling off or showed traces of having been repaired. It was evident that quite a few of them were in foreign languages. Next to the window, a round table was visible in the mottled light, and a fat white cat was asleep on the windowsill, snoring lightly. A thin old lady was sitting in an old-fashioned chair, and next to her there was an ancient urn. The woman was wearing a short Chinese-style jacket with large lapels and a sky-blue border. She had sharp features, with a faint smile, phoenix-like eyes, thin lips, a delicate nose, and a pair of jade pendants hanging from her ears. Time had not completely destroyed her natural beauty, and it was still possible to make out what she must have looked like in her youth. Her snowy-white hair was tied up in a bun, and she was smiling as she poured tea from a white porcelain pot. The tea cups were also translucent white, and looked as though they were made from bone porcelain. The tea had a scent of alcohol, and was clear and fragrant. She said to the man whose face I still couldn't make out, "Ah Hai, why don't you come and have a cup as well?" He agreed in a soft voice, then grabbed a tiny chair from a corner of the room and sat down at the table to her left. Even though his chair was much lower than ours, Ah Hai was still significantly taller than the rest of us. At this point I was finally able to make out his face—and it turned out he was a spitting image of the Japanese movie star Ken Takakura, with the only difference being that his face was as wrinkled as an old gourd.

"Welcome." The woman raised her hand. Her every gesture and expression had an indescribable grace and elegance, as though she were an actress who had undergone a lengthy and very strict training, or alternatively had absorbed that training by osmosis after spending long periods of time engaged in everyday affairs with aristocracy, to the point that her every gesture seemed very natural and furthermore appeared full of significance. "This is Earl Grey tea." She took a sip, and added, "Won't you try some?"

At this point, another old woman with similarly white hair bound up into a bun brought over several small plates of butter biscuits. This other woman's movements, however, were much slower and she appeared more elderly.

I experienced an uncanny feeling that was almost enough to make me pass out—which was that it seemed as though this was not merely just a random stranger but rather someone who had been waiting for this encounter for a very long time. I couldn't quite put that feeling into words—a feeling that I had been trapped (or captured). I didn't dare ask directly—though I had a strong intuition—but it definitely seemed they had been waiting for me for a long time. I became concerned that, in a sense, I would never be able to free myself from that feeling I had that afternoon of being invaded by time. *"I thought I would take this to my grave."* She explained, *"This is because I'm already too old—so old, in fact, that it almost seems as though I already have one foot in the grave."* As we were having tea that afternoon, she remarked, *"I'm already too old, and rarely have a chance to go out. But I do know that people are looking for us. Things have always been this way, but this has particularly been the case since last month."* She directed her gaze to the light sparkling on the windows of a distant building. *"That pale man—you could even call him a young man, as far as I'm concerned—comes to visit me in my dreams every night. He sits in a corner and silently opens his mouth, as though there is something he wants to tell me."* Based on her description of the appearance and expression of that person (who sounded like the sort of jovial uncle one often sees in the sitting room of a Chinese home), it seemed that it could very well be Mr. Yur himself. *"So, I knew that sooner or later someone was going to arrive."*

I felt as though I had suddenly entered the confused mind of the unconscious Mr. Yur.

"I'm already very old." That day, the first time we met, this was in fact the first thing she said. She made this announcement very abruptly, without any context. It sounded like a dramatic monologue, almost as if she wasn't directing the remark to me, but rather to herself. It was only later that I realized that this was how she began every conversation. At the same time, what she said was definitely true. She was indeed very old, and in fact I think she may have been the oldest woman I had ever encountered. But unlike other people, who resemble succulent fruits that become shriveled raisins when they age, she instead appeared to have managed to achieve that legendary process of aging backward. Standing in the sunlight, her skin appeared virtually transparent, and beneath it you could see her blood flowing through her veins. I suspected that this was because she had simply been too well off, and for too long had been caking her skin with natural cosmetics made from ginseng, Chinese angelica, swallows' nests, winter toads, and human placenta. It was true that she was even better preserved than I, and her thin lips were still naturally red. "I became old when I was eighteen," she said. The air was full of the scent of rosemary. "Because after I met Mr. Faulkner," she added with a note of nostalgia, "he brought me from Shanghai to the South Seas." She spoke very deliberately, and even though her voice sounded as ethereal as a dream, she nevertheless enunciated every syllable very clearly, such that you almost felt as though you could see the written characters as she was speaking them.

"This is a long story.

"It was during the war. The army of the Eight Nation Alliance had just entered Beijing, and the entire country was in a state of upheaval. At the time, Mr. Faulkner was a low-level bureaucrat working for the colonial division of the East Indies Company, while also working as a reporter for some newspaper. He was fascinated by Asian affairs, but at the same time was very concerned about my safety. You also know quite well what kind of fate women in wartime could expect, particularly given that my father didn't look after me and instead spent every day smoking opium and hanging out with his concubine. He regarded himself as belonging to the Qing dynasty, and therefore paid absolutely no attention to contemporary affairs. Once, on account of that debased woman, he savagely beat me, and I wanted to get as far away from there as possible. Because I was very interested in the arts, I met the chain-smoking and very elegant Mr. Faulkner in a literary salon. He was a dreamer, and was fascinated by the East. At the time, I really didn't know that he was also selling opium. For us, it was love at first sight, and we were mutually attracted to one

another. At that point I was really still too young, several years younger than you are now. Mr. Faulkner was very concerned about my situation. He predicted that in the 1950s China would undergo tremendous turmoil, and suggested that it would be best for us to leave the country now and go somewhere more stable. We therefore relocated to the South Seas. Before I knew it, I had been waiting for more than a century."

"Time really flies."

She sighed softly. That was the content of our first afternoon tea.

She explained that she was already very old, and therefore would need many more afternoon teas to finish telling her story, like a serialized piece in a newspaper. We proceeded to meet on countless afternoons, although our meeting times became increasingly erratic. The war did in fact break out and soldiers arrived. Wave after wave of immigrants poured in and each day there was a tide of humanity at the airport and the harbor. My work was basically finished, or rather you could say that, now that the nation was on the brink of collapse, anything that hadn't already been completed no longer mattered. Compared with the enormous transformations taking place in front of us, it seemed as though there was nothing that had remotely comparable significance. And yet, I still continued to meet her regularly for afternoon tea, listening as she recounted stories of that bygone era while leisurely sipping her tea, constantly doubling back and forth between these two periods, with many digressions and side stories, deeply shrouded in clouds and fog. In this way we had one rendezvous after another.

I felt as though I were meeting a lover for a tryst. At first, I often lost my way (she didn't—or wouldn't—give me any modern means of contacting her), but Ah Hai would always be waiting expectantly at the crucial juncture. Given that I had free time, every morning I would go see Mr. Yur at the hospital, as previously arranged. I would tell Mr. Yur, lying unconscious in his hospital bed, the stories I had heard the previous afternoon, while also offering him a massage or something. It was as though I were his daughter, visiting him more regularly than his own children. Actually, I hadn't expected that his wife and children would treat him so coldly, as they each focused on their own work and simply hired a Filipina domestic to serve as his nurse. They would only show up twice a week, as if to check to see whether he was ready to be buried. At first the family seemed rather skeptical about my motives, given that I was a young woman with no obvious personal or financial relationship to the patient, who appeared to be wasting her valuable time coming to visit him every day. I think they may have even suspected I was a daughter he had secretly fathered as a young man when traveling away from home (as an academic, he often had to go abroad for conferences), and that I was coming to assess whether or not there was any inheritance. Or, alternatively, they may have suspected I was a young lover who had recently glommed onto him (thank you, but no! he is simply too old), and so forth and so on. Instead, everything was perfectly normal.

I privately suspected that if you were to prick his back with a hot pin, he would probably wake up very quickly.

I felt certain Mr. Yur was listening intently, as though everything I was telling him was already buried in the depths of his consciousness, in the same location to which he himself had now receded. It appeared that a critical link between his consciousness and his physical body had somehow been severed, and it would therefore be necessary to suture them back together. More than anything else, I wanted to be able to call out to him and invite him to join me for afternoon tea.

It turned out that the legend behind Mr. Yur was indeed true.

I didn't know how to retell his story, and because this was all derived from informal chats over afternoon tea, much of it had already been transformed to conform to the structure of the afternoon tea. Some afternoons she would relate many stories, jumping back and forth between one time period and another, while on others she would just simply vent her emotions. Once she merely sighed, and never even got started on her story. . . . So, the question was whether to preserve this fragmentary structure, or insist on giving it some sort of coherence?

For instance, there was one afternoon that she fell into reminiscences about her father, becoming completely entranced with the memory of how good her father had been to her when she was a girl.

"*. . . At that point, my father was still quite young—very handsome and with fine features, having inherited a large set of favorable qualities from his ancestors like a dynastic loyalist. He appeared as white as a sheet, as though he had never spent any time in the sun. At that point he* *had not yet begun smoking opium. He would wake up early each morning and, in the house's brightly-lit library, would teach me calligraphy and Tang dynasty poetry. We would discuss the plot of* Dream of the Red Chamber, *play word games, and answer riddles. We even agreed to coauthor an old-style chapter novel. We had already picked out the chapter titles and decided that I would write the romantic portions while he would write the knight-errant-style action portions. If only he hadn't subsequently encountered that opium-smoking woman at the pleasure quarters. . . .*"

One afternoon, we began with a discussion of how he had once gone on a boat ride along the Mekong River, where they happened to encounter a charming young French woman messing around with her Chinese lover, "*And in front of everyone, the man tried to cover the two of them with his cloak, but you could still see their movements very clearly. Although the boat's engine was running, everyone could still hear the embarrassing sounds they were making. The woman's moans were even louder than the boat's engine. . . .*" She leisurely described that early morning breeze, the scene on the Mekong River, Mr. Faulkner's delighted expression, her own state of mind at the time, together with the situation with Vietnam.

On another afternoon, however, she merely discussed her flowers and the various dogs, cats, fish, and birds that she had kept as pets.

Or, she would be like this . . .

"*I never expected things could change so much in a hundred years, from being a small fishing harbor into a global metropolis.*

"*At first he lived on Quinn Street, which was located in a district with a lot of Europeans. Given his identity as an Englishman, together with his relationship with the British colonial office, his China experience began as a low-level bureaucrat working for a Chinese Affairs Office established by the East Indies government. He was in charge of investigating, inspecting, and managing the Chinese prostitution and gangster affairs of the time. Mr. Faulkner's libertarian tendencies made him poorly suited for this job. Later, he was reassigned to serve as the director of the island's main post office. It was actually kind of funny—given that at the time there was only one post office on the entire island, which was the one on Quinn Street, and there were no postal substations. All that the other regions were able to have was a set of mailboxes. His job could be considered fairly relaxed, in that he simply had to make sure that there was always someone on guard. After he lost this plum job, he explained, 'I couldn't continue waiting on those wretches for every half-cent stamp they wanted to buy,' though the real reason he left was that around that time he had become addicted to hunting, for which he would frequently skip work.*

"He started out hunting wild boars, like the Europeans who lived on the island at that time, but quickly became bored with this and instead switched to hunting tigers. That was the Bukit Timah era, and there were still many primitive forests. It was only decades later that some of these forests began to be converted into rubber tree plantations. The tigers had swum over the strait from Johor, and would feed on the Chinese farmers' pigs, the Indians' sheep, and the Malays' cattle, and periodically there would even be reports of tigers attacking people. But the people injured in these attacks were all either locals, Indians, or Chinese, but never the well-off Europeans. The Colonial Office bureaucrats viewed tigers as a prized commodity, and would frequently meet up with others to go hunt them. There were also many wild boars, pheasants, iguanas, bats, various kinds of monkeys, and countless species of birds. The local ecology was actually not unlike that of undeveloped areas in contemporary Malaysia and Indonesia. In contemporary Singapore, however, these sorts of animals can now only be found in the zoo. Who knew that so much would change in only a hundred years!

"At the time, Mr. Faulkner did in fact succeed in killing several tigers. The pelts were really quite beautiful, and several of them were confiscated by the Japanese, who then gave them to that short and squat figure whom we called the Malaysian tiger.

"Mr. Faulkner eventually lost interest in hunting. This was partially because of me, given that it was around that time that I got pregnant. I therefore begged him to stop killing things, though in the end I ended up losing the child anyway. The next several times I became pregnant also resulted in stillbirths. Eventually, I gave up trying to have children. I myself don't even know why. Later, the Japanese arrived, and Mr. Faulkner didn't manage to survive. Otherwise, I would now be able to see

countless generations of his descendants. This was my and Mr. Faulkner's greatest regret in life. But perhaps a child would not even have been able to survive in that wartime period.

"For my sake and for that of the unborn child in my belly, Mr. Faulkner decided to end his career working for the immigration bureau, and instead come here to start a business. By that point he had spent many years abroad. That was a great era of exploration, and he had managed to accumulate numerous elephant tusks and gold bars, not to mention the several chests of antiques that I had taken from my father's library. This would be enough to permit us buy a four-story house in Singapore's Chinatown, thereby realizing the dream Mr. Faulkner had harbored for many years. You would never guess what that dream was—to put it delicately, you could say he wanted to establish a wine shop, but in reality he was interested in entering the world's oldest profession. As he himself put it, 'I want to offer comfort to those souls wandering far from home.' At that point, virtually all of the Chinese living here were hard-working male coolies who didn't have female companions, since initially women were not permitted to travel abroad. China's long-running war, however, made that kind of enterprise a possibility. At first, I was very surprised by this proposal, because wouldn't this then make me a madam?

"Actually, Mr. Faulkner's real objective was not the brothel itself, but rather to set up an ideal environment within which to realize his dream. His actual goal was to write, and one of his slogans became: 'The best place to write is in a brothel, where it is peaceful during the day and boisterous at night. You can write when it is peaceful, and relax when it is boisterous.'

"I secretly called that place the Red Chamber, because I was exceedingly fond of the novel Dream of the Red Chamber. *In reality, however, it was actually what one would call a 'green chamber,' which is to say a brothel. Singapore's Chinatown had always been an area where Chinese worked, and Mr. Faulkner's decision to live there reflected his desire to distance himself from his fellow Europeans. His storefront sign was also in Chinese, and furthermore was written by a famous Chinese calligrapher. At that point he was very unfortunate, given that while he was supposedly traveling around the world, he was actually in exile. He would leave inscriptions everywhere he visited, and as long as there was a surface that could be written on—be it a rock, a wall, or a column—he*

would leave an inscription. His attendants would therefore always have to bring along several large pots of ink and writing brushes. In Malacca, he transformed a Dutchman's red chamber into a black one, and at Port Dickson he even left an inscription on a lighthouse. If he had left his inscription on a mere wall, that would have been fine, but instead he wrote directly on the light beacon itself, leaving the colonial authorities no choice but to pay to have it replaced, and in the process contributing to a rash of shipwrecks during those years. Despite this fascination with calligraphy, he nevertheless led an incredibly opulent lifestyle, and had clearly arrived with a desire to wine, dine, and find women. He traveled in a sedan chair that was carried by eight men, and the road was lined with people beating gongs and drums, as though he were part of a wedding procession. To his face, we all called him Lord Kang, but behind his back we nicknamed him the God of Wealth. He was very overweight and had a bright red face, and I figured he must suffer from hypertension. He spoke in a loud voice, though it was hard to make out what precisely he was saying. I still remember his voice as if it were merely yesterday. He lived like an emperor, and each time he arrived he would be accompanied by a large retinue, including many local literati. He would always book an entire floor of the Red Chamber, and would spend the entire night drinking and composing poems. Throughout the night you could hear him loudly reciting his poems, or laughing so hard that the walls trembled. It was said that his voice was so loud it could be heard as far away as Johor, on the other shore. Other customers said that every time he showed up, even the tigers in the forest would disappear—probably because they were hiding out in Johor, not daring to emerge even to look for something to eat. We therefore began secretly calling him Loudmouth Kang or Tiger Kang. Eventually someone apparently complained that he was simply too loud, and consequently the colonial government decided to expel him and not grant him another entry visa.

"The words Southern Sky Wine House *are clearly visible on the old sign that was still extant, though now it was in the hands of a museum. At any rate, the name of the establishment had long since been changed, though Mr. Faulkner had become enamored of those four words and he sent Mr. Kang a beautiful tiger pelt, saying that he could use it as a summer quilt. Later, he couldn't resist asking Mr. Kang to write him several pieces of calligraphy—and I know he paid generously for them—featur-*

ing bold and forceful characters, each of which was as large as a person. Sometimes, Mr. Faulkner would look at those inscriptions and mumble to himself, becoming so entranced that he could go an entire day without eating.

"Perhaps that is how he came to fall in love with the Chinese language. At the time, I had no idea to what extent he had become obsessed with Chinese characters—how terrifyingly obsessed he had become.

"By that point he was already a famous novelist back in his homeland, having published several well-reviewed works. He was even dubbed a 'modernist' by a critic within the academy. He originally wanted to establish a newspaper for the British subjects living in the colonies, in which he could then serialize his novels. If he hadn't fallen so hopelessly in love with Chinese characters, perhaps he really would have established the newspaper, in which case everything else would never have come to pass.

"So why did *things unfold the way that they did? I later spent a great deal of time trying to piece together what had happened.*

"Odd things often took place at our Southern Sky Wine House, and if one really wanted it would probably be possible to write dozens of volumes describing them. I, however, can only recount what I remember, which may perhaps be related to what you want to know. For instance, I could tell you about his relationship to Chinese writing.

"Once we opened our wine house, business was extremely good, as you can well imagine. The clientele turned out to be fairly elite. This is not something we had arranged on purpose, but we ended up having many literati come visit us. From the day we opened until two years after the fall of the Qing dynasty, when we closed, Singapore's consul general Mr. Zuo and his cronies would drop by every few days.

"One evening, a couple of visitors came to the wine house. Both of them were short in stature, and they were wearing sky-blue long gowns and cloth shoes. The one walking in the front was wearing a black melon-skin hat, thin-rimmed glasses, and had an extremely sharp gaze. The one in back had hair that was so thick and unruly it seemed as though you could hurt your eyes simply looking at it for too long. Both of them liked to stroll along with their hands behind their backs—with the older one in front sporting a white goatee while the younger one in back had a thick mustache. The two of them went directly to the top floor and sat down

at a table next to the window, where they could enjoy the wind blowing over from Southern China. They ordered some wine and a few dishes of vegetables, chatted a bit, and then fell silent, and it was only after a long pause that one of them said a few more things. The younger of the two was clearly very courteous, and his speech, posture, and even the position where he was sitting, all clearly indicated that he was maintaining respect for his elder. Perhaps he was the other man's student. It was rather hot that day, but up on the top floor where those two guests were sitting it actually felt quite cool.

"It was very odd, but on that day there weren't any other guests on that particular floor until just before midnight. Or, perhaps it would be more accurate to say that there were no other guests who dared come up and join them. As soon as other literati came upstairs they would all hurriedly retreat, and I heard several people whisper, 'Madman Zhang and Lunatic Lu are upstairs in the wine house.'

"This phenomenon made the gregarious Mr. Faulkner very curious, and he seemed to sense that the two of them must be up to something. Therefore, on the pretense that he wanted to 'learn Chinese,' he took something Mr. Kang had written and went up to ask him for advice. When the older of the two visitors saw Mr. Kang's In the Four Seas, *he snorted in disdain. Then, in an enigmatic tone, he told his companion to take a thread-bound book from the cabinet and give it to Mr. Faulkner. He then asked for an inkpot, a brush, and some blank paper, and told Mr. Faulkner to open the volume up to any page and read out loud any three characters selected at random, whereupon he would write out the following thirty pages from memory. If he got a single character wrong, he would agree to have a tattoo artist come and inscribe the entire text onto his back. If there was not enough room on his back—including the backs of his feet, hands, neck, and head—then the tattoo artist could use the front of his body as well, including his face.*

"How could we have known that Mr. Kang and this little old man were actually sworn enemies, or that Mr. Kang despised foreigners on principle? At the time, Mr. Faulkner knew a bit of Chinese, but only enough to be able to read Chinese shop signs with difficulty. He couldn't even read the title on the cover of that book, and therefore he just stood there terrified, like an orangutan. I, however, did know those characters, which were written in ancient seal script, and proceeded to read them

out loud—It turned out that the volume was an annotated edition of the ancient Chinese dictionary, Shuowen jiezi.

"To my surprise, before I had even finished reading the passage, the old man began writing furiously. It was only then that I noticed that his fingernails were completely black and were so long that they looped over several times, such that they inevitably got in the way whenever he tried to do anything practical, such as use the toilet. When he wrote, his fingernails scraped the paper, producing a sound like a cat at a scratching post. His companion smiled grimly as he worked up a sweat grinding ink, and in no time at all the older man had written several pages. He then put down his pen and invited Mr. Faulkner to compare what he had written to the original text. But who would dare to do so? I barely had time to apologize.

" 'Only after having memorized this book, should you then come to discuss wanting to learn Chinese!' the strange old man commanded. No wonder everyone called him Madman Zhang behind his back! The younger man, whose hair was as long as wild grass, merely shrugged his shoulders noncommittally, as though there were a tall young woman waiting for him downstairs.

"Those two odd birds never reappeared. I heard that their life back in China was not ideal either, which is why they had come over to divert themselves in the first place.

"I met many odd people in those years. For instance, there was a tall and thin foreigner who spent the entire night doing nothing other than toss a pair of dice into a green floral bowl while making a squawking sound. Eventually, Mr. Faulkner told me that that man was a famous French poet, and what he was mumbling were the French prepositions de, de, de, des. *That man gave Mr. Faulkner a recently published poetry collection, which contained different-sized characters that were positioned in different locations on the page. It was said that the size and position of the characters was determined by the pair of dice he was holding. It turned out he had been writing poetry.*

"Another time, a fat man with a full beard who looked like a tramp trudged up the stairs carrying two backpacks that were each almost larger than he was—one pack was black and the other white, making him look like a dung beetle. His footsteps echoed throughout the entire building, and we wondered if perhaps he was carrying a dismembered

corpse of which he was trying to dispose. We watched as he sat down and ordered some tea, after which he pulled out a joss stick and carefully lit it. Next, he took out a small knife and placed it on the table, then removed something from his white bag—when we looked closely we saw that it looked like a turtle shell—and heated it with the joss stick. For the rest of the evening, we could periodically hear a strange puk *sound echoing clearly through the building. Eventually, he began using his knife to carefully inscribe the surface of the shell, as though he were inscribing a seal. I couldn't resist going up to chat with him, and ask him a few questions. He said that his name was Ah Kun, and that he was composing an unprecedented literary masterpiece—a novel written entirely in the oldest form of written Chinese, using the oldest form of writing utensils* (writing utensils *was his term), the oldest kind of pen, and the oldest way of expressing Chinese characters—'because this is also the most difficult' He said, 'I've decided that this is the only thing I want to do in life, and if it turns out that I can't finish it or do it well, that doesn't matter.' Upon hearing him say this, I experienced a surge of maternal affection, and felt a strong desire to follow him and help wash his clothes, cook for him, kill turtles, bake their shells, and even assist him—if there is any need—in copying his text onto them, in order to help him achieve this childlike dream. I couldn't stop thinking about him, and distinctly recall not only everything he said, but even his facial expression when he said it. 'So far, I've only inscribed two thousand or so shells,' he said, 'but in all I plan to inscribe at least a hundred thousand.' That is to say, he planned to create more oracle bone inscriptions than all of the ones that had been unearthed up to that point. His earnest attitude was very moving, and also very pure. He said that he was extremely fond of* Dream of the Red Chamber, *and that his greatest hope was to produce a novel that would be as great as that one. He stayed on for about a month and a half, explaining that he really liked the atmosphere of our wine house. I made a point of not charging him, and after he had finished baking his turtle shells he bid me farewell, saying that he was going to Borneo and the Malaysian peninsula to catch more turtles. This time, he hoped to find more giant tortoises, on which he could 'inscribe even more characters.' At the time, I forgot to ask him how he planned to store so many huge 'manuscripts,' whether they counted as being published, or whether he planned to publish them in the future (would he instead bury them?), but as it turns out I never saw him again. For many years I waited for him to return, wondering how many shells he ended up inscribing. I even considered going to a Chinese medicine pharmacy I knew and filling several sacks with turtle shells to help him out. Some people speculated that he might have gone into a forest in search of more shells and gotten killed by a tiger, while others reported that in the forest they had encountered a dark and thin young man who had been bitten by a viper and who was as dark as a Malay. It seemed that this was not the same person. From that point on, however, I couldn't find anyone with any news of his whereabouts. Perhaps he had changed his plans and switched to a different method of writing? Based on my brief encounter with him, he appeared as determined and devout as a pilgrim, and seemed likely to continue his project unless tortoises were to go extinct—and even if they did, he might simply go to the ocean and switch to hunting sea turtles. He was so fervently in love with the past!*

"Perhaps for this reason (because some difficulty may have forced him to switch from using terrestrial turtles to aquatic ones, leading him to board a long-distance fishing boat and sail the high seas), or perhaps because he found a small island that lent itself even better to permitting him to realize his dream (such as an island with an inexhaustible supply of turtle shells), he therefore decided to settle down there to complete his masterpiece. This was a possibility that had never occurred to me.

"Before that, however, I couldn't resist confessing to Mr. Faulkner that I felt as though I had fallen in love with that dream house. I don't know if my confession had anything to do with his subsequent change of heart or with that other person's sudden disappearance? Perhaps the two were unrelated. But Mr. Faulkner was utterly entranced by that other person and his unusual occupation, because otherwise he wouldn't have instantly become fascinated with oracle bone inscriptions. When the great explorer Mark Aurel Stein passed through the region, Mr. Faulkner followed him asking countless questions, eventually purchasing from him some oracle bone inscriptions that had been manufactured by an antiquities store, and which he then proceeded to caress all day long.

"I don't know what, ultimately, was more influential. For instance, there was a period when a Europeanized and familiar-looking Chinese woman and middle-aged foreigner came regularly to our wine house, and she had servants bring several suitcases that she said were full of

lizard skins. Her male companion's belt was fashioned from the pelt of a single lizard. That woman constantly stared at me as though I were her long-lost daughter, and asked countless questions. Mr. Faulkner was very interested in the lizard skins they had brought, and for a long time afterwards he himself wore a lizard-skin belt and tie. He also became fascinated with the patterns on these pelts, which looked as though they were an even more primitive form of written Chinese.

"I'm not sure whether this occurred before or after, because everything happened so long ago that it is difficult for me to remember the specific order of the individual events. Perhaps it wasn't very significant after all, but I do recall that Mr. Yu was present at the time.

"At any rate, one day our wine house was the site of an uproar that almost claimed someone's life. This was a very unusual occurrence. That woman was one of the refugees who entered our territory, and it was not until a long time afterwards that we finally learned of her origins. It turns out she was a famous revolutionary from the Third International, who was known as 'Juice Extractor,' and at that point she must have been trying to raise travel expenses or satisfy a personal need. Because she was young and beautiful, she was warmly welcomed by the other guests, and received countless invitations for dates. However, we attempted to reserve her date for a wealthy guest. It should be someone with a business, such as Boss Gu from Yihe Goods. The other girls often complained he was too rough, and I don't know if he took the wrong medicine that day but for some reason he ended up annoying our Juice Extractor. As you know, you can often make a pretty good determination of someone's fate based on their nickname, and as soon as the white foam was wiped from her mouth, it was clear that she was already dead and her face had already begun to turn purple.

"As all of this was unfolding, a tall and thin middle-aged man wearing a long gown suddenly emerged from the crowd. He rushed up like a tiger and immediately proceeded to bite the invalid's neck while waving a needle he was holding in his hand, and in a matter of seconds he managed to bring her back to life. Screaming, she scrambled up and, grasping the two lines of tooth marks on her neck, ran out of the building. I later learned from some of the other guests that this was a famous Northeastern shaman doctor known as the 'Big Biter,' but I hadn't realized that he really did bite people. Mr. Faulkner seemed to express considerable interest in this entire scene.

"Later, something very peculiar happened. Someone filed a complaint saying that Mr. Faulkner had herded a flock of sheep into a clock store. The sheep, it turned out, were originally being watched by an Indian boy, and because he wasn't paying enough attention they eventually started running around in all directions. But Mr. Faulkner's explanation was that he happened to see a strange boy wandering back and forth in front of a kám-á-tiàm convenience store, and he kept trying to peer inside, and the strangest thing was that the boy appeared to have a fist-sized clock hanging from his waist!

"In any event, that was a very tumultuous period, when anything could happen. As a result, I quickly became accustomed to strange occurrences, to the point that I found it rather odd when things appeared to be perfectly normal. Therefore, when that particular incident occurred, it seemed like just another of those strange things that kept occurring during the period, if viewed from the perspective of our contemporary, relatively uneventful era.

"A short and clear-eyed young man came to stay at our wine house, and the strangest thing was that when he arrived he was leading a female monkey with a bright red bottom. He sat silently at a table in the corner playing with a series of cigarette lighters. At that time cigarette lighters were not yet very common, and consequently he attracted a lot of attention. Eventually, the naturally curious Mr. Faulkner couldn't resist going up and trading an antique he happened to have on hand for an ugly lighter. Later, it was at this man's invitation that we subsequently went to the Mekong River. I don't know if this incident had anything to do with that.

"I never expected that this incident would stimulate him as much as it did, to the point that he would completely abandon his own language and start studying Chinese. It would also be difficult for me to tell you precisely when it was that Mr. Faulkner became obsessed with Chinese characters. Perhaps the change occurred even earlier, when he initially met me—given that I was the one who was taking care of virtually all of his needs, both inside and outside the wine house, so that he could have more time to pursue his dreams. Accordingly, I wasn't very clear on what he was doing outside, and I sometimes suspected that perhaps he was going out to look for women or something, despite the fact that he had me and I am a woman. Later it occurred to me that maybe it was during that period that he ran into trouble. Perhaps he and the world-famous

author Mr. Yu had sunk into the decadence of the South Seas. As I've already mentioned, my wine house was very respectable, and our guests were all literati, government officials, businessmen, or adventurers. Coolies, accordingly, would never dare step inside.

"Because Mr. Yu was already a celebrity the first time he visited our wine house, he arrived accompanied by a large retinue consisting of local literati and other writers. They drank and talked until dawn, discussing domestic and foreign events, joking about poetry and women. Afterward, he was often like this, perennially affable and occasionally manic. Our wine house was therefore often visited by fans of the arts who wanted to become famous. The thing that left the biggest impression on me was that he always insisted on having the ugliest women come drink and sleep with him, explaining that he simply couldn't abide the arrogant attitude of our regular prostitutes.

"It must have been around that time that one or two coolies started sneaking into the wine house through the back door every day to look for women. This is something that I didn't learn about until later. For instance, a guest looking for little Cui might find she was already with another customer, even though according to my own records she should theoretically have been free. The first time this happened, I simply assumed that my records were faulty, since business was very hectic and I had many influential guests whom I couldn't ignore. Another time, I heard a man groaning in the middle of the night, didn't give it much thought. As you know, many of those celebrities and literati are deviants, and some of them even like to have women bite them from head to toe. There are many clues that I didn't pay attention to at the time. I just had the vague impression that Mr. Faulkner rarely appeared in front of me. During the day he would frequently lock himself in his room, staring intently at his turtle shells, his calligraphy, and that Book from the Sky, looking extremely tortured and depressed. He would repeatedly mumble to himself things like, 'What am I to do? What am I to do? What am I to do?' Or, alternatively, 'What is to be done? What is to be done? What is to be done?' Sometimes three or five days would go by without our seeing any trace of him. But there were also periods in which he would fall into a manic state lasting several days, in which he would become frenetically interested in sex, like a mammal in heat, during which he could only be described as 'giving play to his brutish nature.' I couldn't handle him myself, and had no choice but to let him enjoy all of the other women

in the building. Of course, I had to give them an extra bonus, because otherwise who would have consented to be with him? When he entered that kind of state, I'm convinced my life would have been in danger had I not strategically hidden from him. As you know, he was a foreigner, and when he started acting up he was truly a sight to behold. No wonder he continually insisted that this was his ideal writing environment. Nor did I ever really suspect him. I just vaguely assumed he was creating something, and was alternating between making good progress and getting stuck, because otherwise why would he have exhibited such dramatic mood swings? Aren't all artists like this?

"There was a period when I even began to suspect that those growing numbers of coolies entering through the back door were some sort of vestigial remnant from his artistic creation. Given that I had always been partial to him, I therefore turned a blind eye to all of this. Even though I found it completely disgusting, this was nevertheless a place for shitting. Later, however, I couldn't help blaming myself for having had such a delayed response. . . .

"But who could have guessed that it would turn out like that?

"By the time I discovered it, there was no turning back. He had already advanced beyond the experimental stage and begun working on what would be his masterpiece.

"One day, I noticed that in his room there was a large iron cage, in which there was a naked boy. The boy had his face in his hands, and appeared to be crying. I initially assumed that this was another victim of the foreigner's raging hormones, but when I looked more closely I discovered that the boy's back was tattooed with countless tiny Chinese characters that extended from his shoulders all the way down to his buttocks. Mr. Faulkner was sprawled in an armchair puffing on a cigar, looking very pleased with himself.

"I asked him what was going on, noting that it was clearly illegal to imprison someone in a cage and that his own British colonial government could arrest him.

" 'You want to run, run away? I'll teach you to run away!' he screamed at the boy while blowing smoke into the cage. 'If you try to run away, I'll drag you back and lock you up!'

"Then, he proudly explained that he had finally conquered the sense of pressure and insecurity that, for the past several years, the impressive guests in the Southern Sky Wine House had given him on account

of their creative endeavors. He had finally come up with a scheme for how to write Chinese in a uniquely revolutionary and modernist fashion. Using the most modern textual form, a lively writing style, instantaneous publication, and a life-like transience—the instantaneity that exists in the dasein, *this untranslatable singularity that lacks any counterpart and yet has completely surpassed the limits of Chinese writing, which can only be inscribed on paper or other non-living material (the word* released *that one often finds inscribed on the shells of turtles is an exception to this rule, but this would not count as a form of cultural creation). . . . Eventually, he concluded, he felt that he had already captured the most profound meaning of the Chinese written language (this way of putting it sounds almost Japanese, but you can hardly blame him, given that he learned some of his Chinese from the Japanese, and therefore some of what he was learning was actually Japanese written using Chinese characters), which is to say he used corporeal pain to function as an intermediary character—*Human Flesh. *He named his creation* Corporeal Writing [*wenshen*], *and remarked that to call these* wen [meaning "marks"] *would be an anachronistic mistake. Given that virtually all of the characters are inscribed on the man's back, the work should therefore be called* Inscribed Backs. *Either way, it was about the Tao taking corporeal form.*

"Even now, I can still clearly hear his manic tone of voice.

" 'It takes me an hour to inscribe each individual character. Are you surprised?' He pulled aside my qipao *and, with impure motives, began caressing my trembling back with his bony hand. Actually, I had witnessed many strange things in my time, and therefore did not find anything surprising in the fact that someone would not have learned Chinese well. I was however afraid he might try to bite someone again. As you well know, foreigners have big mouths and large teeth, and absolutely no sense of restraint. Therefore, if they bite you, it hurts forever, and it even hurts when you try to walk. He must have noticed that I looked very afraid, so he shouted at me, 'You are also startled!'*

"That time he actually didn't bite me.

"He then proceeded to relate how he had continued experimenting over the preceding several years, and actually got his inspiration upon seeing a crowd of Chinese coolies on the dock (Indian coolies were too dark, he noted) loading and unloading cargo under the blazing sun like so many ants. He felt profoundly moved by the sight of these anonymous laborers

(sometimes he declared himself a Marxist, and other times an anarchist). In those crystalline drops of sweat pouring down the coolies' backs, he glimpsed the earliest form of Chinese writing (he had a very vivid imagination). Therefore, he would approach the coolies and, claiming to be a wine house owner, he would hire them to come to move things around. Then, after he got to know them better, he would invite them over to come eat something, or else he would go out gambling with them. Once, he even smoked some opium. Sometimes he would simply invite them over to the wine house and set them up with a prostitute, thereby encouraging them to develop a sense of indebtedness to him. After they started feeling uneasy and wanted to try to find a way to repay him, he would propose his unusual request (as they do in the mafia). Those coolies were all honest people, and in this way he was able to obtain a large quantity of 'writing material.' He then used the imperfect skills he had learned from the tattoo artist, and although he struggled for a long time he nevertheless ended up producing a few lines of text that looked as though they might have been written by a child, and were possibly even harder to decipher than the oldest Chinese characters inscribed on Shang dynasty oracle bones. Inscribing those miswritten characters on the backs of those young coolies, he carried out his arduous experiment.

"His most terrifying idea was that he wanted to use the backs of a thousand men to write 'a novel as great as Ulysses.*' My god—those were human backs!*

"I subsequently encountered some of his victims—which is to say, what he regarded as his notebooks—and found that they all felt as though they had been 'sodomized.' They all felt acutely ashamed, and were not willing to let anyone else see their backs—not even their own relatives. Their inscribed backs seemed to have become like their private parts. Neither were they willing to talk about their experience. I even suspected that he sometimes—or perhaps often—became excited and helped himself to these human writing materials in other ways as well. Initially, the coolies were like a secret society, not daring to discuss their experience with anyone, but as people began to view him as a sexual pervert it became harder and harder for him to find any more 'paper.'

"The boy locked in the cage, it turns out, had been purchased from a coolie trafficker. Mr. Faulkner regarded the boy as very valuable, since he had been selected for the first section of Mr. Faulkner's novel. As for what Mr. Faulkner actually wrote, I no longer recall. At any rate, I

couldn't understand his Chinese. Sometimes he would break a character up into a number of different fragments, and other times he would mash several distinct characters into one. In fact, I doubted whether he would later be able to read what he himself had written. That boy could really run, and several times he managed to escape, but each time he was brought back and severely punished. He was quite young, but had an old and haggard expression. Eventually, he was allowed to escape for good. Several years later I happened to see him at the zoo. Needless to say, his body had aged a lot and his hair had gone gray, but his face now looked noticeably younger. He was with his family, and pretended that he didn't recognize me.

"In order to justify purchasing such a large number of coolies, Mr. Faulkner acquired a thousand-acre forest in central Johor, which he planned to convert into a rubber tree plantation. For this, he would need at least five hundred coolies, and if the Japanese had not suddenly attacked . . . In any event, it seemed to me that he must have produced quite a few 'manuscripts,' it's just that they are now too hard to find. More challenging than regular archaeology, this sort of investigation required a kind of archaeology of human flesh.

"Over the radio, I heard that the Japanese had already entered northern Malaysia and were rapidly moving south, and it was clear that they would soon cross the strait. During that period, however, Mr. Faulkner stayed locked up in his room, and from the screams I knew he was back at work on his composition. I figured he had probably had a burst of inspiration. When he was at work, he became a tyrant, and even a veritable beast. But the situation was becoming too urgent, until finally I had no choice but to push open his door and go inside. I really can't bear to recall the scene I witnessed when I entered: two bare-butted young men . . . I promptly turned away and told him that Mr. Yu and I had reserved a boat for that evening. That was the last boat, if we didn't leave that night we would have no way of getting out. At that point I really didn't want to look at him, but also didn't expect that I would never see him again. I quickly went into the wine house and took some valuables, and that night I waited until we could hear Japanese gunfire in Johor and could see fires burning, but he still didn't show up. Finally, I couldn't wait any longer and proceeded to flee with Mr. Yu and the others to Sumatra, where I proceeded to spend three years and eight months hiding in anonymity.

"Naturally, I hope he has now managed to return safely to England. I don't even blame him for leaving me in the end. That, after all, was a time of war, and separation was a daily occurrence. However, a reliable source indicated that he and that gentleman had both been murdered. The only thing that has not yet been confirmed was whether they were killed by the Japanese, the Communists, or by those coolies he had been using for his masterpiece and his various drafts. After the war, I petitioned the British colonial government for news about his whereabouts, but their response was very cold and bureaucratic: 'Miss, if we come across any new information, we'll notify you immediately.'"

In the end, she wept elegant tears. Those days, she felt her and Ah Hai's complexion was deteriorating. Their faces had become increasingly gray, perhaps because the story was reaching its conclusion. When she finished, she invited me to go to her wine house the next time I visited, and have a formal afternoon tea. She also had a small parting gift for me.

"Is the wine house still there?"

"Of course, but now it is a high-rise building. After the war, we spent several years working on it, as it developed in step with the nation. Now, it is one of the two largest hotels in the country."

I suddenly remembered the time I glimpsed Ah Hai's back.

"Oh, he used to be a coolie, so he still retains his former humility, and likes to lead a simple life. He was with me during those difficult three years and eight months, and several times I would have fallen into the hands of the Japanese had it not been for him. Since he misses his home, he therefore likes to gaze out over the ocean, even though the family he left behind have all already passed away. With respect to his back, I didn't realize until later that Mr. Faulkner had no lack of followers and imitators. A Peranakan Chinese with a thin mustache had seen some of Mr. Faulkner's creations somewhere, and was deeply impressed. I also knew that even though these Peranakan Chinese didn't know any Mandarin, they nevertheless idolized foreigners and many of them spoke Tamil as their first language if their nanny happened to be Indian. Like some other Peranakan Chinese, the fact that he couldn't read Chinese made him even more fascinated by Chinese characters, to the point that he would treat them as a kind of Taoist charm.

"You could say that Ah Hai was also a victim, albeit a willing one. Fortunately, he was the only one, given that this youngster was not actually very ambitious. Ah, I might as well tell you everything—he actually only knew this one character. From Ah Hai's back, you can observe the course of that youngster's studies. Ah Hai watched him grow up, since he lived right next to us.

"That youngster would often come over to our place, asking a lot of questions. I, however, was not very willing to recall my experiences with Mr. Faulkner, and I would very rarely mention them. I have no idea why, but this youngster completely idolized Mr. Faulkner, whom he had never met, regarding him as his teacher and mentor—to the point that I even began to suspect that he might be Mr. Faulkner's illegitimate son, given that the two of them did in fact look a bit alike. After all, it is never a good thing when one has a child who resembles one's neighbors. Later, the youngster decided he didn't want to inherit the family's business, continually traveling around on the family's behalf. He was convinced that the mentor he idolized was still alive, and he later spent most of his time in China (on account of his love of the Chinese written language). I suspect he went around lifting up people's shirts to peek at their backs. I myself hadn't seen him for more than thirty years, and I hadn't heard of him producing any new works."

The next day, I kept my appointment, as she had instructed, and followed her map. The political situation had become increasingly dire, and the city was now full of refugees. During that period, the city was like the Tokyo rail station, with countless panicked faces. This scene of countless people displaced by war gave me a feeling of ineffable sorrow.

We arrived at the resplendent Singapore Hotel. Because of its name, many war refugees would often meet up there, making it even more crowded. In the middle of the main hall there was someone standing on a wooden chair giving a speech in a hoarse, duck-like voice. When I saw her, I noticed with surprise that she seemed to be the politician we had nicknamed the Hunchback of Notre Dame, who was always laughing. It hadn't been that long since I last saw her, but she had already visibly aged. Was it possible that this might in fact be the Hunchback's mother? But she looked just as I remembered her. But how was it that she had come here? Her hair looked even more messy than before, and it seemed as though no one was listening to her. Among the various things she said, I could just make out a reference to a ". . . government in exile." Then, I felt someone tugging on my sleeve. It was an attendant wearing a uniform like that of a flight attendant, who emerged from the crowd and pulled me over. After confirming my name, she handed me a dark blue box. It was so heavy, it seemed like there might be a gun inside. She whispered into my ear, "The chair of the board wasn't feeling well, and therefore couldn't come. She asked me to come apologize on her behalf."

I suddenly realized what had happened.

Countless anxious people were wandering around the main hall, or waiting with a vacant gaze. Only that woman on the chair kept shouting herself hoarse, like a fish out of water. I could only make out isolated phrases, such as, ". . . United States . . . Taiwan . . . People Stand Up." I suddenly felt extremely weary. At this point, there was a sudden disturbance, as a pair of hands suddenly pulled the refugees apart and a large figure appeared in the doorway. That terrifying figure was none other than the door god, dressed up in the latest fashion. That person pushed open the door and, in a soft voice that was starkly at odds with his appearance, he cried, "Ah Lan, Ah Lan. Has anyone seen my Ah Lan?"

When he turned around to look, suddenly right behind him he noticed there was a koala-like bat, attached to which there was an old lady who looked like a tiny bird that was sleeping soundly.

After we left the wine house through the back door, the scene in front of me became very familiar. Was that not the back alley leading to that place where I had so many afternoon teas? However, unlike that alley that led to a dead end, this one instead had a four-way intersection. The alleys were all extremely narrow, receding to a single vanishing point.

These were truly troubled times. Was it possible that even space itself had been secretly revised?

I felt cold and dizzy. Feeling my way forward, I stumbled out of the alley.

I was jostled back and forth in the crowd, to the point that I had no idea where I had come from or where I was going.

It turned out that I was already overly accustomed to having long afternoons that could accommodate leisurely afternoon teas.

I therefore had no choice but to go to the hospital, even though I had already gone earlier that same morning.

It turned out, however, that Mr. Yur's hospital bed was now empty. At first I didn't register what had happened, and thought that perhaps he had been discharged or transferred to another hospital. . . . After a while, I asked at the reception desk, and learned that he had been moved to another room.

I stumbled over to that other room, just as a middle-aged man wearing black clothing like a priest's was walking out. Behind his black-framed glasses there were a pair of ice-cold eyes. He brushed past me, carrying a very heavy book that must have been a Bible. He swooshed by. Upon pushing open the door to that hospital room, I was astonished by what I saw. The box in my hand fell to the ground, but I didn't even notice. I ran to the bed, and confirmed that that was in fact Mr. Yur, whose body was already cold and lifeless. The old man's naked body was lying motionless on the white sheet. The most terrifying thing was his back. From his nape down to his ankles, his entire back was covered in Chinese characters. Some of the characters were as large as a fist, others were as tiny as the tip of a needle, and they were all written in irregular strokes of different thicknesses. They were, however, all the same character: . They were all written in a very infantile style, as though from a practice book kept by a child who was just learning how to write. It turned out that in a depression at the base of his spine, there was the character inscribed inside a tiny circle.

Suddenly feeling weak, I collapsed onto the cold floor next to the bed.

What *was* this? Who had done this? Was this the only representative work by Mr. Faulkner's unofficial disciple?

It was at that point that an even more startling scene appeared before my eyes, as a large bone rolled out of that box. I saw that it was a vertebra, wrapped in a scrap of tiger pelt. It suddenly occurred to be that this must be a human bone. A foreigner's bone. Could it be . . . I suddenly remembered that large, urn-sized white ♀ symbol that was written in chalk on the old woman's wall.

This bone was covered with Chinese characters, but I found I couldn't decipher any of them. Perhaps they were symbols that antedated the Chinese written language, like the traces left by birds and animals which, legend holds, provided the inspiration for the earliest Chinese characters. The scene before me became blurry, and I suddenly realized that my eyes were full of tears. I felt completely exhausted, as though I myself had become a soft, boneless animal. I suddenly developed an acute pain in my belly, as something warm and sticky began to seep out.